Read W9-BIN-232

"Scott, why don't you just come with me to church?"

His brows furrowed. "No, Frannie. I can't. I'm not ready for that."

"Not ready for what? Mingling with the rest of humanity? What's wrong with you, Scott? Why do you avoid people? Who are you hiding from?"

Scott pushed back his chair, sprang to his feet and strode over to the window. "You don't understand, Frannie."

"Then explain it. We're friends, Scott, and yet I feel like you're a stranger."

He gazed out the window, then back at her. "Someday I'll tell you everything. But until then, you have to trust me. That's all I can say right now."

Books by Carole Gift Page

Love Inspired

In Search of Her Own #4
Decidedly Married #22
Rachel's Hope #40
A Family To Cherish #88
Cassandra's Song #141
A Child Shall Lead Them #150
A Bungalow for Two #159

CAROLE GIFT PAGE

writes from the heart about issues facing women today. A prolific author of over 40 books and 800 stories and articles, she has published both fiction and nonfiction with a dozen major Christian publishers, including Thomas Nelson, Moody Press, Crossway Books, Bethany House, Tyndale House and Harvest House. An award-winning novelist, Carole has received the C.S. Lewis Honor Book Award and been a finalist several times for the prestigious Gold Medallion Award and the Campus Life Book of the Year Award.

A frequent speaker at churches, conferences, conventions, schools and retreats around the country, Carole shares her testimony (based on her inspiring new book, *Becoming a Woman of Passion)* and encourages women everywhere to discover and share their deepest passions, to keep passion alive on the home front and to unleash their passion for Christ.

Born and raised in Jackson, Michigan, Carole taught creative writing at Biola University in La Mirada, California, and serves on the advisory board of the American Christian Writers. She and her husband, Bill, live in Southern California and have three children (besides Misty in heaven) and three beautiful grandchildren.

A Bungalow for Two
Carole Gift Page

Love Inspired®

Published by Steeple Hill Books™

If you purchased this book without a cover you should be aware
that this book is stolen property. It was reported as "unsold and
destroyed" to the publisher, and neither the author nor the
publisher has received any payment for this "stripped book."

 STEEPLE HILL BOOKS

ISBN 0-373-87166-X

A BUNGALOW FOR TWO

Copyright © 2001 by Carole Gift Page

All rights reserved. Except for use in any review, the reproduction
or utilization of this work in whole or in part in any form by any
electronic, mechanical or other means, now known or hereafter
invented, including xerography, photocopying and recording, or in
any information storage or retrieval system, is forbidden without
the written permission of the editorial office, Steeple Hill Books,
300 East 42nd Street, New York, NY 10017 U.S.A.

All characters in this book have no existence outside the imagination of
the author and have no relation whatsoever to anyone bearing the same
name or names. They are not even distantly inspired by any individual
known or unknown to the author, and all incidents are pure invention.

This edition published by arrangement with Steeple Hill Books.

® and TM are trademarks of Steeple Hill Books, used under license.
Trademarks indicated with ® are registered in the United States Patent
and Trademark Office, the Canadian Trade Marks Office and in other
countries.

Visit us at www.steeplehill.com

Printed in U.S.A.

No soldier in active service entangles himself in the affairs of everyday life, so that he may please the One who enlisted him as a soldier.

—*2 Timothy* 2:4

In loving memory of Jason Michael Williams.
February 13, 1981–April 11, 2001
With a heart for God, a passion for life,
great devotion to his family and friends
and an insatiable appetite for adventure,
Jason touched countless lives in countless ways.
All who knew him loved him.

Chapter One

Andrew Rowlands was dreaming. An odd dream really. He was about to be married to the lovely Juliana Pagliarulo, but he couldn't find his darling daughters. Surely the wedding couldn't begin without them. He darted among his smiling, well-attired guests, inquiring, "Have you seen my daughters?"

No one had.

And then amid the cacophony of voices and laughter swirling around him, he heard a familiar voice.

"Daddy?"

It was his oldest daughter, Cassandra, in a mauve bridesmaid dress. She came slipping through the crowd with her handsome husband, Antonio, Juliana's son. In her arms Cassie carried a precious bundle, Andrew's first grandson. "Be happy, Daddy," she said, giving him a hug, and squeezing one-month-old Daniel between them.

"I couldn't be happier than I am today, Cassie. I've got all my family around me."

He spotted his second daughter in the throng. His dear Brianna with Eric Wingate, her dashing groom. Beside them stood their soon-to-be-adopted daughter, Charity, looking like an angel in pink chiffon. Andrew strode over and swung the precocious two-year-old up in his arms. "How's my beautiful little Blue Eyes?"

The child tossed back her blond ringlets and laughed. "I not *little,* Gampaw. I big girl!"

Matching her laughter, Andrew kissed her shiny hair, then set her down. "Yes, you certainly are Grandpa's big girl!"

"Oh, Daddy, isn't she the prettiest flower girl you ever saw?" Brianna said in her lyrical voice.

Andrew winked at his daughter. "No prettier than the bride who's going to be her mother."

Brianna swept into Andrew's arms with a tender embrace, her ivory-white wedding gown swishing around her.

"I love you, Daddy," she whispered, stepping back and blowing Andrew a kiss. "Isn't this a glorious day...the four of us having a double wedding?"

"Wonderful!" Andrew crooned. "Nothing better than standing at the altar with my ravishing bride and my precious daughter and her intended."

"We're all going to live happily ever after, Daddy. Happily ever after..."

The dream darkened after that. The festive crowd in the wedding chapel receded behind a mist of swirling shadows. A storm was gathering, with voluminous clouds rolling over a shrouded earth. The noise was deafening, drowning out the sounds of celebration rising from the chapel.

"Where's Frannie?" Andrew shouted through the gloom. "Who's seen my youngest daughter?"

The murky darkness cleared, as if someone had pulled back a curtain, and Andrew saw her, his beloved Frannie, who had cared for him like a mother hen. She was dressed in black and kneeling at her mother's grave, the grave of his cherished Mandy, gone seven years now.

Andrew held out a hand to his daughter. "Frannie, come! The wedding's about to begin. Your sisters and I are waiting for you."

She stared back with tears in her eyes. "No, Daddy. I can't! I won't!"

"Honey, please! It won't be the same without you."

"How can you do this, Daddy? How can you forsake Mom and marry a stranger? I'll never forgive you, Daddy!"

"No, Frannie, it's not like that." Andrew reached out, but the shadows closed around his daughter, and she was gone.

"Come back, Frannie! I don't want to lose you, sweetheart...!"

Andrew woke in a cold sweat, his heart pounding. Thank goodness, it was just a dream. A silly dream. Everything was okay. Normal as an old shoe. The double wedding had gone off without a hitch nearly two weeks ago, the first of July. And just last night he and Juliana had returned, happy and exhilarated, from their Caribbean honeymoon.

Now he was here in his own home again, surrounded by everything familiar, waking as he always did to the summer sun streaming in his bedroom window. But this time, there was one major exception. Lying in bed next to him was his sleeping bride, the sun casting gold ribbons across her ivory face and bare shoulder.

The warm sunlight reminded him that all was well in his life. Better than it had been in years. He had so much for which to be grateful...a devoted wife and two daughters happily married with families of their own.

He had kept his promise to Mandy. "Find our girls good husbands," she had told him during their last hours together. It had been her dying wish. "And find a good woman for yourself, Andrew. You'll need someone to look after you."

Yes, he had done that too. God had given him his exquisite Juliana.

And now, with his two oldest daughters married, that left just one daughter. Frannie, his youngest. A chill rippled though him as he recalled his unsettling dream. Those shadowy, nightmarish images had captured his underlying concern for Frannie. She had taken Mandy's death the hardest. With everyone else in the family married, she seemed so alone, at loose ends, drifting. Surely one of these days the right man would come along for her. It was one of Andrew's most fervent prayers.

And until then, he didn't want Frannie feeling abandoned, just because he had a brand-new family to fuss over. But the truth was, he would have his hands full with his vivacious Juliana and her grown daughter.

If ever a young woman needed a father, it was shy, skittish Belina. She had already endured enough trials and heartaches for a lifetime—the car crash, her father's death, her own disability and disfigurement. But with surgery, counseling and rehabilitation, she had come a long way over the past two years.

Andrew hoped against hope that Frannie would take Belina under her wing and become a real sister to her. Of course, Frannie was stubborn and headstrong and didn't warm to just anybody. She was possessive and overprotective, too, but that was partly Andrew's fault. He had been so needy after Mandy's death, he had allowed his youngest daughter to pamper and mollycoddle him. While he had thrown himself into his ministerial duties at the church, she had taken over the cooking and household chores like a faithful little trooper.

Even when his two older daughters began making lives for themselves, Frannie was the one who dug in her heels and refused to budge. She was going to stay home and take care of her daddy, no matter what. No wonder she had resisted the idea of him bringing home a new bride and stepdaughter.

But Andrew was just as determined as Frannie.

With Cassie and Brianna married now and establishing homes of their own, he would encourage Frannie to find in Juliana and Belina the motherly and sisterly companionship she missed.

It was a long shot, to be sure. In temperament, Frannie and Juliana were like oil and water. Add to the mix Belina's reclusive personality, and you had a recipe for trouble. But, as he had learned long ago, with God all things were possible. More than once, Andrew had staked his life on that Scriptural principle.

Another unmistakable reality confronted Andrew. The Rowlands household was going to be a very different place from now on. How drastically it had changed in the past seven years, starting with Mandy's death, then Cassie's marriage, then the double wedding of Andrew and Juliana and Brianna and Eric. And now Brianna had moved out just as Cassie had, and Juliana and his new stepdaughter had moved in.

Andrew rolled over and gazed again at his sleeping bride. Lightly he caressed a strand of her shiny black hair that rippled over the pillow. He yearned to sweep her up in his arms, but she looked so peaceful, he was reluctant to startle her.

It still hardly seemed possible that God had blessed him with two remarkable women in one lifetime. Naturally, Juliana was nothing like Mandy; they were as opposite as night and day. Mandy had been quiet, self-assured, delicate, refined. Juliana was fun-loving, flamboyant, larger than life.

Andrew rested his arms under his head and looked up at the ceiling. Over the years he had grown so accustomed to talking to Mandy in his mind that it was a hard habit to break, even with Juliana lying beside him.

Mandy, he mused with a wry half smile, can you believe it? Here I am with Juliana. My wife. She isn't like you, nothing like you. But, oh, I love her. It doesn't mean I loved you any less. No one can replace you, Mandy. But Juliana's a delight. She's full of laughter and exuberance and song. She's impetuous and unpredictable.

Sometimes I wonder if I'll ever keep up with her. I'll never corral her spirit, but that's part of why I love her. She isn't you, Mandy. I knew you like I know my own soul, and I'll never forget you, darling. You taught me what love is all about, showed me how to open my heart and cherish a woman. Because of what you taught me about life and love, I believe I can make Juliana happy. Do I have your blessing, Mandy? I'd like to think I do.

Juliana's drowsy voice inquired, "Andrew? Are you okay?"

With a start he looked over at his wife. She had propped herself up on one elbow, her ebony hair cascading over her milky-white shoulders.

"Sure, I'm fine," he said, running his fingers over her arm. How could he confess to his lovely bride that he had been carrying on a mental conversation with his long-deceased wife?

"You looked so deep in thought. A million miles away."

"Yes, at least that," he conceded.

"Pleasant thoughts, I hope."

"Absolutely. What else on a sunny morning with my new bride beside me?" He reached over and gathered her into his arms. She nestled her head on his bare chest and he caught the scent of magnolias. How good she felt in his arms. He could hold her like this forever!

Being a man over the half-century mark in years, he hadn't expected to feel such a rush of what could only be described as youthful emotions. What a power there was in love. Falling in love was an indescribable intoxicant. With Juliana in his arms, he felt ageless, invincible; there was nothing he couldn't accomplish. He turned her lovely face up to his and kissed her soundly.

When she caught her breath, she murmured, "Andrew, dearest, what a wonderful way to start the day. Maybe we should skip breakfast and spend the entire morning—"

A determined knock on the door jarred them both.

"We're sleeping," Andrew called out, stifling his vexation.

"Not anymore!" The door eased open and Frannie peeked inside, her long blond hair flowing around her shoulders. She was wearing a tank top and cutoffs that showed off her golden tan. "Time for breakfast, you sleepyheads. It's almost nine, and you never go past 8:00 a.m., Daddy."

Andrew released Juliana, and she slipped down modestly under the covers.

Andrew cleared his throat uneasily and folded his arms over his bare chest. "We were thinking of skipping breakfast this morning, sweetheart."

"No, Daddy, it's not good for you to skip a meal. Besides, I have a surprise for your first morning home." Frannie breezed inside with a serving tray and set it on the bedside table.

As Andrew hoisted himself up, he caught the inviting aromas of bacon and coffee. "Honey, it smells wonderful, but—"

Juliana sat up, too, tucking the sheet around her shoulders. "Breakfast in bed? Oh, Frannie, you shouldn't have."

Frannie beamed. "It's nothing really. Just bacon and eggs and cinnamon toast. Daddy's usual."

Juliana gave Frannie a stricken look. "Oh, dear, your father shouldn't be eating such things! Think of his cholesterol!"

Andrew reached for a slice of toast. "My cholesterol is fine and dandy, thank you."

Juliana lifted her chin truculently. "I don't care what you say, Andrew. A man your age should not be eating such fatty foods!"

"What do you mean, a man my age? What's wrong with my age?"

"Nothing is wrong with your age. But I intend to see that you live several more decades."

"By depriving me of bacon and eggs?"

Frannie snatched up the tray. "Listen, I could get

you both something else. How about some cereal and yogurt?''

Juliana tossed back her waves of coal-black hair. ''Thank you, Frannie. I will tell you the truth. I rarely eat breakfast. Maybe a little fruit now and then.''

Frannie stepped back toward the door, her countenance darkening. ''I'll remember that tomorrow, Juliana.''

''Dear, please do not worry about your father and me. I will get our breakfast from now on. I am sure you have more important things to do.''

''Nothing more important than taking care of my dad.''

Andrew winced at the disappointment etched in his daughter's face. ''We just don't want to put you out, honey.''

''Your father is right. You work too hard. From now on I will fix breakfast.''

''That's not necessary, Juliana. Daddy likes me to get his breakfast. Besides, I know just how he likes it.''

Juliana flashed her most winsome smile. ''But now it is time for me to learn.''

Why did Andrew have the uneasy feeling he was witnessing a battle of wills, and he was the prize? With her trained voice and Italian accent, Juliana's words sounded almost lyrical. But Andrew could see them hitting Frannie like barbs. ''You have had to take care of your father long enough, dear girl, and you have done a wonderful job. But you have your

own life to live, and it's time your father let you live
it.''

"Wait a minute!'' Andrew declared, raising his
hands in a conciliatory, if not defensive, gesture. He
could see trouble coming at him like a stampeding
bull. "Hold on! Let's get this straight. I've never said
Frannie couldn't live her own life. And I certainly
never asked her to stay home and take care of me.''

The misery in Frannie's eyes deepened. "You
didn't have to ask, Daddy. I did it for Mother.''

Andrew groaned. His awkward attempt to defuse
the situation was igniting a firestorm too hot to handle. "Doll baby, your mom never would have expected you to sacrifice your life for me.''

Frannie's big blue eyes clouded. "Sacrifice? Is that
what you think I've been doing? Daddy, I thought
you liked the way I took care of you!''

"I did, honey. I do! But I want so much more for
you. Juliana's right. You need a life of your own.''

Frannie balanced the tray and gripped the door-
knob. Her lower lip quivered. "Don't beat around the
bush. Just say it, Daddy! Now that you've got a new
wife and daughter, I'm not needed around here anymore!''

Before Andrew could muster a reply, Frannie pivoted and marched out the door, slamming it so hard
behind her, the walls rattled.

He threw back the covers and was about to go after
his daughter, but Juliana stopped him and coaxed him
back into bed. "You can't go after her dressed like
that, Andrew. Let her be. She will get over it. We are

a new family now. We all have adjustments to make. It will take time." She snuggled against his chest and he caught the delectable scent of her hair.

"Time?" he murmured, closing his eyes and inhaling deeply. That heady, intoxicating feeling was sweeping over him again. "My darling bride, do you suppose we have time for…" He let his words trail off as Juliana raised her face to his and kissed his lips with an ardor that left him breathless.

"My darling Andrew," she said in that throaty, beguiling voice of hers, "for you, there is always time!"

Chapter Two

Panic was growing inside Frannie like mushrooms in the dark. In June she had received a handsome commission to sculpt a bust of Longfellow for the La Jolla Children's Museum—due by the end of summer. It was already July, and all she could do was sit and stare at a mound of lifeless clay.

Try as she might, Frannie couldn't muster a shred of creativity. Her mind felt dry, numb, dead. She wondered if she had ever had a creative thought in her life. Had she ever experienced that flaming impulse to create something from nothing, or nearly nothing? Had she in the past actually molded fine sculptures— not masterpieces, of course, but still quality work— from heaps of wet, shapeless clay?

Where was the artist she had been just a few short weeks ago? How could her talent have fled so swiftly, so completely?

Every time she thought of sinking her fingers into

that formless mass, she remembered something else she needed to do—some mindless chore or task that wouldn't usually demand her attention. With a sigh of resignation, she would drape the clay with a wet cloth, as if covering a dead body with a shroud. Then she would escape to another part of her house and fiddle with something, or busy herself in the kitchen, or stare out the window, or pester her father in his study—anything to keep from facing the task at hand, the challenge of pulling life and form out of that silent blob of gray earth.

Today held the same lack of promise. Right after breakfast, Frannie had gone to the sunroom to work. She had pored over a dozen drawings of the old poet and sketched several hurried renderings of her own. Then she had kneaded the clay until her fingers ached, until she admitted at last that she wasn't in the mood to create. God help her, she had lost her vision for the work.

Once, days or weeks ago, she had felt that creative impulse in her fingers, in her mind, in her heart. But now it was gone. An empty place remained, a vacuum, a hollow in her soul that nothing seemed to fill.

She had heard of writers and artists hitting a dry spell, suffering writer's block and questioning their talent. But it hadn't happened to her. At least, not for several years. Not since…yes, she remembered now…not since her mother's death seven years ago.

For two years after her mother died, she hadn't been able to create a thing. She was seventeen at the time, fresh out of high school and just beginning her freshman year at San Diego State. Majoring in art, of course, as she had always planned. But every time she thought of creating something—a painting, a drawing, a vase or a piece of sculpture, she felt a knot of pain in her heart.

It was as if the idea of creation, even producing something as mundane as an object of art, signified a birth. The paradox was that her heart was deluged with the reality of death. But at last, praise God, when she began her junior year of college she experienced a breakthrough. Her creativity returned in a rush. She changed her major from art education to fine arts and completed her B.A. two years later.

And in the five years since then, her skill and reputation as a sculptor had grown. She was even teaching a night class at San Diego State...and the commissions were coming often enough that she had bankrolled a tidy sum in her savings account.

Yes, her life these days had been good, very good. Even though her evenings were devoid of romance, her routine had been satisfying and stable.... Until the last few weeks, when Frannie's world turned topsy-turvy—the day her father brought home his new bride and stepdaughter. Since then, nothing had been the same.

Take today, for example. In the past (B.J.—before Juliana), Frannie would have risen at seven and fixed her father's and Brianna's breakfast. The three of them would have sat around the table chatting about their plans for the day. They would have held hands and prayed together before going their separate ways.

But now that Brianna was married and setting up housekeeping in her own country estate, Frannie was lucky to see her once a week. And Cassie, with her new baby, stopped by even less often. Even when her sisters dropped in to visit, they chatted only about their happy new lives and then were quickly on their way. They were so busy and preoccupied, they were totally unaware that Frannie felt lonely and left behind.

It wasn't that the house was empty now. Frannie could have tolerated that. She had never minded long periods of solitude. The silence sometimes even stirred her creative juices. Peace and quiet were welcome friends.

But, in fact, the old Rowlands' homestead wasn't silent; it was as bustling as ever. It reverberated with noise and voices and music and laughter. But except for her father, the sounds belonged to strangers, not to the people Frannie loved.

In truth, even her father was different now. The dynamics had changed. He was a man absorbed with pleasing his wife. Where Frannie's happy home had once comfortably contained a father and three daughters, now her father was half of a newlywed couple occupying the premises. And each had a daughter. To complicate matters, Frannie and Belina were virtual strangers and had no desire to be anything more.

These days, Frannie's home was filled with Juliana's laughter and songs. In her youth, Juliana had performed on the New York stage and in the opera houses of Europe. Now her full, lilting soprano wafted through the Rowlands house a dozen times a day…as Juliana cooked and cleaned, as she taught voice lessons to eager children and led a women's Bible study twice a week in the parlor. Juliana was obviously determined to become the quintessential minister's wife—a fact Frannie resented.

But if Frannie begrudged the way Juliana had taken over her home, she was equally disturbed by the stealthy comings and goings of the mysterious Belina. The aloof, raven-haired girl was like a ghost, flitting through the house noiselessly, rarely speaking or making eye contact. She spent most of her time alone in her room doing who knew what.

Frannie was just as glad that she didn't have to make polite conversation with the strange young woman. What would they talk about? They had nothing in common…except that Belina's mother was married to Frannie's father.

Every morning, when Frannie awoke, she told herself, Maybe today things will be different. This will seem like my home again. I'll feel comfortable around Belina and Juliana. We'll begin to be a family at last.

But as quickly as she made her resolves, they were shattered by some minor event that caught Frannie unawares, that brought her up short and reminded her she was living in a vastly different household. It happened again today, the last week of July, just over two weeks since her father had brought Juliana home from their honeymoon.

This morning was the last straw for Frannie, because the incident involved someone dear to her heart.

Ruggs, the family dog, an ancient, longhaired mongrel, had tracked mud all over Juliana's freshly waxed floor. Juliana chased him out the back door with a broom. Frannie had never seen the old dog run so fast or yelp so loud. The sound nearly broke Frannie's heart.

The problem was, Juliana just didn't get it. She considered Ruggs a scroungy old dog that was always getting in the way. She didn't understand that he was as much a member of the family as anyone. When Juliana shooed Ruggs out the door, it was as if she had shooed Frannie out, too.

Ten years ago, Brianna had found the scrawny, abandoned puppy on the street, hungry and shivering. She had brought him home and nursed him back to health, the way she nurtured everyone she came in contact with. And for ten years Ruggs had been king of the castle. There was no way Juliana was going to convince him he was just a mangy mutt.

The incident with Ruggs had left Frannie feeling more resentful of Juliana than ever. How dare that woman take over Frannie's home and chase her dog outside? The trouble was, these days Frannie felt as unwelcome as Ruggs in her own house. No wonder she wasn't in the mood to sculpt Longfellow's bust.

Even as she sat in the sunroom contemplating the mountain of clay on her worktable, Frannie could hear Juliana bustling about in the kitchen, crooning the lyrics from some Italian aria. Frannie worked with the clay for a few minutes, dipping her hands in a container of water and wetting down the gray mound.

It still wasn't taking shape the way she wanted. It was as if the stubborn mass refused to relinquish the form hidden within.

Usually Frannie could work her artistic magic. A mysterious connection formed between her mind and hands; they worked together in a way Frannie herself couldn't comprehend. It was as if some secret force within her recognized the shape inside the mass and freed it, then she molded it until it came to life under her fingers.

That was the way it was supposed to work. But not today. In exasperation, Frannie pounded the clay with her fists, then tossed the wet cloth over it and went to the deep sink to wash her hands. If she couldn't sculpt anything worthwhile, she might as well go help Juliana in the kitchen. She emerged from the sunroom just as Juliana hit a high note that rattled the crystal on the buffet.

Frannie ambled over to the kitchen sink where Juliana was scouring a black kettle, and said, "Looks like you could use some help."

Juliana whirled around and clasped her hand to her ample bosom. "Oh, dear girl, you startled me!"

"I'm sorry. I was going stir-crazy in the sunroom. The Longfellow bust—it's just not working for me."

"Oh, what a shame. Give it time, dear. It'll come." Juliana's rosy lips pursed together, forming a tiny rosebud of sympathy. She extended a graceful hand and touched Frannie's cheek with long, tapered fingers, her perfectly manicured nails a bright vermillion. "I have had many times when the music would not come, when I had to labor for every note. The arts do not give away their secrets easily. We must stretch and strain for every victory. But to create something beautiful is worth all the pain. It is like giving birth. Agony and ecstasy tied together. The agony of releasing something precious from within your secret self. And the ecstasy of holding in your hands a new life that only you and God could have created.''

Frannie nodded distractedly. She wasn't in the mood for a philosophical discussion about creativity.

Juliana set the kettle on the gas range, then reached for a can of tomatoes. Frannie's stomach knotted as she watched Juliana move about the kitchen as if she had already memorized—and claimed—every inch of it. She already considers it her private domain! Frannie noted grudgingly.

How could her father be so captivated by a woman like Juliana? The ebony-haired matron looked nothing like Frannie's idea of a minister's wife. Juliana was a buxom, brassy woman who made a habit of wearing colorful, formfitting dresses that were just short of being tacky. All right, so on Juliana they somehow managed to look classy in a dramatic, theatrical sort of way. That still didn't explain how her father could be so smitten by this flashy woman.

''What are you making?'' Frannie asked as Juliana gathered an array of spices from the shelf.

Juliana paused and smiled at Frannie, her rosy face brightening. ''I'm making spaghetti. Your father's favorite. We are entertaining his ministerial staff here tonight.''

Frannie straightened, suddenly alert. ''Tonight? They're coming for dinner? Why didn't Daddy tell me? He knows I teach my class tonight. There's no way I can fix spaghetti.''

Juliana gently patted Frannie's arm. ''No, dear girl, you don't understand. I will fix the spaghetti.''

Frannie drew back from Juliana's touch. ''But I always fix the spaghetti. Daddy won't be happy if I don't.''

Juliana opened the cupboard and removed several cans of tomato sauce, then turned back to Frannie. ''Well, we will straighten him out, won't we? We will tell him it's time for a change. I will fix my family's secret Italian recipe. I am sure your father will find it delightful.''

Frannie wanted to retort, *It won't be as good as mine!* But she held her tongue. No sense in making waves. Her father would just take Juliana's side. ''Well, let me know if you need any help.''

''Thanks, dear. I'm fine.'' Juliana waved her ringed fingers in the air. ''You go work on your sculpture.''

A storm cloud of resentment swirled in Frannie's chest. Before she said something she regretted, Frannie strode back down the hall to the sunroom. As she looked back, she caught a glimpse of Belina slipping like a silent shadow into the kitchen. *She was waiting for me to leave!* The girl was so antisocial, she made every effort to avoid encounters with Frannie. *What's her problem? Does she hate me? How can I live in* the same house with someone who doesn't even want to look me in the eye or say good morning!

Frannie knew as soon as she sat down and gazed at the leaden mound of clay that she wasn't going to get any work done today. "Might as well take a drive and clear my head."

Frannie ran upstairs to her room and grabbed her purse off the bureau. On her way out the door she noticed Ruggs crouching on the floor by her bed. "Hey, boy, how did you get back in the house? Oh, I bet Daddy let you in, didn't he? While Juliana wasn't looking!"

Frannie knelt down and wrapped her arms around the rangy, mop-haired dog. He made a whining sound and ran his rough tongue over her arm. His shiny black eyes peered yearningly at her through several shanks of sandy-brown hair.

"Poor baby. Are you still smarting from your scolding this morning? Queen Juliana banished you from the kitchen, didn't she?" Frannie stood up, smoothed her jeans and beckoned the shaggy mongrel to follow her. "Come, boy. Let's go for a joyride!"

She scrambled down the stairs, with Ruggs bounding right behind her. She took long strides down the hall, peeked in her father's study and told him she was taking Ruggs for a ride to keep him out of Juliana's hair. Her father looked up from his sermon notes with a distracted smile and told her to have fun.

"Sure, Daddy. See you later." She sighed dispiritedly as she headed out the door. *He doesn't have a* clue how miserable I am since he married Juliana! Not a clue!

Outside, in the driveway, Frannie opened the passenger door of her shiny yellow sports car and coaxed Ruggs inside. "Sit still now and be a good boy."

Out on the open road, she looked over at Ruggs and grinned. Her hirsute pet sat tall, panting happily as the warm breeze rolled through the open window and fanned his heavy fur.

"Let's go to the ocean and be beach bums for a day," she suggested, as if expecting a reply. Ruggs accommodated her with an agreeable yip.

She took La Jolla Shores Drive for several miles, then turned off on a small winding road that led to a lonely expanse of beach. She parked beside the road, let Ruggs out and the two ambled across the sand under a shimmering white-hot sun. At the water's edge, she pulled off her sandals, rolled up her pant legs and waded barefoot into the cool water. Ruggs started to follow, then backed up as a wave rippled over his paws.

Frannie laughed. "Oh, come on, you chicken. Come in the water! You won't melt."

Ruggs took another lumbering step backward and shook himself. No dip in the sea for him. He was staying high and dry.

As if to defy her stubborn pet, Frannie waded out deeper. A ringlet of seaweed caught her ankle. She kicked it away and noticed a creamy white shell in the water. She stooped down, picked it up and brushed off the wet sand. It was a perfect shell. She breathed in the fresh, briny air, filling her lungs. There was something she loved about the beach. A sense of freedom and adventure, as if the world were wide open, boundless, offering endless possibilities. And yet, somehow, standing there, she could stretch out her arms and touch the earth from end to end.

"I could stay here forever," she told Ruggs. "I feel like I could sit down right here and sink my hands in the wet sand and create something beautiful."

Ruggs ignored her and pawed at something slimy on the hard-packed sand. Frannie chose not to look too closely. "Come on, Ruggsy," she urged. "Let's explore!"

She slogged a while through the ankle-deep water, then made her way up the beach and padded across the warm, uneven sand. They had walked a quarter mile when Frannie spotted an old clapboard beach house nestled beside a rocky protuberance. Jutting cliffs dotted with palm trees rose beyond the modest little house. The place looked empty, its door padlocked. A weathered sign stood at an angle beside the house. It said For Rent. Call 555-7878.

Frannie shaded her eyes and gazed into the distance along the isolated beach. There were other houses, but they were far and few between. Anyone living in this house would have complete privacy, not to mention peace and quiet.

"This is just what we need, Ruggs. A place to call our own, with no one to disturb us. What do you say, boy? Shall we check it out?"

Ruggs galumphed toward the house. Frannie caught up with him as he clambered onto the small wood-frame porch and pawed the warped pine door. Frannie rubbed a layer of dirt off the window and peered inside. To her surprise, the little house was furnished. To be sure, the modest furnishings looked a bit dilapidated, but comfortable.

"Wouldn't it be a hoot to move into this place? What do you think, Ruggs?" she asked, as if the pooch might actually respond.

He backed up and let out an approving howl. At least, that's how she chose to interpret it.

"So you like it, too, boy. It's something to think about." She memorized the phone number and gave the house another once-over, then she and Ruggs headed back down the beach to her car.

Until now she had never seriously considered moving out of her father's house. As long as he had needed her, she had vowed to be there for him. But the bitter truth was, he didn't need her anymore. He had Juliana and her strange, reclusive daughter, and he seemed perfectly content to make them his family now.

But maybe her father's marriage was a blessing in disguise. Frannie was twenty-four now, too old to still be living at home under her daddy's watchful eye. Maybe it was time to step out, explore the world and carve a new life for herself. There was no telling what—or who—awaited her in this vast, beckoning land.

Chapter Three

For two days, Frannie put off phoning the rental number to inquire about the beach house. She vacillated between excitement at the prospect of moving into a place of her own and horror at the thought of leaving her father and the home she had lived in all her life. Wouldn't moving out show that she had truly given up on salvaging her family? Or was God trying to tell her something, nudging her to take responsibility for her own life and future?

On the third day, Frannie gathered her courage and dialed the number. She learned the house was still available and the rent was less than she might have expected for beachfront property, even though the house was a bit dilapidated. "I'll take it," she heard herself saying. Her heart began to pound with anticipation and a pinch of anxiety.

What am I doing? she asked herself the next day as she drove to the beach house to meet the real estate agent for an official walk-through. "What could I have been thinking?" she wondered aloud an hour later as she returned home with a signed rental agreement and a set of keys.

That evening she cornered her father in his study and told him the news. By the stunned look on his face, she might as well have told him she was taking the next shuttle into space.

"Aren't you happy here, sugar plum?" he asked blankly.

She fought the tears gathering in her eyes. She couldn't—wouldn't—lose control. All she could manage to blurt out was "You have Juliana now, and you like her spaghetti better than mine!"

He got up from his desk, came around and drew her into his arms. "Spaghetti? This is about spaghetti?"

"No, Daddy. It's just...you don't need me anymore. You have a new family."

He caressed her hair. "I'll always need you, baby cakes. You know that. I need you to be my loving daughter, but not my cook, housekeeper and caretaker. I let you fill those roles much too long." He kissed her forehead. "And who says I like Juliana's spaghetti better than yours? Nothing can top yours."

Frannie sniffled like a sulking child. "You're not just saying that?"

Her father grinned broadly. "Are you kidding? I'm a minister of the Gospel. I'm committed to telling the truth, and only the truth. And the truth is, I saw this coming. I understand why you'd want a place of your own. But I'll miss you like crazy, pumpkin. And no matter where you go or what you do, nobody can take your place in my heart.''

She smiled through her tears. "Then I have your blessing?''

"My blessing, my love and my prayers. I just ask you to make sure this is what you really want. And promise me, anytime you decide this isn't for you, you'll come home.''

"Don't worry. I'll come home to visit. I'll be here so often, you'll get sick of me.''

"Never in a million years.'' Her father kissed her forehead, then clasped her face in his large hands. "This beach house—is it safe? In a good area?''

"Of course, Daddy. It's perfect.''

"Well, I have an idea. Why don't you take Ruggs with you? I'd feel better knowing he's there to protect you.''

"You wouldn't mind?''

Her father winked. "Juliana's not too fond of the old boy anyway. You take him.''

Frannie threw her arms around her father's neck. "Thank you, Daddy! Thank you!''

She turned to leave, but he caught her hand. "You know, there's someone else who's going to miss you. Now Belina won't have anyone in the house her age to hang out with.''

Frannie rolled her eyes. Was it possible her father really didn't have a clue about Belina? "Daddy, she'll be very happy to have me out of here. You just wait and see.''

"I don't believe that for a minute. I think she'd like the two of you to be friends."

"Then she can come visit me at my beach house." Fat chance that would ever happen!

Her father seemed to think that was a good idea. "I'll tell her that. She used to live on the beach. I bet she misses it."

"Whatever," Frannie mumbled. Spooky Belina was the last person she wanted hanging out at her new place, but she couldn't tell her father that.

The next afternoon, after lunch, her father helped her carry her things out to the car. She wasn't taking much—some clothes, toiletries, her Bible, CD player, boombox and enough dishes, pots and pans and utensils to accommodate one person. On the weekend her father and Juliana's son, Antonio, would rent a truck and bring out all her art supplies and equipment from the sunroom.

"Are you sure you don't want me to come with you today?" her father asked as she coaxed Ruggs into the passenger seat. "I could help you settle in. The place might need some work. I could get my toolbox and—"

"No, Daddy, you stay here. I'm fine. I've got to do this myself. I'm grown up, Dad. I'm not Daddy's little girl anymore." She didn't add that she feared her father would have a fit if he saw how desolate and in disrepair the beach house was. She could hear him now. I won't have my daughter living in a hovel like this! And look how isolated you are! It's not safe. What if someone breaks in—?

No, she didn't want him seeing her new home until she'd had a chance to settle in and spruce it up a bit. Once she had all her things in place, her father would be reluctant to insist she move out and come home.

It was late afternoon before Frannie pulled her vehicle into the small, rutted driveway beside her new home. Her heart was pounding with excitement as she slipped out of her car, let Ruggs out and walked across the beach to the modest dwelling. "Well, here we are, Ruggsy. Home at last!" She stuck the key in the lock and turned it, then gingerly opened the door. It creaked on its hinges. She made a mental note: Oil the hinges. She stepped inside and gazed around at her very own domicile.

The thought came to her: Be it ever so humble, there's no place like home. Her gaze flitted over the hardwood floor, the paneled walls, braided throw rugs, pine tables with hurricane lamps and several pieces of overstuffed furniture, worn and sagging, but adequate. Besides the small bedroom and bath down the narrow hallway, the house consisted of one large room, with a breakfast bar separating the kitchen from the living area and a rustic stone fireplace taking up most of one wall.

Frannie sank down on the lumpy couch and bounced gently, testing the springs. "Well, they're right about the humble part. It's not Beverly Hills. But we'll get along just fine, won't we, Ruggsy?"

Ruggs loped around the room, sniffing every corner, then settled on the braided rug at Frannie's feet. She reached down and massaged his floppy ears.

"We can't sit around loafing all day, Ruggs. We've got work to do." She riffled through her purse and found her cell phone. "I'd better call the phone company and see when they can start service. Can't depend on my cell phone forever." She punched in the numbers and waited, then tossed the phone back in her purse. "Might know. In all my excitement, I forgot to charge the battery last night. We're off to a good start, aren't we!"

She got up and went to her kitchenette and turned on the spigot. The pipes groaned and clattered. Rusty water finally sputtered from the faucet. "Doesn't look like this place has been occupied in ages." She opened the cupboards. They would need to be washed out and lined before she stocked them. "Looks like I'd better bring in my stuff and find the detergent."

It took several trips to unload her car. She couldn't believe she had packed so much. And wait till her father came with the rest of her stuff on Saturday! Now that she had boxes, sacks and suitcases everywhere, the place looked smaller than ever. And a bit grungy, if she was honest about it. No second thoughts! she warned herself. You wanted a place of your own, and now you've got it. Make the best of it!

For the next hour she scrubbed the kitchen cupboards. While they weren't exactly gleaming, they finally looked tolerable.

"I'm done! They'll have to do." Wiping her chapped hands on a paper towel, she looked over at Ruggs, ensconced by the stone fireplace. "Guess I'd better make a trip to the grocery store, or we'll be having stale granola bars and rusty water for dinner. You stay here, boy, and keep an eye on the place, and I'll bring you back your favorite doggie treats.''

Ruggs barked and wagged his tail.

Frannie grabbed up her purse, checked for her keys and retraced her steps across the sandy yard to her car. The air had cooled perceptibly and clouds were gathering on the horizon. ''You might know,'' she mumbled as she pulled out onto the street. ''My first day in my new house and it looks like rain. It hardly ever rains in Southern California in July! Hope I'm not stuck with a leaky roof.''

The closest grocery store was a small market several miles away. Hope I don't see anybody I know, she thought as she entered the store. She was wearing formfitting jeans and a white blouse tied at her waist, and her long blond hair looked unattended and flyaway in the rising breeze. Seeing that the store was nearly empty, she gave a little sigh of relief. Thank goodness, she wouldn't be encountering any prospective dates in a place like this.

She bought just enough staples to tide her over for the next few days—two paper sacks filled with milk, butter, bread, eggs, oatmeal, ground beef, salad fixings and a healthy selection of fresh fruits and vegetables. She remembered Ruggs's dog food and treats and even snuck in a bag of chips and munchies for herself, plus a six-pack of diet cola. At the checkout counter, she added a local newspaper, a nice way to keep in touch with the world, since she had decided not to bring a television set.

By the time she returned to the beach house, the clouds had swollen to a threatening black and the wind was rattling the shutters, as if demanding entrance. Balancing her two bags of groceries, Frannie got inside just as the wind banged the door shut behind her.

"Wow! Looks like we're in for quite a storm."

Ruggs gazed up at her and cocked his head in agreement. She gave him a treat, then put the groceries away. She hadn't noticed before how old and small the refrigerator was. She hoped it worked. Why hadn't she been more careful to check things when she'd had her walk-through?

A sudden pelting rain slammed against the roof and rattled the windows. She looked outside and groaned. It was a downpour. The thought occurred to her to go back home just for tonight to get out of this storm. She immediately dismissed the idea. How would it look for her to go hightailing it home her very first day?

She shivered and realized she had no idea how to heat the place. She scrutinized the fireplace. Sure, why not? This was her home now. If she wanted to have a little fire in her own fireplace, who was to stop her? She stooped down beside the hearth and moved the grate aside. To her surprise, it already held several charred logs. Now if she could just find the matches she had packed in one of the boxes.

By the time she located the matches, it was dark

outside and the rain was coming down harder than ever. A bone-chilling dampness seeped through the walls, one of the disadvantages of living in a bungalow perched on the edge of the ocean.

Frannie bent over the fireplace and made sure the flue was open, then took the classified section from the paper, lit it and coaxed the flames until they ignited the blackened wood. After several minutes she had a roaring fire. Frannie stepped back and folded her arms in satisfaction. See, she was a smart, capable, independent woman. She could manage without her father's help!

Feeling a hunger pang or two, she returned to the kitchen and browsed through her groceries. Time for dinner. Maybe she would fix a salad, some broccoli and a hamburger. Not a feast exactly, but certainly adequate.

As she broke open a head of lettuce, she smelled something burning. How could that be? She hadn't turned on the gas range. A crackling noise broke into the distant drumming of the rainfall. Ruggs barked. Frannie spun around and gazed across the room, the lettuce dropping from her fingers. Heavy, black smoke was billowing out of the fireplace and filling the house.

Frannie ran to the fireplace and grabbed the poker. If she could only smother the flames! But her awkward attempts were useless. The flames were too intense and the smoke too thick. Her eyes started smarting, her throat went dry and she began to cough. She couldn't see. The acrid fumes were already stealing her breath. She dashed to the bedroom for her cell phone, then remembered that the battery was dead. She ran back to the living room and stared helplessly at the rolling smoke blanketing the room.

With her heart pounding in her throat, she grabbed Ruggs by the collar. "Come on, boy! Gotta find a phone and call the fire department!"

The moment she and Ruggs stepped out on the porch, she knew her trouble had only begun. The rain was coming down in a blinding deluge. There was no way she could drive.

"Dear God, help us!" She looked around, the rain streaming down her face and soaking her clothes. The world was a mass of liquid shadows and elusive shapes. Then, through the leaden gloom she saw a light flickering in the distance. It was the cottage down the beach. Someone was home!

"Come on, Ruggs!" Frannie broke into a run, her sneakers filling with water, her wet clothes sticking to her skin. She was drenched and out of breath by the time she reached the bungalow. She scaled the porch steps and pounded on the door until her palms ached. It seemed like an eternity before the latch clicked and the door creaked open.

Frannie caught a glimpse of a towering silhouette in the doorway, etched against the rosy glow of lamplight inside.

"I need a phone," she blurted.

"Don't have one."

"Please! My house is on fire!"

The man stepped outside. He was tall and brawny, his face obscured by shadows. "Where?"

She pointed down the beach. "There! The next cabin!"

The man pushed past her and broke into a sprint. She nudged Ruggs and ran after him, her legs suddenly feeling like overcooked spaghetti. She slipped in a puddle and nearly went down. Somehow she caught herself and slogged on through the relentless torrents. She arrived at the beach house just as the man disappeared inside. She clambered onto the porch and pushed open the door. Smoke rolled over her.

Inside, the man's deep, rasping voice bellowed, "Get out!"

She backed away, letting the door bang shut, and waited, holding Ruggs by the collar as the rain pelted them mercilessly. What if the stranger died trying to salvage her cabin? He could be asphyxiated by the fumes. How long did she dare wait before entering the house again?

Her questions were answered moments later, when the man burst out the door, his brawny chest heaving as he sucked for air. He was covered with soot, the stench of charred kindling so pungent on his body that Frannie turned her face away.

He took her arm and urged her away from the cabin. "Come on!"

She dug in her heels. "No—my house!"

"It's okay. I smothered the fire. Nothing's burning!"

"But I can't just leave it."

He stared down at her, impatience etched in his blackened face. "You can't stay, lady. It's toxic in there. We'll air it out tomorrow."

He took her hand and pulled her after him as if she were an obstreperous child. "Let's go!"

She stumbled after him. "Where?"

"My place, unless you've got a better idea."

She followed numbly, Ruggs galumphing after them through the downpour. By the time they reached the man's bungalow, Frannie's teeth were chattering. He opened the door and stepped aside. She hesitated only a moment as she recalled from childhood her mother's repeated admonition *Never go in the house of strangers*. This time there seemed no other choice. Besides, she had Ruggs. He would protect her, unless the man made him stay outside.

She sighed with relief when he held the door for Ruggs, too. After Ruggs bounded inside and shook himself like an oversize mop, spraying water everywhere, the man came in and shut the door behind him. He broke into a spasm of coughing.

She looked at him with concern. "The fumes got to you."

He wiped his red-rimmed eyes. "I'm okay." He pulled a handkerchief from the pocket of his jeans and coughed into it.

Frannie politely looked away. Folding her arms to keep from shivering, she gazed around the cottage and realized how good it felt to be inside a nice, warm house. The furnishings were as spartan as those in her cabin—masculine pine furniture, worn overstuffed couch and chair, hurricane lamps, braided rugs and a red brick fireplace with a crackling fire. The cottage was nothing fancy, but at the moment it seemed immensely inviting.

The man touched her arm, and she jumped. "You'd better get out of those clothes, miss."

She shrank back, her heart pounding. What if this stranger was a homicidal maniac? He was well over six feet tall and close to two hundred pounds. She'd be helpless to fight him off.

"I'm f-fine," she stammered.

"No, you're not. You'll freeze in those wet clothes."

She slipped over by the fire and held out her hands. "I'll just warm up a minute and then be on my way."

The man guffawed. "Really? You'll be on your way…where?"

"Home." They were both in this miserable predicament, and he was laughing at her! "I'll dry off, then go back to my house. The smoke should be tolerable by then."

Even with his face smudged with soot and his eyes tearing, the man managed a twinkle of amusement. "You're not getting rid of that smoke until you open all the doors and windows and air the place out in the heat of day."

Frannie's ire rose. She didn't want anyone telling her something that she wasn't ready to accept—the fact that she was stuck in a strange house with a strange man for the duration of a bleak, rainy night.

"I won't be here long," she insisted. "Once I've dried off, I'll go get my car and drive to my father's house."

"You'd have to be a fool to drive in this deluge."

"Well, I certainly can't stay here all night."

"Have it your way." He pulled his wet T-shirt over his head.

Frannie gasped. "What are you doing?"

"I'm going to go take a shower and see if I can scrub off some of this grime. And make the fire stop burning in my eyes."

As he rolled his blackened shirt in a ball, Frannie couldn't help noticing that he had the muscular build of a football player or weight lifter. He started down the hallway, then paused and looked back at her. "Listen, I've got some clothes you can change into, or a blanket—"

"No, I'm o-okay."

"That's why your teeth are chattering so hard you can't talk?"

He was right. She was freezing inside and out. If she didn't get out of these wet clothes, she'd catch her death of cold. "Maybe...maybe I will change."

He grinned, showing white, even teeth in his smudged face. "Fine. I'll lay some things out in the bedroom and you can change in there. There's a lock on the door, if you're worried. I'll be in the bathroom showering."

It sounded reasonable enough. Maybe the guy was harmless. She nodded. "I'd appreciate some warm clothes."

He disappeared down the hall, then returned a minute later and led her to the bedroom. "My things are way too big for you. But I found a flannel shirt and some sweats with a drawstring, so they should stay up okay. If you're still cold, you can wrap yourself in a blanket. Just take one off the bed."

"Thank you." She was still hugging herself, shivering. As soon as he stepped out of the room, she shut the door and bolted the lock. After removing her soggy sneakers, she quickly peeled off her soaked jeans and blouse and hung them over the metal bedpost. Her underwear was damp, but she wasn't about to part with it. She pulled on the long-sleeve shirt and baggy sweats and pulled the strings until they were cinched around her narrow waist.

For the first time she glanced at herself in the bureau mirror and shuddered. Who was this straggly, ragamuffin waif looking back at her with smeared makeup and disheveled hair? She looked like something out of a fright movie. Oh, well, the last thing on her mind was impressing anybody, especially her churlish stranger.

Gingerly she unlocked the door and peered down the hall. No one in sight. She heard the shower running in the bathroom. And—was it possible?—a deep voice was crooning a country-western song. The nerve of that man, to be singing so nonchalantly when they were in such a dire predicament!

She pulled a blanket off the bed, wrapped it around her shoulders and tiptoed down the hall past the bathroom. When she heard the shower go off, she scurried on to the living room and curled up on the couch before the fireplace—a little bug in a rug, as her mom used to say.

The man's voice sounded from the hallway. "You through in the bedroom, miss?"

"Yes, it's all yours," she called back, quelling a fresh spurt of anxiety. Now what? Was she actually going to spend an entire night in this house? Was she safe?

After a few minutes, the man came striding into the living room in a fresh T-shirt and jeans. He was toweling his dark, curly hair. His eyes were still tearing. But without all the soot and grime, he looked uncommonly handsome. His strong classic features were as finely chiseled as a Michelangelo sculpture—a perfectly straight nose, high forehead and sharply honed cheekbones, a wide jaw and a full, generous mouth. Arched brows shaded intense brown eyes and the stubble of a beard shadowed his chin.

Frannie realized she was staring.

He tossed his towel over a chair and eyed her suspiciously. "Is there a problem, lady?"

Frannie felt her face grow warm. "No, I'm sorry. I was concerned about your eyes. I hope the smoke didn't hurt them."

"They smart a little, but they'll be okay." He sat down in the overstuffed chair and raked his damp hair back from his forehead. "What I want to know is how you got all that smoke backed up in your house like that."

Frannie tightened the blanket around her shoulders.

"I just started a fire, that's all. How did I know it was going to back up into the house?" She tossed him a defensive glance. "I checked the flue, if that's what you're wondering."

He sat forward and held his hands out to the lapping flames. "But did you check the chimney to make sure some bird hadn't built a nest in it? Or the winds hadn't stuffed it with debris? No telling how long it's been since someone built a fire in that place."

Frannie shook her head. "I didn't think of that."

"Next time, get yourself a chimney sweep before you go starting a fire."

She bristled. "I will. First thing tomorrow. Or… whenever the rain stops."

He coughed again, a dry, hacking sound that shook his hefty frame.

"You inhaled too much smoke. Maybe you should see a doctor."

He laughed, and coughed again. "No way to see a doctor tonight. Maybe I'll fix a little tea and lemon. Want some?"

She shivered in spite of the dry clothes and heavy blanket. "Yes, some hot tea would be wonderful."

He stood and gazed down at her. "Listen, neighbor, if we're going to spend the night together, there's something you need to know."

She gazed up at him with a start, her backbone tensing. The rain was still hammering the roof, its relentless rat-a-tat echoing the fierce pounding of her heart. "Something I should know? What's that?"

He held out his hand. "My name. I'm Scott. Scott Winslow. What's yours?"

She relaxed a little and allowed a flicker of a smile to cross her lips. "I—I'm Frannie. Frannie Rowlands." She slipped her hand out of the blanket and allowed his large, rough hand to close around it.

He matched her smile. "Well, Frannie, it's going to be a long night. We might as well make the best of it."

Chapter Four

Frannie was on her guard again. She tightened her grip on the blanket wrapped around her, then glanced over at Ruggs curled contentedly beside the fireplace. If Scott Winslow tried anything suspicious, surely Ruggs would come to her defense. Wouldn't he? Or would he just roll over and go to sleep and leave her to fend for herself?

"Sugar and cream?"

"What?"

"Your tea. Do you want it plain? With lemon? Or with sugar and cream?" A faint smile played on the man's lips, but his eyes held a hint of something darker. Was it despair, nostalgia, remorse? "My mother was an Englishwoman. She always had a spot of cream in her tea."

"Plain is fine for me. Just as long as it's hot."

While he fixed the tea, Frannie gazed around the room, assessing what sort of man she was keeping company with tonight. *Please, dear Lord, don't let him be an ax murderer!* There wasn't much to go on—a few books on a table, a radio on the counter. But no television, stereo or telephone. Nor were there any newspapers, magazines, knickknacks or family portraits in sight. And not even a calendar or a cheap print on the wall.

Who is this man? Frannie wondered. He's anonymous. There's nothing in this room that tells me who he is. Except perhaps his books.

She reached out from her blanket for the nearest book and turned it over in her hands. It looked like a library book, some sort of historical treatise. Did the man possess nothing of his own? As she put it back, she noticed an open Bible lying among the history books, philosophy tomes and suspense novels.

A man who reads the Bible can't be all bad, she mused.

As Scott served the tea, she let the blanket fall away from her shoulders and accepted the steaming mug. With the tea warming her insides, her flannel shirt and sweats should be enough to keep her toasty. She put the mug to her lips and sipped gingerly, then nodded toward the stack of books. "You must like to read."

He settled back in his overstuffed chair and took a swallow of the hot liquid. "Yes, I do. It's one of my favorite pastimes."

"Mine, too. When I have time."

He flashed an oblique smile. "I always have time."

"You're lucky. I'm always juggling a busy schedule."

"And mine is wide open these days."

She ventured another observation. "I see you have a Bible."

He nodded. "It was my mother's."

"Was?"

"Yes." He paused, as if deliberating whether to go on. Finally he said in a low, abrupt voice, "She—she died."

Frannie felt a jolt of emotions—sympathy, empathy, compassion and her own lingering pain. "I'm sorry."

"Don't be. It's been a while."

"How long?"

"Well over six months."

Frannie turned the warm mug in her palms. "My mother died seven years ago, and I still can't believe she's gone."

Scott looked away, but not before Frannie saw tears glistening in his eyes. His voice rumbled. "Seven years? Then it sounds like I've got a long way to go."

Frannie searched for words. "Scott, I hope your mother's Bible has been a comfort for you."

"I'm trying to find in it what she found."

"I'm sure she'd be pleased that you kept it."

His eyes darkened. "It's the least I could do." He leaned forward and set his mug on the table, then folded his hands under his chin. His brows furrowed and the lines around his mouth deepened as he gazed at the flames. He was a young man, surely no more than thirty, but the heaviness in his expression made him look old beyond his years.

Frannie had the feeling he was debating whether or not to say more, perhaps even to open up to her about his feelings. She took the initiative. "Losing someone you love... There are no words for it. But it does help to talk about it, even when you don't know what to say."

His voice was noncommittal. "I suppose you're right."

"And sometimes talking to a stranger is easier than baring your soul to your loved ones."

He nodded. "Ironic, but true."

"When my mother died, I didn't talk about my feelings for a long time. I was afraid my father and sisters would feel worse if they knew how much I was hurting."

Scott gave her a probing, incisive glance. "Then how did you cope?"

She gazed at the flickering fire for several moments. "I don't know. I'm not even sure what coping means. I just tried to make it through each day. I prayed a lot. Cried a lot. Ranted a little." She held up the thumb-worn Bible. "And I looked for answers in this book."

His lips tightened in a small, ironic smile. "So we have something in common. Two motherless orphans with a penchant for the Holy Scriptures. Extraordinary."

"Not really. I've read the Bible all my life. You might say I was spoon-fed from the cradle."

"How so?"

"My father's a minister."

He looked at her curiously, one brow arching. "Is that so? What's it like?"

"Being a minister's daughter?" She chuckled. "Don't get me going on that subject."

"Why not? The rain's not letting up. We've got a long night ahead of us."

Frannie shivered and pulled the blanket back up around her shoulders. He was right. The uncertainty of her situation struck her afresh. She didn't know the first thing about this man. She might have stepped heedlessly into her worst nightmare. She would have to endure an entire night to find out. She drummed her fingers on the mug. "I really need to let my father know where I am. He's such a worrywart. He might even come looking for me."

"He'd be crazy to go out in this weather."

It was true. Her father wouldn't be looking for her. He had no idea she even needed him. Frannie sipped her tea. It was lukewarm now. She glanced at her watch. She had been here for nearly two hours. She was cold and exhausted. All she wanted was to be back in her father's house, in her own bed, safe and sound.

But there was something in the remote, melancholy face of the man sitting in the chair beside her that touched her and piqued her curiosity. Staring morosely into the fire, he looked like the loneliest man in the world. Or maybe that's the way he wanted it... To be alone. He hadn't anticipated that he would have to rescue a damsel in distress and take her back to his cottage for the night.

Frannie shifted uneasily on the couch. She drew her legs up under her and tucked the blanket around her knees. Rain still pelted the roof and windows like an invisible intruder, demanding admittance. She cleared her throat and waited to see if her moody companion would break the silence. The rosy glow from the flames danced on his stalwart features, but he remained tight-lipped, stony-faced.

Finally she spoke his name, startling him out of his reverie. "Mr. Winslow?"

He stared at her as if he had forgotten she was there. "Did you say something?"

"Just your name."

"I'm sorry. My mind wandered. I guess I'm guilty of that a lot these days."

"No problem. It took me a year after my mother died before I could concentrate on anything again. People talked to me and I never heard a word. I'd try to work and end up staring at a shapeless mound of clay all day."

Bewilderment flickered in his eyes. "You stared at a mound of clay? I've heard of many ways to express grief, but that's a new one on me."

Frannie broke into laughter. Scott joined her with a polite, baffled chuckle, but she knew he had no idea what was so funny. She covered her mouth to stifle herself. "I'm sorry. There's no way you could know. I'm a sculptor. The clay had nothing to do with grieving. It's my job. What I do."

He grinned sheepishly. "Now I get it. I'm impressed. I've never met a sculptor before."

She smiled. "Most people look at me with suspicion or pity. They figure I'm in my second childhood or never got out of my first. They can't imagine a grown woman mucking around in clay all day."

"Good training for a muddy night like this."

"I suppose so."

"And you're doing what you love best."

She arched her brows, wide-eyed. "How do you know that?"

He grinned. "I see it in your face. Hear it in your voice. You're obviously passionate about your work."

"I didn't realize it showed."

"Like neon lights."

She felt a warm glow that had nothing to do with the fire. "So what do you do?"

He didn't answer for a full minute. She was about to repeat the question in case he had reverted back into his reverie. But finally he spoke. "What do I do? I walk. I run. I collect driftwood on the beach. I read. I think. Sometimes I even try to pray."

"Sounds like a very peaceful life. But I meant, what kind of work do you do?"

"I just told you."

She laughed lightly. "You know what I mean. I assume you have a job to go to. You're too young to be retired. Oh, I know. You're on vacation. Renting this cabin for the summer."

He shook his head, his expression clouding, as if

he were deliberately stepping back behind a veil. "This isn't a summer cottage. It's my permanent home."

Frannie ran her fingertips over the scratchy blanket that enveloped her. "I'm sorry. I didn't mean to sound nosy. It's none of my business what line of work you're in."

Scott got up and stoked the fire, then sat back down. "I'm not trying to be evasive, Miss Rowlands. The truth is, this is what I do. This is it. I live in this cottage. Sometimes I collect and sell firewood."

Disappointment scissored through Frannie. She had imagined that her handsome rescuer might be a doctor, lawyer or business tycoon. Surely anything but a common beach bum.

"When I'm in the mood, I build furniture out of driftwood, but it's not a profitable occupation. It takes me too long to create each piece, and no one's willing to meet my price."

"I know the feeling," Frannie conceded. "Sculpting is like that at times. It's feast or famine. When I have a commission I'm on easy street. When I don't, I'm on a penny-pincher's budget. It was never a problem when I lived at home, but now that I'm on my own..."

"It can be a challenge," he agreed. "But I always have a few dollars in my pocket. Enough to get by."

"Did you ever think of, um, you know, going out and—"

"Getting a real job?"

"Something like that."

Scott's voice took on an oddly menacing tone, as if he were lashing out at some invisible adversary. "The corporate world is filled with potholes and booby traps. I've seen men swallowed whole by the duplicity and hypocrisy. I've seen them sell their souls and the souls of their families for just a little more power and wealth. It's a deadly, diabolic life. I want no part of it."

There was only the sound of the thundering downpour until Frannie found her voice. "It doesn't have to be that way, Mr. Winslow. I've known some very honorable businessmen. Men who are honest and generous and—"

He stood abruptly. "It's late, Miss Rowlands." He took a step toward her, his towering frame silhouetted against the firelight. "I imagine you'd like to get some sleep."

A knot of apprehension tightened in Frannie's chest as he loomed over her. "Sleep? I—I hadn't thought about it."

"It's nearly midnight."

She shrank back against the couch, her fingers clutching the blanket around her shoulders. What would she do if this strange, agitated man attacked her? Ruggs, asleep by the fire, couldn't save her. And there wasn't another living soul in shouting distance. She might be able to grab the poker, knock him out and run. But where would she go in this deluge? And surely with his strength, he could wrestle the poker from her grip and use it on her.

Her fear crescendoed as he held out his hand and said in a tone both forceful and compelling, "Come, Miss Rowlands. Don't be afraid. You know where the bedroom is."

Chapter Five

"I don't need the bedroom, Mr. Winslow. I'm fine right here on the couch," Frannie declared with all the boldness she could muster.

"Nonsense, Miss Rowlands. You're my guest. You take the bedroom and I'll take the couch. It's the least I can do."

"All right, if you insist."

"I insist."

Relief washed over her. Thank heavens, he meant her no harm. He was just offering her a place to sleep! Still wrapped in her blanket, she got up off the couch and headed for the bedroom. She recalled the lock on the door. It meant she could rest without fear.

But when Scott followed her down the hall into the bedroom, her anxieties sparked again. He went over to the bed and pulled off a blanket. Then, seeing the expression on her face, he held up his palm in a gesture of peace. "Don't worry, I'm just getting myself a blanket." He looked back at the bed. "I could change the sheets if you want to wait a minute."

Frannie waved him off. "No, thanks, I'll probably just curl up on top of the bed."

"Well, make yourself at home. You're the first company I've had here. It's nothing fancy, but I think you should be comfortable. I'll put clean towels in the bathroom. Feel free to shower if you like."

Frannie took a backward step and shook her head. "I'm pretty tired. I'll just get some shut-eye."

"Fine. Mind if I take one of the pillows?"

"Of course. They're yours."

Scott grabbed a pillow and tucked it under his arm with the blanket. He stood beside the bed for a moment, gazing at Frannie. In the soft glow of the hurricane lamp, he looked ruggedly handsome. "So I guess we're all set, Miss Rowlands. Sleep well. I'll see you in the morning."

"Yes. Thank you. Good night." As he started for the door, she said, "Wait! I forgot about Ruggs. I should bring him in here with me."

Scott looked back at her and shrugged. "He's fine sleeping by the fire. I doubt you'll be able to rouse him anyway."

"I know, but I just thought—"

Comprehension flickered in his eyes. "Oh, you think you'll be safer with your dog in here with you. Is that it?"

"I—I didn't say that."

"But I can see it in your eyes. What do you think

I'll do, Miss Rowlands? Attack you in my own home? I assure you, you have nothing to fear from me.''

Her cheeks warmed with embarrassment. ''I didn't mean to offend you, Mr. Winslow. But you must admit we find ourselves in a rather unusual situation.''

''Circumstances always look worse in the midst of a howling storm. Don't worry. Things will look infinitely better in the morning. Good night again, Miss Rowlands.''

As soon as he was outside the door, Frannie scurried over and turned the lock. With a sigh of relief, she sat down on the bed and let the blanket fall from her shoulders. Mr. Scott Winslow would have to break down the door to get to her now. The bedsprings creaked as she moved. She wondered if he was standing outside the door listening. Waiting.

She got up and glanced at her reflection in the bureau mirror. She looked ghastly, her makeup blotchy, her long blond hair disheveled. The flannel shirt hung on her like an oversize nightshirt, and the sweats were baggy. If only she felt free to take a shower and wash her hair. But that was a luxury she couldn't afford right now. Mr. Scott Winslow seemed like a nice enough guy, but one never knew. There was no sense in taking chances and putting herself in harm's way.

The rain was still falling, less forceful than before. It tapped a steady, almost reassuring rhythm on the roof. Weariness enveloped her. She turned off the hurricane lamp and blinked as her eyes got accustomed to the darkness. She climbed onto the bed, curled up on the covers, pulled her blanket over her and fluffed the feather pillow under her head.

For her own safety, she ought to try to stay awake. But the bed felt so comfortable and warm, she could feel her body giving itself up to sleep. "Lord," she whispered, "this isn't how I expected to spend my first night on my own. If Daddy gets wind of it, he's going to tell me to pack up and get myself home. But I can't go back. You know that. Help me, Lord. Sometimes You seem so far away. But I really need You now. I feel so alone. Please keep me safe through the night."

She had intended to say more, but the words died on her lips as she gave herself up to a deep, dreamless slumber.

Frannie's next conscious thought was, Where am I? Sunshine streamed through the windows and sea-gulls screeched to one another in a blue, cloud-studded sky.

Frannie rolled over and rubbed her eyes. She knew she wasn't at home, but this wasn't her little bunga-low either. Then it all came back to her in a rush—the clogged chimney, the smoke, her rescuer bringing her here to his beach house. Everything fell into place. And now it was a glorious morning and she was safe and sound.

A knock sounded on her door, followed by a deep masculine voice. "Miss Rowlands, are you awake?"

She scrambled off the bed and smoothed her rum-pled flannel shirt over her sweatpants. "Yes, I'm awake."

"Breakfast will be ready in about ten minutes."

"Breakfast?"

"Do you like coffee?"

"Yes, but—" She unlocked the door, opened it a crack and peered out. Scott Winslow looked even taller and more athletic than she recalled. "I really don't need anything to eat."

"Well, I'm as hungry as a bear. So as long as I'm cooking anyway, you might as well join me for some bacon and eggs."

She caught the aroma of bacon sizzling in a skillet and realized how ravenous she was. "All right. I'll have a little."

"Coffee, too?"

"Decaffeinated?"

"Sorry."

"That's okay. I'll drink whatever you've got."

"I warn you, it's strong stuff. It'll curl your hair."

She grinned. "Then I'll take it. Always did want Shirley Temple ringlets."

He returned her grin. "And you're welcome to use the shower. I'll be busy in the kitchen."

"Thanks. Maybe I will take a quick shower." Her genteel host didn't seem nearly so threatening in the full light of day.

"Soap and shampoo are in the cupboard. Sorry I don't have any of the nice perfumed amenities. Just the basic masculine stuff."

"I'll get by."

It was the fastest shower she'd ever taken. But at least she was clean and her clothes were dry, she mused as she slipped into her own shirt and jeans. Her sneakers were still soggy, and she would have to forgo any makeup, but she sure could use a hairbrush to get out the tangles in her long, thick hair.

She joined Scott in his kitchenette, her hair wrapped in a towel. He was draining the bacon on a paper towel.

"I don't suppose you have an extra hairbrush."

"Top drawer of the bureau. It's even clean. Help yourself."

She returned to the bedroom, opened the drawer and removed the brush, but not before she noticed a snapshot of a young family. Father and mother and two young sons. Was one of those boys Scott Winslow? There was something oddly compelling about the photo. What struck Frannie was that no one in the picture was smiling. The woman stood gazing solemnly at the camera, with one hand on each boy's shoulder. The father stood apart from the others, frowning, gazing off in another direction. Behind them was what appeared to be an immense house, a Spanish-style mansion. If they were fortunate enough to occupy a house like that, why did they look so glum?

Frannie shrugged. It was none of her business. If she had her way, she would probably never encounter her mysterious neighbor again. And yet, she couldn't help feeling curious about him.

As she was about to shut the drawer, Frannie noticed a sketchbook beside the photo. Did that mean Mr. Winslow was an artist like herself? Should I take one little peek inside? she wondered. Why not? It's not like reading private letters, and it might give me a clue to who this man is.

Gently she removed the book, opened the cover and flipped through the pages. The book was filled with sketches of houses, buildings, gardens, playgrounds and trees. They were the work of an untrained hand, and yet they were quite exquisite in their own way. They revealed a man of extraordinary energy and idealism. Not at all the way she perceived Scott Winslow.

His voice sounded from the other room. "Miss Rowlands, did you find the brush? Do you need some help?"

"No, I found it."

She replaced the book, closed the drawer and returned to the living room. She sat down on the couch, unwrapped the towel and shook her hair. Slowly she pulled the brush through the tangled strands. It felt good to be clean again. Even the masculine aroma of the shampoo on her damp hair seemed pleasantly refreshing.

It seemed equally bracing to hear a man at work in the kitchen. For years now, Frannie had been the one doing kitchen duty at home. This was a pleasant change.

When she had finished brushing her hair, she ambled into the kitchenette and watched as Scott spooned a mound of golden-yellow scrambled eggs into a bowl.

"Looks like you know your way around a kitchen pretty well."

He cast her a boyish glance. "Better wait until you've tried the food before making a judgment call like that."

"If it tastes as good as it looks and smells, you've got it made."

He paused and gave her an approving once-over. "Hey, you clean up pretty good."

She smiled. "That's what my mama always said. Is there anything I can do to help?"

"No, I've got a handle on it."

He carried the eggs and bacon over to a small table by the window. "I've mastered about six dishes, mainly using eggs, potatoes, hamburger and pasta. Anything beyond that and I'm helpless as a baby."

He brought over steaming mugs of coffee and set them down. "As soon as the toast pops up, we're ready to go."

"It smells delicious."

"Then sit down and enjoy it." After fetching the toast, he sat down across from Frannie. "I suppose since you're a minister's daughter, we ought to say grace. Would you like to do the honors?"

She nodded, pleased, and offered a brief prayer. For the next few minutes they concentrated on the food. "It's very good," she told him.

"There's more. Eat up."

"Thanks, but this is plenty. I will have another cup of coffee though. That's potent stuff, but it's delicious."

He got up and filled her mug. "My secret recipe. Actually, I get it at that little market a couple miles from here."

"Oh, yes, I've been there. Nice little place." She debated whether to ask him about his sketches, and decided to chance it. She wouldn't mention the picture though. Somehow she sensed that it was off-limits. "When I got the hairbrush, I noticed your sketchbook. Since I'm an artist, I couldn't resist taking a peek."

He gave her an odd, scrutinizing glance. "So that's what took you so long." She couldn't tell whether he was pleased or upset. "I did those for fun. Just messing around."

"I'm impressed. Have you ever thought about studying art professionally?"

"No. It's just a little hobby of mine. Any talent I have I got from my mother. She was the real thing, an artist of substance. Never got to do much with it, though."

"But you could. I teach an art class at the university. I recognize talent when I see it. You really should consider—"

"I'm not interested, Miss Rowlands."

His tone silenced her. She sipped her coffee, then finished the rest of her eggs.

Scott cleared his throat. "I didn't mean to be so abrupt."

"It's okay. I shouldn't overstep my bounds. Besides, it's time for me to head back to my place and see if I can air out all that smoke."

"I'll help you."

"That's not necessary. You've done quite enough."

He drummed his fingers on the table. "What you said about art classes... I'll give it some thought."

She managed a smile. He was trying to make amends. "Good. I'd hate to see talent like yours go to waste."

His face grew ruddy. Frannie saw something she hadn't seen before—vulnerability, hope, delight. "Nobody ever said I had that kind of talent."

"Well, you do. What about your mother? You said she was an artist. Didn't she praise your drawings?"

"I suppose. But she had her own problems. She was sick a lot. I learned at an early age not to bother her with my concerns."

"Or with your dreams?"

"Yeah, that, too."

"That's a shame. My parents were always there for my sisters and me. We had a very happy life."

"Had?"

"Yes. I'm afraid it's all changed now."

"How so?"

She paused, her spirits darkening. "Daddy's got his new wife and stepdaughter. I really don't feel comfortable with either one of them."

"Is that why you moved into the beach house?"

"That, and the fact that it's time for me to be on my own. I can't be Daddy's little girl forever."

He nodded. "I hear what you're saying."

Frannie sensed that Scott Winslow was speaking

out of his own private pain, and it went beyond the death of his mother. "You really do know what I'm saying. You're dealing with more than your mother's death, aren't you?"

His expression changed, as if a veil had dropped over his features. "We were talking about you, not me, Miss Rowlands."

"I'm sorry. I didn't mean to pry."

"Forget it. I'm a grump in the morning until I've finished my brew." He swallowed the last of his coffee and set the mug down. "There, that's better."

"That's some tonic, Mr. Winslow. If it can change your mood that fast, maybe I'd better get some more for myself."

He sat back in his chair and flexed his shoulders. "Let's drop the formalities. We've spent the night under the same roof…and survived. Call me Scott."

"All right. Scott it is. And I'm Frannie." An idea occurred to her. "You know, if you'd like to earn a little extra spending money, I could use a model in my art class."

He grimaced. "Doesn't sound like my kind of thing. Truth is, I like to keep my clothes on in public."

A crimson flush spread over Frannie's face. "Oh, Mr. Win—I mean, Scott—it's not that kind of class."

His face had turned nearly as red as hers. "It's not?"

"No. We don't use nude models. You'd wear a tank top and shorts."

"It's still not my cup of tea. Or coffee, as the case may be."

"It was just a thought."

He chuckled. "If I get that hard up, I'll let you know."

"You do that." She picked up her dishes and carried them over to the sink.

"Don't worry about the dishes. I'll take care of them."

"I don't mind, really. I'm the proverbial mother hen."

"You're the prettiest mother hen I ever saw."

She came back, took his soiled dishes to the sink and turned on the spigot. "You know just what to tell a girl who's wearing yesterday's clothes and not a stitch of makeup."

He got up and grabbed the dish towel. "It's the truth. I wouldn't lie about a thing like that."

"Thanks. Now I don't feel like such a ragamuffin."

When they had finished the dishes, she glanced over at the fireplace, where Ruggs was ensconced in all his furry glory. "Guess I'd better get my dog and go home. I've interrupted your life long enough, Mr. Wins—I mean, Scott."

"No problem. I had no plans for you to interrupt."

A memory stirred at the back of Frannie's mind. "Your name... It somehow rings a bell. Scott Winslow. It seems like I've seen the name in the news."

He stared blankly at her. "I don't think so. I've done nothing noteworthy, except rescue a lady from a smoking chimney, and if that makes tonight's news, I won't know it. No TV."

Frannie rubbed her chin. "Now I remember. Scott Winslow is that billionaire entrepreneur who owns half the real estate in California." She smiled slyly. "You're not that Scott Winslow, are you?"

He chuckled dryly. "If I were, do you think I'd be sitting here?"

She laughed. "Not unless you were totally crazy."

"I'm not that crazy."

She went over and knelt down beside her slumbering pet. "Come on, Ruggs. Wake up, you lazy dog. Time to go home." As she massaged the dog's floppy ears, she looked back at Scott. "Good thing you're not that rich man. I remember the news clip now. Scott Winslow made his fortune providing low-income housing for the poor. But it was so substandard, he created his own slums. A judge sentenced him to live for six months in one of his own buildings that was infested with rats. Can you imagine?"

Scott's countenance darkened. "No, I can't imagine. What kind of monster lives his life like that?"

"I don't know. It's sad, isn't it? How someone like that can totally miss out on the real meaning of life."

Scott flexed his jaw. "Someday he'll get what he deserves."

Ruggs roused himself and stretched, then clambered to his feet and shook his shaggy frame. He yawned and nudged Frannie with his wet nose, as if to say, Okay, I'm ready to go.

Frannie shrugged. "The boss says it's time to leave."

"Guess we can't argue with the boss." Scott walked her and Ruggs to the door and offered his hand as she stepped out onto the porch. "Now you get that chimney cleaned out before you start any more fires, you hear!"

As his hand enveloped hers, she felt a pleasant tickle in her stomach, as if she'd just crested the summit and was on the downward spiral of a roller-coaster ride.

As she stepped off the porch, she shaded her eyes from the blinding sun. "Don't worry, I'll clean my chimney. I promise."

She walked a few yards across the beach, then paused and looked back as Ruggs bounded on ahead. Scott Winslow was still standing on his narrow porch, one hand on the log railing. Something in his stance touched a deep chord in Frannie. She had no words for it, except that the emotions she felt were strong and puzzling. Scott Winslow had aroused her fears, piqued her curiosity and kindled an unexpected tenderness for the reclusive beachcomber.

Chapter Six

Nearly a week passed before Frannie encountered Scott Winslow again. She and Ruggs were walking along the beach at sunset, when she spotted him jogging in a muscle T-shirt and cargo shorts. He waved, and Ruggs went bounding toward him, as if they were long-lost friends.

Scott stooped down and massaged the panting dog. "Hey, Ruggs, ol' boy, how's it going?"

Frannie, in a halter top and stretch shorts, removed her sunglasses and gazed at the strapping jogger. "Look at this! My dog's crazy about you. He never greets me like that."

"You've got to have just the right touch. See, I scratch his ears exactly at the skull. He loves it."

"I knew there had to be a secret to it. I'll have to try it sometime."

"It's easy." Scott straightened and drew close to Frannie, until she could see the sweat beaded on his bronze forehead. He stretched out his hand and gently brushed her hair back with his fingertips, then touched her head just behind her ear. "Right here. This very spot. You just massage in a circular motion. Ruggs will love it."

Frannie drew back with a bemused grin and swung her hair free. "It might be more effective if you demonstrated on the dog."

Scott's dark eyes crinkled merrily. "No, that was just the effect I wanted." He glanced around. "Where you heading?"

"Nowhere special." She followed his gaze. The sun was a huge red ball balanced on an azure-blue skyline. Gulls were circling and screeching to one another, and the waves lapped up over the sand, bathing the soles of her bare feet in cool, refreshing water. "Actually, I'm heading home. Took Ruggs for his usual evening walk. He loves the beach."

Scott raked his fingers through his damp hair. "Did you get your chimney cleaned out?"

"Yes, but we haven't had a cold night since the storm, so I haven't needed it."

"We will again, one of these days." He reached down and gave Ruggs another ear massage. The dog stood rooted to the spot, panting contentedly.

Frannie laughed. "If he were a cat, he'd be purring."

"He is purring. Don't you hear it? That low growl in his throat? He's saying, 'Don't stop. Don't you dare stop!'"

"I don't blame him. You do seem to have the magic touch."

"I told you."

"I haven't seen you since the storm. Are you hiding out?"

His brow furrowed. "Why would you think that? I've been busy. Reading. Thinking. Building a driftwood chair. Jogging at dawn every morning. I haven't seen you out jogging."

"Not at dawn, I can assure you of that."

"Don't knock it until you try it."

"I've been busy getting settled. My dad brought the rest of my stuff last Saturday and helped me set up my studio, so I'm ready to sculpt again."

"Sounds exciting."

"It is to me. Of course, most people think of sculpting with clay as a kindergarten pastime. But I just ignore the rude remarks of the unenlightened masses. Or in this case, I escape to the beach, where I don't have to face them."

"You sound like a girl after my own heart. The life of a loner has its own rewards."

"Then maybe you'll initiate me into the official beachcombers' society."

"I would, if there were one, but we're all fierce individualists. Couldn't get us all together in one room if you tried."

Frannie slipped her sunglasses back on. "Actually, I do have a proposition for you, Scott."

His lips curved in a wily smile. "Go ahead. I haven't heard a good proposition in ages."

"Stop grinning. I'm serious. Remember when I suggested you do some modeling for my class to earn a little extra money?"

"Yes, I remember, and the answer is still no."

"But you haven't heard my offer."

"I have no wish to pose clad or unclad before a bunch of googly-eyed college students."

"I don't want you posing for my class. I want you to pose for...me!"

Scott's brows shot up. "You want me to pose just for you? You're kidding!"

"No, I'm not. Last Saturday, when my dad brought me my mail, there was a letter from a Riverside cemetery. They want to commission me to do a Vietnam memorial statue. It would be a wonderful opportunity, and I already have some great ideas. But I'll need someone to pose as a Vietnam soldier."

"What about one of your students?"

"They're all busy with their studies. They wouldn't have time to commit to a project like this."

"But you assume I have the time."

"You could do your thinking and reading while you're posing. I couldn't afford to pay you much, but it would be enough to buy a few groceries and keep your refrigerator stocked. How about it, Scott?"

"You're one persistent gal, aren't you!"

"Tell you what. You'll just have to pose for the initial sketches. Then I can do the actual sculpture from my drawings."

"Where would we work?"

"In the back room at my beach house. Like I said, my dad's got it all set up for me."

Scott scratched his head. "I'll have to think about it."

"Fine. If you're willing, just come by my place tomorrow about ten."

He touched her arm. "But I don't want your money. If I agree to pose, then maybe you can give me some art lessons. Unless you were just being nice when you said you liked my sketches."

Frannie's heart soared. "Oh, I loved your sketches. What a wonderful idea! You'll model and I'll teach. That way we both get what we want. A perfect arrangement!" She held out her hand. "So it's a deal? My place at ten?"

He clasped her hand so firmly, she winced. A light sparkled in his eyes that she hadn't seen before. "Ten sharp it is."

Scott posed for Frannie every day that week, arriving around 10:00 a.m. and leaving by three. He wore a tank top and shorts the first few days, then donned a rented army uniform for the next two. Every day they took a lunch break around noon. She fixed tuna fish sandwiches, opened a can of soup or stuck a frozen pizza in the oven. After lunch, with Ruggs loping at their heels, they walked for a half hour on the beach to clear their heads.

By the end of the week Frannie had completed a dozen drawings, showing Scott from different angles and a variety of poses, some in uniform, some not.

By the middle of the second week, she had done enough sketches to convey the correct musculature in her sculpture, the natural flowing grace of tendons, muscles and sinew. Her excitement for the work blossomed. She couldn't wait to begin building the armature and applying the supple, malleable clay.

But Scott was growing weary of posing. "This is hard work," he told her by the end of the second week. "You get to sit there and draw till your heart's content. I have to stand in awkward poses and hold still for hours on end."

"Just one more day," Frannie begged, "and I'll have all the drawings I need to start work on the sculpture."

"One more day? And what do I get in return?"

"More drawing lessons?"

"You already owe me a dozen lessons."

"Then how about a home-cooked steak dinner? Medium-rare filet mignon, grilled mushrooms and onions, baked potatoes with the works and a fresh garden salad? Guaranteed to be delicious. Don't forget, my family considers me a gourmet cook."

"You really know how to tempt a guy, don't you? Who can resist a tender steak smothered in mushrooms?"

The very next night, Frannie fixed Scott the mouthwatering steak she had promised. He arrived at her cottage just as she was tossing the salad. Dressed in a charcoal-gray shirt and sport coat, he could have passed as a high-level executive of a major corporation.

As he stepped inside, Frannie drew back, giving him the once-over. "Wow, look at you!"

His gaze swept approvingly over her. "You're not so bad yourself."

Frannie made a little curtsy in her sleeveless top and sarong pants. "Looks like we should be doing the town and showing off our fancy duds instead of eating in."

"Next time. My treat."

She returned to her salad. "Don't worry about it. I know money's tight. I can be satisfied with a burger and fries."

"Then you've got a date."

"But not until I've got my armature done. I started today. You can take a look at it. Of course, right now it just looks like a bunch of sticks and chicken wire."

"Don't they call that modern art?"

"You can scoff, but wait till you see the finished product. You'll think you're looking in a mirror. Actually, you'll be cast in bronze, and you will be so fine."

"My secret wish, to be bronzed!"

"Not you, silly. Just the clay model of you."

Scott crouched down and stroked Ruggs behind the ears. "What do you think of all this nonsense, boy? You think anybody's going to want to see a statue of me in a cemetery?" The shaggy dog barked, pawed the floor and licked Scott's hand. "Okay, so you approve. I guess it's not so bad."

"The money's not so bad, either," said Frannie. "I really wish you'd let me pay you for posing."

"I said no, Frannie."

"I know you like living the simple life, mean and lean and close to the bone, but even you need to eat. If I paid you what you're worth to me, you could have a telephone installed. You wouldn't feel like you're cut off from civilization."

He chuckled. "Who would I call? And who would I want to call me? It's my own choice not to have a phone."

"Or a television, or a computer, or anything else that connects you to the real world." She eyed him curiously. "I wonder sometimes what has made you turn your back on everyone and everything."

"I haven't turned my back on you, Frannie. I rescued you from a smoking chimney, and I've posed for you for two solid, back-breaking weeks."

"And I appreciate your help more than I can say. But I worry about you, Scott. What kind of life do you have, holed up alone in your beach house?"

"I've got the same kind of life you've got. Peace, quiet, solitude. The freedom to come and go as I please." He ambled over to the counter where she was working and helped himself to a wedge of tomato. "So what's the problem, Frannie? We're in the same boat—a boat of our own choosing, I might add."

She sliced an avocado into the salad. "But I haven't narrowed my world to just this cottage. I have a career and a family. I teach an evening class at the university. I go to church on Sunday. I visit my dad. Or at least I will be visiting him next week."

"What's happening next week?"

"A family dinner." Frannie took the salad over to the linen-draped dinette table. "My dad mentioned that the new music director from church will be there. I have a feeling he's pulling one of his matchmaking schemes again."

"Setting you up, huh?"

"My father won't be happy until he has all of his daughters married. Two down, one to go."

"How do you feel about that?"

"To be honest, I have no desire to be tied down to any man."

"So you don't plan to get married?"

"I didn't say that. Maybe someday the right man will come along, but I've got a whole lot of living to do in the meantime." She placed salad bowls and glasses of iced tea on the table. "What about you, Scott? Are you the marrying kind?"

"I thought I was once. But before I got to the altar, I realized it wouldn't work out."

"I'm sorry."

"Don't be. We would have made each other miserable."

Frannie pulled out the two straight-back chairs. "Let's start with the salad while the steak is broiling."

Scott sat down and spread the linen napkin over his lap. "Smells delicious. Suddenly I'm famished."

She looked across the table at him. "Would you like to ask the blessing this time?"

His face reddened slightly. "I'm a little rusty."

"I'm sure the Lord doesn't mind."

"If you say so." He bowed his head and murmured a one-sentence prayer, then said a relieved amen.

Frannie reached across the table and patted his hand. "Thanks. I love to hear a man pray. Reminds me of my dad."

He grimaced. "I haven't had much practice in recent years."

She handed him the salad dressing. "It's never too late to get back in practice. My father's prayers have seen me through more troubles than I could possibly count."

"My mother was like that when I was young. But I think my father wore her down. He scoffed whenever we went to church, told us we were being brainwashed. Said church makes a man weak."

"Your father must have been a very unhappy man."

Scott nodded and turned his attention to his salad, his dark brows shadowing his eyes.

"But your mother took you to church anyway?"

"Yes, when I was a small boy."

"She must have loved you very much."

"She did." He met her gaze and his expression softened. "I loved going."

"Being raised in the church, I never knew anything else."

"You were very fortunate."

"Yes, I guess I was."

"I remember I was about five when I raised my

hand in Sunday school and asked Jesus into my heart.''

Frannie smiled. ''I was five, too. I didn't understand it all, but I knew something was different in me. I didn't feel lonely anymore. You know, the way you feel alone in the midst of a crowd.''

''Yes, I do know.''

''It's amazing how you can be so young and yet know that something special has happened to you. I knew Jesus was with me. It was like I was carrying around this special secret in my heart. I wanted to tell everybody. Did you feel that way?''

''I suppose I did. But now, as an adult, I've come to believe that experience was just part of the magic of childhood.''

Frannie stared wide-eyed at him. ''You can't mean that. Are you saying you've lost your faith?''

''No, not lost it. Just put it in its proper perspective. It was special to me as a child, but not especially relevant to me as a grown man.''

''How sad. I admit I haven't felt as close to God these past few years, but the Lord is still very real in my life.''

''Good. Don't let anyone talk you out of it.''

''You mean...like your father talked you out of it?''

''I didn't say that.''

''Yes, you did, in so many words.''

He nodded toward the broiler. ''You'd better check those steaks. Smells like they're done.''

For the rest of the meal, they talked about superficial things—the sweltering August heat, the good buys on vegetables at the farmers' market and Frannie's upcoming family dinner.

"So you really think your father is trying to set you up?" asked Scott between bites of baked potato.

"I don't think, I *know*. There's no other reason he would invite an eligible man to dinner. I just wish I could figure out some way to send him a message that I'm not interested."

"What about the direct approach? Just say no."

"Wouldn't work. My father would smile and nod, and then set me up with his version of Mr. Right anyway."

"Then just don't show up at the dinner."

"I can't do that. It would hurt my dad and embarrass his guest. I have no choice but to go and endure the evening."

"Who knows? Maybe you'll like the man."

Frannie speared a tender morsel of steak. "How many ways can I say it? I'm not interested in finding a husband right now. I've got a long way to go to establish myself as a sculptor. What husband will want to wait on dinner while I muck around in the clay?"

A sly smile played on Scott's lips. "If he loves you, he'll have dinner ready for you when you get through mucking around."

Frannie grinned. "Now that sounds like a man I could love!"

"Maybe this fellow your dad picked out is that man."

"No, I don't think so. The thing is, my dad won't even tell the poor guy that he's matching him up with his daughter. It'll all seem like an innocent, ordinary evening. But under the surface my father will be orchestrating everything."

"One of those control freaks, huh?"

"Only when it comes to his darling daughters."

"Can't you just go along with it for one evening?"

"I suppose. I just wish I could show up with a date of my own and cut my dad off at the pass. Then he wouldn't dare try his matchmaking tactics anymore."

Scott chuckled. "Now who's conspiring?"

"Wait, I've got it!" Frannie reached across the table and seized Scott's hand. "You'll be my date!"

He stared blankly at her. "Me?"

"Please! As a favor. Just this once."

"Let me get this straight. You want me to go to your house for dinner and pretend that we're dating?"

"Yes! It'll stop my dad in his tracks. If he thinks I've already met Mr. Right, he won't keep trying to match me up. He'll leave me alone."

"I won't do it."

"Why not?"

"Because I won't lie to your father."

"We won't lie. I'd never lie to him. We'll just act like we like each other and let him draw his own conclusions."

"I do like you, Frannie. I don't have to pretend that."

"And I like you too, Scott. So will you do it?"

"I'll think about it."

Frannie gave him her most beguiling smile. "I made chocolate cheesecake for dessert. Do you suppose that could persuade you?"

Debra Clopton 88

Chapter Seven

Andrew Rowlands was on a mission—to bring his wandering daughter back into the fold and get her headed down the matrimonial path. He had even found the perfect mate for his fiercely independent daughter—Wesley Hopkins, the new minister of music at Cornerstone Christian Church. Wesley was a solid, reliable man with a stellar background and an impressive future. Just the sort of man who would take good care of Frannie and balance her mercurial personality with his dependable character.

Of course, if Andrew were honest with himself, he knew he was doing this for himself as much as for Frannie. Since her departure to her beachfront bungalow, Andrew's home wasn't the same. As much as he loved Juliana, he couldn't quite get used to the fact that his house was now occupied by an entirely new group of people. At times, the thought occurred to him, Where have all the others gone—my wife,

Mandy, and three daughters? What happened to that life? How is it that I'm still here, but everyone else is different?

It wasn't that he was unhappy with Juliana. He adored her. But since their wedding, she had spent so much time and effort trying to be the perfect minister's wife that she had filled his house with people and activities he didn't recognize—visitors he hardly knew who seemed drawn to Juliana like a magnet, neighborhood women who came for a weekly Bible study and young people who seemed to like congregating at his house after their youth meetings.

It wasn't that Andrew didn't like people. He cared deeply for them. He had been called to serve them as a minister of the Gospel. But he wasn't used to them flocking in and out of his home day and night. At times he quipped that if it got much worse, he would have to install a revolving door.

The simple fact was Andrew was a man who didn't take easily to change. Once the furniture was placed in a certain spot in his house, he wanted it to remain there always. When he had established a daily routine that worked well, he wanted to keep that routine permanently.

But Juliana thrived on rearranging schedules and furniture. Even the sounds and smells in his home were different these days, the voices and conversations louder, the aromas stronger—spicy, garlic-filled pastas, heavy, flowery perfumes.

Juliana was a presence to be reckoned with; with her buoyant personality and natural charisma, she captivated people with a word or a smile. When she entered a room, she took charge of it, dominated it. All eyes turned her way.

Compared to Juliana, his beloved Mandy had been hardly more than a background shadow, small and unassuming, deferent, gentle, quiet, compliant. Of course, Mandy had been a powerhouse of prayer and had accomplished much for her faith, but her deeds were all done behind the scenes, often unnoticed. Andrew hadn't realized Mandy's many achievements until she was gone. The void she had left was enormous.

But now Juliana was the love of his life, and Andrew had to learn a whole new set of responses and expectations. It wasn't that he wanted to tame or change Juliana or make her a carbon copy of Mandy. It was just that he had spent most of his adult life with one kind of woman, and now he had to find a way to accommodate himself to someone exactly the opposite.

Often these days he found himself thinking that life would be easier if Frannie were still at home. All the changes would be balanced with a presence from the past, a familiar face in the kitchen, his own flesh and blood who knew his ways and anticipated his wishes even before he did.

So, even as he invited Frannie to a special family dinner to get acquainted with the new minister of music, he knew his motives weren't unsullied. He wanted his daughter to move back home and begin an approved courtship that he could keep his eye on. He longed to renew that special father-daughter closeness he had come to depend on after Mandy's death. He simply didn't like his youngest trying her wings and soaring into an unknown future without him. The scope of his manipulations made Andrew uncomfortable, but he reminded himself that he had Frannie's best interests at heart. And didn't that justify all his paternal machinations?

The dinner was set for Saturday night, the last week of August. When Frannie mentioned bringing a friend, Andrew had discouraged her, reminding her that the dinner was in honor of the new minister of music. It was a half-truth, the other half being that Andrew was matchmaking again. But neither Wesley nor Frannie needed to know that minor detail. "Wesley is young and talented and all the way from Michigan," Andrew had told Frannie, "so he doesn't know anyone in California. We want to make him feel welcome, so he'll stay at our church for a long time."

Andrew wasn't sure Frannie was convinced. But tonight he would find out. Now that the big night was here, Andrew felt as nervous as a cat on a hot stove. And it wasn't just because he was afraid Frannie would see through his ploy and resent his meddling.

There was another unknown factor—his reclusive stepdaughter, Belina. As gregarious and outgoing as Juliana was, her daughter was equally withdrawn and aloof. Andrew wasn't even sure she would come to the table. Often she hid out in her room when company came. But perhaps this time Andrew could persuade her to join them. If Frannie saw that Belina missed her and wanted to be friends, perhaps she would give up her beach house and come home.

These thoughts tumbled in Andrew's mind as he showered and dressed for dinner. He knew he should pray about this evening, but he couldn't quite bring himself to say, *Lord, Thy will be done.* His anxieties mounted as he went downstairs and checked on Juliana in the kitchen. She had baked lasagna, her family recipe, and now she was tossing a salad with vinegar and oil.

"It smells delicious in here." Andrew kissed her cheek. "Anything I can do?"

"Take the bottles of sparkling cider out to the table while I put the garlic bread in the oven."

He picked up a bottle in each hand. "Will Belina be joining us for dinner?"

Juliana pursed her ruby-red lips. "I hope so, Andrew. I told her this is a very important dinner for you, that you want her and Frannie to be friends, and you want to make the young music minister feel welcome to our community. So we shall see if she comes down."

The doorbell rang. Andrew glanced at his watch. Someone was ten minutes early. He hoped it was Frannie. But when he opened the door, there stood Wesley Hopkins, tall and lanky as a reed, with a bouquet of yellow roses in his hand and a wide smile on his lips. He looked a bit nervous, but wholesomely attractive in his navy blue blazer, blue shirt and maroon tie. Yes, indeed, he was good son-in-law material—neat, courteous, respectful and dependable.

"I hope I'm not too early, Reverend Rowlands."

"Not at all, Wesley. Come on in. And, please, this is a social evening. Call me Andrew."

"Yes, sir…Andrew." With an awkward thrust, he stuck the bouquet under Andrew's nose. "These are for Mrs. Rowlands."

Andrew drew back, rubbed his nose and smiled. "Juliana's in the kitchen working on dinner. But I'm sure she'll love them."

"I hope so. I couldn't decide between pink and yellow. I hope she likes yellow."

"Loves yellow! By the way, my daughter Frannie should be here any moment. I don't think you've met her yet."

"No, sir. I'm looking forward to it. You have a fine family."

"Thank you, Wesley. I'm sure you'll like Frannie. She's a wonderful artist…and a superb cook. Almost as good as Juliana. Follow me. We can chat in the living room until dinner's ready."

Andrew stuck the flowers in a glass vase on the buffet, then showed Wesley into the living room. But before they could settle on the sofa, he heard the front door click. He tried to hide his enthusiasm as he said, "Oh, that must be Frannie now."

He strode back to the foyer and arrived just as Frannie stepped inside. She looked stunning in a simple, belted black sheath and pumps. Wesley couldn't help but fall for her. Andrew was about to give his daughter a welcoming hug when he realized there was someone else just behind her. Andrew gaped at the

tall, imposing stranger. He was dressed in a black
V-neck shirt and blue blazer and had the tanned face
and sun-streaked hair of a surfer.

Andrew gave Frannie a questioning glance.

Embracing him, she whispered, ''I said I might
bring a friend.''

He whispered back, ''I assumed you meant someone of the female persuasion.''

''Sorry, Daddy. Guess it was a lack of communi-
cation.'' She turned to the robust man beside her.
''Scott, this is my father, Reverend Rowlands.
''Daddy, this is my friend Scott.''

Andrew vigorously shook the man's hand, but in
his mind's eye he was watching his carefully orchestrated evening collapse around him. ''Didn't catch the
last name,'' he murmured politely. But Frannie was
already leading her rugged companion into the living
room, her arm twined in his. Andrew followed and
dutifully introduced Wesley, but his heart wasn't in
it now. The evening would be a fiasco, unless he
could pawn off this beach bum on someone else…like
Belina. It was a long shot, but worth the effort.

Slipping his arm around his capricious daughter,
Andrew assumed a confidential tone. ''Honey, would
you mind going upstairs and seeing if you can persuade Belina to come down to dinner? You know how
she is around company.''

''Sure, Daddy.'' Frannie turned to her escort. ''Be
right back, Scott. I want you to meet my stepsister.''

By the time Frannie returned downstairs with Belina timidly following behind, Juliana was already

putting the salad on the table. Andrew made introductions, giving Belina a fatherly embrace as he did so. She looked quite lovely in a white blouse and pleated jumper, her long black hair framing her delicate, ivory face. These days not even Andrew could tell where her facial scars had been.

But Belina's emotional scars couldn't be erased so easily. She shyly lowered her gaze and kept her hands at her sides as the two men greeted her. Andrew's heart ached for her. If only his stepdaughter could find the courage and confidence to face life head-on. Until she learned to smile and reach out to others, it was unlikely she'd ever find a proper suitor.

The thought made Andrew groan. It struck him suddenly that he had not just one daughter left to marry off, but two! And they both presented him with a monumental challenge.

Juliana's voice broke into his thoughts. "Dinner is served, Andrew. Please bring our guests."

They all gathered around the table and took the chairs Juliana assigned them. Frannie and her young man sat opposite Wesley and Belina. It wasn't the way Andrew had planned, but perhaps Wesley and his daughter would hit it off anyway. Anything was possible.

"Juliana, is there anything I can do to help?" Frannie offered.

"No, dear. Everything is ready. This time you do no work. You just eat and enjoy the meal."

"But what about our spaghetti bibs?" Frannie turned to Scott. "We always wore these huge, home-made bibs on spaghetti night. It was a family tradition.''

"Because I am such a klutz," Andrew interjected.

"No bibs anymore," said Juliana with a bright smile. "To me, they are unsuitable for a formal dinner."

After Juliana returned to the kitchen, Frannie mused under her breath, "I always thought they were kind of cute."

Andrew patted his daughter's hand. "Me, too, sweetheart. But let's abide by Juliana's wishes."

Frannie didn't reply, but Andrew could see a shadow of resentment darken her face. Would his darling daughter ever accept Juliana as his wife and the new lady of the house?

"Shall we pray?" he said in his most reverential tone. When he was stymied, he always resorted to his comfortable clergyman's role. Everyone held hands as Andrew said grace. He made a point of asking God's blessing on his two first-time dinner guests, Wesley and Scott.

Minutes later, as his guests consumed their salads, Andrew said conversationally, "So, tell me, Scott, what do you do?"

Scott's eyes remained on his salad as he speared a tomato wedge. "I live in the beach house down the way from Frannie."

"No, I mean, what do you do for a living?"

A long pause. "I'm between jobs right now."

"I see." Andrew's irritation flared. Why wouldn't

the man look him in the eye? "I'm curious. What are you trained to do?"

Finally Scott looked up, his brows shading his dark eyes. "I have a business degree from Stanford."

Andrew whistled through his teeth. "Impressive. A real accomplishment. But I should think, with your background you would have major corporations lining up at your door. And yet you say you're out of work and living in a cottage on the beach?"

"I didn't say 'out of work,' sir. I said, 'between jobs.'"

"Isn't that one and the same?"

Frannie glared at him. "Daddy, please! You're giving Scott the third degree."

Andrew winced inwardly. He knew he was crossing the line, behaving like an overprotective dolt. And yet there was something about this elusive young man that didn't add up. "Sorry, Scott. I didn't mean to be rude. I just like to get to know Frannie's friends. Fathers are like that, you know."

Scott sat back and put down his fork. His expression was inscrutable, but his voice sounded conciliatory. "No problem, Reverend Rowlands. The truth is, my mother died not long ago. We were very close. I needed some time off to regroup and figure out what I want to do with my life."

"I didn't know. I owe you an apology, Scott."

"No apology needed, sir. I trust you can see now why I need some downtime."

"I certainly can, Scott." Andrew sipped his sparkling cider, then asked with a casual air, "So what do you hope to do when you get back into the swim of things?''

Frannie interrupted. ''Scott's quite an artist, Daddy. You should see the buildings and houses he draws. And the lovely gardens and trees.''

''An artist, are you? That's quite a leap from a business degree.''

''Art is my hobby, Reverend Rowlands. Only a hobby. And I'm really not very good at it, no matter what Frannie says.''

''That's not true, Scott. You have a lot of natural ability. And by the time we've finished our lessons, you'll be drawing like a professional.''

Andrew's eyes narrowed. ''You're giving him art lessons?''

''Yes, Daddy. And he's posing for me.''

''Posing for you?''

''Oh, Daddy, it's just for the commission I'm doing for the Riverside cemetery. I needed someone to pose as a Vietnam soldier. Scott is an excellent model.''

Before Andrew could utter another word, Frannie looked across the table at Wesley Hopkins. ''So, Wesley, how do you like California?''

A wide grin spread across the man's narrow face. ''I have mixed feelings, Miss Rowlands.''

''Frannie, please.''

''I love the weather and the scenery, Frannie. The ocean and palm trees and mountains. But I haven't got the hang of the freeway system yet. I hold my breath every time I head for an on-ramp. And the traffic! I don't know how veteran commuters stand it.''

"It can drive you to distraction," Frannie agreed. "That's another reason I love living at my beach house. I can pretend I'm the only person in the world."

Wesley beamed. "You make it sound quite appealing, Frannie."

Andrew knew the young music director was hooked when he added, "Maybe I'll drop in on you sometime and see what it's like firsthand. I'd phone first, of course."

Andrew could see that Wesley's offer didn't sit well with his daughter.

Frannie cast a quizzical glance at Scott, then looked over at Belina, who was staring down at her plate and seemed unaware of the entire conversation. In an excessively bright voice, Frannie said, "Belina, didn't you say you wanted to come see my new beach house?"

Belina looked up in bewilderment, as if rousing herself from a daydream. "Did I say that?"

"I'm sure you did." As Frannie rushed on, Andrew could almost see the gears turning in her mind. "Why don't you come and bring Wesley sometime, Belina? Maybe Scott could come over too, and the four of us could have lunch or dinner together."

Belina's hand flew to her mouth. "No, I couldn't, really."

"Oh, but it would be fun!" said Wesley, his face lighting up. "Please, Belina. I would be honored if you'd accompany me to your sister's place. I'm even willing to tackle these crazy freeways, if you'll be my navigator.''

Belina's face reddened. She seemed to be shrinking in her chair. Andrew had the surreal sensation that if she continued recoiling into herself, she would simply disappear. He wanted to rescue his mortified step-daughter, but, for once in his life, his mind was a blank.

Juliana spoke up and saved the day, her voice ebullient as a song. "That is a wonderful idea, Frannie. Of course you will go, Belina. You will have a splendid time. You and Wesley are very much alike.''

"Oh, Mama, please! You're embarrassing me!''

"But it's true, child. You both love music. You both have fine voices. You will be good for each other!''

"Then it's settled.'' Relief colored Frannie's voice. With a glance at Andrew that blended triumph and defiance, she placed her hand over Scott's, as if the two were certainly more than friends. "The four of us will have great fun together, Daddy.''

Andrew couldn't help noticing the way Scott slipped his arm possessively around Frannie's shoulder, as if they were already a couple planning a future together. A sour taste rose in his throat. Juliana hadn't even served the lasagna yet, and already he had indigestion.

And no wonder! For all of his matchmaking efforts, it appeared that his precious daughter was going to end up at the altar with a shiftless beachcomber!

Chapter Eight

When Frannie awoke the next morning, a smidgen of guilt pinched her thoughts. She couldn't get back to sleep. Last night she had deliberately misled her father about Scott, and now he was probably afraid she would marry a drifter. If she wanted a clear conscience, she would have to phone and reassure him that she and Scott were only friends. But maybe she'd give her dad another hour or so to stew about it first.

Since she couldn't sleep anyway, Frannie got up, put on a halter top, shorts and sneakers and roused Ruggs from his bed by the fireplace. "Come on, boy. Let's go take a run on the beach. We'll both feel better with some sun and fresh air."

The sun was already shimmering on the waves as she and Ruggs tromped over the packed sand to the water's edge. She kicked off her sneakers and waded into the water. "Try it, Ruggsy. The water's warm."

With a low growl, Ruggs backed up and pawed at the ground.

She ruffled his furry head. "Don't worry, I'm not going to drag you in. Come on, we'll jog in the sand."

She broke into a run along the beach and Ruggs bounded after her, yipping happily. The salty breeze caressed her face and fanned her hair as she quickened her pace. No ambling gait today; she was ready for a brisk sprint.

Suddenly she was aware of someone running with her, just a step behind. She slowed and glanced back, then stopped in her tracks. "Scott, you startled me."

He grinned and raked back his hair from his tanned face. He was wearing sweats and a tank top that showed off his glistening muscles. "Didn't mean to scare you. Just surprised to see you on the beach this early."

She looked up at him, shading her eyes from the sun. "Couldn't sleep. So thought I'd take Ruggs for a run. He's getting to be such a lazy pooch."

"Mind if I join you?"

"Be my guest."

"I'll race you to that palm tree by the rocky ledge."

"That's a good half mile."

"Too much for you, huh?"

"I didn't say that."

"Then let's try it."

They bolted forward at the same time and ran side by side, with Ruggs bringing up the rear. All too quickly Scott raced ahead and kept the lead by several yards. He was waiting for her at the palm tree, smiling triumphantly. By the time she reached the tree, Frannie's rib cage ached. She bent over, her hands on her knees, panting, catching her breath. Then she collapsed on the sand and lay on her back, her heart pounding like a jackhammer.

Ruggs assumed this was a game and plopped his shaggy hide down on top of her. "No, Ruggsy, get off!"

Scott came to her rescue. "Move it, boy. The lady said no!"

As Ruggs skulked off to examine a soggy rope of seaweed, Scott stretched out on the damp sand beside Frannie. He cupped his hands behind his head and gazed up at the sun-washed sky. "Guess I gave you a run for your money."

She turned her face to his. "Didn't know there was any money involved."

"But if there had been—"

"What? You would have let me win the race?"

"No chance. I have a very competitive spirit."

"So I see."

He grinned. "Don't tell me you're upset with me."

"Of course not. Why would I be upset?" She gave him a sly grin. "But if you were a gentleman, you would have let me win."

"No way!" He tossed a handful of sand on her bare legs. "You're just a poor sport!"

"I am not!" She grabbed a fistful of sand and threw it at his chest.

He rolled over on one elbow and shot her a challenging glance. "So you wanna fight?"

"Sure!" She scooped up more sand. Before she could toss it, he lunged forward and grabbed her wrists. "Oh, no, you don't!"

She struggled to free herself, but he held her fast. She kicked at his shin, but he rolled over and pulled her with him until she found herself in his arms, their faces only inches apart, his breath warm on her cheek.

Promptly she wriggled free and he released her. He hoisted himself up and brushed off the sand. He looked as taken off guard as she was. "I'm sorry, Frannie. I didn't mean to—"

She scrambled to her feet, her pulse quickening. "It's okay, Scott. I'm fine. No harm done."

"Good. I hope you didn't think I was—"

"No, I didn't. Didn't think a thing."

"Because I wasn't trying—"

"Of course you weren't." She turned to Ruggs, who had his nose buried in slimy green seaweed. "Come on, boy. Time to head home. I've got work to do."

Scott fell into step beside her. "I'll walk you back."

"You don't have to."

"I'm going in the same direction."

"Okay. But let's take it at a slower pace this time."

He nodded. "Much slower."

She glanced over at him. "I hate to say this, but I'm feeling a little guilty this morning."

"Guilty? Why?"

"For giving my dad the wrong impression about us."

"You said you wanted to discourage his match-making schemes. And I think we were quite convincing, don't you? He's expecting wedding bells any day now. He's not a happy camper."

"I know. But I handled it the wrong way. I shouldn't have misled him. He's a wonderful father, and I adore him."

"Then tell him the truth. We're friends. Period."

"I will. I'm going to phone him today. But he's got to understand that I'm a grown woman who wants to make her own choices. He can't keep interfering in my life and thinking he knows what's best for me."

"What about this double date you've set up with your stepsister and that Wesley fellow?"

"Oops, I forgot. I should keep my word. Would you mind?"

He winked at her. "What are friends for?"

"I'll talk to Belina when I phone my dad. She may back out of the date anyway. She's so painfully shy. You'd think she was still disabled and disfigured."

"Maybe she is. On the inside. Emotional wounds take a lot longer to heal than physical ones."

Frannie flashed Scott an approving smile. "You're pretty wise for a man who claims to be a simple beachcomber."

"Solitude is good for the soul."

"Yes, I'm learning that, too."

They had arrived at Frannie's bungalow, and Ruggs was pawing at the door.

Frannie opened it, then glanced back at Scott. "What about Friday night? We could barbecue steaks outside on the grill."

"Sounds good to me. Run it by your stepsister and let me know."

To Frannie's surprise, Belina agreed to the double date. "Do you want to phone Wesley," Frannie asked her, "or should I call him?"

"Would you mind phoning him? I don't think I could work up the courage."

Frannie smiled at the undercurrent of excitement in Belina's soft, breathy voice. "Don't worry, I'll arrange everything. I'll tell Wesley to pick you up around six. Is that okay?"

"Yes, Frannie. Thank you. You don't know what this means to me."

"No problem, Belina. I'm looking forward to it."

As Frannie clicked off her cell phone, she felt a peculiar sense of satisfaction. This date obviously meant more to Belina than Frannie could have imagined. Maybe Belina wasn't the sour-faced stick-in-the-mud that Frannie had assumed. Maybe it wasn't her choice to be a recluse. She had lived a solitary existence for so long, maybe it was all she knew.

The thought passed through Frannie's mind, Maybe it's not too late to be a sister to this reclusive girl. But did she even want to be close to Belina? She had moved out of her father's house partly to get away from her remote stepsister. But what if Belina wasn't really odd at all? What if she was just sad and lonely and afraid?

All day long on Friday, Frannie kept expecting Belina to phone and say she had canceled her dinner date with Wesley. But no call came. Looks like the dinner is on, Frannie mused as she put large russet potatoes in the oven to bake, then changed into a mint-green halter dress.

At six-thirty, Scott arrived, looking startlingly handsome in a blue sport shirt and navy khaki slacks. He handed Frannie a bouquet of yellow daisies and salmon-pink baby roses in a clear, cut-glass vase. "Fresh flowers for the hostess," he murmured as he stepped inside.

Ruggs bounded toward him and eagerly licked his hand. Scott's fingers moved instinctively to the back of Ruggs's ears.

"Am I early? Or has the other couple bowed out after all?"

"No, I'm expecting them any moment now." Frannie took the vase of flowers and set it in the center of her linen-draped table. "Thank you, Scott. Now the table is perfect! That was so thoughtful of you."

He grinned and nudged her chin playfully. "I figured we might as well do this evening up right. This might be our only official date, since, as we agreed, we're just friends."

She stifled a chuckle. "That doesn't mean we can't see each other. Friends spend time together."

"Good. I'm glad we clarified that, because solitude has lost its luster since you came along."

She met his gaze with a sly grin. "Are you saying you enjoy my company?"

His dark eyes crinkled. "And that's quite an admission coming from a confirmed hermit like myself."

"Really? Well, I—"

Ruggs severed their conversation with a sudden frenzy of barking. He dashed back and forth from Frannie to the door, his thick fur flying.

"Looks like we've got company." Scott followed Frannie to the door. Her two guests stood on the small porch—Wesley, in a pullover brown shirt and slacks, towering over Belina in a simple blue A-line dress and sandals. With her long ebony hair curled around her delicate face, Belina had never looked prettier.

Frannie smiled. "Welcome to my humble abode!"

As they stepped inside, Belina uttered a little exclamation of pleasure. "This is so quaint. And the ocean is just outside your door. I see why you love living here."

Wesley handed Frannie a box of foil-wrapped chocolates. "Hope you have a sweet tooth."

"I do, but I don't mind sharing these with everyone."

"You've got a charming, comfortable little place here."

"Thank you, Wesley. I like it. Please, sit down. Dinner's almost ready."

"May I help?" Belina asked, her voice almost a whisper.

Frannie nodded toward the kitchenette. "There's not much room for two cooks. But you could toss the salad while I sauté the mushrooms."

Scott placed a hand on Frannie's shoulder. "And I'll get the fire started in the grill. You bring out the steaks."

To Frannie's relief, the meal went without a hitch, and everyone seemed to enjoy it. While she served a fresh strawberry pie for dessert, Belina cleared the table.

When they were out of earshot of the men, Belina said under her breath, "Frannie, I've never had so much fun. Thank you for inviting us."

"I'm glad you could come."

"I can see why you love Scott. He's such a kind, charming man. And I can tell he's very fond of you, too."

Frannie's breath caught momentarily. She nearly dropped the steaming coffeepot she held in her hand. How could Belina think she loved Scott or that he cared about her? "Didn't my dad tell you? Scott and I were just pretending to be a couple to get my dad off his matchmaking high horse."

Belina's dark eyes met Frannie's, then her lashes lowered diffidently. "I don't mean to speak out of turn. But perhaps you two are fooling yourselves, not your father. When I look at you, I see a couple."

"I'm sorry, Belina. You're mistaken." Frannie hurried back to the table with the coffeepot, but Belina's words lingered in her mind: *I can see why you love Scott.... And I can tell he's very fond of you, too.*

"Who wants coffee?" Frannie asked, too brightly. Scott held out his cup. "I'll have some."

Frannie's hand shook slightly as she poured, and

the hot liquid sloshed outside the cup. "I'm sorry, Scott. I'm suddenly all thumbs."

"No problem. Want me to pour?"

She gave him the coffeepot and sat down, hoping he wouldn't think her nervousness had anything to do with him.

Wesley gave Frannie an approving nod. "This strawberry pie is out of this world. You should go into business."

"Then I'd never have time to sculpt."

Wesley forked up another ripe, red berry. "If you show the world what you can do with a mound of berries, men will beat a path to your door."

Frannie laughed. "My reason for moving here was to find some peace and solitude. Men beating a path to my door definitely doesn't fit that image. Besides, I'd much rather sink my hands in a mound of clay than a mound of strawberries."

"But the clay isn't nearly so delicious," said Scott, tossing her a sly smile. "Believe me, I know."

"Scott is posing for me," Frannie explained. "Before you go, I'll show you the sculpture. It's nearly completed."

"I would love to see it." Belina's voice was hushed, soft as the air.

Wesley turned to Belina and said, "But first, it's your turn. You haven't told us much about yourself, Miss Pagliarulo."

"It's Belina, please."

"Very well, Belina. What's your favorite pastime?"

Her face reddened. "I don't know. I love to read. I love to dream. And I love music."

"Do you sing?" Wesley leaned close to Belina with a conspiratorial air. "You must sing. You're a member of the Pagliarulo family. Your mother and brother have exceptional voices. Surely you sing, too."

Belina lifted her fingers to her lips, as if to muffle her reply. "I sing a little. But only for myself."

"That's hardly fair," said Wesley, "to deprive the world of your singing voice. Would you consider joining the church choir?"

Belina lowered her head and rocked back in her chair. "I couldn't. I'm sorry."

"No, I'm the one who's sorry," said Wesley. "You would add so much to our choir." He glanced over at Frannie. "Some of our choir members have more enthusiasm than talent."

"Yes, I've heard them." Frannie reached over and patted her stepsister's hand. "Couldn't you just think about it, Belina? Give it a try. You might enjoy it."

"I—I'll think about it, but I can't promise—"

"Wonderful!" Wesley clasped Belina's arm with an exuberance that startled her. "I welcome you to the choir of Cornerstone Christian Church!"

Scott raised his coffee cup in a congratulatory salute.

Belina shook her head. "I didn't say yes."

Wesley reminded her, "But you didn't say no."

When they had finished their dessert and coffee, Frannie suggested, "Why don't we take a walk on the beach? The house is a little warm, and there's a full moon out tonight.''

"A wonderful idea." Wesley pushed back his chair, stood and pulled out Belina's chair. "A moonlight stroll is the perfect way to end the evening."

Frannie and Scott exchanged amused glances, as if to say, Look at this! A romance is brewing! Scott got up and helped Frannie out of her chair, and the foursome headed outside, with Ruggs trotting close behind them.

They walked down to the beach and stood close enough to the water to feel the salt spray from the whitecaps rolling in. Belina slipped off her sandals and waded into the water, holding her skirt up.

"Be careful." Wesley followed her to the water's edge. "Don't fall in."

"Don't worry. I love the water! It's still warm from the heat of the day. Come join me!"

With a titter of laughter, Frannie kicked off her sandals and waded into the sea. "Come on in, you guys. It's great!"

Scott and Wesley exchanged dubious glances, then shrugged, removed their shoes and rolled up their pant legs.

"No splashing," Scott warned Frannie as he slogged out to meet her. "I don't want a replay of the night we met."

"What night was that?" asked Belina.

"The wettest night of the year." Frannie gave a quick recap of how Scott had saved her from her smoky cottage and the two had gotten drenched in the downpour. "He was a regular Sir Galahad. I don't know what I would have done without him."

Scott clasped her hand and swung it loosely between them. "But she had to promise not to set any more fires."

"And I haven't touched so much as a match since then." Frannie bent down and ran her fingers through the foamy waves that crescendoed against her bare legs. "Isn't this the best? Having the whole Pacific Ocean for a front yard?"

"I love it!" Belina raised her arms to the sky, her long raven hair rippling in the breeze. "Look, the moon is so bright, the ocean looks like it's glittering with diamonds."

Frannie lifted her skirt and waded in deeper, one hand still holding Scott's for support. "We should change into our swimsuits and have a midnight dip."

"No way." Scott's fingers tightened around her hand. "This is as far as I go."

She playfully yanked his hand. "Come on. I dare you. Just a little farther." She took another step and the sand gave way to a slippery patch of seaweed. As the slimy tentacles wrapped around her ankles, she swayed and nearly lost her footing.

Suddenly two strong arms seized her around the waist and held her fast. Flustered, she gazed up into Scott's dark, snapping eyes. "Didn't I warn you? You almost went under."

She clung to him as she kicked away the stringy seaweed. He kept his arm around her as he led her back to shore. Belina and Wesley followed. They gathered their shoes, socks and sandals, and when they reached dry sand, they sat down.

Wesley unrolled his pant legs and wiggled his bare toes. "Got to dry these tootsies off before I put on my socks."

"It's nice here," said Belina. "I don't want to go back inside." She looked at Wesley, beside her. "When I couldn't walk, my brother would carry me in his arms on the beach. Sometimes we'd go out in the middle of the night, when no one was around. Those times on the beach are my best memories."

Wesley moved closer. "I'd like to hear more about your life, Belina."

Frannie nodded. "You've never talked much about the past."

Belina drew a circle in the sand and turned it into a sad face. "Most of it was too painful. It's not easy to find the words. It was a very lonely existence."

"But not anymore, Belina. We won't let you be lonely." Wesley leaned over, erased the lines in the sand and made a smiling face. "God willing, from now on, there will be only happy faces for you."

Belinda looked around at each of them, tears glistening in her eyes. "I have never had friends. Until now."

"You not only have friends," said Frannie over a sudden lump in her throat. "Don't forget, you have a sister, too."

Belina's countenance shone, as if illuminated with moon glow. "Thank you, Frannie. I didn't think you wanted another sister."

Frannie blinked self-consciously. "I didn't know it, either, until now."

"This is turning into an evening of quiet revelations," noted Wesley. "Say, I have an idea. Why don't we play one of those silly ice-breaker games they play at parties?"

"What?" Frannie challenged. "You mean, truth or dare?"

"No, not exactly." Wesley sat forward and wrapped his arms around his long, narrow legs. "We'll all answer the same question, something philosophical, like 'What is your secret desire?'"

"Count me out," said Scott. "I'm not good at party games."

Wesley made a soft chuckling sound low in his throat. "Come on, it won't be so bad. How about this? What achievement would you most like to accomplish in your lifetime if money and circumstances weren't an issue?"

"And talent weren't an issue, either?" Scott smirked.

"Whatever. Okay, it's my idea, so I'll start. I'd like to compose a work of music, an oratorio, that would turn people's hearts to God the way *The Messiah* has."

Belina touched his arm. "What a wonderful goal, Wesley."

"Thank you." He clasped her hand, intertwining his fingers with hers. "Okay, who's next?"

Frannie lifted her hand. "Okay, I've got it. I would

like to create a work of art that points people to God, like Michelangelo's Sistine ceiling.''

Scott squeezed her shoulder. "And you may do that someday with your sculpture."

"I hope so. What about you, Scott?"

"No, let's just skip me, okay? It's not worth mentioning."

"Of course it is," said Wesley. "Come on, Scott, we'd all like to hear."

Scott looked thoughtful for a minute. When he finally spoke, his voice was husky. "I'd like to create housing developments where even poor people would be surrounded by beauty. Mothers would have their own gardens, children their own playgrounds, teenagers a place to play ball. And there would be a park where lovers could stroll, people could jog and old men could sit on benches and watch the world go by." He paused and looked away, as if embarrassed by his own impassioned words.

Frannie reached over and turned his face toward hers. "That's a beautiful thought, Scott. Who knows? Maybe someday you'll make that dream come true."

He grinned sheepishly. "Not at the rate I'm going."

"We all have to live by our dreams," said Frannie softly. "When we stop dreaming, we're dead."

"What about you, Belina?" said Wesley. "We haven't heard your wish."

She lowered her gaze. "It's nothing so grand as yours."

Wesley urged her on. "Let us be the judge of that."

"All right, I will tell you. But don't laugh."

"We would never laugh," Frannie assured her.

"It's just a little thing." Belina's voice was as soft and light as the breeze. "I would like to find the courage to stand before a congregation and sing without terror in my heart."

"Beautiful, Belina. Such a pure, sweet wish." Wesley moved beside her, until their arms were touching. "If you let me, I will help you make that wish come true."

As Wesley and Belina exchanged lingering smiles, Frannie had a sudden insight into what inspired her father's matchmaking efforts. Making someone happy—or even better, *two* someones—gave a person a real adrenaline rush.

Or was this rush of emotion coming from somewhere else? Frannie looked up at Scott. He was smiling down at her. Something in his eyes transfixed her. It was as if he were reading her very thoughts, listening to her pounding heart. The silent beat was saying, Frannie, this is a man you could love!

Chapter Nine

To keep her mind off Scott, Frannie threw herself into her work. She completed her bust of Longfellow and delivered it to the La Jolla's Children's Museum the first week of September. Her sculpture of the Vietnam soldier was due at the kiln by the middle of September, where it would be fired and then cast in bronze for the final memorial statue. But Frannie couldn't get the finishing touches just the way she wanted them. There was something missing in the soldier's face—a rugged intensity, a raw courage that she had been trying for days to capture. Her sketches weren't enough to go by now. She needed a flesh-and-blood person for the subtle nuances of shape, form and expression. She needed Scott.

Early on a Tuesday afternoon she tramped over to his cottage, wishing as she trudged under the blazing sun that the man would at least invest in a cell phone.

It was ridiculous that there was no way to contact him, except to show up at his door.

As she scaled his sagging porch steps, it occurred to her that he probably wasn't home anyway. In midday he would probably be out collecting driftwood for his innovative, one-of-a-kind furniture. Or selling firewood to passersby on the street. It was odd that a man of Scott's refinement and intellect was satisfied living the life of a beach bum.

But who was Frannie to judge? Hadn't she chosen the same sort of life for herself? Still, it bothered her that Scott didn't aspire to a higher calling or a professional career. If she were honest with herself, she had to admit that Scott's lack of ambition vexed her not just for his sake, but for her own.

Ever since the night of their double date with Wesley and Belina, Frannie hadn't been able to get Scott out of her mind. What concerned her most was that she found herself thinking of him, not just as a neighbor and friend, but as a man she could fall in love with.

Naturally Frannie had experienced her share of high school and college crushes. But until now she had never found a man she seriously considered spending her life with. It amazed her that she was entertaining such thoughts about Scott, a man seemingly without a past, without a career, without a future. In the few weeks she had known him, she knew almost nothing about him.

Maybe she was just going through a phase, or subconsciously retaliating against her father for his matchmaking schemes. Maybe she was drawn to Scott simply because he was so mysterious and charming. Whatever was prompting this silly infatuation, she knew one thing for sure: Scott Winslow was definitely not husband material.

As she knocked soundly on his door, she chided herself for harboring such foolish sentiments. If Scott guessed what she was feeling, he would probably burst into laughter or take off running in the opposite direction. There was no way on earth she would ever confide her schoolgirl fantasies to him.

The door opened suddenly, catching Frannie unawares. She stepped back, startled, her hand flying to her throat. Scott stared back at her, a puzzled expression on his face.

"Frannie, you okay?"

She caught the wood railing and inhaled sharply. "I—I'm fine. I didn't expect to see you there."

"Then why are you here knocking on my door?"

"I mean, I needed to see you. But I didn't think you'd be home."

He shrugged and stepped aside. "You're not making any sense, but come on in."

She entered the small bungalow and gazed around, as if looking for clues. There had to be something in this house that told her who this man was. Someday she'd find it. "I hope I'm not disturbing you." She noticed his open Bible on the table. "Were you reading?"

"As a matter of fact, I was. Sit down at the table and join me."

She pulled out the chair and sat down. "You seem to spend a lot of time reading the Bible."

"I've read it through twice since I moved here seven months ago."

"Really? I'm impressed. It takes me a year to read through it once."

He thrummed his fingers on the tissue-thin pages. "I came to this cabin to search for truth. And this book is the only place I know to find it."

She nodded. "My father would be pleased to hear you say that."

"Your father?" He eyed her curiously. "What about you, Frannie?"

"I'm pleased, too."

"Being a minister's daughter, you must know the Scriptures very well."

She shifted uneasily. "Not as well as I should. Being a minister's daughter doesn't give me an inside track with God."

"I know that. Scripture says that whoever will may come. Even a beachcomber who hasn't been to church since he was young. But you have a head start on most of us, Frannie. You've been brought up in the church."

"Sometimes you take for granted what you've always had."

"Is that what you've done with your faith?"

"I suppose so. I figured Daddy would get it right for the rest of us. It's not that I don't believe all the right things. But, to be honest, God has never seemed especially close."

Scott flipped through several pages. "I've been reading the letters of the apostle Paul. He talks about knowing Christ personally and having daily fellowship with Him. He says when we become a believer, Christ's Spirit comes and resides within us and communes directly with us."

"Yes, that's true."

"I experienced that when I was a child and invited Jesus to be my Savior. For a long time after that I felt His presence. But somewhere along the line, I lost that sense of Him in my life."

"He's still there, Scott. Maybe you just stopped listening."

"Yes, I'm sure that's it. Because I've started listening again, Frannie, and I know He's still there." He tapped his chest. "He's still in here. And, incredibly, I've begun to feel His love again. But I've got a lot of catching up to do."

"I'm happy for you, Scott. Having faith is a wonderful gift. Sometimes I wish I could be more like my father and experience that kind of vibrant, personal walk with God."

Scott's dark eyes drilled into hers. "Why can't you?"

She shrugged, suddenly uncomfortable. "I suppose I could. I guess I just haven't made God my priority."

Scott pushed the Bible toward her. "Let's work on it together, okay?"

She gave him a baffled look. "What are you talking about?"

He flashed her a bemused grin. "I'm suggesting

we get together and study the Bible now and then. You could share your vast wisdom with me, and I could be, um, immensely grateful. And who knows? Maybe we could even try praying together. Like they do in church.''

"Scott, why don't you just come with me to church?"

His brows furrowed. "No, Frannie. I can't. I'm not ready for that."

"Not ready for what? Mingling with the rest of humanity? Exposing yourself to the civilized world?" Her frustration spilled out in a rush of words. "What's wrong with you, Scott? Why do you avoid people? Who are you hiding from?"

Scott pushed back his chair, sprang to his feet and strode over to the window. "You don't understand, Frannie."

"Then explain it so I can understand. We're friends, Scott, and yet I feel like you're a stranger."

He gazed out the window, then back at her. "Someday I'll tell you everything. But until then, you have to trust me. That's all I can say right now."

"You haven't said anything. How do I know you're not a—an ax murderer or something?"

He came back over to the table, sat down and clasped her hands in his. "Do I look like an ax murderer?"

"I don't know. I've never met one."

"Well, take my word for it, I'm not. You say I'm a stranger. But you know all the important things about me. I mind my own business and don't bother anyone. I take pity on strangers who knock on my door in the middle of the night. I love God and the world He's created. I love your friends. I love your dog. I love you.''

She gaped at him, speechless.

A wily smile played on his lips. "I didn't mean to let that slip out. Forget I said it, okay?"

She looked away, heat rising in her cheeks. In a high, thin voice she said, "I'd be glad to get together and study the Bible with you, Scott."

"Great! We can start now if you like."

"I would, except…I came to ask a favor."

"Well, one good turn deserves another."

"I need you to pose for me again. Just for a day or two. I'm completing my commission for the Riverside cemetery, and I have some finishing touches. I can't get the face quite right. My Vietnam soldier just doesn't look soldierly enough. Would you mind coming over?"

Scott gave her a sly wink. "Another thing you know about me, Frannie. When a lady's in distress, I always come running."

True to his word, the next day, Scott showed up at Frannie's beach house at 10:00 a.m. sharp to pose for the sculpture. Frannie's delight knew no bounds. Being able to study—and actually touch—the solid planes and angles of Scott's sturdy face gave her exactly what she needed, what she had been struggling to achieve. As her trained fingers massaged the supple clay, she began to capture the pathos, strength and rugged humanity of her soldier.

Two days later, when she gazed at the final result, she felt the keen inrush of satisfaction, gratitude and pride. She had been true to her original vision. She had poured herself into this work of clay, had given it everything she had. It was part of her, an expression of her very soul, that part of herself that she couldn't express in any other way.

But what struck her most of all was that her clay soldier represented her blossoming feelings for Scott Winslow. The affection she had for the work, she also had for the man. By creating his image in clay, she had glimpsed the inner person, as well. And she liked what she saw.

"So what do you think of it?" she asked Scott as she washed the clay from her hands.

He walked around the nearly life-size sculpture, studying it from different angles as he rubbed his broad chin. "So that's how you see me? I'm impressed. And flattered. You have me looking downright heroic, noble, larger than life."

She gave him a teasing smile. "Are you saying you aren't all those things?"

He grimaced. "Not by a long shot."

She removed her smock and tossed it on her worktable. "Come with me. You deserve some sustenance after all your hours of posing."

He followed her down the hall to her kitchenette. "What about you? You did all the work. Let me take you to dinner."

She looked at him in surprise. "You're going to

give up your solitary existence long enough to eat dinner in a public restaurant?''

''You make me sound like an eccentric old hermit.''

She laughed. ''Aren't you? Not old, of course. But a hermit, for sure.'' She paused. ''But you haven't always been, have you?''

''Neither have you.''

''Touché.''

''So do we go to dinner or not?''

She peeked inside her cupboard. ''I guess so. Unless you'd like some boxed macaroni.''

''I pass.''

''Okay, dinner out, then. But I'll have to get cleaned up. I've got clay in my hair and up to my elbows.''

He stepped forward and swiped his index finger across her cheekbone. ''And you've got a streak or two of mud—I mean, clay—on your face, young lady.''

''So give me an hour to shower and change clothes.''

''That'll give me time to change, too.''

She walked him to the door. ''Where are we going?''

''I have a place in mind. It'll be a surprise, okay?''

She smiled, noticing the way his eyes twinkled when he said the word *surprise*. ''I'm looking forward to it, Scott.''

''I'll pick you up in an hour.''

She had just put the finishing touches on her makeup and run a brush through her long blond hair, when she heard Scott's familiar knock. Ruggs bounded to the door and barked while she stole a glance in the mirror at her tailored crepe blazer and trousers. The dusty rose outfit was elegant and yet feminine, exactly right for their first official date.

She tried to ignore her quickening pulse as she greeted him. Why was she feeling nervous when she had just seen him an hour ago? Maybe because he looked stunning in his casual brown shirt and tan sport coat. He ambled inside, stroked Ruggs behind the ears and bent over and brushed a kiss on her cheek. Another first!

She felt the color rise in her face. "You look great. Must be we're passing up the fast-food joints tonight."

He touched her hair with the tips of his fingers. "The way you look, there's not a restaurant in town ritzy enough."

She laughed lightly. "I bet you say that to all your dates."

"You're my first date in over six months."

"I'm flattered."

He walked her out to his vehicle, a vintage black sports car, and opened the door for her. As he pulled out into the street, she ran her hand over the leather upholstery. "With a classic car like this, you must have won some sweepstakes."

"Not really. This is my one and only indulgence."

"I've seen you driving by. I wondered if I'd ever get to ride in it."

"You should have asked."

"I wasn't sure it was yours."

"You think I stole it?"

"Of course not. But it's not the sort of car you can afford on a beachcomber's salary."

"I don't know. I've made some pretty good money on some of my driftwood furniture."

"Maybe I'd better give up sculpting and start collecting driftwood with you."

"Anytime."

She gazed out the window. "Where are we going?"

"To Diego's, a little Mexican restaurant in Del Mar. You do like Southwest cuisine, don't you?"

"Love it." She nudged him playfully. "And it's got to be better than boxed macaroni."

"You can say that again."

Twenty minutes later, they entered the small stucco café and were shown through the dusky candlelight to a small table in a private corner. Surrounding the simple wicker furnishings were huge colorful clay pots with cactus and palm fronds. Completing the south-of-the-border decor were Aztec-style stone fountains and colorful wall hangings portraying California missions.

After they were seated and given menus, Frannie leaned across the table and whispered, "The atmosphere here is wonderful! Why didn't we come here weeks ago?"

A sardonic smile flickered on his lips. "I was your hired model. I wasn't sure you wanted to mix business and pleasure."

She flicked her menu at him. "Scott Winslow, you're a big tease!"

"And you love it!"

She grinned. "I guess I do."

He opened his menu. "So what are you having?"

She scanned the menu items and the prices. "Scott, this place is a little pricey. I can help with the tab, if you—"

"No, this is my treat. Order whatever you like."

When the waitress came, Frannie ordered the *camarones al pescadore*—breaded shrimp, wrapped in bacon and sautéed. Scott chose the *carne asada,* with rice, beans and guacamole.

While waiting for their order, they helped themselves to warm tortilla chips and fresh salsa. As they chatted about inconsequential things, Frannie found that she couldn't take her eyes off Scott. The candlelight did amazing things to his ruggedly handsome face. And her stomach did somersaults over the way his eyes danced when he smiled at her.

After their meals had been served, Scott reached across the table and touched her hand. "I'll say grace this time, Frannie."

"All right. That would be nice."

As they bowed their heads, he took both her hands in his and offered a simple, earnest prayer.

The warm, fuzzy feeling that had started in Frannie's midriff was spreading to her heart and extremities. She liked being here with Scott, liked the way he spoke her name and the way his eyes moved over her with silent approval. Was she falling in love with him? She had suspected some days ago. The answer appeared to be a resounding yes.

And yet, how could she love him when she still knew so little about him?

He leaned across and table and said confidentially, "A penny for your thoughts."

She smiled. "Oh, it'll cost you more than that."

"How about an I.O.U.?"

"Deal. I was just thinking how much fun this is. I hope we can do it again."

"I don't see why not."

She poked idly at her shrimp. "Scott, I hope you don't mind my saying this, but I feel as if I'm seeing you in a whole new light."

"How so?"

"I don't know if I can explain it."

"I'm no longer the crazy drifter on the beach?"

"That's part of it. I don't want this to sound off the wall, but I feel a connection between us. As if we're kindred spirits. Soul mates somehow. Even though I don't know much about your past, in some ways I feel as if I know you better than anyone I've ever met. Does that sound bizarre?"

"No, Frannie." He clasped her hand in his. "I feel as if I know you, too. I know your heart, and it's pure and sincere and beautiful. I've never known a woman like you."

"You sound like you've known a lot of women."

"I've had my fair share of relationships, but they never worked out. When I moved into the beach house, I resolved to keep my distance from all women. Permanently. Then you came pounding on my door." He lifted her hand to his mouth and kissed her fingertips. "Now, dear Frannie, you've got my head spinning. I don't know what to think."

Her voice escaped in a baffled whisper. "Neither do I, Scott." Did she dare tell him she felt as bedazzled as he?

Chapter Ten

Almost unnoticed, September had settled in with a relentless shimmering heat. Frannie was caught unawares. Where had the time gone since she had moved here to her beach bungalow? How could summer be over and autumn already in the wings?

For two weeks now Frannie and Scott had been meeting every day for devotions on the beach. At midmorning, after a brisk run with Ruggs, they would spread out a blanket on the sand and put a praise tape in her boom box. Then they would sit together under the blazing sun and take turns reading aloud from the letters of the apostle Paul.

Often, Scott would interrupt the reading to insert a comment or a question—"What do you think Paul meant by this?...This Paul was quite an opinionated guy....Hey, he could have been writing about our world today."

When they had finished reading the Bible and discussing the verses, they would hold hands and take turns praying. At first, their prayers were brief and a bit self-conscious, with awkward pauses and a fumbling for words. But then something happened. One day Frannie noticed that their prayers had become earnest and impassioned. They were no longer aware of the time. And most important, she felt a closeness with God she hadn't felt before.

These devotional times that had begun almost out of a sense of duty had now become the most important part of her day. Not only was she cultivating a closer relationship with God, but she and Scott were developing a closeness she hadn't anticipated, as well. Other than occasional prayers with her father, Frannie had never revealed her spiritual side to another person, and certainly not to a handsome young drifter on the beach.

Today, Frannie found herself waking at dawn and counting the hours until her special time with Scott. Nothing else seemed as important, not even her work. She hadn't started a new sculpture since finishing the soldier, even though she had a new commission for the bust of a child. To her consternation, if she wasn't sculpting Scott, her heart wasn't in it.

As she showered and dressed in a sleeveless blouse and cutoffs, she mused that she had never experienced a friendship like Scott's. He not only nurtured her emotions and her spirit, but his very touch was electrifying.

Now, as she and Ruggs crossed the beach to their usual morning rendezvous, she told herself that she couldn't be in love with this man, even though her heart told her she was. Surely he was just a friend, a cherished confidant during this changing phase of her life. They were good for each other on a temporary basis. As she helped nurture his budding spirituality, he was helping her regain a passion for her faith and a hunger for God's presence in her everyday life. They had both been careful not to mention anything that would suggest a more permanent relationship.

No matter how much Frannie cared about Scott, she had to remember that he was a man without a past or a future. He had made that clear to her often enough. He refused to divulge any details of his personal history just as he avoided speculating about the future—his or theirs. They shared these present, fleeting days of summer, and that had to be enough.

Accept him as he is, Frannie. Don't ask questions. Just enjoy his company for as long as it lasts. She gave herself this little pep talk every day as she walked across the beach to their special meeting place. She reminded herself that she had to be on her guard and keep her emotions in check. Otherwise, when Scott greeted her with a friendly embrace, she would imagine him smothering her with kisses and be swept up in a delirium of bliss. And that would spoil everything.

Today she found Scott already ensconced on the blanket, reading his Bible. Ruggs bounded over to him and licked his face.

With a bemused laugh, Frannie sat down cross-legged beside him. "You can see how much Ruggs has missed you. He can't stop kissing your whole face.''

Scott gave the panting dog a playful hammerlock and rumpled his fur. ''What about his master? Did she miss me?''

''Not that much.''

Scott winked. ''Too bad.''

Frannie elbowed him. ''Don't get smart, mister.''

Scott released the dog and sent a broken shell skittering over the sand. ''Go get it, boy!''

They both laughed as Ruggs scrambled after the shell. Frannie rose up on one knee. ''Are you ready for our jog?''

''Let's jog later, okay? I'm reading some good verses here.''

Frannie sat back down and peered over his shoulder at the open book. ''Which ones?''

''The first letter to the Corinthians. Chapter thirteen.''

''Oh, the love chapter. That's a beauty.''

''It says there's faith, hope and love, but the greatest of these is love.''

''Yes, everything else is pretty empty without love.''

Scott gave her a long, scrutinizing look. ''Do you really believe that?''

''Yes, the Bible says it. It must be so.''

''Do you think it's talking just about our love for God? And His love for us?''

''Partly. The Great Commandment says we should love God with all our heart, mind, soul and strength.

I don't know if any of us really try to do that. We would have to galvanize all our senses, our thoughts, our emotions, and our energy to love God that way."

Scott nodded. "Yeah, I've got a long way to go on that one."

"It also says we should love one another as we love ourselves. That's a hard one to manage, too."

"It's not something we can do by ourselves."

"True. We can love like that only when God fills us with His love."

Scott's eyes moved over her with an odd expression, as if he were debating whether to say something more, and then thought better of it.

"Something on your mind, Scott?"

"No, just pondering these concepts. Trying to decide how they fit in with everyday life."

"Your life?"

His jaw tightened. "Maybe."

She searched his dusky eyes, her courage growing. "Scott, can't you trust me enough to tell me who you are?"

A guarded smile twisted his lips. "You know who I am. Scott Winslow, your number one rescuer."

"I need more than that, Scott. Why won't you tell me?"

He closed the Bible and set it on the blanket, his troubled eyes avoiding hers. "You know everything you need to know about me, Frannie. You know the person I am today. Anything else is irrelevant."

"Not to me. I can't help feeling there must be something terrible in your past to keep you so secretive, even after all these weeks when we've become so close."

He twisted a corner of the flannel blanket into a jagged snake. "I never deliberately hurt anyone, but I made many mistakes that caused people pain. I'm not proud of my past. I don't want to talk about it, because I'm not that man anymore, and I don't want to be reminded of him."

"I understand that, Scott, but—"

"Frannie, can't you accept me as the person I am today—a simple, ordinary man who wants to live close to the earth and close to God?"

"I do accept you, Scott. But you can't live the life of a reclusive drifter forever."

"I'm not reclusive. I made friends with you, didn't I?"

"But who else, Scott? You've isolated yourself from the rest of the world. You talk about wanting to know God better, but you won't even go to church with me. And what about a real job? Are you satisfied just being a beach bum?"

He ran his hand along her arm. "Is that how you see me? As a worthless beach bum?"

"No...yes...I don't know." Tears welled in her eyes. "I care so much about you, Scott. You're sensitive, witty, intelligent and creative. But you're also totally disengaged from the real world. Don't you have any ambition for a career, a future, a home, a family?"

He was silent for several minutes as he moved his

palm idly over the sand, forming little ridges beside the blanket.

Frannie wondered if he had withdrawn so far into himself that he had forgotten she was there. Had she pushed too hard, gone too far? Would he close her out forever now?

Finally he looked at her. Something had shifted in his face. It was as if the mask had dropped, revealing a naked, raw vulnerability. "Do you know, Frannie, what it's like to be trapped in a life you can't change? To be riddled with guilt? To feel your life isn't your own?"

"I suppose I don't."

"Because every detail of your existence has been orchestrated by powers beyond your control? Do you know what it's like to feel disgusted with yourself, because you've allowed others to define who and what you are? You're repulsed by the person you've become, but you're too weak to do anything about it."

"That would be very painful."

Scott continued, his voice solemn, fervent. "I wasn't just making conversation when I said I've hungered all my adult life for spiritual fulfillment, for something to explain and justify my existence in this world. I had to cut every tie to the past to be strong enough to make that search. Now I'm finding the answers I need. You've helped me, Frannie. You've helped me find the God of my childhood, a faith I thought had been snuffed out years ago. I know someday I have to make my peace with the past. But not until I know I'm strong enough to hold on to the person I'm becoming…a man of conviction and integrity. Do you understand, Frannie? Does any of this make sense to you?''

She moved closer and placed her hand on his arm. ''In a strange way, I do understand. And if you're asking me to have faith in you, I do. I won't ask any more questions until you're ready to tell me.''

He slipped his arm around her shoulder and she nestled her head against his sturdy chest. She could feel his pounding heart through his tank top and smell the suntan lotion on his warm skin. They sat like that, pensive and silent, until Ruggs came leaping back with the shell in his mouth.

They both laughed as Scott wrestled with the playful canine and pretended to grab for the shell. Finally Ruggs dropped it on the ground and waited, tail wagging, for Scott to throw it again. Frannie watched the two interact, her heart swelling with affection for this intriguing man with the mysterious past. Someday he would open up to her, and whatever he was hiding, it wouldn't change how she felt about him.

Scott looked at her, his eyes crinkling merrily. ''Guess we'd better get back to our study.''

She chuckled. ''If Ruggs will let us.''

''Oh, he'll let us. Come here, boy!'' Scott pulled Ruggs down beside him on the blanket and kneaded his ears. ''Watch, he'll be in a trance before we know it.''

By the time they had finished their devotions,

Ruggs was snoozing beside them, his legs twitching as he dreamed.

Frannie hoisted herself up and brushed the sand from her bare legs. "Time for our jog, but I hate to wake Ruggs."

Scott stood, too. "Let him sleep. We won't be gone long."

"Are you sure? I never let him outside alone."

"He'll be fine. He can catch up with us. But my guess is he'll still be sawing logs when we get back."

Frannie gave her pet a lingering glance. "I guess you're right. I must sound like an overprotective mother."

Scott fingered a strand of her flyaway hair. "It becomes you. Ready to go?"

"You bet. Better watch out. I'll leave you in the dust."

"Not a chance. I'm in top form today."

"You say that every day!"

"And every day I win."

"Not today!"

They broke into a run and raced side by side for nearly twenty minutes, neither speaking. When they reached their usual spot, a balmy palm tree beside a rocky bluff, they stopped and collapsed on the sand, shoulder to shoulder, both gasping for breath. Scott gave her a sidelong glance, his chest heaving. "I won."

"I did!"

"Okay, it was a tie."

"Poor sport!" Frannie licked her dry lips. "Can't stand to have a woman beat you."

Scott leaned up on one elbow and looked at her. "You can beat me any day you please. But you've got to do it fair and square."

"I did!"

"Did not!"

She gazed at him, savoring his closeness and the way his dark eyes crinkled and his tanned face glistened under the hot sun. They exchanged companionable smiles.

"What are you thinking?" she asked.

He twined a lock of her hair around his finger. "Nothing much. Just noticing how beautiful you are with the sun's healthy glow on your skin."

She laughed. "You mean, I'm perspiring."

"I didn't say that. I'm saying I like what I see."

She lifted her fingers to his stubbled chin. "So do I."

He bent his face to hers and lightly kissed her lips, then looked at her as if to say, Do you mind? Before she could utter a reply, his mouth came down on hers with a firmness that stole her breath. The kiss deepened as he gathered her into his arms and held her close. The moment was everything she had imagined it to be, and more. She wound her arms around him and returned the kiss, her senses igniting like fireworks.

Frannie lost track of time in his arms.

When she heard the distant sound of a dog barking,

she rallied and looked up at Scott. "How long have we been here?"

He kissed the top of her head and tightened his embrace. "I don't know. Time stopped the first time I kissed you."

She pulled away and sat at attention. "That dog barking. Could it be Ruggs?"

"I don't think so. We wouldn't hear Ruggs from here. Besides, he's probably still dozing."

"Still, we'd better get back." She jumped up too fast and felt a lightness in her head. She swayed, her knees buckling.

Scott sprang to his feet and caught her. "You okay?"

"Too much sun."

"Or too many kisses?"

She leaned into him. "Never too many kisses."

He slipped his arm around her waist. "You've had enough running. We'd better walk back."

What had been a twenty-minute jog became a forty-minute walk back up the beach. Frannie had butterflies in her stomach. She couldn't be sure whether they were the result of too much sun, jogging without eating or being dazzled by Scott's closeness.

When they reached the blanket, the Bible and boom box were still there. But not Ruggs.

Frannie looked around. "Where is he?"

Scott gathered up their belongings. "He probably wandered back up to the house."

Frannie ran across the sand to her beach house and searched the yard. She put her hands to her mouth and shouted Ruggs's name. She was met with only a deafening silence. "He's not here, Scott. Where could he have gone?"

"Maybe to my place." He put their gear on the porch. "Let's go."

As they ran along the beach, they took turns calling for Ruggs. They searched the area around Scott's bungalow, but again, no sign of the shaggy dog.

"Scott, do you think someone took him?"

"I don't know. Our stuff was still there on the blanket, untouched. Doesn't seem likely someone would come by and snatch a pet."

"Then where is he?" Hysteria was edging Frannie's voice.

Scott gripped Frannie's shoulders. "Listen, why don't you go back to your house and wait there? Ruggs may have wandered off or come looking for us. He'll probably come home anytime now. Meanwhile, I'll keep looking for him."

"You'd do that?" Tears glistened in her eyes. "You'd spend your day looking for my dog?"

He touched the corner of her lips. "I'd do just about anything to make you smile again."

Frannie returned to her bungalow and busied herself in her kitchenette, scouring the countertops. Then she rearranged the magazines and junk mail on the small desk in her living room. Between tasks, she stared out the windows, first one window, then another, watching for Ruggs. She couldn't concentrate on anything except the fact that she had somehow lost her precious pet, the animal that had been with her since before her mother died.

She had suffered enough casualties. Ruggs was a loss she simply could not tolerate. He was her dependable companion, the one constant in her life these days, other than Scott and her revived faith. Surely now that she felt close to God again, He wouldn't hurt her by taking Ruggs away.

For the umpteenth time she stared out the front window. "Lord, please bring Ruggs home to me. I'm sorry I let my love for You grow cold after Mama died. I'm sorry I resented You for taking her away. I'm sorry I disappointed Daddy by moving out when Juliana and Belina moved in. I'll do anything You ask if You'll just let Ruggs be okay."

Later that afternoon Scott arrived at her door, solemn-faced and empty-handed. "I'm sorry, Frannie. I couldn't find him." He held out his arms to her. "I searched every inch of this beach for a mile in both directions."

She sank against him and covered her mouth to stifle a sob.

"But I'm not through looking. I'm taking the car out and checking the streets beyond the beach, outside our neighborhood."

"You think he ran away? That he's wandering some street somewhere?"

"There's a chance. When he awoke and we weren't there, he might have gone looking for us and gotten lost."

"He's not used to being out alone."

He held her at arm's length. "Do you want to go with me?"

"Absolutely!" She hurried to the bedroom, grabbed her purse and followed him out the door.

They drove up and down every street within two miles of her beach house. Scott drove slowly, keeping his eye on traffic, while Frannie scanned the road-sides. For an hour they drove, retracing the streets closest to home, going up and down boulevards so that Frannie could search both sides.

The sun was setting in a brilliant red sky, the day-light waning, and still no sign of her cherished pet.

A knot tightened in Frannie's chest. "He's gone, isn't he, Scott? I'm not going to find him."

"We'll keep driving as long as we have enough light."

"What then? We just go home and forget about him?"

"We pray that he's waiting for us on the porch."

Frannie breathed the words, "Please, God, let it be!"

Scott sat forward, suddenly alert, his hands gripping the steering wheel. "What's that, Frannie? There, by the side of the road." He slowed the vehicle to a crawl, and they both stared at the furry mound beside the curb.

Frannie gasped, her stomach clenching, a sour taste rising in her throat. "No, Scott, no! It can't be Ruggs! Please don't let it be Ruggs!"

Chapter Eleven

"Frannie, it's Ruggs!" Scott was down on one knee, examining the stricken animal.

She got out of the car and approached, covering her mouth lest the nauseous spasm in her stomach turn to retching. "I can't bear to look. Is he dead, Scott?"

"No, Frannie. He's still alive!"

She stooped down over the wounded dog and touched his matted fur. He was panting hard and made no effort to raise his head. "He's hurt bad, isn't he?"

"Looks that way. A car must have hit him and kept going. Let's get him to the animal hospital."

"Scott, it's a good ten miles from here."

"Then let's go. We have no time to waste." Scott gathered the limp dog up in his arms and placed him in the back seat of his car.

As Scott drove, Frannie reached into the back seat

and stroked Ruggs's ears. He made a high-pitched moaning sound and tried to wag his tail. Frannie kept up a steady stream of conversation, her voice shrill, tremulous. "You'll be okay, boy. Just hold on! You're a good dog. Don't die, Ruggsy. Please don't die!"

The drive seemed to take forever, even though the dashboard clock told her it was less than twenty minutes. Scott pulled into the first parking spot, threw open the car door, scooped Ruggs up and carried him inside.

"We need some help here!" he called to an attendant in the modest waiting room. The wiry man dashed to Scott's aid and helped carry the burly animal into an examination room.

Frannie started to follow, but the receptionist at the desk—a stout woman with cropped brown hair—called Frannie back. "Sit down, miss. The doctor will be out shortly."

Frannie started to protest, then sank down wearily in a straight-back chair. Her knees were shaking, her arms shivering—a case of nerves and the frigid air-conditioning. She was still dressed in her cutoffs and sleeveless blouse.

After a minute, Scott came out, his shirt smeared with blood, his expression inscrutable. "The doctor's checking him over. He'll give us his diagnosis as soon as he can. I'm going to go wash up. Be right back."

She nodded and turned her gaze back to the closed door. Ruggs was in there, hurt and bleeding, maybe dying. She should insist that they let her in. She needed to be with her pet, comforting him. If she held him, maybe he wouldn't be afraid.

Scott returned and sat down beside her. He took her cold hand in his warm one. His eyes were shadowed with concern. "You okay?"

She nodded, not trusting herself to speak.

He slipped his arm around her shoulder and pulled her against him. "Ruggs is going to make it, Frannie. We've prayed for him all day. God can take care of him."

She sniffled. "I know God can, but that doesn't mean He will."

Scott nuzzled her hair. "We've got to trust Him to do what's best for us, Frannie, even if we don't understand it. You're the one who taught me that."

She brushed away a tear. "Every time I start trusting God again, He takes someone or something I love away from me. How can I believe He really loves me?"

"Well, you convinced me. You helped me see that God doesn't promise us a perfect life, but He promises to see us through the hard times. You said it yourself. He'll never forsake us, no matter what."

She smiled up at him through a blur of tears. "I did teach you well, didn't I?"

He squeezed her arm. "I couldn't have asked for a better mentor."

"I talk a good fight but don't do so well in the heat of battle."

"You're doing fine, sweetheart. Just keep hanging in there."

"I'm trying, but I feel so weak right now. I hate being such a wimp."

"You're the cutest wimp I ever saw." He massaged her shoulder. "Seriously, you're stronger than you think you are. Remember what Paul said, 'When I am weak, then I am strong.'"

"I know. When we give God our weaknesses, He turns them into His strength. I just don't know how to give them to Him."

"We start by asking." Scott bent his lips to her ear and whispered a prayer for healing for Ruggs and strength for Frannie.

When he had finished, she lifted her face to his. Even in the fluorescent glare of this spartan office, he looked wonderful—his dark eyes full of sympathy, his full lips arced in a smile. No wonder she was falling in love with this man. He made her feel cherished and protected. No man, except her father, had made her feel that way before.

"A penny for your thoughts," he murmured.

She managed a smile. "They're worth much more than a penny."

"How about a million dollars?"

She ran her fingers over the stubble on his cleft chin. "I'll tell you one of these days…when the time is right."

"I'll hold you to that promise."

A deep, thickly accented voice interrupted. "Miss Rowlands?"

Frannie looked up into the face of a bald, portly man in a lab coat, a clipboard under his arm.

"I am Dr. Augustino." He pulled a chair over and sat down, facing her, his shaggy brows crouching over black, bespectacled eyes. "I have finished my examination."

Frannie sat forward, all her senses alert. "Will Ruggs be okay?"

Dr. Augustino drummed his fingers on the clipboard. "Your dog was apparently struck by an automobile. He needs surgery to repair a broken leg and a fractured hip. With your permission, we will operate tonight. Barring any complications, he should make a full recovery."

Frannie sank back in her chair and folded her hands under her chin. "Praise God!"

"If you agree to the surgery, Miss Rowlands, you will need to sign these papers."

"I will. Just tell me when Ruggs will be able to come home."

"In a few days. Again, assuming he responds well to the surgery."

Her fingers stiffened. "Is there a chance he wouldn't do well?"

"There are no guarantees, of course. But I anticipate no problems. You may go home, if you wish, and we will call you."

"No, Doctor," Scott replied. "We'll wait here until Ruggs comes out of surgery."

"Very well. It will take some time. You may wait in the consultation room. The couch there is more comfortable than these chairs."

Frannie held out her hand for the clipboard.

"Thank you, Dr. Augustino. I'll sign those papers now."

Afterward, the receptionist led them to a cozy room with an overstuffed sofa, armchairs and end tables with bell jar lamps.

"A little touch of home," Scott mused as they settled on the couch. He slipped his arm around her. "Put your feet up, Frannie, and catch a few winks, if you like."

She nestled her head in the crook of his arm. "I'll put my feet up, but I can't sleep. Not when I'm so worried about Ruggs."

"He'll be fine. The doc says so."

"He has to be okay. This never would have happened if I hadn't taken him away from home. He always had a fenced yard. We never let him out on the street, except on a leash."

"It's not your fault, Frannie. Don't blame yourself."

"But it is my fault. I got so caught up in my own freedom, I didn't see the danger in letting Ruggs be free, too. All because I wanted to get away from home." Her hand flew to her mouth. "Oh, Scott, I just remembered. I should phone my dad and sisters. They need to know what happened."

"Let's wait until after the surgery. Then you can give them the good news."

"You're right. We'll wait." She rested her palm on his arm. "Thanks for being here with me. I couldn't have gone through this alone."

He lifted her face to his, his eyes searching hers.

"I'll always be here for you, Frannie, for as long as you want."

A shiver of excitement danced along her spine. "What if I say...forever?"

"Forever's a long time. You'd get tired of me."

"No, I wouldn't. I'd never stop learning fascinating things about you. It would be a wonderful adventure."

Scott flinched, and a shadow crossed his face. Frannie couldn't be sure, but she had a feeling he was withdrawing from her in some secret way she couldn't comprehend.

She studied his solemn face. "Did I say something wrong?"

"No. What makes you think that? I just..." His voice trailed off.

"What is it, Scott? Am I reading the signals wrong? These past few weeks, you've made me believe there's something special going on between us. And then today, when you kissed me...that wasn't the kiss of a casual friend."

"I know. I let my guard down, Frannie. I shouldn't have. It's not fair to you."

She bristled. "Not fair? What do you mean?"

"I can't explain it. It's just that I would never want to hurt you. You mean more to me than anyone."

"And you mean the world to me, Scott."

He pulled her closer. "If I could, I would keep our lives exactly as they are today—the two of us living in our beach bungalows and shutting out the rest of the world. In my dreams, I even imagine a little bungalow for two. Just you and me, Frannie. And Ruggs, of course.''

''That's a beautiful dream, Scott.''

''But it's only that. A dream. I can't turn it into reality.''

''You can't?'' A sliver of hurt pricked her heart. ''Why not, Scott? What aren't you telling me?''

His eyes grew distant, clouded. He had slipped away to some other place, a world he still refused to divulge to her.

''Scott, why can't you talk about the past? I know it haunts your every waking hour. Please tell me. How can our relationship go to the next level if you don't let me see who you were before you came here?''

His voice took on a defensive edge. ''And what if that man isn't the person you think you know?''

''Whoever you were before isn't as important as the man you are today. But I want to care about the whole man, not just facets you choose to reveal. I want to know your history, your heritage, all the experiences that make you the man you are.''

''Are you so eager for the truth that you'd risk destroying what we have together?''

An icy chill swept over her. ''Are you saying I wouldn't want to be with you if I knew the truth?''

''I didn't say that. It's just that my life is—*was*—very complicated. And once the genie is uncorked from the bottle, you can't get him back inside. Everything changes. Everything reverts. The fantasy is gone, and I'm back to reality.''

"You're not making any sense, Scott. You keep talking in riddles, metaphors."

"Because I'm trying to protect what we have here, Frannie, this beautiful, delicate thing, whatever it is, between us."

"So am I, Scott. That's why I need you to be honest with me."

"Honesty, huh? Remember what happened to Eve in the garden of Eden?" His voice took on a bantering tone, but she knew it was just another delaying tactic. "Eve was determined to eat from the tree of knowledge, to learn the difference between good and evil. And look what happened to her. She ended up with a snake in the grass."

"That's not funny, Scott."

"I'm not trying to be funny. I just don't want to lose you, Frannie. We can't change the past or predict the future. All we have is today, and no one knows how long it will last."

"God knows."

"Yes, He does. I just pray He's not telling us it's over already."

Shivering, she folded her arms across her chest. "You scare me when you talk like that."

"You wanted honesty. I'm being honest. I'm on borrowed time, Frannie. Delaying the inevitable. One day I'll be sucked back into the vortex of my past, and the Scott Winslow you know will cease to exist. And, believe me, you won't like the person in his place."

"Stop it, Scott. I won't listen—"

"I'm just saying, midnight will come. You'll turn into a pumpkin, and I'll turn into a rat. So much for fairy tales and 'happily ever after.' Is that the truth you want to hear?"

In a small, hushed voice she asked, "Are you telling me you're married?"

He heaved a careworn sigh. "No, I'm not married. How can you even ask that? If I were, I wouldn't have allowed things to progress the way they have between us."

"Then whatever your problems are, we can deal with them together, Scott. Please, let me help you."

He released her and shifted so that they were no longer touching. "There's nothing you can do, Frannie. I have enough entanglements to sink even an honorable man in the mire. I won't bog you down with my troubles. You don't deserve it."

"I don't deserve this, Scott." Tears pressed behind her eyes. "I'm worried sick about Ruggs. I can't deal with anything else tonight. And now, when I most need your comfort, you insinuate all these horrible things and make me doubt you. Make me doubt *us!*"

"I'm sorry, baby." He gathered her back into his arms and kissed her forehead, her cheeks, her lashes. "I don't know how we got off on this tangent, sweetheart. Forget I said anything, okay? We'll keep things just the way they are. We'll make the rest of the world go away, and it'll just be the two of us for as long as you want."

Frannie nodded, reveling in Scott's warm embrace.

Yes, God willing, it would be just the two of them, forever.

But a shadow of doubt lingered. How long could she and Scott keep the rest of the world at bay? And what dark secret from his past threatened their happiness, their future?

Chapter Twelve

Ruggs was coming home today. After three days of recuperation, he was ready to be released from the animal hospital. Scott had suggested that he and Frannie go together to pick up her recovering pet and bring him home.

But that wasn't what had Frannie's anxiety level hitting the ceiling. It was the anticipation of being with Scott. Several times over the past few days, he had insinuated that tonight would be more than just Ruggs's homecoming. He had all but admitted that he would divulge the secrets that had shrouded their communication from the beginning.

Just last night he had said, "I think I'm finally strong enough to face the ghosts of my past. Once we have Ruggs settled back at home, maybe we can talk. You need to know everything. We can't begin to plan our future until we've made peace with the past."

His words echoed in her mind all last night and

all day today, igniting her hopes and coloring her dreams.

Now Scott was due to arrive at any moment.

Frannie couldn't contain her excitement. She paced the floor of her beach house, watching out the window and stealing glances in the mirror at her sleeveless shell top and white stretch jeans. For once, she liked what she saw. Usually she wore her long blond hair straight, with a carefree, unattended look. But today she had taken her curling iron and coaxed her silky locks into luxuriant, cascading curls.

Surely Scott would approve. She could almost picture the look of delight on his face as his umber-brown eyes swept over her. Time and again today she had mentally rehearsed their conversation. She heard herself confessing to Scott that she was in love with him. Surely he suspected, but she had never actually said the words. She was convinced he loved her, too, and wanted to tell her so...except for that dark chapter of his life that held him back.

Perhaps it was more than a chapter. An entire book perhaps. But whatever it was, surely, with God's help, they could deal with it and pave the way for a future together. After all, knowledge was power. It was not knowing the truth that undermined their closeness. But tonight everything would be disclosed and there would be no more secrets between them.

Frannie heard a car in the driveway. She slipped on her sandals, grabbed her clutch purse and flung open the door with a cheerful "Scott, you're right on time!"

But it wasn't Scott. A tall, statuesque woman stood on the porch in a rust-red blouse and matching herringbone skirt and jacket. Her red hair was swept up in a twist and her makeup was dramatic and flawless. She couldn't have been more than twenty-five, even though she exuded an aura of jaded sophistication.

"I'm sorry," Frannie blurted. "I thought you were someone else."

"Obviously." The woman's voice was heavy with sarcasm.

An alarm went off somewhere in Frannie's mind. "May I help you?"

"Yes, but he's obviously not here."

"Who?"

"Scott. Scott Winslow. He is the man you thought you were greeting at the door, is he not?"

Frannie hesitated, then conceded, "Yes. I'm expecting him at any moment."

The woman gazed around curiously. "Then he doesn't live here in this dreary little cabin?"

Frannie swallowed her rising indignation. "No, he certainly doesn't. Are you a friend of Scott's?"

A Mona Lisa smile flickered on the woman's full crimson lips. "Yes, you could say that."

"Well, if you'll give me your name, I'll tell him you stopped by."

The woman's cool sea-green eyes drilled into Frannie's, unnerving her. "May I come in and wait?"

"I'm not sure that's a good idea. If you'll just leave your name—"

"He hasn't told you about me, has he?"

Frannie managed to keep her voice steady. "That depends on who you are."

"I'm Vivian LaVelle. Does that ring any bells?"

"No, it doesn't. But I'd be glad to give Scott a message for you."

The woman scowled. "You can do better than that. You can tell me which scummy, decrepit little cabin he lives in on this asinine beach. And don't tell me he doesn't live here. My sources have reported that he's here, living like a foolish, eccentric hermit."

Frannie said coolly, "Why should I tell you anything about Scott?"

Vivian raised one finely plucked eyebrow. "You are a simpleton, aren't you? I bet Scott hasn't even told you who he is."

Frannie wavered. "He's told me everything I need to know."

"And haven't you wondered why a man in Scott's position would be living in a hovel on the beach?"

"Scott's position?"

"He hasn't told you, has he? What did he do, lie about his name?"

"He wouldn't lie about that. He's Scott Winslow."

"And the name means nothing to you?"

"What are you getting at, Miss LaVelle?"

"For most people, the name Scott Winslow summons images of a billion-dollar real estate empire. Or don't you read the newspapers?"

The skin prickled on the back of Frannie's neck. "Of course, I read—" The truth struck her like a fist in the stomach. She nearly doubled over.

"Maybe...maybe you'd better come in after all, Miss LaVelle."

"I figured you'd want to hear more." The woman stepped inside and gazed around with a detached nonchalance. "The detective I hired observed Scott in this very cottage, coming and going several times. For the life of me, I don't know what Scottie was thinking, pretending to be a common beachcomber."

"Sit down, Miss LaVelle. Please, you obviously know more about Scott than I do. Tell me everything."

In a smooth, graceful gesture, the woman sat down on the couch and crossed her long legs at the knee. "Since it appears we have something in common, call me Vivian. And you are...?"

"Frances Rowlands. Frannie. A friend of Scott's."

"A good friend, by the reports I've received. If Scott doesn't live here with you, he must live in one of the other beach houses nearby."

Frannie sat down in the overstuffed chair by the fireplace. "I assure you Scott doesn't live here. But we did spend a lot of time together this past summer. I'm a sculptor. He was my model."

A brittle smile crimped Vivian's lips. "How quaint...and how convenient for Scott."

Frannie chose to ignore the coarse insinuation. "Tell me how you know Scott."

Vivian lifted her tapered fingers and examined a long polished nail. The color was fire-engine red. "Isn't it obvious how I know him?"

"No, it's not. You haven't told me anything you couldn't have read in the newspaper."

Vivian sat forward and glared at Frannie, her face as cold and unyielding as a painted porcelain doll's. "Then listen carefully, Miss Frances Rowlands. Scott Winslow lives in a multimillion-dollar mansion on the Santa Barbara coast. His family is one of the wealthiest in America. They own half the real estate between San Diego and San Francisco. In fact, they own this dilapidated joint you're living in, plus every other rinky-dink bungalow on this beach. They don't always play by the rules, but they are ruthless and they always win, no matter who gets hurt."

Every word Vivian spoke felt like a slap across Frannie's cheek, a dagger to her heart. She struggled to find her voice, her defenses crumbling. "The man you're describing…he isn't anything like the Scott Winslow I know."

"Isn't he? Did your Scott Winslow move to the beach about seven or eight months ago? Has he told you some irrational story about wanting to get back to nature and live the simple life? Has he been secretive about his past?"

"What if he has?"

"I'll tell you why." Vivian's green, thickly lashed eyes narrowed. "Last year Scott began to complain about his rich, privileged life. He joked about running away from all his responsibilities and becoming a carefree vagabond on some exotic beach. I didn't take him seriously. But apparently he wanted a taste of the humble, unadorned life before taking the big plunge."

"The big plunge?"

Vivian's crimson lips tightened against perfect, white teeth. "Scott Winslow is my fiancé. Our wedding is next month."

Frannie flinched, as stunned and disoriented as if a lightning bolt had struck between her eyes. "You're Scott's fiancée?"

"That's what I've been trying to tell you." Vivian's lips puckered in an exaggerated pout. "Obviously my naughty little Scottie wanted some time to himself—or should I say some time to play—before we get married. I'm really going to have to give him a slap on the wrist for letting me worry about him all these months. Just you wait until I get him back home!"

Frannie's head spun. This moment couldn't be real. Surely she was dreaming, trapped in the worst nightmare of her life. *Dear God, let me wake up, please!*

"You look a bit pale, Miss Rowlands, I mean, Frances. You did say that was your name, didn't you?"

"Frannie. They call me Frannie."

"Yes, of course. Now, Frannie, if you'll just tell me where I can find my roguish swain, I'll be on my way."

"He—he lives in the next cottage. Just down the beach. You can see it from here."

Vivian stood up and smoothed her expensive jacket over her shapely hips. "Thank you, Frannie. You've been very helpful. I hope my naughty Scottie didn't lead you on or fill your sweet head with sentimental nonsense. He's a very shrewd, hardheaded entrepreneur. But once in a while he gets these romantic notions that he has to rescue some damsel in distress. He's a bit like Don Quixote tilting at windmills. I have to go out and bring him back to reality. But I adore him, no matter how flawed he is. I'm sure he captivated you too. For a scoundrel, he can be disarmingly charming. Don't you agree?''

Frannie's thoughts were racing pell-mell. This had to be a terrible mistake. But it appeared that the biggest mistake was Frannie's, for trusting a mysterious man named Scott Winslow.

"Since it doesn't appear that Scott is coming here, I will go to him. You said the next beach house?''

"Yes. You can get there by the beach, if you don't mind walking. Or you can go back out to the street and drive down. It's about a quarter mile.''

"I'll drive. Thank you, Miss Rowlands. You've been very helpful.''

In a daze Frannie escorted the woman outside to the porch and stood watching numbly as she strutted out to her vehicle, a foreign red convertible. With a haughty nod in Frannie's direction, she climbed in, backed out of the driveway and headed down the street in the direction of Scott's house.

What just happened here? Frannie asked herself as she went back inside and shut the door. Who was this woman? Was she a crackpot, a deranged troublemaker, a stalker? Perhaps everything she had told Frannie was a lie. Why did I let her in my house?

Why did I even admit I knew Scott? Why did I tell her where he lives?

There was no way to phone Scott and warn him. And what if the woman wasn't lying? What if she actually was Scott's fiancée? Frannie sat down at her small kitchen table and massaged her knuckles. What should she do now? Run the length of the beach to Scott's house to see what kind of reception he gave this bizarre woman, Vivian LaVelle?

Frannie stood up and went to the window. "Where are you, Scott?" she said aloud, her voice sounding hollow in the empty room. "You were supposed to be here by now. We're supposed to pick up Ruggs. Don't you remember?"

She had to do something, had to make a decision. Go pick up Ruggs by herself, or drive over to Scott's to see what was keeping him, or take the twenty-minute walk along the beach to Scott's bungalow and size things up, unnoticed. She decided against driving over, lest she encounter the lady LaVelle at his door. Better to go by way of the beach, a more private and circuitous route.

She went to the phone and dialed her home number. After several rings, her father answered. "Daddy, it's me, Frannie," she said, a nervous tremor in her voice. "Listen, Daddy, I was supposed to pick up Ruggs at the animal hospital, but something came up. Would you mind getting him and taking him back to your house?... Thanks, Daddy. I'll come by in the morning and get him... No, Daddy, I can't explain it right now. But I'll tell you everything when I see you.''

She hung up the phone, went to the bedroom, kicked off her sandals and slipped on her sneakers. She grabbed a lightweight sweater, tossed it around her shoulders and headed outside. It was dusk now, and the ocean air was cooling quickly as the crimson sun lowered, hugging the horizon.

What am I doing? Frannie asked herself as she tramped across the beach toward Scott's cabin. I should have stayed home and waited for him to come to me. I'm going to feel like a fool if I arrive at his door and he's with this strange woman, his supposed fiancée. *Please, God, just let it be a big misunderstanding. Don't let that rude woman be the one Scott loves.*

She quickened her pace, her rubber-soled sneakers scudding over the hard-packed sand. Maybe Scott would be at home and greet her as if nothing had happened. Maybe he would have some perfectly good explanation about the nauseating, abrasive Miss LaVelle. She was someone I once knew, and she went off the deep end and got the wrong idea about us. She won't listen to reason, but just ignore her. She's no one really, she doesn't matter....

By the time Frannie arrived at Scott's bungalow, the salmon-pink sky had given way to deep streamers of blue. The last faint rays of sunlight had been swallowed by ever-widening shadows. There were no lights on inside.

Frannie knocked anyway—once, twice, three times.

Then, impulsively she tried the door. To her surprise, it opened. She peeked inside and called Scott's name. There was no reply. Gingerly she stepped inside and turned on the wall switch. The room was flooded with light. She looked around, blinking against the brightness.

No one was home.

A chill shot through her. She shouldn't be here checking up on Scott. She felt like an intruder, trespassing where she didn't belong. But something didn't feel right. What if Scott needed her? She called his name again as she walked down the shadowed hall to the bedroom. Her heart raced as she entered and flipped the switch. Everything was in disarray—drawers pulled out, the closet door open, toiletries and clothing on the floor and bed.

Frannie's breath caught as she looked in the closet. Most of Scott's clothes were gone. And his shoes. And luggage. Some of the drawers had been emptied, others had been left untouched. He had obviously packed in a hurry. Had he been that eager to get back to the life he had left behind?

"No!" Frannie covered her mouth with her hand. Tears stung her eyes. "He wouldn't leave like this without saying goodbye!" She ran to the door and looked out at the driveway. Scott's vintage car was still there. That meant one thing, one terrible, indisputable fact. Without a parting word or a backward glance, Scott had gone off with the woman who claimed to be his fiancée, the brassy, outrageous Vivian LaVelle.

Chapter Thirteen

For a mellow, unassuming minister of the Gospel, Andrew Rowlands's life was getting increasingly complicated. Just when he had finally adapted himself to the household routine of his lovely new bride and his taciturn stepdaughter, his youngest offspring had moved back in with a broken heart and a lame dog.

For several days after her return, Frannie wouldn't say a word about what was troubling her. But Andrew could see in her eyes how much she was hurting, and he knew the source of her pain had to be that beach bum Scott Winslow. Andrew could only imagine the loathsome things that man might have done. He hadn't trusted the evasive drifter from the beginning. There were too many unanswered questions, too many glaring gaps in his background.

Andrew should have been more forceful in warning Frannie about him. But, for a change, he had resisted the impulse to meddle. After all, he had already batted zero in trying to set Frannie up with Wesley Hopkins, the new minister of music.

But to his own astonishment, Andrew had inadvertently achieved another matchmaking coup, pairing Wesley with his bashful Belina. The two were quite an item these days. Wesley had even persuaded Belina to start singing in the church choir, and Andrew had a feeling Wesley would even have her doing solos one of these days.

Now if Andrew could just help his youngest daughter find the man of her dreams...but it certainly wouldn't be the likes of Scott Winslow! The contemptible cad even had the nerve to keep phoning Frannie on both her cell phone and at Andrew's house. But at least his daughter had the good sense to refuse to speak to the man.

On the morning of Frannie's fourth day at home, as Andrew and his daughter lingered over a second cup of coffee, he seized the opportunity to question her about her plans. "Are you thinking of moving back in here for good, honey, or is this just a respite before you return to the beach house?"

"I don't know, Daddy." Frannie pushed a wisp of flaxen hair behind her ear. In spite of her tan, she looked pale and drawn and several pounds thinner. "I know I can't stay in limbo like this forever, but I honestly don't know what to do."

"If you want to come home, we can rent a truck and bring all your stuff home. I imagine you want to get back to your sculpting, and you can hardly do that with all your equipment at the beach house."

"To move home would be a step backward, Daddy, like conceding defeat. I would be admitting I can't make it on my own."

"I don't see it that way, sweetheart. You'd just be agreeing that the beach house wasn't the right choice at this time."

Frannie's eyes glistened with tears. "But I was so sure, Daddy. I was really happy there. It felt so right."

He reached across the table and covered her hand with his large palm. "Why don't you tell me what happened, honey? I know it has to do with Scott."

"I never said that."

"You didn't have to. You've refused his calls all week long. Tell me what he did to make you so unhappy."

Frannie lowered her gaze. "I didn't want you to know what a fool I've been, Daddy."

He squeezed her hand. "You know I'd never think that. I love you, baby. You'll always be my little sunshine girl, even when your smile is turned upside down."

Frannie's lips turned up in a droll little grin. "Oh, Daddy, you always know what to say to make me feel better."

"I could do an even better job if I knew what has you so upset. What did that scoundrel do to hurt you?"

Frannie sipped her coffee. Andrew could see that something was going on—the way she blinked back tears and her chin puckered, as if she were wrestling with herself. Finally she licked her ashen lips and drew in a deep breath. "Okay, Daddy, I'll tell you." Something in her guileless tone and melancholy expression reminded him of the cherub-faced little girl who used to climb on his lap for bedtime stories.

"Take your time, honey. I've got all morning."

"It's about Scott, but you already know that."

Andrew's ire was rising. "What did he do?"

"He—he made me fall in love with him." She brushed at a tear. "I thought he loved me, too, and that we had a future together."

"What changed your mind?"

"A woman came to my door. She was looking for Scott. I found out she's his fiancée."

Andrew sat back and rubbed his jaw. "That had to be a shock."

"There's more, Daddy." She gazed at him, her eyes glassy pools. "He's not the man I thought he was."

"I guess not—leading you on, with a fiancée in the picture!"

"That's not all of it." Frannie ran her finger over the rim of her coffee cup. Her lower lip was trembling.

Andrew winced. It hurt him to see his little girl suffering like this. "You don't have to go on, honey. I get the picture. Scott Winslow is a big-time jerk."

Frannie inhaled deeply and looked at him, her eyes filling with seething fire. "It's worse than that. Scott Winslow is a fraud, Daddy. He's not a poor beach-comber wanting to live the simple life close to nature.

He's the notorious Scott Winslow with the billion-dollar real estate empire!''

Andrew sat back, startled. No, his reaction was stronger than that. He was appalled. He had been prepared to hear just about anything concerning Frannie's deceitful Lothario. But not this. "You're telling me your drifter friend is Scott Winslow, the billionaire entrepreneur who owns half of California?''

Frannie began to weep. "Yes, Daddy. He fooled us all. He spouted all these platitudes about wanting to help the poor and make life beautiful for them. And here he's the man a judge sentenced to live in his own shabby, substandard tenement for six months. Maybe that's why Scott was living in that dilapidated beach house. The law made him!''

Andrew whistled through his teeth. "I knew the guy was hiding something, but I never dreamed his secret was this big.''

"That's why I can't take his calls, Daddy. I can't bear the thought of facing him again after the fool he made of me.''

Andrew pushed back his chair and went around the table. He wrapped his arms around his daughter and kissed the top of her head. "I know it hurts, honey. I'm so sorry. If there was anything I could do to make it better...''

She patted his arm and looked up at him with tearful eyes. "Thanks for not saying 'I told you so.' ''

"Sweetheart, we're going to do everything we can to help you forget that turncoat. We've got Ruggs to nurse back to health, and I'm sure Belina will welcome your company, especially now that she's coming out of her shell.''

"It's because of Wesley, isn't it? She cares about him a lot, doesn't she?''

"And the feeling seems to be mutual.'' Andrew massaged his daughter's shoulder. "I hope you don't regret encouraging that little romance.''

"No, Daddy, I'm happy for Belina. I could never have cared about Wesley the way I...'' As she let her words trail off, tears slid down her cheeks.

Andrew filled the awkward silence with a booming, "Come on, kiddo. Let's think of something fun to do today. Drive into San Diego and take in a play. Or go out to eat at that fabulous seafood grotto in Del Mar. Or how about the zoo? You wanna go see some silly orangutans, hippos and chimpanzees? What do you say, kid? You wanna do something crazy and fun with your ol' man?''

She managed a lopsided smile. "Shouldn't you be working on your sermon for Sunday morning?''

He waved his hand breezily. "I've got time. And right now I think my daughter needs some old-fashioned TLC. How about it?''

She gave him an appreciative hug. "Thanks, Daddy, but I'll be fine. Maybe I'll go upstairs and visit with Belina. She's probably dying to tell someone about her new romance.''

"Someone her age, you mean.''

Frannie nodded. "She's probably never had a girlfriend to share things with.''

"Nor a sister,'' said Andrew meaningfully.

Frannie carried their coffee cups over to the sink, then gave Andrew a wistful smile. "Maybe Belina and I will have a chance to get closer now that I'm back home."

"I hope so, baby cakes. Just don't spend all day up there. I'm sure Juliana could use a hand in the kitchen. Don't get me wrong. She's a wonderful cook, but I'm sure she'd welcome a night off. Besides, we haven't had your spaghetti and meatballs for ages. I'll even get out the big bibs, if you like."

Frannie laughed. "Oh, Daddy, I've missed you!"

He winked at her. "And I've missed you, too, sweetheart."

After Frannie had gone upstairs, Andrew sauntered down the hall to his study and sat down at his large mahogany desk. He needed to work on his sermon notes, but he wasn't in the mood. He still couldn't reconcile the idea that the young drifter who had visited his home with Frannie was indeed the ruthless billionaire entrepreneur whose name was so often in the news. Nor could he imagine that his bright, sensitive daughter could have fallen in love with such a cold, calculating man. As elusive and puzzling as Scott Winslow had seemed that night, he seemed a thousand times more baffling and incomprehensible in light of this new information.

Andrew was scratching out a few mindless notations when the phone rang. His habit was to let someone else get it when he was working on his sermons. He waited for Juliana to pick up, then remembered that she was at the beauty parlor for her weekly hair appointment. When the girls didn't catch it on the third ring, he grabbed the receiver and said hello with exaggerated politeness, to disguise his impatience.

"Reverend Rowlands?"

The voice was familiar. Unmistakable, in fact. Andrew's outrage took over. "Scott, is that you? Scott Winslow?"

"Yes, sir. Please, don't hang up."

Andrew snapped the pencil in his hand. "You have a lot of nerve calling here after what you've done."

"I know, sir, and I'm sorry. I never intended to deceive Frannie. Or hurt her. It was the last thing I wanted to do."

"It's a little late for regrets now, don't you think? The damage is done."

"I know she hates me, but I can't let things end this way. If I could just talk to her and explain—"

"I don't think there's anything to explain," Andrew interrupted. "She doesn't want your sorry excuses. Just leave her alone, you hear me? She'll be okay."

"I can't do that. She deserves to hear the whole story."

"Do you honestly think the details of your deception will make her feel better? Give her a break, man. Make it a clean cut. Don't draw out the agony."

Desperation colored Scott's voice. "Sir, please, just tell her I called. Tell her I need to talk to her. I had to leave the cabin so quickly that night, I know I left her hanging. She must be thinking all sorts of terrible things."

"She wouldn't be thinking such terrible things if you had had the decency to tell her the truth in the first place."

"I know. I was wrong. And I need to tell her so myself."

Andrew drummed his fingers on his desk. Why was he even talking with this rapscallion? "I'll tell her you called, Scott, but I can guarantee she won't call you back."

"Reverend Rowlands, wait. Don't hang up yet. Please, listen to me. I know you're a godly, compassionate man. Would you just take down my phone number and address and tell Frannie she won't regret contacting me."

Andrew grabbed another pencil. "Go ahead, but it won't make any difference." He scribbled the information on a notepad, then said through clenched teeth, "Is that it?"

"One more thing, Reverend." A slight tremor rippled through Scott's voice. "If you believe nothing else I've said, sir, believe this."

Andrew blinked, surprised. The man sounded like he was ready to cry. "What is it, Scott?"

"I love your daughter, sir, and that's the truth."

The line went dead after that. Andrew sat for several moments replaying their conversation in his mind. The whole thing was bizarre. It made no sense. Why would a man in Scott Winslow's position care so much about a girl he had met on the beach, and betrayed? Another strange thing. Andrew didn't have the feeling that he had been talking with a cold, heartless tycoon in his lofty ivory tower. Scott Winslow had sounded like a needy, broken, remorseful human being.

Andrew raised his hands in a gesture of helplessness. "What do I do now, Lord? Throw this paper away, or tell my darling daughter this Winslow fellow may have something to say that she needs to hear?"

Chapter Fourteen

Frannie missed the beach more than she could have imagined. So did Ruggs. Now that his cast was off and his leg and hip on the mend, he was eager to romp and play in the sand again. Frannie could see it in the way he tilted his head just so and gazed dolefully at her. She nearly melted when those enormous mahogany peepers peered at her through that rag-mop of hair, as if to say, When are we going home where we belong?

It seemed strange to her that she thought of the beach house as home. But it was true. Her father's house was just a place to visit. She had been here for over two weeks now, and it was time to go before she wore out her welcome.

So on a brisk, October day with just the hint of scudding clouds on the horizon—she packed her bags, loaded her belongings into her trunk and told her father goodbye.

He and Belina walked her out to her car. She opened the passenger door and let Ruggs inside, then gave Belina a hug. "Keep me posted on how things go with Wesley, okay?"

"I will, Frannie. Thanks for listening to all my silly chatter about him. You've been a good friend."

"So have you, Belina. I'll miss you."

"I'll miss you, too. Come back soon."

Frannie's father stepped forward and gathered her into his sturdy arms. "Listen, kiddo, just because you're moving back to your beach house doesn't mean you can't come visit as often as you like."

"I know, Daddy. I'll be back soon. But right now I need some time alone to think...and pray."

"I'll be praying for you, too, baby doll." His eyes crinkled with a mixture of smiles and tears. "You know your ol' dad loves you."

"And I love you, Daddy. More than I can say." She lifted her face to his and kissed his cheek. "Take care of yourself."

"That goes both ways." He held the car door open for her. "Maybe I shouldn't bring up the subject, but it's been over a week now. Have you decided whether to contact Scott?"

She shrugged. "I've still got the paper with his address and phone number in my purse, but I don't know whether to call him."

"Give it time. And give it to the Lord. He'll show you what to do."

Minutes later, as Frannie drove away from her father's house, she realized this was a more painful farewell than when she first moved out. Maybe it was because she had left the first time with an innocence and expectations that had since been dashed by her disappointment in Scott.

A half hour later, Frannie pulled into the driveway beside her beach house. She could still visualize Scott's fiancée standing on the rustic porch in her expensive clothes and fancy hairdo. She pushed the image out of her mind as she carried her things into the house. Ruggs clambered in after her, still limping on his bad leg.

"Well, here we are, boy. We may be a little worse for wear, but we're home. After I get my stuff put away, we'll take a little walk on the beach and watch the sunset."

In the days that followed, Frannie made it a point to take Ruggs for a walk every evening at sunset. Sometimes weary from working on her latest commission, she would wade into the water and let the foamy waves wash over her bare legs. At other times she and Ruggs would stretch out on the sandy beach and watch the fiery sun become a crimson balloon on the deep blue horizon. She loved burrowing her toes into the warm sand while Ruggs chased a seagull or sniffed at a questionable object the waves had washed ashore.

Sometimes she brought her Bible and read or memorized verses while Ruggs dozed beside her. She loved the sense of peace and tranquillity that washed over her at moments like this. In these solitary days when she had no human support group surrounding her, God was becoming increasingly real to her. She found it easier to pray as she sat by the ocean, watching the frothy tide roll in and the sky change colors as if God were spreading his multicolored palette across the heavens.

She often talked aloud to the Lord, as if He were sitting beside her. She would pour out her heart in a blitz of words, her voice becoming one with the rushing waves, the screeching gulls, the whistling wind. But even as her spiritual life deepened, her emotions vacillated between joy and despair. On the days when her faith was strong, she released her hurt and anger to God and felt His sweet consolation. But on other days her faith wavered and she found herself giving in to desolation.

Ten days from the day she had returned to her beach house, she received a call from Scott on her answering machine. "Frannie, I've been waiting for you to return my call. As each day passes I realize I may never hear from you again. Please give me a chance to tell my side of the story. After I've had my say, if you wish, I'll never bother you again."

Hearing Scott's voice resurrected all the painful emotions she had nearly convinced herself she no longer felt. The truth was, she still loved him, would perhaps always love him. And yet she couldn't be sure the man she loved even existed. She had fallen in love with someone that a man named Scott Winslow had carefully, deliberately manufactured. And this man—the Scott Winslow who could undertake such a cruel hoax—she hated with every fiber of her being. How could she ever again trust another man? Or even herself? How stupid and gullible was she that Scott could sweep her off her feet and convince her he was a believer like herself, compassionate and altruistic, when in reality he was a ruthless, lying fraud?

After hearing Scott's message, Frannie escaped to the beach. She walked for a long while, arguing with herself, arguing with the Lord. "What am I supposed to do? I'm caught in limbo, Lord. I can't go forward and I can't go back. I can't even concentrate on my work. All I can see is Scott's face. When I wake in the morning I think of him. When I go to sleep at night, I dream of him. How can I get my life back, heavenly Father, when Scott still controls my emotions and rules my heart?"

The thought came to her, Go see him. Settle this once and for all. Yes, it suddenly seemed so simple. She would drive up the coast to Santa Barbara and confront Scott Winslow on his own turf. She would tell him in no uncertain terms how he had hurt her and warn him that he had better straighten his life out if he wanted any peace of mind. Perhaps by putting him in his place, she would save some other unsuspecting woman from suffering the same heartbreak.

But Frannie's bravado was short-lived. When she woke just before dawn the next morning, doubts assailed her. Surely she wouldn't have the strength and courage to face Scott again, let alone give him a piece of her mind. But as she scrambled herself an egg and brewed a pot of coffee, her old resolves returned. She would make the trip, no matter what.

After breakfast she got online and mapped out her trip to Santa Barbara. Amazing these days how she could plot the course from her door to his. She phoned her father and told him she would be dropping Ruggs off for a day or two. When he inquired where she was going, she said simply, "To take care of some old business." Her father didn't ask any more questions, but she knew he suspected what was up.

By 7:00 a.m. she had thrown a valise into the back seat and was on her way. When she dropped Ruggs off at her father's house, Belina came out to the car to collect the dog. "Your dad hinted that you're going to see Scott. Are you sure that's a good idea?"

"I have to," Frannie told her in a matter-of-fact voice. "I can't live like this, wrestling with all these conflicting emotions. Scott has to know he can't treat people this way. Until I tie up these loose ends, I can't get on with my own life."

Belina nodded. "I'll pray for you. See you soon, okay?"

"You bet."

As Frannie wended her way up the coast to Santa Barbara, she seesawed between anger and panic. One minute she was rehearsing what she would say and giving Scott a mental tongue-lashing. The next minute she was asking herself what on earth she was doing, driving up to his Santa Barbara mansion to confront him. "I must be a crazy person, thinking I can accomplish anything by facing him. I'll just make matters worse. What kind of fool am I anyway? Oh, Lord, I'm a lovesick fool, for crying out loud!''

Her hands tightened on the steering wheel until her knuckles gleamed like smooth white stones. ''Dear God, I'm doing this because I believe it's the right thing. I'm going with fear and trembling, but I believe You're leading me. If I'm wrong, let me run out of gas or have a flat tire or put a stop sign in my path. Please, don't let me see Scott unless it's Your will!''

It was shortly after noon when Frannie followed the winding driveway up a rugged bluff overlooking the Pacific. Scott's sprawling, Mediterranean-style mansion was reminiscent of a grand villa in Barcelona, with its white stucco exterior, terra-cotta tile roof, high arched windows and spacious balconies. Colorful gardens accented the manicured lawn. Towering eucalyptus, swaying palms and gnarled oak trees circled the estate. Behind the villa rose the majestic Santa Ynez Mountains.

Frannie's knees felt like jelly as she climbed the steps to the expansive front porch. She breathed another prayer as she knocked soundly on the wide double doors. After a moment, a door opened and a stout, pleasant-faced matron greeted her. The woman's gray-black hair was tied back in a bun and a scalloped apron covered her crisp blue housedress. Her voice was softly lyrical, yet professional. ''Yes? May I help you?''

Frannie straightened her shoulders. ''I'd like to see Mr. Winslow, please.''

''Mr. Winslow?''

"Yes, it's quite urgent."

"Are you here for the wedding?"

"The wedding?"

"If you're a guest, the wedding isn't until this evening. The invitation distinctly said six o'clock."

Frannie felt faint. "You mean, Mr. Winslow is getting married...today?"

A frown creased the woman's brow. "You didn't know? You are a friend of the family, aren't you? If not, I really must ask you to—"

"Yes, I'm a friend of Mr. Winslow's," she said quickly. "But we've been out of touch lately. I didn't know about the wedding."

The maid looked relieved. "Oh, I'm glad you're a friend and not some nosy reporter. The family is trying to keep the wedding under wraps, you know. It's just going to be a simple affair with a few close friends and family. They don't want the press getting wind of it and swarming all over the place."

Frannie struggled to keep her voice steady. "Who—who is Mr. Winslow marrying?"

"Why, Miss Vivian LaVelle, of course. That woman is finally going to have the Winslow name. She's done everything in her power for years to become a Winslow, and now she's finally succeeded. Don't you dare tell a soul I said this, but I pity poor Mr. Winslow when he finds out what she's really like."

Frannie reached for the doorjamb and leaned against it for a moment. She refused to pass out on Scott Winslow's porch.

The maid stepped closer, a pinched expression on her face. "Miss, you look ill. You're white as a ghost. Can I get you something? A cup of tea?"

Frannie inhaled deeply. "Yes, that would be good."

The woman led Frannie across the wide marble entry and through a spacious, two-story great hall into a sprawling kitchen. While Frannie sat down at a massive teakwood table, the maid brought her a cup of steaming tea and a slice of buttered toast. "While you drink your tea, I'll go fetch Mr. Winslow for you. He should be back from picking up his tuxedo."

Frannie held up her palm. "No, don't do that. I don't want to disturb him on his wedding day. I'll just drink my tea and be on my way."

The woman shrugged. "Okay, miss, if that's how you want it. I've got lots to do today. The caterers are due anytime now. So I'll check back on you in a few minutes."

It's not how I want it, Frannie reflected darkly, *but it's the way things are. It's too late for me to change things now.*

As she sipped her tea, she gazed around at the ultra-modern, Spanish-style kitchen with its custom appliances and polished cherrywood cabinetry. As hard as it was to admit, the luxury and opulence of this immense show place reflected the real Scott Winslow. Not the man she knew.

Still, she couldn't help remembering the fun and laughter she and Scott had shared in her bungalow's modest kitchenette. They hadn't needed a wealthy lifestyle or an extravagant residence to be happy. They had enjoyed being together, no matter where they were or what they were doing. At least that's how it had seemed to Frannie. Or maybe she had been so blindly in love, she had missed all the warning signals.

Frannie took another sip of tea, lost in her own reverie, when a familiar masculine voice cut into her thoughts.

"Frannie?"

She whirled around, nearly overturning her cup.

Scott stared down at her, looking as if he had seen a ghost. "Frannie, oh my goodness, it is you! What are you doing here?"

She pushed back her chair and stood shakily, facing him, her face flaming with embarrassment. "I asked your maid not to bother you. I'm not staying, Scott."

He held his arms out, as if to embrace her, but when she backed away, he let his hands fall at his sides. "My maid didn't say a word. I just came in to see if the caterers were here yet."

She took another uneasy step backward, hoping to make her escape before her mortification grew. "For the wedding, you mean."

"You know about the wedding?"

"Yes, your maid told me." Her voice thickened with sarcasm. "Miss LaVelle must be very happy."

Scott grimaced. "She ought to be. She's marrying into a billion dollars."

Frannie grabbed her purse off the table and started

for the door. "I'm sorry, Scott. I should never have come. I'm very embarrassed by my bad timing."

He stepped in front of her, his hands raised in a gesture of conciliation. "You can't go. You just got here."

Tears blinded her eyes. "I was a fool to think we still had anything to say to each other. But you kept phoning my house, so I thought maybe—"

"You thought right, Frannie. I've been wanting to talk with you since the night I left the beach house. Why wouldn't you take my calls?"

"How can you ask that? I didn't want to feel humiliated, the way I do right now. A woman does have a little pride, you know. Besides, what was there to say? You lied to me about everything. You deceived me, and I was fool enough to believe you."

"I didn't lie exactly, Frannie. I just omitted some very important details about my life. I had my reasons, and that's what I wanted to tell you on the phone."

"Well, Miss LaVelle told me everything I needed to know, and more. So I don't think there's anything you can add, Scott."

He gripped her shoulders. "Please, Frannie. There's so much more to say. Give me a chance."

Tears coursed down her cheeks. "Nothing you say matters now. You made me fall in love with a man who doesn't exist. I'll never be able to trust my own instincts again."

He ran his palm over her arm, his own eyes glistening. "Frannie, please, I'm sorry I hurt you. I never meant to. I wanted to tell you the truth, but I was afraid it would destroy everything we were building together.''

"And it did!''

"Dear Frannie, my wealth has always been a scourge on relationships. I've never known a woman who loved me just for myself. She always saw me through that hideous green filter of my money.''

"That's no excuse. I'm not like that.''

"I know. I loved the relationship we had. I didn't want to lose it. I thought if I went on pretending I was the man you thought I was, I would eventually become that man. And I did, Frannie. You helped me become the kind of man I always wanted to be.''

His closeness taunted her, tantalized her, but she dared not give in to his charm. "You didn't become that man, Scott. You were playing a role. Underneath you were an entirely different man, a man I could never love or respect. Please, let me go!'' She pushed against him, but he held her firm.

"I can't let you go until I'm sure you know the whole story.''

A sudden weariness overtook her. "Scott, don't tell me any more. I can't bear to hear it. Just let me walk out of your life and forget you ever existed. And you forget about me and go on with your wedding.''

He stared quizzically at her. "My wedding?''

"Yes, your wedding to your fiancée, Vivian La-Velle.''

He shook his head. "She's not my fiancée.''

"Of course she is. She told me so herself.''

"She was my fiancée once, but not now."

"I don't understand. She is the bride, isn't she?"

Scott's eyes crinkled with comprehension. "Yes, she's the bride. But I'm not the groom."

Frannie pulled herself free and walked back to the table. She needed to hold on to something for support. "I don't understand. You're talking in riddles. Your maid told me there's going to be a wedding here tonight. She said very definitely that Mr. Winslow is marrying Vivian LaVelle."

"He is." Scott gave her a wry, whimsical smile. "Mr. Winslow *is* marrying Vivian. Mr. *Jason* Winslow is marrying Miss LaVelle."

"Jason?"

"My younger brother. We're a year apart. He and I have sparred back and forth for Vivian's hand for nearly a decade. I'm glad to say that he won the honor, not I."

"You—you're not getting married today?"

"Not unless you want to make it a double ceremony."

"Scott, don't make jokes like that, please. It's too painful."

"Who's joking? I'm dead serious."

She tucked a strand of golden hair behind her ear. "Even if you're not getting married, there's no way I could marry you. You're nothing like the husband I want."

"Are you sure? Will you listen to my story before making such a sweeping judgment?"

She set her purse back on the table. "I suppose. I've come this far."

While she sat down, he went over to the coffee-maker and poured himself a cup of coffee. He brought it over to the table, along with a porcelain teapot. "Frannie, this is going to be a long story. Would you like more tea?"

Chapter Fifteen

"I'm listening, Scott."

He swallowed a mouthful of coffee and set the cup back on the table. In his casual shirt and slacks, with several dark curls straying over his forehead, Scott looked like the carefree beachcomber she remembered. A painful yearning twisted in her heart. If only Scott could say something that would make things right again!

His gaze met hers. "Frannie, I never planned to deceive you. When I moved to the beach, I got caught up in the mystique of being someone else—a carefree drifter, spontaneous and without responsibilities."

"You've told me that already."

"Okay, so I have." He turned the handle of his coffee cup, his thoughts turned inward for several moments. When he spoke again, his voice was husky. "People think being rich is this magical answer to all of life's problems. But in some ways you get caught up in a system where everything is already in place, and you can't change anything. It's bigger than you are, and it takes over your entire existence. For most of my life I accepted the hand fate dealt me, a very lucrative hand, to be sure. I allowed myself to be swept along in the tide of events, because I thought I had no choice.

"But after my mother died I started remembering all the things she had taught me as a child. I recalled the Sunday school class I attended. I knew it wasn't fate I had to reconcile myself to—it was God. I didn't know how to begin that journey back to Him. I just knew I had to separate myself from my life as I had always known it.

"So I broke up with my fiancée, packed a bag and left a note for my family telling them they'd have to manage without me, because I didn't know when I was coming back. I knew we owned some beach houses in Del Mar, so I rented one under another name. It happened to be the one next door to you."

"Until Vivian told me, I never knew I was renting my house from you. But you knew all along."

Scott nodded. "If I had let you know who I was, it would have changed everything between us. My wealth and position would have come between us and kept us apart. I had to see what life could be like without all the baggage. Don't you understand, Frannie? I just wanted us to be two footloose sojourners on the beach getting to know ourselves, each other and God."

"Stop it, Scott." Frannie pushed her teacup away.

"All of this idealistic talk is just a subterfuge for your duplicity and deceit. I don't want to hear any more."

He massaged the back of his neck, as if trying to alleviate some deep inner exhaustion. "You win, Frannie. I guess there's nothing I can say to make things right between us again."

"No, Scott, there's not," she replied in a small, pained voice. "Our values are just too different. I admit I don't know a lot about your real estate empire. I've never been one to follow the business reports and newscasts."

"Then how do you know what my moral values are?"

"Your reputation precedes you." She rubbed her knuckles with a nervous agitation. "Even I know about the substandard housing you built and the properties you've allowed to fall into decay and ruin. I know that you have so little compassion for your impoverished tenants that a judge forced you to live in one of your own rat-infested buildings for six months. And, from what I understand, it's still business as usual for the Winslow enterprises. You take advantage of the poor, Scott. You've made your wealth and power by shortchanging the needy and powerless."

Scott's brows knit together, shadowing his eyes. "Those are broad, sweeping judgments, Frannie. Be sure whereof you speak."

"I am sure, Scott. These are things you can't deny." Her words were coming in a rush now; she couldn't hold them back. "And the most unforgivable thing about you is that while your company is fleecing helpless people, you talk so convincingly about the beautiful parks and gardens you want to provide for them. I can't love a double-minded man like that, Scott. All I can feel is pity and disgust—"

Frannie's words broke off. She was on the verge of tears again. She closed her eyes and covered her face with her hands. She hadn't meant to rage on like this, but someone had to put a corrupt man like Scott Winslow in his place. Now maybe she could go home in peace and get on with her life.

"Are you finished, Frannie?" he asked with unexpected patience.

She picked up her purse and held it tightly in her hands. "Yes, I think I've said quite enough."

He nodded. "I think so, too." He heaved a deep sigh. "As far as I can tell, you've made only one glaring error in your grievous assessment of the Winslow name and empire."

She blinked rapidly. "An error? What was that?"

He pushed back his chair. "I'd rather show you than tell you."

"Show me?"

"Yes. Would you be willing to accompany me to a destination I can't disclose in advance? I promise you'll be safe with me. I'm not a complete ogre."

Her face warmed. "I never said you were."

"But you just painted me as a cruel, despicable man."

"Yes, I suppose I did."

"And yet you feel safe going somewhere alone with me?"

"Yes, but if you keep questioning me, I may change my mind."

Scott went over to an intercom system on the wall and pressed a button. "Dorothy, I'll be going out for a little while. Will you check on the caterers and the flowers? They should be here by now. And you might want to check up on Jason. He should be back by now with our tuxedos."

Scott turned to Frannie. "Ready? Let's go."

Wordlessly she followed him outside and around the villa to a six-car garage where his familiar vintage sports car was parked. "I should have known an out-of-work drifter wouldn't own a rare car like this," she remarked dryly as she slid into the passenger seat.

Neither of them spoke again until they were on Shoreline Drive heading into downtown Santa Barbara. "It's beautiful here," she murmured as they passed gardens, museums, wineries, historic missions and colorful adobes. "I can see why you built your home here."

He nodded. "Yes, it's a little patch of paradise, isn't it?" A hint of cynicism colored his voice. "Hard to believe we have all this beauty and history sandwiched between the mighty ocean and the magnificent mountains. You'd think this would be enough for any man."

"I'm surprised you would want to leave it."

"It wasn't the scenery I was trying to escape." He turned off the road into a short driveway and parked beside a stucco, mission-style building with a wide courtyard, stone arches and a red-tile roof.

Frannie gazed up at the sign over the massive double doors. "I don't understand, Scott. It says Sea Coast Convalescent Hospital. What are we doing here?"

He helped her out of the vehicle, then took her arm and led her inside. "You want to know the real Scott Winslow, don't you?"

They walked the length of the formal lobby, passing a reception desk where a woman looked up and smiled pleasantly. "Hello, Mr. Winslow. Nice day."

"Hello, Denise," he replied. "Yes, it's a very nice day."

Scott held her arm firmly as he escorted her down a long hallway past elderly and handicapped people on crutches and in wheelchairs. "Hello, mister," one cadaverous woman crooned from her chair. "You come to see me, mister?" She reached out a skeletal hand to Frannie. "How about you, dearie?"

Frannie smiled warmly. "I'm sorry. Maybe another time."

At the end of the hall Scott stopped by a closed door, lowered his head and drew in a deep, shuddering breath.

Frannie could see that he was summoning all of his reserves of mental and emotional strength to open that door. She wanted to ask him who was in there. But she held her tongue.

Finally Scott pushed open the door, took her hand and led her inside. A strong medicinal smell hovered in the air. The room felt too closed, stuffy, the light too scant in spite of the open drapes.

Frannie blinked, her eyes taking in the hospital bed, and beside it, an old man in a wheelchair watching a wide-screen TV. A talk show was playing, the volume turned too low to hear. It was a large, uncluttered room, with two brocade armchairs, a cherrywood dresser and bureau with several bouquets of fresh flowers and a nightstand with a water pitcher, Bible and serving tray with uneaten food.

Scott went over and turned off the television set, then opened the drapes a little wider so that thin sunlight seeped over the stooped figure in the chair.

Frannie stood rooted to the spot, clutching her handbag, her senses alert, anticipating…what?

Scott bent over the old man and brushed a kiss on his stubbled cheek. "Hi, Dad. How are you today?"

The grizzled man, dressed in a white cotton gown, velour robe and leather slippers, kept his glazed eyes turned toward the blank television screen. Scott dragged the two armchairs, one at a time, over beside the wheelchair. He nodded for Frannie to take one and he sat down in the other. He leaned forward and took the man's limp hand in his own. "Dad, I want you to meet Frannie. She's a good friend. I know you would like her."

The man didn't move, except to make a clicking sound with his teeth. His gray-white hair erupted from his high, shiny forehead in unruly tufts. Frannie could see now that the old man's mouth was twisted, the left side of his face paralyzed, so that the two sides of his face seemed to have been brought together unevenly.

She could imagine sculpting such a face, her fingers deftly forming his clean, classic features. And then her hand would slip, and the planes and angles of the pliant clay would be displaced just enough to disturb the balance and make the features asymmetric, disturbing. That was what she saw now—a face once strong and remarkable, but something had slipped, shifted, been dislodged, broken.

With his free hand, Scott took Frannie's slim fingers and squeezed them gently. His voice caught with emotion as he said, "Frannie, I'd like you to meet my father, Scott Winslow Sr."

A shiver of shock traveled down Frannie's spine. As her astonishment cleared, comprehension swept in. This was the man who had given the Winslow empire its ignoble reputation. This was the heartless, oppressive land baron whose name had been desecrated time and again in the press and the media. He had been reduced to *this!*

But he wasn't the Scott Winslow Frannie had fallen in love with!

Frannie touched the man's arm and bent close to his ear. "Hello, Mr. Winslow. I'm pleased to meet you." She looked questioningly at Scott and mouthed the words, "Does he understand what I'm saying?"

"I don't know, Frannie. No one knows. I pretend he does. I have to believe he hears me." Scott leaned in close to his father's contorted face and carefully articulated each word. "I love you, Dad. I wish you could come home with us."

The man sat motionless except for a slight bobbing

of his head, his eyes still drifting toward the television set.

Scott's voice rose. "Listen, Dad. Jason is getting married tonight. He's marrying the woman you always wanted me to marry. Vivian LaVelle. He's very happy, and so am I."

Still no response.

"Dad, I want you to know, I've found the woman I want to marry, too. She's sitting right here, Dad." Scott cast a sidelong glance at Frannie and smiled. "I'm hoping someday she'll agree to be my wife."

Her face reddening, Frannie gave him a quick, surprised look. She wanted to comment, to say something, anything, but no words came.

"Dad, would you like me to read to you?" Without waiting for the hint of a response, Scott got up, took the Bible from the nightstand and returned to his chair. He thumbed through the pages, then began reading Psalm 23, his voice resonant with feeling. When he had finished, he closed the book.

Frannie sat unmoving, holding her breath, her hands folded tightly in her lap. Her gaze flitted from father to son and back again. Although the old man's jaw remained slack and his eyes unfocused, Frannie was convinced she saw tears. Tears glazed Scott's eyes, too.

Frannie choked back a sob. She had never felt so deeply moved. She could feel Scott's grieving heart as if it were her own. She had known that pain when she lost her mother. Now, in a different way, Scott had lost his father. How she longed to go to him and take him in her arms and comfort him. But she forced herself to remain silent and still. She sensed that Scott still had more to say to the broken man in the chair.

Scott moved closer to his father's ear, his arm circling the old man's sagging shoulders. "Dad, I don't know if you can hear me or understand me, but I have so much to tell you. Things I never had the courage to say when you were well. I've come to know God in a way I haven't known since childhood. I've gotten acquainted again with the God that Mother loved."

Scott's voice rumbled with emotion. "Listen, Dad. Try to hear me. Jesus loves you. He wants to forgive you for all the wrong things you've done. If somewhere in the depths of your mind you can understand me, please accept God's love and ask Him to forgive you."

Scott took his father's hand in his. "If you understand, Dad, squeeze my hand. Please, Dad."

Frannie met Scott's gaze. His desolate eyes told her there was no response. Scott released his father's hand and stood up, arching his broad shoulders. "We'd better go, Frannie. I've got a wedding to attend."

After saying goodbye to the silent figure in the wheelchair, they left the hospital and headed back to the villa in Scott's vintage automobile. Frannie was still too stunned to absorb all that had just happened. She kept her gaze on the road ahead. Once she murmured, "I never dreamed..." But the words eluded her. Finally she remarked, "I wouldn't have expected a man of your father's wealth and position to be in an ordinary hospital like that."

"It's the closest medical facility to our home. I wanted to be able to go see him every day. When he's well enough, I'll bring him home."

Frannie studied Scott's sturdy profile. He was more handsome to her now than he had ever been. "I loved the way you were with your dad. You obviously love him very much."

Scott flashed a wan smile, then turned his gaze back to the road. "I read Scriptures to him every day. Every time I go I tell him Jesus loves him. He would never listen to such talk when he was well. I just pray that he comprehends something I'm telling him now."

"I have faith that he does." Frannie drew in a deep breath. "I'm sorry I misjudged you, Scott. I still think you were wrong to mislead me about your identify, but I understand better why you did it. And I'm relieved to know you aren't the Scott Winslow who built substandard housing and fleeced the poor."

"Don't be too generous with your praise, Frannie. I'm not guilt-free."

She gave him a guarded look. "What do you mean?"

His knuckles tightened on the steering wheel. "I mean, as his elder son and an executive officer of the company, I should have done more to oppose my father's decisions. I let him and my brother do things their way. They cut corners, overlooked problems and walked a fine line between honesty and fraud. Oh, I protested often enough and threatened to make the truth known. I even said I'd wash my hands of the whole business. But I never put actions to my words."

"But you did, Scott. You finally left. You came to the beach and lived the kind of simple, ordinary life you wanted. That was a means of protest, wasn't it?"

He gave a sardonic chuckle. "Dear Frannie! That was cowardice, plain and simple. Rather than fighting my father and brother, I retreated. Rather than staying and changing the system, I deserted the system. Maybe if I had stayed and fought harder and made things better, my father might not have had his stroke."

Frannie reached over and squeezed his arm. "You can't blame yourself for that, Scott. Your father made his own choices. You had nothing to do with his stroke. Don't take responsibility for something that rests in the hands of God alone."

"I suppose you're right. But I hate feeling so helpless. You don't know what it does to me to see my father—a man who was so strong and powerful—reduced to a feeble invalid." His voice broke on a sob. "Every time I visit him, it tears me apart inside. My brother won't even go see him. Says he wants to remember him the way he was. To me, that's a cop-out."

"It is, Scott. And it's selfish too. I respect you for putting your father's welfare ahead of your own feelings."

"I'm just doing what I have to do. But it's painful to lose someone you love to a slow death."

"I know. My mom had cancer. That was seven

years ago. Sometimes I think I still haven't gotten over it. Maybe some things you never get over.''

They were both silent for a while. She gazed out at the scenery they had passed before—the wineries and museums and lush landscapes. Everything looked the same. But something within her had changed, and she wasn't sure what it was. It was a bittersweet sensation, as if something had been lost but also gained. Finally she broke the silence with, ''Scott, when did your father have his stroke?''

He looked curiously at her. ''I thought you knew. It was the day Vivian came to your house looking for me. She brought the news. That's why I left the beach house so quickly. I just threw things in a bag and left with her.''

''You left to be with your father? I thought you left to be with her. She never mentioned your father's stroke.''

He sighed. ''That sounds like Vivian. She deliberately misled you. No wonder you wouldn't take my calls.''

''She said she was your fiancée and the two of you were supposed to be married next month.''

Scott shook his head. ''I broke up with that woman last year before I ever left Santa Barbara.'' He reached over and took her hand. ''Let me get this straight! You thought I was romancing you while I was engaged to someone else?''

Her voice came out light and breathy. ''That's how it looked.''

"After all that, I'm surprised you came to Santa Barbara to see me."

She twisted her purse strap. "I couldn't get you out of my head, Scott. I thought if I came up here and gave you a piece of my mind, I could go home and get on with my life."

"And now what do you think?"

"I wish I knew." She studied the way the sun etched a golden glow over Scott's rugged profile. Just being with this man stirred a pleasant warmth in her heart. Whenever their eyes met, something tickled inside her. But that didn't mean it was love.

"Things are definitely more complicated than I expected," she admitted. "Nothing's the way it seemed. How can I know how I feel, Scott, when my ideas about you keep changing?"

"I can't answer that, Frannie." His voice was gentle, almost solemn. "But I can tell you how I feel. You heard me tell my father I'm in love with you. And I meant it. The question now is, Where do we go from here?"

Chapter Sixteen

When they arrived back at the villa, the house and grounds were a buzz of activity. The florist was delivering huge bouquets of orchids, carnations and azaleas, along with lush garlands of white roses for the gazebo in the backyard. The caterers were setting out chafing dishes, punch bowls, utensils, silverware, china and crystal on linen-draped tables in the garden. And a technician was adjusting the sound system for the combo that would be performing later.

Scott left Frannie standing alone in the great hall for several minutes while he spoke with Dorothy and the various service people. When he returned, he seemed preoccupied, almost brisk in his demeanor. "They're concerned about whether to have the wedding outside as planned," he told Frannie, "or whether to move everything into the house."

"It's a warm, pleasant day, Scott, and it promises to be a balmy evening, even for October."

"That's what I told them. The white gazebo and exotic gardens are perfect for a wedding. It's where I'd like to be married someday." He gave her a meaningful glance, then rushed on. "So we're going to keep the festivities outside unless a cold front comes in. Or rain. But I don't see a cloud in the sky."

"Neither do I. It should be a wonderful evening for your family, Scott." She turned and took a tentative step toward the foyer.

Scott seized her arm. "Where are you going, Frannie?"

She stopped and looked up at him, her heartbeat accelerating. "It's time for me to go home. If I leave now I may get back to La Jolla before dark."

His grip tightened. "You can't go now. We've just begun to talk. We still have so much to say to each other."

She tried to pull away, but he held her fast.

"Please, Scott, you're going to be busy tonight with the wedding. I'd just be in the way."

"You can't be serious! I want you here. You'll be my guest. Spend the night. We have plenty of rooms. You can have any suite you please. Just say you'll stay."

A thousand arguments collided in Frannie's thoughts. So many pros and cons. There were reasons why she should stay, but even more reasons why she should flee now, before her emotions became more entangled with the cryptic, complex, captivating Scott Winslow.

She looked down at her tailored shirt and stretch jeans. "I don't have a proper outfit for a wedding."

"You didn't bring a change of clothes?"

"Yes, I have some things in the trunk left over from moving…a plain black sheath and pumps in the car, but they're not dressy enough for—"

"They'll be perfect. One of my mother's diamond necklaces and earrings will dress it up. You'll be the belle of the ball."

"Scott, I can't!"

"Of course you can. It's settled, Frannie. I've just got you back. I'm not going to let you out of my sight until we've resolved things between us."

The sound of footsteps on the spiral oak staircase distracted them from their conversation. Frannie turned and looked up as a shorter, leaner version of Scott descended the plush stairs in a black tuxedo. The young man's face was narrower than Scott's, but his high cheekbones, straight nose and full lips were unmistakably part of the Winslow heritage. He came striding toward Scott and Frannie with a mischievous smile on his bronze face.

He winked at Scott as he extended his hand to Frannie. "So what have we here, big brother? Is this the mystery woman you've been pining for?"

Scott ignored the innuendo. "Jason, this is Frannie Rowlands. Frannie, my zany brother, Jason. The groom."

They shook hands and exchanged pleasantries for a moment.

"Jason, you don't look half-bad in your tuxedo," Scott observed.

"Thanks, I think. You know how I hate these monkey suits. Good thing I picked up the tuxes myself. When I tried mine on, it needed more alterations. Trousers were too long. I made them do a rush job, or I'd still be there waiting. Hope you have better luck with yours. It's upstairs in your room."

"Guess I'd better go change. The guests will start arriving in another hour."

Jason smiled at Frannie. "You are staying for the nuptials, aren't you, Miss Rowlands?"

"Yes, I guess I am. Scott convinced me. If you have room for another guest, that is."

Jason held out his hands, palms up. "Look at this place. We could invite half of Santa Barbara if we wished."

"We're only expecting a hundred of our closest friends and colleagues," Scott told her, winking. "We want to keep this simple and private. Not a media event."

Frannie stifled a chuckle. "I've put on a lot of dinner parties, and this is definitely not small or simple."

Scott gently took Frannie's arm. "Let me get Dorothy to show you to your room. And if you give me the keys, I'll get your travel bag from your car. Then you can dress at your leisure and come downstairs when you're ready."

Minutes later, Frannie found herself standing in the midst of a luxurious bedroom with plush white carpeting, a pink canopy bed, floor-length antique mirrors and white French provincial furniture. Off to one side was a sitting room with a balcony overlooking the garden; on the other side was a spacious powder room and bath with a sunken Jacuzzi tub surrounded by tropical fauna.

Frannie kicked off her sandals and did a little pirouette in her bare feet. "I can't believe this! I feel like Cinderella about to go to the ball with Prince Charming!"

She removed her black dress from her travel bag, hung it on the door and examined it closely. "Please don't be too wrinkled. And my pumps...I hope they're not scuffed."

After a leisurely bubble bath, Frannie applied her makeup, adding a little extra eyeshadow and mascara. She curled her hair and slipped into her black sheath and pumps. The outfit looked nice enough if she were going to a church social, but hardly fitting for a billionaire's wedding. "How did I get myself into this?" she wondered aloud. "I should just sneak out now, and maybe Scott won't even notice I'm gone."

But moments later, as she descended the spiral staircase, she saw Scott, stunning in his tuxedo, waiting for her, one hand on the oak banister. With a little flourish he held out his hand to her and bowed as if she were a princess. "You look lovely, Frannie. Exquisite. Only one thing is missing."

"What's that?"

"My mother's necklace." He produced a diamond choker from his pocket and fastened it around her neck. Then he handed her two diamond earrings and watched with a smile as she slipped them on.

She tilted her head slightly. "How do I look?"

He beamed. "Like an angel swathed in stars."

She felt color bloom in her cheeks. "No one's ever given me a compliment that was quite so poetic."

"I can't help it. You bring out the poetry in me." He tucked her arm in his. "I think we're ready to join our guests."

Frannie's gaze had been so unswervingly on Scott that she hadn't noticed the wedding guests in all their finery. They were mingling in the foyer and drifting through the great hall toward the stained-glass doors that led to the patio.

"Scott, they're all in formal wear. I can't go out there in this dress."

"Of course you can. You're more beautiful than any woman in the place, including the bride." He led her outside to the gazebo where chairs formed a semi-circle around a rose-covered altar. The band was already playing and guests were taking their seats as the setting sun turned the sky a flaming red.

Scott squeezed her arm affectionately. "Frannie, I'm afraid you'll have to survive the ceremony without me. I am the best man, you know. And I'd better give my brother the moral support he needs, considering whom he's marrying. But I'll join you immediately after." He showed her to the first row. "For tonight you'll be family, sitting close to the altar, close to me." His lips curved in a wry smile. "I hope it's a sign of things to come."

She ignored his comment and sat down in the chair he offered. "You go join your brother, Scott. I'll be fine here."

The wedding proceeded without incident. The ceremony was brief, formal and romantic. Even the vain and insufferable Vivian LaVelle looked quite lovely in her designer-original gown. But Frannie hardly heard a word the minister said, for in her imagination, it was she and Scott standing at the altar saying their vows. The fantasy sent her thoughts reeling and her spirits soaring. Oh, if only!

The stars were out and the garden lights twinkling as the reception got in full swing. As the band played an upbeat tempo, Scott escorted Frannie around the garden, introducing her to friends, colleagues and relatives.

But Frannie drew back uneasily when Scott led her over to Jason and his new bride. After Vivian's visit to the beach house, Frannie had no desire for another nasty encounter with the woman. But to her surprise, the bride smiled politely and said, "How nice that you could make it, Miss Rowlands."

"It was a beautiful wedding," Frannie said sincerely.

But while Scott and Jason chatted confidentially, Vivian's smile turned brittle. She leaned close to Frannie and whispered, "You may think you've won, but you'll never have Scott. He's infatuated, but he's no fool. Give him up while you still have your dignity and self-respect."

Frannie rocked back on her heels momentarily,

then said through clenched teeth, "I have no designs on Scott. We're friends. That's all." As the men rejoined them, Frannie told Vivian brightly, "I hope you and Jason will be very happy together. You must love him very much."

Vivian turned sharply, picked up her crinolines and flounced away. Jason shrugged and followed after her. Scott drew Frannie into his arms and pulled her close. "What was that all about?"

Frannie averted her gaze. "Nothing important."

"It was something. I saw that look in Vivian's eyes."

"Let's just say your brother's bride isn't too fond of me."

He chuckled. "That's no loss. Say, are you hungry?"

"Famished."

He steered her over to the buffet table. "We'll fill up our plates and see if we can find the most secluded table in the garden."

The long, linen-draped table was brimming with luscious delicacies—beef bourguignonne, glazed ham, Cornish game hens, baked whitefish, shrimp scampi and chicken Parmesan. Candied yams, green bean casserole, rice pilaf, small red potatoes and vegetable lasagna rounded out the menu, along with a variety of salads and breads.

Frannie vowed to try just a little of this and that, but soon her plate was heaped with goodies. She looked helplessly at Scott. "This is a banquet. Too many tempting things I can't resist."

He waved his hand. "Eat all you like. I like a woman who isn't afraid to enjoy her food."

She laughed. "Good thing. Because I may go back for seconds!"

"Don't forget there's all that gooey sweet wedding cake."

"How could I forget? It's as big as a tower and smothered in mounds of icing and little sugar rosebuds. Totally irresistible to someone with a sweet tooth like mine."

"I'm right there with you. Looks like we're both in for a sugar high."

She elbowed him playfully. "At least we don't have to eat and drive."

Scott took both plates and led Frannie to a table at the outskirts of the garden. While Frannie sat down, Scott went to the punch bowl and brought back crystal goblets of sparkling cider. They ate with only the glow of the flickering candlelight between them.

Frannie loved the burnished glow that shimmered over Scott's handsome features. He looked dapper and dashing in his black tuxedo, his chestnut-brown hair swept back, with a single curl straying over his forehead. His dark eyes glinted with merriment as he held up his goblet and toasted her. "To the most beautiful woman under these stars. And to our first wedding together, Frannie. I pray it won't be our last."

As they sipped their drinks, he reached across the table and clasped her free hand firmly in his. "You know, now that I have you here, my dear Frannie, I'm not going to let you go."

She gave him her most guileless smile, bating him. "You mean you want me to stay here forever?"

"Why not? Every day I'm more convinced we belong together. I'm not just making conversation or handing you a line. I'm speaking from my heart, Frannie."

Her smile faded. "I'm flattered, Scott, but..."

"But you're not ready for a commitment, is that it?"

She traced the rim of her goblet. "You must admit we haven't had a typical relationship. Just when I think I know you, something happens and I realize I don't know you at all."

"That's not true. You know me better than anyone. You know the man I want to be. You know me without all the trappings and accoutrements of the Winslow wealth. You know the inner man, the private person I've never revealed to anyone else."

"It's true that I saw a side to you today I loved. The way you were with your father. Your deep compassion for him, even though I know he's disappointed you in so many ways. I love that about you, Scott, that you could reach out to your father at his lowest point, and be there for him."

"I wasn't trying to impress you. I do care deeply for him."

"I know. It was so evident. That's a wonderful trait."

"But it's not good enough, is that it?"

"It's not enough to base a marriage on. Or a future together. Don't you see, Scott? No matter what you say, you're not the man I grew to love during our months on the beach. That man was poor and idealistic, filled with dreams but without the resources to make them come true. But I was convinced he would have done anything in his power to turn them into reality. He would have fought everyone and everything to fulfill his goals. He would have given his very life to make the world a better place for the poor, forgotten people of this land."

"I still feel that way, Frannie. It's my heart's passion."

"Maybe, or maybe not, Scott. You're a man with resources beyond anyone's imagination, but your dreams are just pleasant ideas tucked away for safekeeping. You haven't tried to make them come true. You haven't put everything on the line, you haven't risked all for them, because you're too rooted in your own reality. You say you don't approve of your father's business practices and decisions, and yet you're still part of the company that does things you don't approve of."

Scott released her hand and sat back, a frown creasing his brow. "It's not easy being a man in my position, Frannie. I'm entrenched in this company. It's my life's blood, my past, my future. I'm a vital cog in the machinery that keeps it going, functioning smoothly. Especially now, with my dad incapacitated, I can't just walk away from it and let it flounder. And someday maybe I'll be able to exert the kind of influence that will make a difference."

Frannie fought against a niggling disappointment. She looked away and back again. "See what I mean, Scott? The man I see before me now isn't the impoverished, passionate idealist I knew last summer. The man I see sitting before me now is the rational, pragmatic son of one of America's wealthiest families. How can I relate to you, Scott, when I don't know which man you really are?"

He shrugged. "I guess I'm both men. And, frankly, I don't know how to reconcile the two into the man you want me to be."

"I'm not asking you to change to fit some mold I've created. I want you to be yourself. But don't ask me to commit to you until you know for sure who that man is."

Scott swallowed the last of his drink and pushed back his chair. "This conversation has gotten entirely too solemn for a wedding celebration. Would you like me to show you the rest of the garden under a brilliant ceiling of stars?"

With a titter of laughter, she got up and joined him. Arm in arm they strolled along the narrow footpath through the lush foliage and sheltering oak and eucalyptus. The band was playing romantic ballads in the distance, the music blending with the muffled voices of the wedding guests. The melodies wafted on the same crisp sea breeze that rustled Frannie's hair and brought out goose bumps on her bare arms. Or was it Scott's closeness that electrified her senses?

After a while, he stopped and pointed to the sky. "Do you see the Big Dipper up there?"

"And there's the North Star. They're so clear to-night."

His arm encircled her waist. "I ordered them just for you."

She gazed up at him, studying the way the shadows and moonlight played on his face. "You didn't have to do that for me, Scott. I only needed a star or two, not a whole sky."

He pulled her against him, so close that she could feel his heart beating against her breast. "I'd give you the galaxies if I thought it would make you happy, Frannie."

Her lips parted to offer a response. But before she could make a sound, his lips came down on hers, soft, gentle, moving over her mouth with exquisite tenderness. In that blissful moment, she yearned for nothing more than to melt in his arms, as pliant as the supple clay she molded with her fingers.

"I love you, Frannie," he whispered against her ear. "I need you more than life itself. Tell me you love me. too."

Dazzled, delighted, she struggled to catch her breath. "I do, Scott. I love you with all my heart."

"That's all I wanted to hear, my darling." He kissed her earlobes, her eyes, her hair, then moved back again to her lips. She relaxed, returning the kiss, luxuriating in the taste of his lips, the encompassing warmth of his embrace.

This was where she belonged, where she yearned

to remain forever…with this man she cherished and adored. Even with her eyes closed, she saw the spangling stars, flaming and bright, exploding like fireworks. They were more brilliant in her heart than they had ever been in the heavens.

It occurred to Frannie that maybe it was time to listen to the yearnings of her heart rather than to the cold voice of reason. Maybe Scott Winslow was the man for her after all.

Chapter Seventeen

Frannie lost track of time in Scott's arms. Had they been lost in their embrace for mere moments, or hours, or forever? At last she pulled away, her senses still reeling, her legs unsteady.

Scott kept his arms loosely around her waist. "Are you okay?"

"Yes." She rubbed her forehead. "Just a little dizzy."

"It can't be the sparkling cider." He smoothed her hair back from her forehead. "Maybe it's the intoxication of love."

She smiled. "That must be it."

"We'll go back and sit down." He kept his arm around her as they walked back to their table. "Would you like something more to drink?"

"No. Actually, I think I'll use the powder room."

"It's right off the great hall, to the right. Would you like me to show you the way?"

"No, I'll find it."

Wending her way through the milling guests, Frannie returned to the villa and found the powder room. To her amazement, it looked like a fancy sitting room, with velvet wallpaper on three walls and a floor-to-ceiling mirror on the fourth. She uttered a little exclamation of admiration as she gazed around at the posh furnishings—an overstuffed sofa and love seat, polished end tables and ruffled lamps. "This gives new meaning to the term, 'reading room,'" Frannie remarked to another guest, who was on her way out.

The stout, middle-aged woman checked her hem in the mirror and smiled. "If you're looking for the bathroom, this is it. Just keep going around the corner."

"Thanks. I was afraid I had stumbled into the wrong place. The maid's quarters, or something."

"This house is like that. Incredible. They could turn it into a hotel and still have room to spare." The woman patted a curl into place, then headed for the door. She paused and looked back at Frannie. "That's what you get when you're filthy rich. Makes the rest of us look like paupers, even with our million-dollar estates."

Frannie held back a chuckle. What would the woman think if she knew Frannie's "luxury mansion" was a modest rented beach house with a tiny bathroom, sagging porch and clogged chimney?

Moments later, Frannie was washing her hands when she heard two women enter the powder room. She couldn't see them, but they were talking loudly and sounded as if they had been celebrating a little too heavily.

Frannie was about to leave when she heard one woman call the other, *Vivian*. Frannie's breath caught. Not Vivian LaVelle! She was the last woman Frannie wanted to face again. Stepping back into the shadows, Frannie waited, hoping she could slip out unnoticed after the two women left. But they showed no signs of hurrying, so Frannie gritted her teeth and listened.

"Oh, Vivian," one woman exclaimed, her voice slurring, "why did they put a mirror like this in here? What woman wants to see this much of herself?"

"Miranda, you look gorgeous. You just want somebody to tell you so."

Yes, Frannie acknowledged silently, withdrawing farther into the shadows, the second voice was definitely Vivian's.

"Of course, darling. And you look absolutely ravishing in that wedding gown. I bet it set Jason back a pretty penny."

"He wanted me to have the best. Who was I to argue?"

"That husband of yours is a gem. Always extravagant. And generous to a fault. He's a treasure. Hold on to him."

"I intend to."

There was silence for a moment. Frannie wondered if they were leaving. Then the first woman spoke again.

"I'd better sit down here a minute, Vivian. That champagne! You know me. I couldn't get enough of the bubbly. You tell Jason I'll come to his wedding every day if he puts on a spread like this."

"I think you had a little too much, Miranda."

"Way too much. Sit here with me for a minute, Vivian."

"Just for a minute. I have other guests, you know." A pause, then: "Speaking of guests, Miranda, did you see that woman with Scott Winslow?"

"A pretty thing. Who is she? I haven't seen her before."

"She's nobody you'd know...nobody you'd wish to know. She's a charlatan if I ever saw one. A real gold digger. Did you see those diamonds she was wearing? I happen to know those belonged to Scott's mother."

"You can't be serious."

"I'm dead serious. I'd seen the old woman wear them a hundred times."

"My goodness, Vivian, how did she get her hands on them?"

"I don't know. But she's got Scott duped—you can be sure of that."

"I'm shocked. The woman has no shame, flaunting the Winslow jewels like that. And at a Winslow wedding! Can you imagine such audacity?"

"Mark my words, Miranda. That shallow twit doesn't have the slightest idea what it means to be a Winslow."

"I'm sure she doesn't, Vivian."

"You can tell she has no class or breeding. If she marries into this family, she'll be swallowed up. Her life won't be her own. The Winslows will devour her and spit her out."

"Like an eggshell in an omelet. That's what my mother used to say, Vivian. You know how distasteful finding an eggshell can be."

"I'm going to keep my eye on that woman, Miranda. I swear I will. I haven't given up ten years of my life to let some other woman get her hands on the Winslow money. Miranda, are you ready to go yet? Jason will be looking for me."

"Yes, Vivian, I'm feeling better. Who knows? Maybe I'll have another glass of champagne."

"Miranda, you take the cake." She gave an icy little twitter. "Speaking of cake, it's time to cut mine. Come. It'll go well with your champagne."

"Oh, heavens, yes. Cake and champagne. Delightful!"

After the two women had gone, Frannie remained for several moments in the shadowed corner of the powder room before stirring. Her body felt as paralyzed as her mind. The women's conversation echoed inside her like a death knell. How could they have been so vicious? What had she done to elicit such cruelty? Worse than their arrogance was the frightening possibility that they could be right. To involve herself with a Winslow man could spell heartache and calamity for her just as it had for Scott's mother.

Frannie gazed at her reflection in the mirror. Her face looked blanched, her lips tight, her eyes wide with alarm. Her stricken expression reminded her of a deer caught in the blinding glare of headlights just before it's struck. The analogy was all too real, the bitter truth staring Frannie in the face. Entertaining the idea of a life and future with the wealthy, powerful Scott Winslow was like walking into the path of an oncoming truck. There was no way she could survive intact. At least not as the person she was now. To fit in with these affluent people and become part of this lavish lifestyle, she would have to become a different person, someone she wasn't sure she could respect, someone like Vivian.

With her spirits ebbing, Frannie returned to the garden, but she no longer felt like partaking of the festivities. If only she could leave right now and drive home. But the hour was late, and it had already been a long day. She looked among the throng for Scott and spotted him zigzagging through the crowd balancing two plates of wedding cake.

"Here you are!" he said as he handed her a plate. "I thought maybe you had gotten lost. I hope my directions weren't that misleading."

"No, they were fine. I'm sorry. I lost track of time."

"No problem." His eyes crinkled with warmth. "I missed you. I'll get us some punch and we can go back to our table."

"No, Scott. I'm really not hungry for cake. I was thinking of...of going to my room and making an early night of it."

He looked dumbfounded. "Aren't you feeling well?"

She touched her forehead. "I do have a headache. I hope you don't mind, Scott."

He set their cake on the table, then slipped his arm around her shoulder and drew her close, his chin nuzzling her hair. "I was counting on spending a few more hours together in this romantic setting, but I do understand."

"Thanks, Scott. I'm sure I'll be fine in the morning."

"I hope so. We still have a lot to talk about. And plans to make, now that we know how we feel about each other."

"Plans?"

"For our future. I want us to make a life together, Frannie. Surely you want that, too."

Her muscles tensed. "I can't think about it tonight, Scott. Too much has happened. I can't take it all in."

He turned to face her and took her hands in his. "Would you like me to walk you up to your room?"

"No, I can find it. Oh, and one more thing." She unfastened the diamond necklace, removed the earrings and placed them in Scott's hand. "These belong to you."

"You don't have to take them off now. You can leave them in your room, if you like."

"No, Scott. I don't want to pretend to be someone I'm not."

His brows furrowed. "You didn't enjoy wearing them? They looked stunning on you."

She struggled to keep her lower lip from quivering. "I guess I'm just one of those plain-Jane girls. What you see is what you get. I don't need million-dollar diamonds, Scott. I'm happy in rhinestones and dime store jewelry.''

Bewilderment shadowed his handsome features. ''That doesn't mean you can't get used to the real thing.''

''That depends on what the real thing is, Scott. For me, the real thing is what we had together on the beach when we were counting our pennies, trusting the Lord and surviving on a pittance. We were thriving then, Scott, having the time of our lives. That was real to me. But now I realize that this is your real world and that was just pretend. I'm not sure this could ever be my world, Scott.''

''It can be. Just give us a chance, Frannie.'' He wrapped her in his arms and kissed her cheek.

She broke away, blushing as she noticed other guests glancing their way. ''We have to pray about it, Scott,'' she said in a small, hushed voice. ''We need to put our future in God's hands.''

''I agree. I promise you, I'll be doing a lot of praying tonight.''

''Me, too.'' She pivoted before he could notice the tears in her eyes. ''Good night, Scott.''

As he caught her hand for a lingering moment, she realized he had never looked more handsome and debonair. ''Sleep well, my darling.'' His gentle, resonant voice wrapped itself around her heart. ''I love you, Frannie. I'll see you in the morning.''

With blinding tears, she slipped awkwardly through

the press of laughing, partying guests, and made her way up the grand spiral staircase to her room.

After locking the door, she undressed and slipped into her cotton nightgown, suddenly too tired even to wash off her makeup. She climbed into bed, pulled the downy comforter over her and tried to sleep. But as exhausted as she felt, sleep eluded her. She could hear the band playing in the garden, the sweet, sentimental ballads accented by garbled voices and laughter. It was as if the world were going on without her, and she had no idea where she belonged in that opulent, paradoxical sphere. Or whether she even belonged at all.

Finally, growing restless, she got up and walked over to the sliding glass door and looked out. The sky was still ablaze with stars. Quietly she opened the door and stole out onto the balcony. It was amazing. Like a tiny bird perched on a limb, she could look down on the entire wedding celebration, and no one could see her watching.

For a long while, she observed the festivities below in curious fascination—dozens of guests milling about, chatting, dancing, laughing, eating and drinking. It was as if God were giving her a glimpse of a world she had never inhabited. She spotted Scott in the crowd, moving from table to table, conversing with guests, smiling, chuckling, as if he had forgotten she had even been there.

Her curiosity gave way to a sense of loneliness and isolation. What was she doing in this place? She surely didn't belong here. But if not here, then where?

The question of where she belonged plagued her these days.

Frannie stepped back inside her room and curled up in a velvet love seat beside the open sliding door, where she could still feel a refreshing breeze. It was time to take her eyes off people and circumstances and focus them on her heavenly Father.

"Lord, I really need to talk with You," she said aloud, her tenuous voice jarring the stillness. "You know how confused I've been since Daddy remarried. I don't know where I belong anymore. I can't go back home and be Daddy's little girl, taking care of him the way I did after Mother died. He has Juliana now. And Belina. A whole new family. He doesn't need me anymore.

"But I can't stay here with Scott in his palatial villa, surrounded by his snobbish friends and all the trappings of wealth. I know now I don't belong in his world, either. I could never be a jaded, society-minded rich girl.

"But who am I then, Lord? I don't know anymore. Maybe all I want to be is the girl on the beach, with just the sun and sea and my sculptures around me, and no one to answer to but You, Father. Is that what You want for me? Help me to know what to do."

When she had finished praying, Frannie climbed back into bed and slept soundly until the first rays of dawn washed over her. She got up and looked out the sliding door at the red streaks breaking through the azure heavens. The world was a silent place this morning, devoid of humanity. God alone was evident

in the vivid splendor of His sunrise. Apparently no
one else in the house was up yet.

A thought occurred to Frannie. If I leave now, I
won't have to face Scott and all his questions. I won't
have to give him an answer about committing to a
relationship, or see the disappointment in his eyes
when I tell him I have no idea what God wants for
us.

Frannie dressed quickly and threw her things into
her travel bag. She found a sheet of stationery in the
dresser and, with a trembling hand, scribbled a note
to Scott.

"I'm sorry. This was a mistake. It's over, Scott.
Please don't call me or contact me. Don't make it any
harder for us than it is. Frannie."

Gingerly she stole downstairs. The house was silent, no one in sight. She slipped out to her car, tossed
her things in the trunk and minutes later was on the
freeway, heading south to San Diego.

As she drove, she vowed that she would forget
Scott. She would throw herself into her work—her
sculpting and her classes at the university. She would
spend more time in church, and with her father and
sisters, and Belina. And she would learn to accept
Juliana as part of her family. She would carve out a
productive, worthwhile life for herself and have no
one to answer to but God.

Whatever it took, she would put Scott Winslow out
of her mind forever. But, even as she made her resolves, she knew that getting him out of her heart
would be infinitely more difficult.

Chapter Eighteen

Last night I dreamed my mother was still alive.
We were sitting in the garden talking together,
and I kept marveling at how wonderful it was
to see her and be able to tell her all the things
I felt about her, and how much I loved her. I
touched her skin and looked into her eyes, and
told her how strange it was that I had somehow
believed she was dead; I had dreamed her death,
and now I knew it wasn't so. She was still here
with me; we still had time together for all the
things I yearned to do with her.

And then suddenly I awoke, and she was gone.
I realized with an ache in my heart that the reality
was reversed. My mother was dead, buried over
seven years now, and alive only in my dreams.

Frannie set down her journal and let the pen fall
from her fingers. She hadn't written in this thumb-

worn book in months, maybe even years. She had packed it and brought it with her to the beach house, then stuck it in a drawer and forgot about it. Now that she had come across it again, she felt compelled to write and express the inexpressible in her heart.

Why was it, in the two months since she had fled Scott's Santa Barbara villa, she grieved her mother's death as much as she mourned losing Scott? Hadn't she already anguished over her mother for seven long years? Why were the memories assailing her afresh— the haunting images of that slow, dreadful dying and her own helplessness as she watched the cancer ravage her mother's body? There had been nothing she could do but stand by and watch. God help her, she lost her mother bit by precious bit and couldn't change a thing. How she hated being powerless. To this day the idea plagued her that there must have been something she could have done.

But now she couldn't stop wondering why the one loss had become entangled with the other, so that she wasn't sure which one she mourned the most.

She hadn't lost Scott, of course. She had deliberately set him free, and herself free, as well. After all, they came from two vastly different worlds. To try to blend their lives would only have brought heartache and pain. And she had had enough pain for two lifetimes.

Scott had phoned the day after his brother's wedding, but she had told him she didn't want to see him. It had to end here and now, because she couldn't imagine the two of them becoming husband and wife.

Better not to draw things out, she told him, because the misery would only be worse.

His reply still tolled in her mind. ''You're making the biggest mistake of your life, Frannie, and someday, when it's too late, you're going to realize it.''

Since then, every morning when she awoke, she silently told herself, Letting Scott go wasn't a mistake. I did the only thing I could do. It's for the best. She had to believe it. The alternative was unthinkable.

On most days she refused to let her mind dwell on Scott and what might have been. She kept herself busy with her art classes and a new commission for the La Jolla library. But now, with Christmas in the air, she was feeling a tad sentimental. She would probably leave the beach house and move back home for a week or two, to enjoy the holidays with her family. Her father always insisted on a live, ten-foot tree, decorated to the max, with loads of presents piled high around it.

Besides, the beach house was drafty these days, as the seasonal winds and rains assailed it. It had become a lonely place, especially without Scott in the neighboring bungalow.

So, on a Tuesday morning, one week before Christmas, Frannie phoned her father and said, ''Daddy, how would you like a house guest over the holidays? Two, in fact, if you count Ruggs.''

As she expected, her father was overjoyed at the prospect of having his little girl home again. And Frannie had to admit, she was looking forward to it as much as he.

"Well, Ruggs, Daddy wants us home for Christmas." Frannie tossed her empty suitcase on the bed and opened it. Item by item, she folded her garments and laid them in the case. Shirts, jeans, dresses, sweaters, nightwear, lingerie. Just enough for a two-week stay.

Just as she was deliberating whether she would need a second travel bag, there was a loud knock on her door. She brushed back her tangled hair and looked down at Ruggs. "Looks like we have company, boy. What do you wanna bet it's someone selling something?"

Ruggs barked, made a little circle, then bounded out of the bedroom, yipping eagerly. Frannie followed him to the door and grabbed his collar. "Quiet, Ruggsy. You'll wake the dead!"

She opened the door and stared up into the face of Scott Winslow. He stood on the porch in a navy business suit and tan overcoat, looking as if he had stepped out of a sophisticated men's fashion magazine.

"Scott!" Frannie gazed down at her own rumpled flannel shirt and clay-streaked sweatpants. She tucked a flyaway strand of gold hair behind her ear. "What are you doing here?"

"I'm a man on a mission, Frannie. May I come in?"

She backed awkwardly into the room and swept out her hand. "Of course. Come in. It's cold out there."

He strode immediately over to the fireplace and

held out his hands before the crackling flames. "I see your chimney is working well these days."

She smiled wryly. "Someone once gave me good advice about keeping the flue clear." She approached him. "May I take your coat?"

He shrugged off his overcoat and handed it to her. She hung it on a hook by the door. "Please sit down. May I get you something to drink? Coffee? Hot cocoa?"

He settled on the couch. "No, thanks, Frannie. I'd just like a little conversation."

She sat down on the overstuffed chair. "If I'd known you were dropping by, I would have… Well, I wouldn't be looking like this."

He grinned. "You look great. Fresh and natural and very attractive."

Her face warmed. "I was just packing…."

"You're leaving the beach house?"

"Just over Christmas. Going home to my dad's for the holidays."

"That's good. It's exactly what a daughter should do. How is your father?"

"Fine. Healthy. Happy with his new wife." She paused, her forehead creasing. "How is your father?"

Scott gazed down at his hands. "He died a week after you saw him."

"I'm so sorry," she said compassionately.

"I hope something I said about accepting Christ's love got through to him."

"We have to trust that it did."

"I'm trying. It's hard. My father and I were never

close, but I grew up thinking of him as invincible and indestructible. He was the captain of our ship, so to speak, our inveterate taskmaster and a crafty old curmudgeon. He ruled with an iron hand, and I never found the courage to cross him. But I miss him more than I ever thought possible.''

Instinctively Frannie leaned over and squeezed Scott's hand. ''I know. After all these years, I still miss my mother.''

''I know you do. I guess it's just going to take time for both of us.''

''They say time is the great healer, but I'm not so sure.''

''Neither am I. But I do believe God is.''

Frannie nodded. ''Yes. He walks us through the darkness, holds our hand through the shadow of death.''

Scott sat forward and folded his hands in a businesslike fashion. ''I didn't come to talk about my dad, Frannie.'' He cleared his throat and assumed a professional tone. ''I have a proposition for you.''

Frannie winced inwardly. She wasn't up for any verbal sparring over their relationship. She had struggled too hard these past two months to distance herself emotionally from him. ''Please, Scott, don't dredge up the past.''

''That's not what this is about, Frannie. I have a business proposition for you.''

''Business?''

''Yes. I'd like to commission you to do a sculpture of children at play. It could be three children, five, whatever you choose. We would like sketches of your design by the end of January, if possible. And if our committee likes what they see, we'll offer you a hefty sum that I hope you won't be able to resist.''

Frannie's mind whirled with questions. "I don't understand, Scott. What do you want this sculpture for?''

He gave her a cryptic smile. "It's a long story, Frannie. My brother and I inherited our father's company. To my surprise, my father gave me controlling interest. I let my brother know there would be sweeping changes. I would no longer support my father's shady practices or heartless tactics. I appointed a new board of directors and new executive officers, men of honor and integrity. From now on, Winslow Enterprises will be a company I can be proud of.''

"That's wonderful, Scott. It sounds like you have your work cut out for you.''

"Well, I've put good men in charge so that I can focus my attention on a personal project that's dear to my heart.''

"What's that?''

"Remember my sketchbook of drawings? The community I wanted to create for people who can't afford housing in today's overpriced market?''

"Of course, I remember. You wanted to build parks and playgrounds and make a beautiful place for poor families and children to live.''

"And that's what I'm going to do, Frannie. I'm going to build a planned community with quality homes, apartments, parks and walking areas, plus neighborhood shops and businesses that will offer local job opportunities.''

"What a wonderful idea, Scott. Where will you build?"

"Actually, it's not terribly far from here. Maybe a two-hour drive."

"Then you'll be commuting from Santa Barbara?"

"No, I'm hoping to move to this area."

"Well, then tell me! Where is it?"

"I've purchased a large piece of property in the desert, near Yucca Valley. It's a prime area for future home developments. It offers gorgeous scenery and wide open spaces, but it's a close commute to nearby cities. The houses will cost half as much in the desert as they do in Los Angeles. And we'll offer low-interest loans and special endowments to needy-but-deserving families. It'll be a prototype of the kind of housing developments I want our company to build from now on."

"That's fantastic, Scott. I'm so proud of you. And you want this sculpture of children for your planned community?"

"Exactly."

"I'm finishing a commission now, but I should be able to have preliminary drawings to you by the end of January."

"Great. That's what I wanted to hear." Scott shifted, as if mentally switching his concentration to something else. He looked at her, his gaze frank, unnerving. "Listen, Frannie, there's something else."

Oh, no, here it comes! She steeled herself.

"I just wanted to tell you that you were right about me."

"Right about...what?"

"You told me once that it was time to follow my passions and stop living in the shadow of my father and brother. It was time for me to find the work and life that God had planned for me."

"I don't remember saying that exactly."

"But that was the message I got. And since my father's death, I've done that, Frannie. For the first time in my life I'm excited. I'm eager. I have a driving desire for the work God wants me to do."

"I'm glad for you, Scott."

"The motivation started with you, Frannie. In a sense, you've given me back my life. You've made my life richer, because I've tapped into a passion and joy for the work I was created to do."

"Scott, I think you're giving me way too much credit."

He stood and walked over to the window and looked out. "I love being back in this cottage, Frannie. It reminds me of our days here on the beach last summer. Those were the best days of my life."

"They were good days, but like everything, they came to an end."

He strode back over to her, seized her hands and pulled her to her feet. He fingered her tousled hair and touched her cheek with his fingertips. "I've missed you, Frannie."

She turned her face away. "No, Scott, please. Let's keep our visit casual, uninvolved."

"I can't do that, Frannie. I tried coming in here and acting businesslike. I tried pretending we're only friends. But it's not working."

"That's all we can be, Scott. That's why I left the villa without saying goodbye. I knew you would try to persuade me…"

"Don't you see, Frannie? All the good things…I want to share them with you—every exciting adventure, every joy and surprise, every rare and wonderful experience that God has planned for us."

"Please, stop it, Scott. Don't include me in your plans."

"But I must, Frannie. I can't imagine my life without you." He clasped her face in his hands. "Look at me, Frannie. Tell me you don't feel the love. It's like static electricity. It makes the air between us sizzle."

"Scott, don't—"

"I haven't finished telling you my plans. I've purchased a beach house near here. Actually, my company already owned it, and now I'm buying it for myself. For us. It's bigger than this one. A bungalow for two. You and me, Frannie. You see, I want to live the simple life just as you do."

"That's just a dream, Scott."

"No, not anymore. I have people in place in my company to execute my plans, so I can be with you in our beach house. While you sculpt fine works of art, I'll plan and design breathtaking communities. Together we'll make life more beautiful for so many people. But I want to start with us. I want to marry you and give you and our children a beautiful life. Please say you'll at least think about it...and pray about it.''

Tears welled in Frannie's eyes. ''Scott, I told you it wouldn't work between us. Why won't you believe me?''

''Because I don't think you believe it yourself, my darling.'' He removed his handkerchief and gently blotted the tears in her eye. ''I think you're responding out of fear, not conviction.''

''How can you say that? You don't really know me.''

''I think I do, Frannie. Tell me if I'm wrong. You've always had to be in control. After your mother died, you took care of your father. You ran the household, planned and fixed the meals. You had to be in charge of your environment and of all the people in your life.''

''That's not fair, Scott. You make me sound obsessive—''

''When your father remarried, you moved out of the house because it meant you would no longer be in charge, no longer running the show. So you moved to this isolated beach house where you could be in charge again, and not have to answer to anyone else.''

''It wasn't like that.''

''You told me once that you wouldn't marry me because you couldn't accept my lifestyle. But aren't you really afraid it would mean subjecting yourself to a world you can't control?''

''That's ridiculous.''

"Is it? I think you're afraid to step into an uncertain, unpredictable world. You're afraid of being hurt again, the way you were hurt when you couldn't control the circumstances of your mother's death."

Frannie was weeping now. "How dare you compare my mother's death to this!"

Scott led her over to the couch, and they both sat down. He handed her his handkerchief, then slipped his arm around her and drew her against his chest. "I'm not trying to open old wounds, sweetheart, but I've been thinking about this for a long time, and the pieces are beginning to fall into place. You lost the person most precious to you. Since then, if you can't control every detail of your circumstances, you run."

"I do not!"

He tilted her tearstained face up to his and lightly kissed her lips. "My darling girl, it's as if you're holding a bird tightly in your hand because you're afraid of losing it. What you're really doing is smothering it, killing it. You need to open your hand and let it fly where it will. Being fully alive means taking risks, Frannie. Loving someone means risking being hurt, risking losing them someday. But to never take the risk is to deny yourself the happiness God wants you to have."

He took her hands and opened her fingers, one by one. "You need to open your hands and receive what God has for you. He's offering you a wonderful, unpredictable life and a man who loves you with all his heart. I confess that the man's not perfect. He's made mistakes and will make mistakes in the future. But

he's a man who loves you and loves God and wants
to make his life count for something."

"Scott, you're making this so hard. I just don't
know—!"

"It's not hard. Open your hands, Frannie. Open
your heart. Let God show you the way. Relax in Him.
Accept what He brings you, with open arms. Accept
me, Frannie. Let me be part of your life. Let me take
care of you the way you've always taken care of others. Let me love you with all the love I have to give."

She wiped the tears from her eyes. "I do love you,
Scott, but I can't let down my guard and agree to
something I may regret later. I'm sorry. I have to be
sure."

With a heavy sigh, he stood and gazed down at
her. "I'm sorry, too. I can offer no guarantees, Frannie. Except this. You can't enjoy life until you release
yourself to it, just as you can't trust God until you
surrender yourself to Him. It's a lesson I'm still learning. Happiness and fulfillment come when you give
yourself unreservedly to God, to the person you love
and to life itself."

He crossed the room and collected his coat, then
pulled it on and walked to the door. Ruggs bounded
over to him and barked. Scott bent down and
scratched the dog's ears. "Do me a favor, Ruggsy.
Take good care of your master, okay? That's a good
boy."

Scott looked back at Frannie with tenderness and
yearning. "I'm going over to my bungalow for an
hour or two to clear out my things. Then I'll be driv-

ing back up to Santa Barbara. If you change your mind, you know where I'll be.''

She got up and walked to the door. She felt as if she were moving in a dream. She didn't want him to go, but she couldn't ask him to stay. Impulsively she kissed him on the cheek. He pulled her to him and kissed her hard on the mouth, then released her. He pushed open the door and stepped out onto the porch. ''Goodbye, Frannie. You'll always be in my prayers.''

''And you'll be in mine.'' She covered her mouth as he turned and descended the steps. She watched until his car pulled out of the narrow driveway and disappeared down the road.

After Scott had gone, Frannie slipped on her windbreaker and went outside, Ruggs following at her heels. She couldn't stand the confines of her cabin. She had to get some fresh air to clear her head.

She walked down to the beach and gazed out at the cold, muted blue ocean, the spumy tide rushing in, covering the sand, then retreating, to start the process all over again. Back and forth, an endless pattern, the rhythm of life. It was the way she felt. She kept going back and forth, stepping out in faith, then drawing back in fear. Where was she going, and would she ever have the courage to reach her destination? She gazed up at the huge dome of sky, cloudy and gray, stretching from horizon to horizon, a vast, unremitting gray. Like the sky, her life felt shrouded in gray, murky shadows. When would the sun come out? When would she see things clearly?

She folded her arms to stave off the biting wind,

but still she shivered with a deep, bone-chilling cold. As she watched the slow, graceful dance of the waves, she imagined herself lying on a surging swell, floating, letting the tide take her where it would. Trusting God was like that. Relaxing on His promises, His truth, His Word. The apostle Peter was afraid, but he stepped out by faith and walked on water to Jesus. Could she do that? Step out in spite of her fears?

She remembered Jesus' words, "I will never leave you, nor forsake you....My peace I give to you; not as the world gives....Let not your heart be troubled, neither let it be afraid."

Looking up at the ashen sky, she whispered, "Dear God, what do You want me to do? I love Scott, and I don't want to lose him, but I am so afraid...." Even as she said the word, the fragment of another Scripture came to her. "Perfect love casts out fear." The truth hit hard. She would never be able to love fully until she released her fear.

The thought came to her. What do you really want, Frannie? If Scott is the man you love, don't run away. Run to him. As fast as you can.

She walked back to her cottage, but she couldn't bring herself to go inside. Instead, she stooped down and gave Ruggs a hug around the neck. "What do you think, boy? Do you want Scott to be your master?"

The shaggy dog barked loudly.

She smiled grimly. "I should have known better than to ask you." She straightened her shoulders, sucked in a breath and lifted her chin. "Okay,

Ruggsy, maybe it's time I stepped out and walked on water. Come on, boy!''

As she hiked down the beach toward Scott's bungalow, she became aware of a growing excitement, a sense of anticipation filling her heart, replacing the fear. She was shivering with cold when she finally knocked on Scott's door.

He answered with a smile of surprise. "Frannie!"

She kept her arms folded across her chest, but couldn't stop trembling. Flustered, she blurted, "I, um, have this chimney that's clogged. And the smoke…the smoke is coming into my house. And it's really not a safe place to stay…you know, with all that smoke billowing in. And I know you're an expert with blocked chimneys. So I was wondering if you'd like to help a damsel in distress."

His grin widened. "I'd be more than happy, if that damsel is you."

Her teeth chattered. "W-well, maybe I c-could just come inside while the smoke clears."

He stepped aside. "I think we can arrange that."

She drew back. "I don't want to trouble you. I know you're packing."

"No trouble at all. I can pack anytime."

"Well, maybe you wouldn't have to pack at all."

"Really? Maybe you'd better come in and we'll discuss it." He took her arm and led her inside. Ruggs scurried in after her.

"What a nice, roaring fire." She walked over and put her palms up to the flames. "Ah, that feels good."

He came up behind her and helped her off with her jacket. "You won't need this. It's very warm in here."

She nodded. "Yes, very warm."

He turned her around to face him, then ran his hands up and down her arms. "You are cold."

She gazed up at him, searching his eyes. "I walked on water to get here."

"Did you now? That took an amazing amount of faith."

"Did it? I just relaxed, opened my hands wide and stepped out…and here I am."

He smiled, his eyes glistening. "I'm very proud of you, Frannie." He smoothed back her hair, tipped her chin up to his and kissed her tenderly. "Do you have any idea how much I love you?"

"As much as I love you?"

"Maybe we should sit down and discuss it." He led her over to the sofa and they sat down. Ruggs came bouncing over and laid his head on Scott's lap.

"He's part of the package. You know the old saying, 'Love me, love my dog.'"

Scott massaged Ruggs's head. "I think I can manage that. How about it, Ruggsy? Do you approve of me marrying your master?"

Ruggs lifted his head and gave a long, ear-splitting howl.

Frannie and Scott both laughed.

He drew her close and murmured against her ear, "I'll take that as a yes."

Epilogue

December Twenty-five

Dear Family and Friends,

I'm usually too busy writing sermons to write Christmas letters. But so much has happened in the Rowlands family this year that I figured I'd better send a letter to catch you up on the latest news.

It's been an exciting and eventful year for the Rowlands clan. In June, Cassandra and Antonio had their first child, a boy, little Daniel Pagliarulo, a fine, handsome lad with his father's dark hair and his mother's blue eyes. It's quite an experience being a grandfather.

I became a grandfather again in July when Brianna married attorney Eric Wingate and the two of them adopted his little niece, Charity. What a joy that precious child is—only three years old and yet she carries the wisdom of the ages in her eyes. And she's a mischievous little bundle to boot, playing hide-and-seek with her grandpa and looking for candy bars in my shirt pocket—naturally, I always keep a stash of goodies for when she comes to visit.

Speaking of weddings, the Rowlands family did a double take. We geared up for a double wedding in July. Not only did Brianna marry Eric, but after seven long years as a bachelor, I tied the matrimonial knot myself. My beautiful bride is Juliana Pagliarulo, a talented performer like her son. That's right, she's Antonio's mother. And, Juliana's daughter, Belina, moved in with us, too—a quiet, gentle girl—and I've grown to love her as if she were my own.

This Christmas we are celebrating not only two summer weddings and the addition of two grandchildren to our family, but we are also rejoicing over two Christmas engagements. Two weeks ago, Belina announced her engagement to Wesley Hopkins, the minister of music at our church. I've never seen Belina look more radiant.

On Christmas Eve, as all of my daughters and their families gathered for our holiday celebration, my youngest, Frannie, announced her engagement to real estate mogul Scott Winslow. They seem very much in love and have expressed their desire to serve God together in whatever way He leads.

Frannie and Belina are considering a double wedding in June. Of course, they want me to officiate, and I couldn't be more honored. Now I just have to figure out how to walk two brides down the aisle at once!

My dear friends, I'm not a man given easily to tears. But my heart is filled to overflowing this Christmas season as I think of the ways God has blessed our family. On Christmas morning, as we all gathered around the tree to open gifts, I realized that the good Lord had already given me the best gifts of all—His love revealed in the birth of a Babe in Bethlehem, and the enduring love of my cherished family.

Amid the laughter and chatter, the baby cries and child squeals, the carols and feasts and presents and prayers, I thank God for His great abundance to us. I have so much to rejoice over—the precious memory of Mandy and her caring influence on our family; my devoted wife, Juliana, who delights me with her spontaneity and spirit; and my three—no, four—exquisite daughters who have found the men of their dreams and are creating their own happy families.

Maybe it's time for me to settle back and relax a bit, now that each of my girls has someone to watch over her. I'm not getting any younger, so I suppose it's time to leave the matchmaking ploys to someone else. Then again, with the grandchildren coming, maybe I'd better keep on my toes. I want to be sure the next generation has a taste of all the joys and happiness our family has known.

Wishing you the Spirit of Christmas all year long,
Andrew Rowlands (and his bountiful brood!)

* * * * *

Dear Reader,

Shortly after writing this book, I heard devastating news: Jason, the love of my daughter's life, was dead. For over a year Heather and Jason Williams had an on-again, off-again relationship. Through all their ups and downs, I found myself loving Jason like a son and secretly rooting for him to become my son-in-law someday.

But that was not to be.

The dashing, irrepressible Jason, who had stared death down so many times, was killed in a motorcycle crash. He died as he had lived, confronting life head-on, flying free. Those of us who loved him will never forget him. He gave 100 percent of himself to his family and friends, and oh, how they all adored him.

But the most remarkable thing about Jason was his passionate abandon to Jesus Christ, his Savior. Jason sang and played guitar and led worship for youth groups in several churches. His Bible was thumb-worn, its pages scrawled with his handwritten study notes. He knew he was in this world for one reason and one reason alone—to serve God.

In my story, Frannie Rowlands and Scott Winslow come to recognize the same truth that Jason lived by: We were put on this earth to love and serve God for whatever span of time He gives us. Dear Reader, I pray that you, too, will let God ignite the flames of His Spirit in your heart. I'd love to hear from you. Write me c/o Steeple Hill Books, 300 East 42nd Street, 6th Floor, New York, New York 10017. I hope you've enjoyed sharing the lives and loves of Reverend Rowlands and his three devoted daughters.

With my love and prayers,

Carole Gift Page

Next Month From Steeple Hill's

Love Inspired®

A LOVE FOR SAFEKEEPING

by *Gail Gaymer Martin*

When Jane Conroy is targeted by a stalker,
loyal policeman Kyle Manning vows to protect
her from harm. Before long, he finds himself
captivated by the courageous schoolteacher.
But the impending danger threatens their
newfound happiness. Can they trust in
God's love to show them the way?

Don't miss
A LOVE FOR SAFEKEEPING
On sale January 2002

 *Love Inspired*®

Visit us at www.steeplehill.com
LIALFS

Next Month From Steeple Hill's

Love Inspired

A FAMILY FOR JANA

by *Eileen Berger*

Sequel to *A FAMILY FOR ANDI*

Jana Jenson has her hands full juggling
motherhood and the demands of college.
She doesn't have the time—or inclination—
to nurture a new romance! But then dynamic
professor Ray Hawkins comes into her life—
and slowly dismantles the barricades
around her distrusting heart....

Don't miss
A FAMILY FOR JANA
On sale January 2002

Love Inspired

Visit us at www.steeplehill.com
LIAFFJ

*Next Month
From Steeple Hill's*

Love Inspired®

A FAMILY ALL HER OWN
by *Bonnie K. Winn*

Minister Katherine Blake's life changes forever when she falls head over heels for disillusioned single dad Michael Carlson, who is struggling to do right by his motherless daughter. Can Katherine restore Michael's lost faith—and realize a cherished dream in the process?

Don't miss
A FAMILY ALL HER OWN
On sale December 2001

Love Inspired®

Visit us at www.steeplehill.com
LIAFAHO

Next Month From Steeple Hill's

Love Inspired®

JUDGING SARA
by *Cynthia Rutledge*

When there are threats on Sara Michaels's life, the beautiful Christian singer reluctantly accepts the protection of her gruff, hard-to-please bodyguard. The two share an immediate attraction, but they couldn't be more different! Can this unexpected love survive a shocking deception?

Don't miss
JUDGING SARA
On sale December 2001

Visit us at www.steeplehill.com
LIJS

Next Month From Steeple Hill's

Love Inspired®

FINALLY FOUND

by *Lyn Cote*

Book #2 of
BOUNTIFUL BLESSINGS miniseries

When Spring Kirkland visits her aunt, she discovers
that her former college sweetheart, Marco Da Palma,
is her aunt's devoted doctor. Years ago, their
starry-eyed love floundered because they came
from different worlds. Still, their mutual attraction
has never waned. Can they set their differences
aside and forge a fulfilling future together?

Don't miss
FINALLY FOUND
On sale January 2002

Love Inspired®

Visit us at www.steeplehill.com

LIFF

W9-BIN-225

1.75

"What the hell do you think you're doing?"

"I treat my female guests in exactly the way their body language leads me to believe they expect," Saul murmured, his voice as soft as velvet now. "The invitation you posed was impossible to resist. And as for what I was doing—"

Fen's eyes went wide and wild. Her body seemed scorched by the imprint of his....

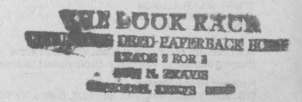

THE BOOK RACK

USED-PAPERBACK HOME

TRADE 2 FOR 1

N. ERAVE

DIANA HAMILTON is a true romantic at heart and fell in love with her husband at first sight. They still live in the fairy-tale Tudor house where they raised their three children. Now the idyll is shared with eight rescued cats and a puppy. But despite an often-chaotic life-style, ever since she learned to read and write Diana has had her nose in a book— either reading or writing one—and plans to go on doing just that for a very long time to come.

Books by Diana Hamilton

HARLEQUIN PRESENTS
1588—SAVAGE OBSESSION
1641—THREAT FROM THE PAST
1690—LEGACY OF SHAME
1716—THE LAST ILLUSION
1732—SEPARATE ROOMS
1775—NEVER A BRIDE

Don't miss any of our special offers. Write to us at the following address for information on our newest releases.

Harlequin Reader Service
U.S.: 3010 Walden Ave., P.O. Box 1325, Buffalo, NY 14269
Canadian: P.O. Box 609, Fort Erie, Ont. L2A 5X3

Diana Hamilton
Waiting Game

Harlequin Books

TORONTO • NEW YORK • LONDON
AMSTERDAM • PARIS • SYDNEY • HAMBURG
STOCKHOLM • ATHENS • TOKYO • MILAN
MADRID • WARSAW • BUDAPEST • AUCKLAND

If you purchased this book without a cover you should be aware
that this book is stolen property. It was reported as "unsold and
destroyed" to the publisher, and neither the author nor the
publisher has received any payment for this "stripped book."

ISBN 0-373-11858-9

WAITING GAME

First North American Publication 1997.

Copyright © 1994 by Diana Hamilton.

All rights reserved. Except for use in any review, the reproduction or
utilization of this work in whole or in part in any form by any electronic,
mechanical or other means, now known or hereafter invented, including
xerography, photocopying and recording, or in any information storage
or retrieval system, is forbidden without the written permission of the
publisher, Harlequin Enterprises Limited, 225 Duncan Mill Road,
Don Mills, Ontario, Canada M3B 3K9.

All characters in this book have no existence outside the imagination of
the author and have no relation whatsoever to anyone bearing the same
name or names. They are not even distantly inspired by any individual
known or unknown to the author, and all incidents are pure invention.

This edition published by arrangement with Harlequin Books S.A.

® and TM are trademarks of the publisher. Trademarks indicated with
® are registered in the United States Patent and Trademark Office, the
Canadian Trade Marks Office and in other countries.

Printed in U.S.A.

CHAPTER ONE

THE group of photographers and reporters outside the highly exclusive, highly expensive West End restaurant snapped to attention as the taxi rumbled to a halt.

'You were right, they did follow.' Fenella wriggled along the seat, closer to Alex, her golden eyes smiling wickedly into his, slipping into a warm Cornish drawl as she tacked on, trying to help him loosen up, 'Brace yourself, me 'andsome!' Picking up languages had always come as easily as breathing, so regional dialects were an absolute doddle, and Alex grinned back at her.

'I'm always right, sweetheart, you should know that by now. Come on, let's strut our stuff!' He had his hand on the door release but despite his jokey tone the interior light picked out the lines of tension around his mouth.

Fenella felt her own lips tighten. At fifty-five Alex was still a handsome man, his considerable talent as a light entertainer still very much intact. She didn't know how Saul Ackerman, that hard-nosed business mogul, had the gall to try and put him down. And out.

What would he know about anything? Alex's talent was creative; Saul Ackerman wouldn't know anything about that because his head would be stuffed

with columns of figures, and big profits were the name
of the game.

But her triangular, cat-like smile was firmly in place
again as she stepped out on to the pavement and
simply stood there, illuminated by the soft lights beneath the awning, one slender hip elegantly tilted
forward, her honey-gold head tipped slightly to one
side, her slumbrous golden eyes almost taunting the
jackals of the Press as Alex paid off the driver.

Her height gave her an advantage—helped by the
ridiculously high heels she was wearing—and the tight
sheath of her low-cut evening dress gave an elegant
emphasis to the width of her white shoulders, the
black silk clinging lovingly to understated yet exquisite curves.

As the taxi slid away the activity among the waiting
Press men became frenetic as they recognised her
companion. Having followed Saul Ackerman's party
from the theatre, got photographs, and possibly comments from him and the leading lady he was squiring,
they had probably decided to call it a day. There was
only so much they could milk from a first night, a
brilliant young Cornish playwright and a leading lady
whose name was a household word on both sides of
the Atlantic.

Her smile firmly in place, Fenella swayed over to
Alex's side, felt his arm snake possessively around her
narrow waist and tried not to flinch as the flashes exploded around them.

'You were at the opening, Mr Fairbourne?'

'What do you think of VisionWest's new
boy genius?'

'Now Ackerman's consortium has the franchise do you see your programme continuing in the same format?'

Questions were bitten out thick and fast and Fenella gave Alex full marks for his performance. There was no sign of that tension as he picked his answer, his voice as smooth and rich as ever.

'I would hardly call Jethro Tamblyn a boy, but he is certainly a genius. As you know, VisionWest has him under contract to produce two new dramas for us a year, which will, of course, be sold to the networks. A scoop the board is justifiably proud of.'

This was common knowledge, safe stuff. VisionWest had had their own camera crew outside the theatre, making sure everyone in the west country knew that their regional commercial television station was backing the Cornishman to the hilt, Saul Ackerman, the chairman, attending the first night, wining and dining the author, his wife, and Vesta Faine, the glamorous leading lady, in high style after the performance.

'And will the networks continue to buy *Evening With Alex*? Are you worried by reported falling ratings?'

'Darling,' Fenella interjected with a tiny pout and a manufactured shiver. 'Do we have to hang round here? It's cold.'

It wasn't. The mid-May evening was unseasonably warm, if anything, but she wasn't going to see Alex savaged by this mob. She moved subtly closer to him, as if seeking his warmth, his protection. In the whole of her twenty-five years she couldn't remember needing or wanting a man's protection. But she would do anything to save Alex from having to answer that particular question.

And then a voice, coarser than the rest, heavy with salacious overtones, drawled out, 'Couldn't your wife make it tonight, Alex? Did you leave her tucked up in bed with a good book, in case she cramped your style?'

Fenella felt Alex's arm tighten around her waist and glared at the reporter who was pushing a notepad under her nose. She knew they had a job to do, a living to earn—but did they have to be so despicable?

'Jean is visiting her mother in Edinburgh,' Alex said uncomfortably. 'Now, if you don't mind——'

But they were like hounds on the scent and one of them bayed, 'And you are a keen theatre-goer, Ms——? Or is it Mrs? Or are you just a wannabe?' The voice persisted as Fenella refused to give her name. 'A model, perhaps, just itching to break into television?'

'Oh, Alex——' Fenella hid her twitching mouth against his broad, dinner-jacketed shoulder just as the flash lights exploded again.

Alex said toughly, 'That's enough. Go hassle someone else.' And he swept her forward into the luxurious foyer.

A breathing space, if only brief. While Fenella got her heartbeats back under control Alex's deep blue eyes raked her pale face with deep concern.

'You all right, sweetheart?'

'I'm fine.' Golden eyes sparkled into his. 'You did warn me what to expect. I think I could get hooked on living dangerously!'

And there was no time to say any more because they were being whisked through to the main restaurant area, all soft lighting and wickedly sumptuous décor and potted plants like a miniature exotic jungle flanking delicate Japanese silk screens painted with golden dragons with glittering ruby eyes.

And full of beautiful people. And the table they were deferentially conducted to was within spitting distance of Saul Ackerman's party. If she looked to the left of Alex's shoulder she would be staring straight into the chairman's face.

A quick, encompassing glance told her he had even more presence than she had realised when Alex had pointed him out to her during the interval back at the theatre. Somewhere in his mid-thirties, he had the type of hard, slashing features that could never be overlooked. But it was more than merely the striking combination of a strongly modelled bone-structure, thick black hair and piercing silver-grey eyes. It was the sheer unadulterated power of the man.

She didn't look his way again. She concentrated on Alex. A tiny muscle was twitching at the corner of his mouth and that only happened when he was nervous. Gently, she laid her hand over his.

'Don't worry, everything will be fine. I promise.'

'Of course it will.' There'd been only a momentary hesitation preceding his answer and then he was smiling into her eyes and he was back to being the urbane, self-confident man she loved. 'Now order something fabulous, Fen, my darling, and we'll have the best champagne on offer.'

'Well . . .' She could hear the note of doubt in her voice and deplored it. But the menu she'd been handed was almost too heavy to hold, and nothing was priced. 'Can you afford it?' Which was even more deplorable, but she couldn't help it.

'Look on it as payment for services rendered and those yet to come.' Alex leaned back expansively in his chair, the look in his eyes, the play of that smile across his mouth making her understand why women had literally thrown themselves at him during his live stage performances a decade or two ago, why his records had once regularly featured high in the charts. 'And if I can't afford it, Jean can.'

'Say no more!' Fenella buried her head in the menu. She was famished. And it was common knowledge that Jean was fabulously rich. She'd inherited a fortune from her father and was due to inherit another when her mother died. Not an event Jean was anticipating, Fenella knew, but the old lady was over ninety. So the price of a meal in a place such as this wouldn't cause Alex's wife any hardship!

'Has Ackerman noticed us yet?' Alex asked quietly as soon as he'd given their order. 'Too obvious if I turned round. I don't want him to think our being here was anything other than coincidence.' He leaned forward, trailing a finger down the side of her face. 'Look over to their table in a moment or two; make it natural. I don't think there's a man in the room who could have failed to notice you, sweetheart.'

Fenella wasn't so sure about that, but she knew the trouble Alex had gone to to discover which restaurant Ackerman intended to bring his party to tonight in time to reserve a table himself.

Strangely unwilling to meet those silver-grey eyes, she waited until the champagne was brought to their table, breaking up their intimately whispered conversation. Then slowly, as if wanting something to do while Alex's attention was no longer given exclusively to her, she allowed her eyes to wander idly over the animated group at Saul Ackerman's table.

Vesta Faine was as lovely close to as she had been on stage, her dark beauty enhanced by the dramatic lines of the white satin of her gown, her vivacious chatter obviously holding Jethro Tamblyn in thrall. The playwright was leaning forward, his arms folded on the table, his ruggedly striking features animated as he listened to every word. He looked as if he had been running both hands through his dishevelled, wiry chestnut hair for at least a couple of hours. In contrast, his wife looked out of her depth in her unimaginative chain-store dress, her pale blue eyes fixed anxiously on her famous husband. Had she married the boy from her own Cornish village when he'd been nothing more than a struggling, impecunious writer only to find him leaving her behind? Would she be able to withstand the pressures of his newly found fame?

Aware that these idle musings were merely delaying tactics, she reluctantly glanced at the head of the table. Saul Ackerman was probably just as riveted by the actress as Jethro was. But she met the silver-eyes head-on and the mocking awareness in them made her face go hot.

She looked away quickly, expelling the breath she hadn't realised she'd been holding, dipping her head on the slender stalk of her neck, feeling the long ornate drop-earrings brush against her skin, restraining the desire to remove the irritants. She had only worn the outlandish things to soften the effect of her starkly modern hairstyle. Cut very short into the shape of her head at the back, it was long on top, falling forwards into a honey-gold fringe that brushed her eyebrows in a heavy, well-defined curve.

'Well?' Alex arched a brow. 'Have we been noticed?'

Hastily banishing any trace of discomfort or wariness from her eyes, she gave him her most brilliant smile, the discreet, muted lighting making her shoulders gleam like oiled satin above the rich black silk of her low-cut dress as she leaned forward, her voice low and intimate as she told him, 'Yes. I don't think anyone, even someone as tunnel-visioned as Saul Ackerman, could fail to recognise your impressive profile!'

'Never mind that.' The blatant flattery left him visibly unimpressed. 'The bastard knows every line on my face! It's you I want him to see, Fen. I want him to recognise you when he sees you again.' He took her hand, rubbing his thumb across her knuckles. 'I want him so he can't take his eyes off you.'

Involuntarily, her gaze slid to the other table and her breath caught in her lungs. Even through the thick veiling of her long dark lashes there was no mistaking the speculation in those flat silver eyes. Saul Ackerman was leaning back in his chair, making no attempt now to join in the conversation that was flying around his table, the fingers of one hand idly playing with the stem of his wine glass as he watched her, his eyes unnerving.

Two thunderous heartbeats later Fenella dragged her attention back to Alex. It would appear that his wish had been granted. Ackerman would know her if he saw her again. Something fluttered inside her breasts, something uncomfortable and alien. Vowing not to look Saul Ackerman's way again, she made a determined and happily successful effort to flirt with Alex across the table but could make little impression on the superb meal she had been hungry for only a short while ago.

What a waste of Jean's money, of good food, she sniped at herself. She didn't know what was the matter with her. She would have thought it would have taken very much more than the impudent stares of a strange man to deaden her always hearty appetite.

'Won't you introduce me to your companion, Alex?'

Fenella didn't have to look up to know whom that voice belonged to. It was cool, authoritative steel, very slightly burred with dry, amused confidence. The fingers that held the fork she'd been using to push her food around her plate started to shake. Very carefully, she put the implement down as Alex hurriedly pushed back his chair and stumbled to his feet.

'Saul. How's this for a coincidence! I saw you at the theatre—only had to look for VisionWest's camera team——' His expansive smile was shaky round the edges, the sudden pinkness of his face emphasising the beginnings of a sagging jawline, the pull of gravity that was wrecking the face that had had women of all ages drooling in the aisles. He was making a too conscious effort to straighten his shoulders and pull in his stomach muscles, Fenella noted, her heart twisting with anguished love.

Ackerman, though, had no need to try to project an image. There wasn't a superfluous ounce of flesh on that tall, aggressively masculine frame. Not even the suavely styled immaculate dinner-jacket could disguise the potent rawness of this prime male animal, she thought with disgust, hating him.

He had a cruel mouth, she decided, refusing to flinch away from the eyes that were consciously and compellingly holding her own. He was totally devoid of compassion, sympathy or understanding. The un-crowned head of the consortium which had recently made a successful bid for the VisionWest franchise, he had more clout than was good for him. Already his business empire encompassed publishing, an airline, communication systems; he had forgotten the meaning of compassion—if he had ever known it in the first instance—and would break poor darling Alex without a second thought.

'How did you rate tonight's performance, Miss——?' Very briefly, his cold gaze spiked towards Alex, reminding the older man of the neglected introduction. No one, especially someone he had already put down as a has-been, neglected his commands.

'Fenella Flemming—my—my niece.' Alex went crimson, shifting from one foot to the other. He couldn't have looked more ill at ease if he'd tried. 'Fen, sweetheart, this is——'

'I know who it is, darling,' she cut in, sounding bored, the downward twist of her mouth, the golden glitter of her eyes letting him know she wasn't impressed, catching her breath a split-second later as she saw the gleam of pure cynicism in the blackly fringed silver eyes, the scornful knowing curve of his mouth as he repeated softly,

'Your niece? But of course—who else could she possibly be?'

Which meant, of course, that he didn't believe it for one instant.

She held his eyes with cool defiance. 'We enjoyed the performance immensely, didn't we, Alex?' She wished he would sit down, stop fidgeting from foot to foot. But maybe no one, but no one, sat when in 'the Presence'! She made a mental note to ask him some time and then went icy cold as that cool voice commanded,

'Then why don't we discuss it? Join me for coffee and brandy and I'll introduce you to the author and Vesta.'

No mention, Fenella noted sourly, of the author's wife. People wouldn't count with him unless they were famous, at the top of their own particular ladder.

'Some other time, maybe.' Fenella rose languidly to her feet, her eyes on Alex. He was probably itching to take up the invitation but not even for his sake could she endure to spend a moment longer in

Ackerman's company. One delicate brow rose and disappeared beneath her glossy, honey-gold fringe. 'It's time we were tucked up in bed, isn't it, darling?' Her mouth curved in a slow smile that couldn't be misinterpreted. 'Excuse me just for a moment while I freshen up before we leave.' And then, not giving her courage chance to desert her, she made herself encounter Saul Ackerman's icy stare. 'So nice to have met you, Mr Ackerman.'

And she walked away, heading for the rest-rooms at the rear of the restaurant, threading her way through the tables, aware as never before of the way her body swayed within the clinging confines of the black silk sheath, uncomfortably sure that the monster's eyes were following her every inch of the way.

The door closed behind her with a soft, expensive thud and she leaned gratefully against the cool, aqua wallpaper, her fingertips to her throbbing temples.

What had started out as a fun, if mentally challenging evening had ended on a quite different note, a note she couldn't really define—even if she'd wanted to. From the moment she'd learned what the chairman of VisionWest was planning to do to Alex she had disliked the man. But seeing him, meeting him, had affected her more strongly than she had bargained for.

Shuddering, she pushed herself away from the wall and effected a few minor repairs to her make-up in front of one of the softly lit mirrors. Saul Ackerman was nothing to her, simply a man she despised. He was planning to axe Alex's programme, strip him of his self-respect, toss him into an empty, financially barren future.

So it was perfectly natural that she should dislike the man so intensely. Sheer, gut-wrenching hatred was something she had never experienced before. No wonder it had a strange effect on her!

Relieved that that was sorted out, she dropped her lipstick into her slender evening purse and snapped the clasp with a defiant click. The sooner she and Alex were out of this place, back in the flat, alone together with all the time they needed to chew over the evening's happenings, the better.

She marched out into the silent, thickly carpeted corridor and almost scurried straight back in again when she saw Ackerman waiting for her, his face blank.

Sinkingly prepared to brazen it out, she gave him the ghost of an acknowledgement and stalked past him. But, levering himself away from the wall he'd been so casually leaning against, his hand shot out, clamping around her upper arm, dragging her to a teetering halt. Her breath froze in her lungs as she swayed on her impossible heels. At a distance he was lethal enough; at such close quarters he was pure poison.

'Do you make a habit of grabbing every passing female?' She managed to sound frosty but she was boiling inside, her temperature rising through the roof. How dared he waylay her? Touch her?

'Do you make a habit of being rude to strangers?' he countered, his mouth indenting sardonically. 'Or is it only me?'

'I don't know what you mean.' She glanced pointedly at the hand that manacled her arm. His fingers looked strong and lean and dark against the whiteness of her skin. 'Please let me go; you're hurting.'

'I don't think so.' There was a trace of wicked humour in his voice, making it richer, deeper, too intimate. 'I might touch the goods before I buy, but I never damage them.'

And what the hell did he mean by that? She had a sneaking suspicion but she wouldn't give him the satisfaction of asking. And there was far too much exposed flesh above the low-cut bodice of her dress to give her any hope that he had failed to register the increase of her breath-rate. And he was certainly looking, those silver eyes making a thorough scrutiny of everything exposed or otherwise.

Quickly putting a lid on her temper, she made a futile effort to pull away, hating the way the pressure of his hand increased immediately, loathing the way his touch made her feel. As if she was burning up inside. With outrage. What else?

Those wandering eyes fastened on her lips and she turned her head quickly, scanning the emptiness of the lush corridor, wishing a whole horde of other diners would come through to use the facilities.

'What do you want?' She made herself sound cool, as if nothing he had to say could possibly interest her, and heard him laugh, a warm sound low in his throat. She hadn't expected that and, just for a moment, it threw her, so when he said,

'To know who you are, for starters. There's much more you could supply me with, but that can wait,' she was unguarded enough to turn again and seek his eyes, her own wide beneath the thick golden fringe.

'You know who I am. My uncle——' her tongue tripped over the word but she ploughed quickly on before her teeth started to chatter in her head '—Alex introduced us. And if you don't mind, he'll be waiting. I——'

'But I do mind,' he cut across her. 'I didn't swallow that old chestnut. What kind of fool do you take me for? And the thought of that delectable firm white flesh tangled up with the folds and wrinkles of an ageing pop star does not bring tears of joy to my eyes.' The voice was infinitely sharper now, the silver eyes glinting like the edge of a bright steel blade.

'You're obscene!' He made her feel literally ill. 'Unc—Alex is in his prime! Pop star doesn't come into it, ageing or otherwise.'

She threw her head back, the better to glare up at him along the length of her nose, unaware that the defiant gesture afforded him an unimpeded view of her long, slender throat, the tantalisingly revealed upper curves of her breasts.

'He's a highly talented, all-round entertainer. All he needs is a new vehicle for those talents, but you're too blinkered to see it!' She drew in a great, shuddering breath, almost sobbing with the hatefulness of being held so near to that vibrant body. She had never encountered a man who exuded such power. It came off him in waves, swamping her.

But she wasn't going to drown in such a potent deluge without struggling, and she ground out between her teeth, 'VisonWest's not the only TV company in the land. There's not a damn thing stopping him from moving on and up—going where he'll be appreciated!'

'Such loyalty. I envy the man his ability to earn it,' he said grimly. The hand on her arm dropped away and his face was rigid, his eyes bitter as he subjected her to one lancing look before he turned on his heels and strode away.

Fenella knuckled her mouth, her eyes anguished as she watched the door back into the restaurant swing to behind him. Oh, God, she had probably killed off any faint hope Alex had had for his programme! She, with her big mouth, had finally wielded the axe that had been hovering over his head ever since Saul Ackerman's lot had taken over the franchise!

And even an abject, squirming apology would do no good. Ackerman's mind had already been made up. He simply hadn't got around to burying *Evening With Alex* yet. All she had done was drive the final nail in the coffin with her outspoken tongue!

She didn't know how she was going to tell Alex what she had done.

CHAPTER TWO

'I'M SORRY, you probably wanted to join Ackerman's party,' Fenella mumbled unhappily as the taxi sped towards Hampstead. Alex hadn't said a word since they'd left the restaurant and, in view of her rudeness in refusing to accept his boss's invitation, was probably deeply regretting ever having let Jean talk him into this.

'About as much as a sharp kick up the backside!' Alex sighed gloomily, giving her hand a gently reassuring pat. 'We were both brilliant, all evening, but I doubt if we could have actually sat down with them and socialised without giving the game away. We need a whole load more confidence for that.'

'I expect you're right,' she conceded, sagging back against the upholstery and closing her eyes. But she didn't feel any less miserable. Alex didn't know what had been said out in the corridor and she didn't know how she was going to tell him.

'We achieved what we set out to do—one of the sleazier tabloids will pick up on the "scandal" and splash it all over the front page. And I'll be famous— or rather, notorious—for all of five minutes. And Ackerman himself saw us together. So the old has-been who once pulled record-breaking female audiences with his sex-appeal will be judged to have regained some of his touch,' he said, sounding tired and

uncharacteristically cynical. 'As they say, even bad
publicity is good publicity. I thought Jean was mad
when she came up with the idea but I think we were
even crazier to go along with it.'

Fenella couldn't argue with that so she said nothing.
But as soon as they were back in the flat her aunt
Jean had bought with a minor part of her inheritance
from her father she drew the curtains in the long
living-room, poured her uncle a large slug of whisky
and pointed him at the telephone.

'Phone her now; she'll be dying to know how
everything went. I'll lay a penny to a pound she's
sitting up in Edinburgh quite convinced we didn't have
the bottle to go through with it because she wasn't
around to make sure we did.'

Easing her feet out of her ridiculous shoes, she said
goodnight and left him to it, confident that a nice
long natter with his wife would cheer him up. She
hated to see him so depressed. She thought the world
of both of them; in some ways they meant more to
her than her own parents. Which was why she'd agreed
to go along with the crazy scheme in the first place—
much against her better judgement.

The guest bedroom was furnished with Jean's unmistakable stamp of elegant style and home-from-
home comfort. Six years ago, when her uncle had been
signed up for the hour-long, prime-time *Evening With
Alex*—a combination of his light-hearted interviews
with celebrities from the entertainment world, plus a
couple of comedy sketches and, naturally, half a dozen
of his own songs performed in his own inimitable

style—the couple had bought a house on the outskirts of Tavistock to be near the main studios in Plymouth.

But Alex had missed London and when Jean had received her inheritance she had immediately bought this flat, which they used when he wasn't recording his show.

They were a devoted couple, and it showed. And that, Jean had stated, was half the problem. The viewing public saw him as a middle-aged pipe, slippers and comfortable old cardigan man, never seen anywhere without his equally middle-aged and unspectacular wife. Now, if they could see him as a bit of a dog, some lovely young thing on his arm as they emerged from some rackety night-spot or other, then people might sit up and take notice, and his female audience might again tune in to his show and realise he hadn't lost all the sex-appeal that had drawn them in adoring droves in the first place!

And it might have worked, too, if she hadn't wrecked everything by the way she'd reacted to Saul Ackerman, she thought wearily, padding out of the *en-suite* bathroom packaged in an old towelling robe as she heard a light knock on her bedroom door.

'She's put us to the top of the class!' Alex was smiling now. He looked relaxed and a good ten years younger. He and Jean had never spent a night apart in the whole of the thirty years of their marriage and he was missing her.

When Jean had stated firmly that she would visit her aged mother in Edinburgh—alone—leaving the field clear for him to 'misbehave' at home he had

almost vetoed the whole idea, she remembered,
forcing herself to return his smile.

'Good. How is her mother?' She had only met the
old lady once, years ago, and remembered her as being
quite alarming, and she couldn't have changed much
because Alex pulled a face as he told her,

'As intractable as ever. She still stubbornly refuses
to make her home with us and insists that "Young
Elspeth" can look after her. "Young Elspeth" must
be knocking eighty!' He puffed out his cheeks in
exasperation. 'Talk about the blind leading the blind!
But never mind that; Jean's given me a whole list of
things we have to do, places we have to be seen at.
Shall we chew them over now, with a nice mug of
drinking chocolate, or would you rather we left them
to the morning?'

'They'll keep,' Fenella told him with a sick smile.
Before they worked out tactics for the coming two
weeks she would have to confess that they would be
a complete waste of time. After her outburst to Saul
Ackerman earlier this evening Alex's programme
would be trashed—no matter what happened! No need
to depress him tonight. Tomorrow would be soon
enough.

'We did it, sweetheart!' Alex bounced into the kitchen,
his arms full of newspapers. 'This one's a blinder!'
He dropped a folded tabloid on the table in front of
her. 'Any coffee left in that pot?'

'Plenty.' Fenella made a gulping sound in her
throat. When she'd crawled out of bed half an hour
ago the flat had been silent. Believing her uncle to be

safely asleep, she'd sat at the kitchen table, drinking coffee and trying to decide exactly how she would tell him of her run-in with his boss.

It wasn't going to be easy, especially as he was looking so pleased with himself, delighted now because the plan to kick him back into the public eye seemed to be working.

'Well—aren't you going to read it?' He had pulled out a chair opposite her, cradling his coffee-cup, his eager grin and boyishly rumpled blond-streaked grey hair reminding her of how attractive to women audiences he had been in his heyday.

Feeling sick inside, she unfolded the paper and ran her fingers over the newsprint. Foreign wars, the balance of payments deficit and the latest cowardly IRA bomb attack had been relegated to a few square inches of print, the majority of the front page sporting the moment when the cameras had caught her hiding her mischievous smile in Alex's jacket. It came over as a snuggling embrace, Alex's arms curved protectively around her slinkily clad body and the huge caption read: "Has-Been Has-Got?"

'Don't look so shattered!' Alex grinned, swinging the paper round on the table-top, and read out the article, with plenty of hysterical expression.

Alex Fairbourne, whose top-spot TV show is to be axed—or so rumour has it—pictured outside one of London's most exclusive restaurants, finally sheds his dull-dog image. His lovely young companion coyly refused to state her name or business. Maybe his wife could throw light on the identity of the Mystery Mistress? But poor old Jean, we hear, has been conveniently banished to the wilds of Scotland. Did she go willingly, or was she pushed?

'Grief! "Mystery Mistress"! How tacky can you get?' Fenella giggled. 'But Aunty's not going to like that "poor old Jean" bit.'

'She's going to love it,' Alex contradicted. 'And since when did you ever call her Aunty?'

Since never, Fenella admitted, her face straightening out. Alex, her mother's younger brother, and Jean had always seemed more like an older brother and sister. It had nothing to do with their ages, more to do with their boundless capacity to enjoy life. Only people as perpetually optimistic as they could have devised such a scheme when faced with the persistent rumours—plus a very definite hint from Saul Ackerman himself—that *Evening With Alex* was to be axed. And, what was more, put it into practice.

And now she was going to have to tell him that she, who had promised to help, had thrown a ten-ton spanner into the works!

'We'll put in an appearance at Tinkers tonight,' Alex told her, pouring more coffee for them both. 'You won't have heard of it—how long is it since you were last in England? But it's the night-spot of the moment,' he burbled on jovially. 'The newshounds are always sniffing around, waiting for something to happen. Only a couple of weeks ago there was a deplorable fracas involving a minor Royal and a lady whose credentials are far from being unimpeachable. One of the pack earned himself quite a scoop that night. Since then there's always someone hanging around, waiting for something they can blow up into a scandal.' He pushed his chair away from the table. 'Now, what shall we have for breakfast?'

'Wait; there's something you should know,' Fenella said heavily. She felt awful. She'd let him and Jean down. She hadn't felt happy about the idea of putting on a deception for the sake of the more gutter-bound Press but once Jean had talked him round Alex had been just as enthusiastic as his wife, pointing out that Fen was the only answer—part of the family, utterly trustworthy and, almost as important, she looked the part.

'Well?' Alex prodded. 'What should I know?'

'I argued with Ackerman last night.' She took the plunge, her tongue feeling like wood. 'In the rest-room corridor, of all places. He accused me of being rude when he invited us to join his party.' She met his eyes miserably. 'And he was right. I was rude. Then I lost my head and accused him of being blinkered. I said there was nothing stopping you working with another company where your talents would be appreciated. I'm sorry if I've blown it.' She lowered her head dejectedly. 'He didn't come over as the type of man who would take any kind of rudeness or criticism lying down. There'll probably be a letter in tomorrow morning's post telling you your contract won't be renewed. So carrying on with this——' she flicked the tabloid disgustedly with her fingernail '—would be a total waste of time and effort.'

There were two more pre-recorded shows to run before the end of the current—and rumoured final—

series. He would be on tenterhooks to see if all this
publicity halted the abysmally falling ratings. 'Nothing
will save the show, after what I said. A flicker of public
interest because you appear to be running around with
a woman young enough to be your daughter won't
alter a thing.'

She had said as much when her aunt had first enlisted her help but once Jean had persuaded Alex to
take the idea on board there had been no dampening
their enthusiastic optimism.

And no dampening now, either, she thought de-
spairingly as Alex hooted, 'Rubbish!' and started to
make the belated breakfast. All that stuff in the papers
this morning had made him see himself as a celebrity
again; he was, once more, the idol women had
scratched each other's eyes out to be first in the queue
for his autograph, a lock of his hair, the clothes off
his back!

'Saul's too astute a businessman to let something
like an insubordinate female affect his judgement. He
was probably intrigued by the way you stood up to
him. He's used to having females at his feet, not at
his throat. And I'd lay odds you were the first ever
to turn down an invitation from him!'

'If you say so.' Fenella was too dejected to argue.
Alex might be her uncle but right at this moment she
felt more like his grandmother. Pushing her fringe out
of her eyes, she laid the table while he toasted
wholemeal bread and scrambled the eggs; she took
over as the phone in the living-room warbled out and
was still half-heartedly stirring when he rushed back
in again, rubbing his hands.

'What did I tell you? That was Saul on the phone—not his secretary, mark you—the great man himself. I am commanded to attend the open day tomorrow in my best bib and tucker. And you, my dear Fen, are likewise commanded! "Bring your niece", he said!' He bounced over and ruffled her hair affectionately then snatched the pan from the burner. 'Good God, Fen, these eggs are like case-hardened rubber!'

But even the ruination of his breakfast couldn't wipe the beam from his face and she felt a complete spoiler as she pointed out, 'He doesn't believe I am your niece.'

'Of course he doesn't. He wasn't meant to, was he? But he still wants you along. Most insistent.'

Fen wanted to ask why but glumly decided she wouldn't like the answer—supposing Alex knew it, which she doubted. She asked instead, 'What is this open day? Anything important?'

'The best news I've had in six months, sweetheart!' Alex abandoned all attempts to eat his breakfast, leaning back and smiling expansively. 'Part of the studios will be open for members of the viewing public to meet the regular presenters and the back-room crews. It's an annual thing but this year the board, in their wisdom, decided to throw a garden party, issuing the invitations as if they were made of diamond-studded gold. Much more exclusive. Backers and advertisers in the main with a sprinkling of show-biz names. A few selected members of the viewing public—they've been running a competition for the past three months. Twenty-five lucky winners re-

ceived a couple of tickets apiece. Not forgetting the
performers in, and writers of, the most successful
series we produce. I wasn't asked. Not until today!
It's a public-relations stunt, of course—make the
viewers feel part of the network. Not to mention
making the invited advertisers feel important.'

'And you!' Fen pointed out with an indulgent smile.
His high spirits were infectious and at least last evening's piece of rudeness hadn't produced the backlash
she'd expected. That made her conscience easier.

'Ab—so—lutely!' His blue eyes were gleaming like
sapphires. 'Clear up, would you, Fen? I'll phone Jean
and tell her the good news. The whole thing's beginning to work like a dream. Oh, and——' he was
halfway out of the room before he turned '—we'll
have to scrub Tinkers tonight. Pity, but it can't be
helped. We'll drive down to Tavistock this afternoon
and be nice and rested for tomorrow's high jinks. Be
sure to pack something sexy to wear.'

By no stretch of the imagination could the simple,
wrap-over amber silk dress be called sexy, Fen consoled herself as the Daimler Jean had given Alex for
his last birthday swept over the Tamar into Cornwall.

She had happily dressed for the part she'd been al-
lotted when they'd attended the first night and shown
up afterwards at the restaurant. But for some unknown reason she could no more bring herself to dress
the part of a *femme fatale* this afternoon than fly.
Long sleeves looked demure enough and the narrow
belt was tied tightly around her waist to ensure that

neither the bodice nor the cleverly draped skirt would gape.

A floppy-brimmed hat in fine amber straw, festooned with huge cream silk roses, completed the ensemble and, emerging from the guest room in the Tavistock house, she had blinked in surprise when Alex, looking very elegant and Fred Astaire-ish in a morning suit, had told her, 'You look fantastic!'

It was probably the hat, she decided edgily, not looking forward to the coming afternoon one tiny bit. Certainly nothing to do with the dress which covered her from her neck to just below her knees as effectively as a shroud.

'Don't forget to stick to me like glue,' Alex said tersely as he slowed down for the turn-off on to a decidedly minor road. 'I'm beginning to get butterflies. I'll need you to hold my hand for that reason alone.'

He was beginning to look white around the mouth, Fen noted, giving him an narrow-eyed glance as the car swept between high hedges filled with the foam of Queen Anne's lace and pink campion. It was a beautiful blue and green afternoon, as perfect as only an English early summer could be, and everything seemed to be going to plan, so why should the pair of them be so uneasy?

'I've suddenly developed a split personality,' he confided. 'One minute I'm up in the air and thinking all this is a superb idea—especially when it's bringing results—and the next I'm wishing we'd never started it. Trouble is, Fen, I can't come to terms with the thought of being on the scrap heap, reduced to earning my crust advertising somebody's frozen dinners in some ghastly commercial.'

About to point out that he didn't need to work at all, that Jean's fortune would keep them both in reasonable luxury for life, she thought better of it. Jean loved him to bits and wouldn't begrudge a penny—as the gifts she showered on him so lavishly testified. But Alex had his pride. His ability to keep himself and support his wife was important to him.

'But we won't get anywhere if we back out now. And Jean would clobber us senseless if we did,' he chuckled softly, his mood swinging again as he slowed down, looking for signposts.

Fen had imagined that the garden party would be held in some suitable spot near the main studios and the information that Saul Ackerman's country home was to be the venue had only added to the niggling sense of unease she'd been suffering ever since she'd had to admit there was no backing out, no way of rejecting the invitation to attend.

Though it was more like a royal command, she decided edgily as the high hedges gave way to a wall of rough-grained quarried stone and then to a pair of massive iron gates flung open in well-bred invitation. Uniformed men who looked suspiciously like security guards directed them along a track that branched off from the main gravelled drive to an area of grassland that served as a temporary car park.

Big white vans bearing the distinctive VisionWest logo left Fen in no doubt that the television crews would be prowling, getting the glittering occasion on film to be relayed to the viewers through the local news programme this evening. And there was well over a million pounds' worth of motorised status symbols lined up on the crushed dry grass, she noted, which meant that everyone here was a 'somebody', and that sent her tension-reading up another couple of notches.

Just why had Saul Ackerman changed his mind and invited Alex along at practically the last moment? He couldn't have had second thoughts about tossing him on to the scrap heap on the strength of a few scandal-mongering write-ups in the tabloids, surely?

Ducking her head as she got out of the car, she still managed to knock her hat to a rakish angle. Muttering under her breath, she righted it. She wasn't used to wearing any kind of headgear; she felt like a mushroom. Hitching up her skirts, she spindle-heeled her way to Alex who was pocketing the keys to the Daimler, her tawny eyes wary as she told him, 'I don't want to spoil your moment of triumph, but have you stopped to wonder why you're here? We never thought about the possibility of Ackerman being disgusted by what he must have read in the papers—he might not want to employ a man who is seen publicly to be cheating on his wife. We could be letting ourselves in for a highly public snub. Have you thought of that?'

'Yes.' Alex smoothed down his hair then took her hand and tucked it into the crook of his arm. 'It's always a possibility, but a remote one. Publicity and top ratings are the name of the game, and besides, he's no saint. He's rarely seen with the same woman twice. Whatever he is, I don't think he's a hypocrite.'

'Is he married?' Fen spiked her heels into the grass. For some unknown yet powerful reason she needed to know more about the man. A case of 'know your enemy', she supposed.

'He was.' Alex gave her a look that carried a hint of impatience. 'But it ended very messily. There was someone else involved—there always was someone else involved during the short lifetime of that marriage. Do come on, Fen!'

More cars were arriving, sunlight glittering from their faultless bodywork, more frivolous hats and sleek-faced men in morning suits. Fen gave in and fell in step beside her uncle as they gravitated towards a gateway in the fuchsia hedge, a graceful figure in the amber silk that emphasised the slenderness of her hips and long, long legs, blissfully unaware that each step she took afforded the onlooker a tiny tantalising glimpse of creamy thigh and intriguing stocking-top.

Alex's brief words had told her as much as she wanted to know about Saul Ackerman, and left her even less endeared to him than before. His poor wife was well rid of him; Alex had spoken of the marriage ending—so presumably that meant divorce. Because he couldn't keep his hands off other women? It certainly sounded like it.

Fen couldn't understand why any right-minded woman wanted to get married at all. Why put yourself in a position where your happiness depended on the good nature and fidelity of one man? Generally speaking, she liked men, enjoyed their company and valued their friendship. But she would never surrender her independence to one; she knew what it had done to her mother and, in consequence, to her. And had heard enough about disastrous marriages to make any sensible female wary.

So footloose and heart-free she would remain, a citizen of the world, a happily independent lady answerable to no one but herself.

'Fen!' A sharp nudge in her ribs brought her wandering mind back to present circumstances. Blinking, she focused on the tray of glasses, the white-shirted, impassive-faced waiter who held it. Then, champagne in hand, she took in her surroundings. Acres of emerald-green, closely mown grass quartered by stone-flagged paths, parterres of flowers cut into the sward, punctuated by tall trees, their leaves whispering softly in the gentle summer breeze. And, beyond and above the long sweep of a closely cut yew hedge a few hundred yards away, the glimpse of the tumbled roofs of an impressive Tudor house.

Some country pad, she thought sourly, contrasting it with the humble stone cottage, the only place that had ever remotely come to resemble a home, a bare twenty miles away as the crow flew.

But at least there was no sign of the owner, so be grateful for small mercies, she told herself, wondering if they could possibly manage to avoid him all afternoon.

'What do we do now?' she asked. 'Plant ourselves in front of the camera crews and grin?'

'We circulate and give each other adoring glances,' he said firmly. 'Drink your fizz; it might put you in a better mood.' He whisked her along paths and over expensively maintained lawns, mingling with various groups of guests, introducing her simply as Fenella, doing nothing at all to dampen the often openly inquisitive stares she was getting, speculative eyes watching her every move. She could almost hear them thinking, debating whether she was with Alex for love or for money.

There was a lot of well-mannered back-slapping, a lot of preening and a fair amount of talking shop and by the time they had worked their way through to the terrace beyond the hedge Fen had had more than enough.

The paving ran along the entire frontage of the spectacularly lovely house and was set with white-clothed buffet tables and bars, all perfumed and punctuated by terracotta pots brimming over with stately lilies. And in the middle distance, surrounded by a group of obvious sycophants, was Saul Ackerman.

Fen recognised him with a curious jolt right in the pit of her stomach. He was easily the most impressive male around—the handful of sexily handsome actors she had encountered notwithstanding.

Oh, drat it to Hades! She had really hoped she wouldn't have to see him. Guilty conscience, she supposed. She had behaved badly that first time they'd met. Which didn't mean she wouldn't behave twice as badly if there happened to be a second time. And that wouldn't do Alex's career prospects a whole heap of good, she admitted. But then, she had never encountered anyone, male or female, who had aroused her to such a pitch of unthinking animosity. Her blood boiled whenever she thought of him!

'We could leave now,' she whispered to Alex out of the side of her mouth. 'You must have spoken to everyone here.'

Except Saul, and she wasn't about to remind him of that. She was sick of being on show, being talked about. Most of the people here would have read at least one scandal-mongering piece of so-called journalism. Most of the men, with varying degrees of interested speculation, had ogled her, while she was sure all the women were bitching about her inside their heads. She was getting paranoid, she recognised, but that didn't stop her wanting to hit Alex when he scoffed, 'What, and miss out on all that gorgeous food? Besides, I haven't paid my respects to Saul yet. Got to keep a high profile. If Jean were here she'd say the same.'

'Go ahead,' Fen told him, feeling tight-lipped. 'You'll deserve a medal if you can drag him out from under all those female admirers.' She had just recognised the lushly sensual, scarlet garbed figure of Vesta Faine hanging adoringly on to his arm. No doubt she was his current lady. Seen twice already in his company, she must be all set to break the record—if what Alex had said about the staying power of his ladies was true. 'And I need to go to the loo,' she grumbled untruthfully. 'Where is it?'

'Go to the house. You'll find doors if you look for them. Saul won't have Portakabins labelled "His" and "Hers" on his sacrosant property.' He gave her arm a little squeeze. 'Don't be long. I'll get us some food and try to grab Saul's attention. After all, he did expressly invite you to come.'

Which wasn't what she wanted to hear, Fen thought as she swayed her way along the terrace, skirting the lily pots and knots of festively dressed personalities with an empty smile fixed on her face.

She had no need to find a bathroom—just a bit of empty space. And she had no intention of returning before she had got herself nice and calm again. Alex could manage on his own; she'd done quite enough.

To the side of the house she found a swimming-pool complete with loungers and white-painted wrought-iron tables. And people. Quickly, she withdrew her inquisitive nose from the trellis of billowing roses that formed part of the pool surround and explored further.

And eventually found just what she'd been hoping for: utter seclusion. A small secret garden, enclosed on three sides by tall yew hedges, the fourth side open to a vista of sweeping fields and the thickly wooded river valley below. No one in sight. Just the sun, the warm soft air, the patchwork of greens, the song of the birds. Heaven.

Ignoring the stone bench seat, strategically placed for peaceful contemplation of the breathtaking view, she kicked off her shoes and sank down on the soft, sun-warmed grass, pulling her hat down over her face to shade her creamy pale skin from the damaging rays.

If she weren't so tense she would be asleep within seconds; she hadn't realised just how exhausted she was. The past four years she'd been travelling round Europe, flitting from one job to the next like a demented gnat, enjoying every hectic moment. Eighteen months ago, after her father's sudden and unexpected death from a heart condition, she had taken two months off to get her distraught mother settled with an old schoolfriend—recently widowed herself—in Australia. And that had been no easy ride.

She had grieved for her father, of course she had, her sorrow taking the form of deep regrets. Regret that he had barely ever acknowledged her existence and, when he had, only because of her nuisance value. A selfish man, there had been no room in his life for anything outside his work as a highly respected travel writer. He'd travelled the world, dragging his wife along behind him and, much later, the child he had never expected or wanted. Not that he'd had to drag his wife, exactly. She'd been too dependent on him, too besotted, to let him out of her sight! And now that he had gone, her mother didn't know what to do with her life. So no, that two months spent trying to help her mother come to terms with the loss she vowed she would never be able to accept had not been a picnic.

And a few weeks ago, during one of the frequent calls to Australia she made from wherever she happened to be, her mother had instructed mournfully, 'When you're next in the UK I want you to arrange for the cottage to be sold. I couldn't bear to go there again, not without your father. It would kill me. You can crate up any of his books and papers that are still there and send them out to me. I'd ask Alex and Jean, but you know how busy they are. Alex has better things to do with his time than bother himself with my affairs.'

And so, after a job that had taken her to the English Midlands, Fen had dropped in on Jean and Alex in Hampstead, intending to spend a few days with them before hiring a car and driving down to Cornwall, promising herself that before she did anything about disposing of the cottage and its furnishings she would give herself a full week simply to laze around and recoup her energies. Instead, she had found herself drawn into playing the part of Alex's mistress, all thoughts of a much needed breathing space pushed into the background.

Sighing gustily, she wriggled herself into a more comfortable position, feeling her skirt ruck up around her thighs and not caring. There was no one to see her, after all. If she was going to have to spend the next couple of weeks racketing around notorious night-spots with her uncle, pretending they were having an adulterous fling, she would need to unwind.

She made a conscious effort to relax, to push everything out of her mind, and succeeded, feeling her body go boneless, sleep pulling at her eyes, pulling her deeper and deeper . . .

'Can anybody join in, or is Alex the only man who's allowed to sleep with you?'

The steel-sharp voice cut through the layers of sleep as a hand flicked the silk and straw confection away from her face. Fen went rigid with shock, then wriggled frantically, trying to get upright without sacrificing too much of her dignity. But a warm hand—a burningly warm hand—on her thigh sent all thoughts of dignity scattering in the ether, her temper and temperature going through the roof.

Not only had her skirt rucked up to an indecent level, it had also gaped embarrassingly. And that lean, olive-toned hand was curved around her thigh, on the soft white flesh above her stocking-top.

'How dare you?' She slapped fiercely at his hand, but it didn't budge an inch. The pressure of his fingers increased by a fraction and Fen pulled in a scorching breath, appalled by the electrifying sensations that spread all over her body. Then she twisted away, ending up on her hands and knees, hardly knowing how to contain her fury when he simply reached for her, dragging her down on to the grass, his arms pinioning her beneath him.

Down, but not out, she glared into his unsmiling eyes and tried to control her hectic breathing as she rasped out, 'What the hell do you think you're doing, Mr Ackerman? If this is a sample of the way you treat your female guests I'm surprised you weren't locked safely away years ago!'

And then he did smile, a sweet, slow smile that took her breath away all over again, a smile that touched his eyes like the rays of the moon on a silver sea and made the harshly modelled planes of his face seem far less uncompromising.

'I treat my female guests in exactly the way their body language leads me to believe they expect,' he murmured, his voice as soft as velvet now. 'The invitation you posed was impossible to resist. And as for what I was doing——' He moved off her and her eyes went wide and wild. Why, her body seemed scorched by the imprint of his, as if she would never be able to rid herself of the way all that power-packed

virility had felt as it had crushed her into the grass!
'I was looking for you. Alex has been going frantic.
And having found you, pinned you down so to speak,
I wasn't willing to risk losing you again.'

He got to his feet, as if nothing had happened, as
if he tumbled women he barely knew in the grass every
day of the week, insulted them and put his hands . . .
Oh, it was unendurable! And if he touched her again
she would kill him!

But she didn't. Because when he hauled her to her
feet, and smoothed down her wrinkled skirt, pulled
together the gaping bodice of her dress and settled her
silly hat on her head, his touch was completely impersonal, as if he were dressing a tailor's dummy,
making it fit for the public gaze. And that, strangely,
was miff-making enough without his almost curt
command, 'Come. Alex has something he wants to
tell you. Besides, if you're missing for much longer
he'll get withdrawal symptoms.'

CHAPTER THREE

SAUL didn't touch her as he walked her back to the party, not even a hand beneath her elbow as they mounted the flight of stone steps that led up from the lower walkway to the pool and terrace level.

Which didn't mean a thing. Because Fen couldn't have been more aware of him if his hands had been all over her. Her body was burning, her mouth suddenly dry, her breath thick in her lungs. Yet she was shivering, quivering all over like a startled mare. But that was just a symptom of the tension she'd been under ever since she and Alex had started out on this mad charade, she informed herself tartly, trying to wipe away the memory of being pinned beneath Saul Ackerman's hard male body, the way his hand had felt on the soft warm flesh of her thigh.

But the memory wouldn't go away and she had never been as pleased to see anyone in her life as she was to see Alex when he met them at the end of the now almost deserted terrace.

'So there you are!' His face lit up with relief. 'I thought you'd run out on me, sweetheart.'

'Never!' In her eagerness to reach him and the safe normality he represented, one of her spindly heels twisted beneath her and only Saul's lightning-fast reactions, the hand that snaked out to steady her, prevented her from falling in a heap and saying

43

goodbye to what little was left of her dwindling composure. 'If you're this eager in bed I can understand why he hates you to be out of his sight,' Saul murmured close to her ear, his breath fanning her thick honey-gold fringe beneath the dipping, rose-laden brim of her hat.

Fen shuddered with scalding outrage. She wanted to tell him to shut his insulting mouth but the words wouldn't come. Her tongue was stuck to the roof of her mouth. And the hand that had steadied her relaxed, just a little, his thumb making lazy circles on the inside of her arm, scorching her through the thin silk sleeve. And the most bewildering, the most horrible thing of all was the way she was just standing there as if turned to stone, letting him do it. Enjoying——

No! Never!

She slapped that thought away smartly then went hot all over as he released her arm, his hand brushing her silk-clad bottom as it fell back to his side, brushing against her so lightly that she could almost have imagined it.

'Excuse me for a moment; there's someone I must have a brief word with,' Saul said, turning away, his movements very fluid for a man whose body packed so much power. And Fen gave him a sourly reluctant ten out of ten for urbanity, for behaving as if nothing had happened, as if he hadn't foully insulted her with both word and touch!

'Can we go now?' Fen glared at her uncle, unfazed by the way his eyebrows shot up to his hairline at her tone. He hadn't been close enough to catch Saul's low-voiced insult, and the touching had gone on out of sight!

'Not yet.' Alex pulled her out of the way of the waiters who were already dismantling the buffet tables. The party was long over. She must have slept for longer than she'd thought. 'Listen,' he began in a rush, his flushed face close to hers, 'while you were missing I had a word with Laurence Meek—he's the director of programmes, the man who can put 'em on and take 'em off. And the only living soul who can sway the decisions he makes is——'

'Saul Ackerman,' Fen put in drily, hatred bubbling up inside her all over again at the mere thought of him.

'Dead right. Anyway, Laurence gave me a very strong hint that, after all, my show mightn't get the shove. His actual words were, "Don't go anywhere else with your c.v., old man. There's a big decision in the offing and I think it will go your way."'

'That's great news!' Fen's golden eyes shone, her bad mood disappearing like mist in the summer sunshine. She was really pleased for him. His own show meant a lot to him—his pride, his self-respect, his sense of worth. Slowly, she walked over to the stone balustrading that edged the terrace and gazed out over the now deserted gardens, Alex at her side. His good news meant that soon they would be able to stop the pretence of a torrid, adulterous relationship. She had never been wildly ecstatic about the idea but she hadn't foreseen how tawdry and besmirched it would make her feel. The relief was heady.

The Ackerman monster certainly had a beautiful home, she decided, the tranquillity of the scene soothing her. She could almost imagine herself putting down roots if she owned something like this. Almost. She sighed. No, she couldn't see herself putting roots down anywhere, any time. She couldn't really see the point. There was always something new over the horizon, something to draw her wandering feet onwards...

'And when's this big decision to be taken?' she asked.

'I'm not sure. But soon. And when it's made, either way, we can drop this act.'

'But it can't have had anything to do with their change of mind, surely?' Fen looked at him worriedly. 'One scandalous story in print...' Her voice trailed away. From what she'd gathered, the viewing figures for Alex's show had been falling steadily for some time, and dropping like a stone just recently. Could their altered decision be based on what was, after all, simply a piece of sleazy journalism and salacious speculation? It didn't make a whole lot of sense.

But Alex didn't care why he had been offered a reprieve, only that it seemed that he had. He was smiling expansively, his face too flushed. Fen suspected he'd been celebrating ever since he'd had that talk with the director of programmes. The champagne had been flowing like water, after all!

'Shall I drive us home?' She didn't want to offend his male pride by suggesting he might be over the legal limit—well over!—but it was time they made a move.

She didn't want to face Saul again, not after what he had said and done. Especially not after what he had said and done!

'We'll see. Later. Saul's asked us to stay to dinner—I've been trying to tell you.'

'What?' Fen shook her head decisively. 'No. Oh, no!' She had had more than enough of his company. Several others would have been invited, too, she was sure of that. A select few. Definitely including the lovely Vesta Faine! But she had no wish whatsoever to be part of the élite around Saul Ackerman's dinner-table tonight.

'Fen!' Alex looked pole-axed. 'Don't be like that! I know it's been difficult—being taken for my mistress, and everything. But it won't be for much longer, I promise, and then we can come clean. And it's important to me; you must see that. We got away with refusing his invitation once; do it twice and I can kiss all hopes of a change of mind goodbye!' He put his hand over hers as it clenched and curled around the sun-warmed stone. 'I can't afford to ruffle his feathers, at least not until that decision's been made. And he might want to discuss it over dinner. Please, sweetheart, try to endure it. For me?'

It was emotional blackmail and she knew she had no choice. But, just to get her own back, she snapped out, 'Couldn't we just tell him we can't wait to get back to your place and dive into bed?' Saul would understand something like that—the arrogant, insulting, over-sexed monster . . . !

She saw Alex's face go purple, and knew why when, from just behind her, that hated voice said, in a tone like steel cutting through stone, 'Shall we go in? We've time for a drink before dinner. And perhaps your niece . . .' his voice hovered damningly over that word ' . . . would like to freshen up before we eat?'

He had heard what she had said; no doubt about it. Trying to hide her flaming face beneath the brim of her hat, she had no other option but to keep pace with the two men as they walked towards the house. But once inside she could have wept with relief as he introduced his housekeeper, Mrs Pringle.

'Show Fenella to the blue guest room, Prinny. And hold dinner for an hour, would you? We'll be watching VisionWest News in the den.'

How many others would be watching, too? How many invited guests for dinner? Would they all be wondering what she and Alex got up to in bed? Wondering if his wife knew exactly what was going on?

Fen felt dreadful. She wasn't cut out to be a mistress, even a pretend one! Hysterically, she wondered if she could tell the housekeeper she'd got a sick headache and was going to have a nice lie-down. No, she would never get away with it. Saul Ackerman would be up like a shot to soothe her fevered brow. He probably knew a few good variations on the game of doctors and nurses!

Oh, she was getting sex on the brain! she howled at herself after the housekeeper trotted off, having deposited her, as ordered, in the blue room. She, who rarely gave the subject a moment's thought in her busy, restless life, preferring to be celibate rather than risk catching some dreadful disease. In any case, she didn't know what the fuss was about. She'd tried it once and had found it to be about as exciting as reading the back of a bus ticket.

True, she'd been only eighteen at the time. Eighteen and lonely, during her first year working for her degree in modern languages. The other female students had all fancied Ray Gordon, but he had picked her and it had gone to her head. She had imagined herself in love with him, and he banished the loneliness, and she had fancied herself as a modern, liberated woman, with a partner—modern women didn't use words like 'lover' and 'mistress'. But six weeks after their first date he had taken her back to his flat and into his bed. And she'd hated every moment of it and had decided that, after all, she didn't need a partner, not if it entailed putting up with all that rather embarrassing business between the sheets.

She would rather handle her life all by herself, make it how she wanted it. With her first-hand knowledge of other countries, their customs and languages, she could be as fancy-free as she chose, and she need never be lonely while there were places to go, people to meet, while she kept a lively, enquiring mind in her head.

So why did sex keep raising its contentious head now? Nothing to do with Saul Ackerman, the way he had touched her? No, of course not. She despised and hated the man.

Tossing her hat on the graceful half-tester bed, she scanned the room sourly. Blue. A misty, pale blue combined with soft greys and cream. Very tasteful. Rather fine antiques, too. But, what was more to the point, an elegantly appointed bathroom with everything a female guest might need to help her freshen up for the fray. For fray it would be, she acknowledged as, twenty refreshing minutes later, she reluctantly made her way back downstairs.

Not knowing where to go, she stood for a few moments in the centre of the huge, jonquil-scented hall. There were big bowls of the delicate, late spring flowers everywhere. And there was an undertone of beeswax, too, and carefully tended great age. The mellow panelling seemed to surround her protectively and the lovingly polished antique furniture looked like old and valued friends. It was a house that had lived through history, sheltering many souls through the ages, and it seemed to welcome her, offer her a gracious, gentle haven . . .

'Through here, miss.'

Fen blinked rapidly. It wasn't like her to come all over fanciful. In fact, it was unheard of. She was probably the most level-headed person she knew.

'Thanks.' She summoned a wavery smile for the housekeeper who had just come through one of the doors, a tray of used glasses in her capable hands. 'I was a bit lost.'

Lost in a load of nonsense, she informed herself witheringly. A house was a house, when all was said and done. Nothing to get all dewy-eyed about! Trying not to look as apprehensive as she felt, she approached the door Mrs Pringle was patiently holding open for her. From the number of the glasses on that tray there must be quite a crowd through there.

Bracing herself to endure more speculative looks and loaded questions, Fen took a deep breath and sailed into the room, her eyes going wide as she saw Alex sprawled comfortably in a leather club chair, a glass in his hand, Saul on a two-seater sofa, and not another soul.

Alex was too intent on the TV set to have noticed her but Saul got immediately to his feet, motioning her to the sofa as he moved to the drinks tray.

Fen's eyes raked the room for somewhere else to sit and decided that perching herself on the edge of the hard-backed oak chair by the bookshelves, removing the stack of what looked like high-quality trade magazines in order to do so, would look childishly defensive.

She had nothing to be defensive about, she assured herself, sinking down on to the sofa. So she wasn't going to act as if she had. It was a comfortable, booky room, very relaxing, and the fact that she didn't have to face a horde of other guests was an enormous relief. She took the flute of champagne Saul handed her with a cool murmur of thanks and watched him top Alex's whisky glass to the brim and wondered just what it was about the man that made her come out in goosebumps whenever she looked at him.

He had discarded the jacket of the formal suit he'd been wearing this afternoon, removed his tie, and the crisp white fabric of his shirt skimmed wide, hard-boned shoulders and the dark, close-fitting trousers emphasised his tall leanness. He was a sexy-looking brute, she admitted, taking a gulp of champagne to moisten her dry throat. He had the look of a man who would never take no for an answer, had probably never had to even try. He blatantly exuded that type of arrogance.

Perhaps that was what made him appear so dangerous—that and the way he moved, the way his eyes seemed to be able to reach right inside her head and read her thoughts, the way the hard mouth could suddenly, unexpectedly smile and make the recipient believe the sun had come out, shining brilliantly just for them, on even the darkest, dreariest of days.

But the threat he posed was not to herself; how could it be? As far as she was concerned he was no threat at all! No, it was Alex she had to think about. The threat to his programme, his standing in the entertainment world. So she would try to forget the brute's insults and do her best to be cool and polite, and eat his wretched dinner and say goodnight and goodbye very nicely, like a well-brought-up young lady. For her uncle's sake.

She shot the object of her concern a frowning look. And he caught it as he momentarily looked away from the screen, lifting his glass in an absurd salute and grinning foolishly. He was drinking far too much. She would definitely have to drive him home. She wished Jean were here to take him in hand. His hoped-for reprieve had gone to his head and knocked out all his common sense!

As Saul joined her on the sofa Fen braced herself. If he tried to touch her again she would scream! But he simply topped up her champagne and concentrated on the small screen.

Fen sipped and tried to convince herself that the crackle of electricity between them existed only in her

imagination, that her minute awareness of him was a
perfectly natural reaction to the insults he had heaped
on her. She had every right to be wary of him after
the things he had said and done. But once dinner was
over they could leave and she would never have to see
him again.

On that comforting thought, she, too, concentrated
on the screen. After the commercial break the second
half of the regional news programme began and she
watched without much interest the shots of members
of the viewing public being shown around some of
the studios. And only when the scene shifted to the
garden party did she begin to sit up and take notice.

As an exercise in corporate back-slapping it was very
well done. Loads of famous faces looking as if they
were having a whale of a time and the director of programmes explaining just how many exciting packages
the viewing audiences could look forward to in the
future. But in the background of many of the shots
she could see herself and Alex, she clinging to his arm
as if glued to his side and—horror of horrors!—every
step she took revealed an outrageous glimpse of legs
and stocking-tops.

And she had congratulated herself on managing to
dress so demurely! Her face on fire, she surrep-
titiously tugged at the traitorous wrap-over skirt and
hoped she had imagined the wicked, low chuckle at
her side.

'Marvellous publicity!' Alex slurred as the credits
began to roll. 'Great idea of yours, ol' man!'

And not bad publicity for him, either, Fen thought
sourly. There wouldn't be many viewers who would

have missed the sight of Alex Fairbourne with a doting dolly on his arm, flashing her legs and smiling dotingly into his handsome, distinguished face.

'The idea was a collective one,' Saul said dismissively. But there was not a hint of the expected censure in his tone. He sounded faintly amused, indulgent even. Fen wondered what he was up to because he didn't seem the type to suffer tipsy maunderings from an underling gladly.

'Shall we go through?' Saul rose to his feet, pressing a bell-push discreetly hidden away at the side of the stone fireplace. 'Prinny will be serving dinner.'

She would be now, Fen thought tartly. The housekeeper had probably been waiting, like an athlete on the starting-block, for just such a summons. Putting her glass down on a side-table, she noted with mild shock that it was empty again. How many glasses of champagne had she gulped her way through? How many times had he silently topped the thing up?

And Alex was definitely unsteady on his feet as Saul ushered them into a small, intimate dining-room that had open French windows leading out on to the terrace. And throughout the beautifully served and prepared meal Saul kept the wine flowing.

One glass was all Fen allowed herself and Saul, she noted, had scarcely touched his. Was he deliberately trying to get his guests drunk? she wondered hysterically. But what would be the point?

Whatever his host's intentions, Alex was definitely under the weather. Twice she had kicked him under the table but it hadn't made a scrap of difference to his alcoholic intake. She would have to pour him into the car! That was if she could ever get him to stop talking!

And it was all Saul's fault! He was the one who was plying the wine, leading poor old Alex on to talk about past triumphs, the celebrities he'd met in his long and—up until fairly recently—successful career. He was being manipulated, made to feel fêted and important. Fen would have dearly liked to shove one of those dratted wine bottles right down Saul Ackerman's throat!

She didn't know what he was up to, only that it was something despicably devious, and she was proved horribly right when, coming through with the coffee, Prinny was instructed in that 'won't take no for an answer' voice, 'Show Mr Fairbourne to his room, would you? He's had a long day.' He got to his feet with a movement that combined ease with purpose and helped his almost paralytic guest to stand upright. 'That's all right with you, Alex? I wouldn't want one of our star performers to fail a breath test.'

'His' room! Thus implying that the housekeeper had known the guests would be overnighters. Oh, the tricky bastard! And Alex said nothing, not a word, just gave her a cross-eyed, fatuous smile before staggering out behind the stone-faced Mrs Pringle. He would fall asleep repeating that 'one of our star performers' like a litany, she just knew he would, the poor old love. Saul Ackerman had been using him, playing on his insecurities. And she thought she was beginning to understand why!

So when Saul turned back to her after closing the door behind his inebriated guest and his housekeeper she was already on her feet.

'Thank you for dinner, Mr Ackerman.' Never let him be able to accuse her of having no manners again! 'I'll collect Alex in the morning. About eleven?'

Her uncle wouldn't have surfaced much before then, the state he was in. And by then Ackerman should be about his business, stamping around, playing God around one of his business enterprises. The haughty glare she gave him belied the way her heart was thumping about. His reaction would tell her whether her suspicions were true, and the tiny, frozen moment of utter silence was straining her composure to the limit.

And then that breathtaking smile, those molten silver, magnetic eyes. Fen shuddered, pulling in air, and Saul said softly, 'How unnecessary, Fenella. You'll be staying, too. Or hadn't I mentioned it?' He moved closer, his nearness intimidating. She stood her ground, her pride not allowing her to give way. He knew damn well he had mentioned no such thing. 'I wouldn't like to see you up on a drink-drive charge, either.'

One insult too many! Fen's nostrils flared. He really was despicable!

'I'm within the legal limit,' she snapped at him, not so sure about that, though. She'd had one glass of wine with dinner but couldn't be positive about the amount of champagne she'd gulped down while they'd been watching that programme. And she felt perfectly clear-headed. In any case, if she had any doubts at all, she was perfectly prepared to drive to the nearest lay-by and sleep in the car.

'Debatable.' His purring voice underlined her own doubts and her eyes fell from his. Immediately, she felt more sure of herself. He couldn't make her stay. But, 'Sadly—or not—it depends on the way you look at it——' the fingers of one hand brushed her thick fringe away from her eyes '—Prinny has a streak of Puritanism a mile wide, so, for the sake of the proprieties, you and Alex have separate rooms. Not——' his fingers slid down the side of her face, feathering along her jawline '—not that he would be much good to you tonight.'

Fen choked. She felt as if she was drowning in agitation. All down to the way he was touching her, his insults. Not that he would think of them as insults, of course. Everyone was supposed to believe that she was having an affair with Alex. But that didn't excuse him!

She jerked her head away but he moved closer, much closer, and she found herself backed against the table with nowhere else to go. About to tell him she had no intention of staying under the same roof as him, she opened her mouth to yell at him and found the words pushed back into her throat as he laid a silencing finger against her lips.

And she didn't know whether her stunned and shattered inability to move a muscle was due to the way her senses were swimming at the intimacy of his touch, or the way he imparted conversationally, 'Let me warn you against refusing my hospitality again, Fenella. You wouldn't want me to feel insulted, would

you? It might make me take my understandable
feelings of pique out on your "uncle". And that would
be a shame, especially after I've convinced Laurence
Meek that we should reconsider our decision to cut
such dead wood as *Evening With Alex* out of our
schedulings. Shall we take our coffee out on to the
terrace?'

CHAPTER FOUR

ALMOST spitting with outrage, Fen flounced down on to one of the sumptuously upholstered patio chairs and watched Saul put the tray of coffee things on the white-painted wrought-iron table. While he poured, she brooded.

Out-and-out blackmail. Do as I say, or else . . .

Do as I say. And no Brownie points for guessing what that might be! He probably thought she was a career-mistress; had seen her with Alex, fancied her, and decided he wanted a piece of the action for himself!

She remembered precisely how many times he had touched her, and where, and how. Her skin tingled, all over her body, and she was sure her face had gone scarlet. And if he so much as laid one finger on her she would scream the house down. Hadn't he imparted that Mrs Pringle had a mile-wide Puritanical streak? She would come to her rescue, surely she would? In any case, she would scream her lungs out until she did!

But he didn't attempt to touch her, or make any further insulting remarks about bed. He put her coffee in front of her, offered cream and sugar, which she stiffly declined, and sat down opposite, leaning back and looking enviably relaxed.

'So—tell me something about yourself.' No trace of steel in his voice now. It was liquid gold as it trickled into her consciousness, making her nerve-ends tingle all over again. And he sounded as if he was truly interested, and that, she assured herself, was simply a trick of the seasoned womaniser's trade.

But, what was worse, she almost wanted to talk to him, relax with him in the soft, flower-scented evening. But only almost. She wasn't that much of a fool. And, in any case, the desire, if indeed it was there, had come fleetingly into being merely because she was sick and tired of the deception, the part she was playing.

'Why?' The question was baldly put and cold, letting him know she wouldn't be that easy to trick. She braced herself for an abrasive return to her far from subtle put-down and found herself gaping at him, flummoxed, as he told her softly,

'Because I'm interested; why else would I want to know anything at all?' In the mellow light spilling from the open French windows behind them she could see the amused slant of his mouth. He shifted into a more comfortable, fluid position, his long legs stretched out in front of him, the diluted light out here on the terrace painting the austerity out of his memorably attractive features. He looked completely, utterly lazy, contentedly at peace with himself. In complete contrast to the slashing authoritarian she'd come to expect. 'Or maybe intrigued is the more apposite word,' he suggested, his eyes drifting in her direction, silvery and soft and beguiling. 'Whatever.' A minimal shrug that barely moved the soft white fabric that covered his hard, wide shoulders. 'I want to know all there is to know about you.'

He was, she recognised hollowly, beginning to fascinate her. And that didn't feel comfortable.

'Then want must be your master.' How many times had she heard her mother say that? Every time she had childishly tried to wiggle her way past the blinkers that had effectively cut out everything, even her own daughter, enabling her to concentrate her entire attention on her slavishly adored husband.

Fen smiled fatalistically at the memory, and that softened the rebuff, made her voice marginally less tart as she added, 'There's really very little to tell.'

'That can't be true.' He lifted his arms and crossed them behind his head, the watchful silver eyes never leaving her face. 'Let's kick off with where you live, shall we? You must have a bolt-hole you go to when you're between lovers.'

Anger shook her like a rough hand and the only thing that kept her in her seat was the memory of the reluctant promise she'd made to Jean. She'd agreed to help Alex by going along with this hateful charade and she wished to Hades she had flatly refused.

'Nowhere special,' she mumbled, finishing the last of her coffee and placing the wide-bowled cup back on its saucer with a hand which shook with all that pent-up inner ire. And that was the truth because she went where her work took her, never stayed anywhere long enough to make anything remotely resembling a settled home.

'Then let me put it another way.' Suddenly, he looked taut and dangerous, and the thread of steel was back in that honeyed soft voice. 'What will you do and where will you go when Alex tosses you out? We can dispense with the polite fabrication of a blood tie, don't you think?' There was no hint of laziness in his pose now. He hadn't moved a muscle but he still looked like a tiger ready to pounce and snarl and rend her apart. 'And he will ask you to leave, you know. You are simply an aberration. Put it down to the male menopause, if you like. One thing is for sure, though. Deep down he's devoted to Jean. He would never leave her. But then, I'm sure you already know that. Women who—attach themselves to much older, married men—preferably men in the public eye with money to throw around—usually know the score.'

Not even for the sake of Alex's career would she put up with this! She stumbled to her feet.

'You assume far too much! I take it I'm to use the blue guest room,' she said harshly. 'Goodnight, Mr Ackerman. I wish I could say I'd enjoyed the evening. But I haven't.'

He was on his feet just as suddenly, moving in on her, blocking her way. This close, he was far more than merely disturbing and when he touched her, his hands closing round her elbows, she knew she couldn't have moved even if she'd wanted to. Her head was spinning, her legs shaky and she raised wide, disconcerted eyes to his as he reminded her silkily, 'You haven't answered my question. What will you do? Where will you go when Alex comes to his senses?'

It had been on the tip of her tongue to ask what made him think Alex was her lover. Silly question! She knew exactly why he and the readership of a few

trashy tabloids thought that! She was going to have
to watch her tongue around him. The trouble was,
his hatefulness drove everything sensible out of her
head. Glaring at him, she amended glacially, 'What
makes you think I have lovers in the plural? Maybe
Alex is the one and only. Have you thought of that?
And take your hands off me.'

He ignored her request, his eyes gleaming in his
shadowed face as the pressure of his fingers increased
just a little.

'How old are you? Twenty-four? Twenty-five?
Don't tell me you reached that age in a state of blissful
chastity, Fen, because I won't believe it. Not with your
looks, that aura of sexual excitement you carry around
with you. Plenty of men must have made a play for
you.' His voice was suddenly huskily seductive and
she shivered uncontrollably, unconsciously lapping her
dry lips with the tip of her tongue, a revealing gesture
he didn't miss. 'Don't tell me our ageing pop star was
the first man you allowed past first base.'

He was crude. He was a devil. And she hated him!

'It's none of your damned business, is it?' Her tone
was passionately acid. 'You deliberately made Alex
drunk, forced us to stay here——' She broke off
jaggedly, her words choking her, and he gave a soft
laugh and pulled her slowly against the hard length
of his body, his arms sliding around her as he said
with a fierce tenderness that utterly bemused her,

'He made himself drunk. He's been under a lot of
strain recently. The guy was celebrating. Why should
I try to stop him? Poor baby...' One of his hands
slid up to cradle the back of her head, easing it

forward to rest against the hollow of his shoulder. 'If you thought I'd plotted to make him incapable, just to get you alone and jump on you, forget it. I don't operate that way.'

Didn't he? Had she misjudged him? No, how could she have done? She hadn't forgotten the insults he'd handed out, even if he had. And what was she doing here, staying so passively in his arms, breathing in the subtle male muskiness of him?

Alarm bells jangled in her brain and her mouth went dry as, agitatedly, she wrenched her head back, dragging herself away as she asked crossly, 'Just how *do* you operate?'

'Ah.' His eyes gleamed wickedly. 'Have patience. You'll find out.' Slow words, softly spoken, slow, soft movements of his hands as they slid down to prevent her wriggling attempts to distance herself, pressing against the small of her back, anchoring her lower body to the masculine jut of his pelvis.

Fen's eyes went wide with shock, her body going totally still. The heat of all the world seemed concentrated in that one region, explicitly concentrated. She simply couldn't believe such a sensation possible, couldn't believe the scorching heat that seared through her loins and made her ache with something she had never experienced before, forcing her to recognise instinctively that the only way to assuage that ache was to press her body closer to his, closer...

'Let's say, for now, that friend Alex is walking a very thin line indeed and you would do well to remember it. Shall we have more coffee and resume our conversation?'

She heard his words as if from a great distance and when he released her she felt disorientated, her veins still running with fire and anguish. It was as much as she could do to stay upright and, more out of necessity than desire, she sank back down on to the chair and inwardly cursed him for being such a bastard.

He was as good as telling her that he called all the shots and, until a decision had been reached on Alex's future with VisionWest, she supposed he did. And yes, she would do well to remember it. She and Alex had come this far with their distasteful charade, and she, personally, had endured much that she would have preferred not to. It would be an appalling waste of effort if she were to tip the balance the wrong way simply because she wasn't tough enough to handle a man who, for some reason of his own, seemed determined to throw her off balance.

So she would grit her teeth and try very hard not to be hostile. Grit her teeth and try to smile. And think of her uncle.

'So where did you meet Alex?' he asked neutrally. She watched his hands slide over the coffee-pot and wondered, chaotically, what it would feel like to have his hands move so gently and so exploratively over her. 'It's cold,' he told her lightly, his mouth curling knowingly, exactly as if he could read her thoughts. 'Shall I ask Prinny to bring fresh?'

'Not for me.'

She sounded breathless. She shook her head to clear it and he sank down into the chair beside her, not opposite, as before, and prompted, 'Well?'

Fine brows peaked above golden eyes, and then she remembered. He had no right to question her, of course, and she had every right to refuse to tell him anything. Except that the wretch held her uncle's professional future in the palm of his hands

But how to answer?

Stick to the truth. She wasn't an easy liar. Thinking back quickly over the years, she told him, 'On a beach in Jamaica. I was fooling around in the water. Topless. I asked him to play with me.' Some inner devil made her add, 'How could he resist?' And she saw his eyes go bleak and hard, the tiny movement of a muscle at the side of his mouth. She had told him the truth and it was too bad if he didn't like it.

What she didn't tell him, had no intention of telling him, was that she'd been six years old at the time, splashing in and out of waves wearing a pair of navy blue knickers.

Her father had rented an old plantation house for three months, presumably to get to grips with the book of the moment. They'd been living out of suitcases for as long as she remembered. Having a settled home, for three whole months, had been quite an experience in her young life. And meeting her uncle and aunt for the first time, down there on that lonely beach, had been quite an experience, too.

Real family. Even at that tender age she had stopped thinking of her parents as family at all. They had always excluded her, her father wrapped up in his work, her mother wrapped up in him, perfectly content to hand her over like an unwanted package to whoever could be hired, or persuaded, to keep an eye on her for an hour, a day, or a week or two.

And her uncle and aunt had come halfway across the world to see her, tired of merely hearing about her in the scrappy and very occasional letters from her mother. It had made her feel beautifully important. And for four lovely weeks they had played with her, cuddled her, made sure she had proper meals at regular intervals, tucked her up in bed and told her stories until she fell asleep. For the first time in her young life she had felt she mattered to someone. When they had returned to England she had grieved.

And if the little she had told him merely served to reinforce his low opinion of her morals then what did she care?

But he said, his voice deceptively mild, 'Did it ever occur to you to keep yourself? You spend your life skimming around the world, from what I can gather. Yet you're highly intelligent, fluent in six languages——'

'Who the hell told you that?' She was appalled that he should know even that much about her. The fact that he knew anything at all made her feel threatened! Quite why that should be so she couldn't work out, and now wasn't the time to try, especially when he reached out for her hand, took it and turned it palm upwards as if trying to see her future in it.

'Alex, who else?' He gave her a glinting underbrow look and she snatched her hand away. So he'd been plying her uncle with questions as well as strong liquor while she'd been innocently freshening up. 'Does it matter? It's not a state secret, is it?'

'No, of course not,' she said stiffly, and got quickly to her feet. 'But what I do with my own life is my business.'

'It could be mine, too. Think about it while I walk you to your room.'

'How can I think about it, if I haven't the least idea what you're talking about?' she came back hoarsely, wishing quite hopelessly that she'd never allowed herself to get into this mess.

The house was utterly silent. Just the sound of their measured footsteps and the thunderous beat of her heart. She was quite sure he must be able to hear it and would put it down to raging sexual excitement, or something just as degrading. And he said softly, a smile in his voice, 'Of course you do.' His hand slipped round her waist as she stumbled on shamingly weak and unsteady legs at the top of the stairs. 'I've already said you intrigue me. And as I'm always honest, or at least I try to be, I'll admit that I want you.' His arm tightened around her waist as he swung her round, and the way his eyes probed hers, as if he could see something that was a secret even from herself, took her breath away. 'And if you'll stop pretending you don't feel the same we could begin to make progress.'

Fen was stunned, almost too dizzy to speak. But she forced herself, pushing at him with her hands bunched into fists.

'Stop mauling me! Is this how you get your women? No wonder none of them can stomach your company for more than a couple of days!'

For a moment he looked nonplussed and then he smiled grimly, subduing her useless struggles by wrapping his arms around her, his mouth a whisper away from hers as he murmured, 'Don't believe all the rumours you hear, Fen. You know nothing about my private life. But you will, you'll be part of it.' His voice thickened. His hands shaped her back, rising to her shoulders and down again, cupping her taut buttocks, scorching her skin through the silk of her dress. She was boneless and breathless, giddy and confused. She didn't know what was happening to her, why she should allow him such liberties. Quite probably, she thought wildly, she was going mad!

'Shall I show you how much you want to be part of my life, Fen?' His voice was a seduction in itself. She tried not to hear him but that was impossible. 'Shall I prove it to you, beyond any shadow of doubt?' His lips brushed hers. They were sweet, like honey, burning like a flame. She thought she was going to die. 'Shall I, Fen?'

She moaned thickly. He had relaxed his hold on her, his body brushing hers from her breasts to her thighs. It was torment. A sob of deep repudiation built up inside her, making her voice disgracefully thick as she managed, 'No! Don't!'

He thought she was easy, anybody's—providing the price was right! And the only way she could get herself out of this hateful mess was by telling him the truth, spelling out exactly how she and Alex had set out to get him back in the public eye, convince everyone that he wasn't a boring old has-been but a man in his prime, capable of attracting and holding female attention.

She had never liked the idea but never, in her wildest nightmares, could she have imagined it would rebound on her like this!

Just being seen with Alex at fashionable night-spots and restaurants would have been enough to boost his image and titillate the interest of female viewers. That was what Jean had said. And now look what had happened!

But she couldn't run the risk of explaining to Saul. He would believe, quite rightly, that he'd been made a fool of. And his monumental ego would demand revenge. Nothing would save Alex's programme if that happened!

And what would save her if she didn't? she thought wildly. The hateful man only had to touch her to take every last one of her senses by storm, to drive her customary cool composure deep underground and make her forget every single one of her firmly held principles.

He terrified her!

'You're quite right, Fen.' He released her, his hands sliding away slowly, with aching reluctance. 'Not with Alex under the same roof.' He made an abrupt, dismissive gesture with one hand. 'When I've squared it with him I'll move in for the kill.' The same hand lifted to trail slowly over her cheekbone to the corner of her mouth. His silver eyes gleamed, his lips curving wickedly. 'I'll make you admit you want me as much as I want you.'

Fen twisted her head away, her heart thundering mercilessly as she tried to armour her self-betraying senses against the silken threat of his touch, the things he was saying. And she saw him smile, intimately, as if they were sharing a delicious secret, her eyes going wide with something that was shamingly more than disbelief as he opened the door to the bedroom she'd been given, flicking on the lights and then walking away without another word.

Jerkily, she dived into the room and closed the door, locking it behind her. She was shaking all over, her breath coming in jagged, uneven gasps.

Relief, she told herself a little desperately. Just that. Relief that she had survived this evening relatively unscathed.

The man was a devil; she wouldn't be at all surprised if the elegant, hand-crafted leather shoes he wore covered cloven feet!

Normally, of course, she would have been able to handle him with as much cool indifference as she handled any man who tried to make a pass at her. Saul Ackerman wasn't in any way special, or different. And the fact that he had sent her haywire, made her experience sensations that were as previously unknown as they were unwanted, was nothing to do with him personally. It was the situation that was out of the normal, the games she and Alex had been playing, her inability to put him straight about her morals—or supposed lack of them—without landing her uncle in the soup. That was why the loathsome Saul Ackerman had been able to shake her composure. Nothing else.

'We have to leave. Right now, Alex,' Fen hissed into her uncle's ashen face as she smartly exited her room. 'If Mrs Pringle offers you breakfast, refuse.'

At the mention of breakfast Alex's face turned a delicate shade of green but he did manage, 'But Saul—I can't just walk out without——'

'He left hours ago,' Fen said tightly, wishing her uncle could make himself move just a little faster than a geriatric snail. She was sure their host had left just before nine. She'd been awake for hours, her ears straining until they ached. She'd heard firm, decisive steps moving down the corridor outside her room at around eight and three-quarters of an hour later the sound of a car engine, tyres scattering gravel on the drive. And then the drone of vacuum cleaners, then nothing until those slow, shambling steps approaching her room.

And who knew when Saul was due back? She couldn't face him. She wouldn't face him! As far as he was concerned it was a case of out of sight, out of mind. And the sooner they were off his premises, the sooner she would be able to forget his very existence.

'I'll drive,' she asserted firmly as she chivvied Alex down the stairs and out into the sunlight. He groaned and screwed his eyes shut against the glare but Fen growled, 'If you don't hurry I'll leave you here and you can darned well walk home!' treating him like a naughty child because she could be tougher and more determined than most when it was a matter of her survival.

And although she wasn't prepared to question herself too closely she knew that her survival depended on never seeing Saul Ackerman again!

CHAPTER FIVE

TOMORROW couldn't come soon enough!

Fen finished the dusting and mooched through into the kitchen to make coffee, wondering whether to spend the day in town or simply curl up with a good book.

Apart from being an ancient market town nestling comfortably beneath the frowning mass of Dartmoor, with a history stretching back a thousand years, Tavistock, as she knew, had a fine covered pannier market where one could buy anything from a cushion to a cod fish and, even more temptingly, there was a newly opened and exceptionally good boutique, or so Jean had told her. And Fen itched to go shopping. She always did when she was miserable or on edge. Other women might munch through pounds of chocolate, or fall on the gin bottle; she went shopping.

But she couldn't really afford to indulge herself, not and stay solvent, and her next job wasn't until the end of June when she was due in Milan to translate a book of children's modern fables into English for an Italian publishing company. The trouble with accepting only work she really enjoyed was the occasional shortage of funds. Which could mean that if she didn't harbour her resources she might have to take on a stint of private language tuition, her least favourite means of earning her bread because it meant staying put for longer than she was comfortable with, she thought gloomily as she waited for the kettle to boil.

So shopping was out. And in any case, there was no reason on earth why she should feel despondent and edgy, was there? She and Alex between them had sorted everything out.

She'd been very near to panic when she'd driven her uncle away from Saul Ackerman's home yesterday. She who never panicked, who took life and turned it into something that suited her, who did her own thing and was accountable to no one, panicking because a man had said he wanted her! She dismayed herself!

She would have preferred to drive through the afternoon to reach the relative safety of Hampstead. But Alex, slumped in the passenger seat had groaned pathetically, 'Not Hampstead. I can't sit in the car for hours. We'll stay in Tavi. God, I made a fool of myself last night! He'll think I'm a lush. Did he say anything to you? No—don't tell me! I need to get back to bed. And quick. It'll be a week before I feel human again!'

So the Tavistock house it had been, and was, and Alex's dire prognosis had proved incorrect because when he'd come down to breakfast this morning he'd looked perfectly human again, his heavy eyes the only sign of his unaccustomed drinking session.

'Am I forgiven?' He'd accepted his toast and coffee with chastened gratitude.

'Of course. You're entitled to kick over the traces once in a while. But I've been thinking...' She had been, all night, or so it seemed. 'I don't believe there's any point in our going back to Town again and haunting the fashionable night-spots on the off-chance we'll be photographed together. I know we said we'd give it a couple of weeks before I slid off the face of the earth and you went back to Jean. But——'

'I know.' He cut her short and patted her hand across the breakfast-table. 'You never liked the idea, but once you'd agreed you threw yourself whole-heartedly into the part and for that alone Jean and I will always be grateful. And I agree with you. I've no stomach for it now, either. And, whatever decision is reached regarding my future with VisionWest, more scandalous publicity isn't going to make a jot of dif-ference.' He swallowed his orange juice and then his coffee and poured himself another of both, looking better by the second. 'I'll drive into Plymouth this morning; I've an idea there's a board meeting and there's a chance Saul will be there. I need to see him and apologise for my lapse and the way we left without so much as a thank-you. I'd offer to take you along, too, but I don't think it would be wise. From the way he was questioning me about you the other evening I've got the feeling his interest is more than merely academic. I told him as little as I could, of course, without seeming to snub him. But the less you see of him the better, I think.'

He was getting ready to leave, pulling on his suit jacket and patting his pockets to find his car keys. And Fen went very still, a shiver icing its way down her spine.

'What do you mean?' Her voice came out sounding tinny.

Alex shook his head at her wryly.

'It's not hard to tell when a man fancies a woman, Fen, only you're such an innocent, you probably wouldn't have picked it up. And despite his looks, not to mention all that wealth and power, a fling with him is not what I'd prescribe for you. He's tough and he's bitter. Not the type I want around my little girl.'

'And never seen with the same woman twice,' Fen supplied stiffly, feeling sick inside.

A relative innocent she might be when it came to intimate relationships with the opposite sex, but Saul had left her in no doubt at all that he wanted her and meant to have her.

But she couldn't tell Alex that. He was as protective of her as if she had been his own daughter and he would go straight to Saul and admit the deception, tell him that his niece was not that kind of woman, was not the type to indulge in lustful flings between the sheets with any man who cared to ask. And in doing so he would make Saul feel a fool, an importuning fool, and could wave any hopes of a renewed contract away. So she would cope with it on her own, make herself scarce until Alex had received the decision the director of programmes had promised. And she wasn't really listening when Alex answered her.

'That's more or less true. But it doesn't mean he's sleeping with them. He keeps his private life to himself. Even when his marriage was breaking up he didn't betray a thing. And on the day after his wife died he was back in harness as if nothing had happened.'

Then, seeing the sudden, stinging attention, the stunned pallor of her face, he shrugged. 'That's hearsay, of course. I'd never met him until the consortium he headed won the franchise. But it comes from a reliable source.' He smiled, attempting to lighten the atmosphere. 'Not that it matters. You're not likely to see him again. And even if you did, forewarned is forearmed, as they say. So.' He straightened his tie. 'What are you going to do with yourself today?'

His wife was dead and he hadn't blinked an eye! What had she died of? A broken heart and disillusionment? He was more than a sex-mad bastard—he was evil! Gathering herself, Fen began to stack the used breakfast china, forcing herself to answer lightly, 'I'll get my things together—I'll pick up the stuff I left at Hampstead in a week or two—and hire a car. I thought I'd go down to the cottage and clear it out, ready to put it on the market. I'll drive down tomorrow.'

Out of that devil's way. Always presuming he'd meant what he'd said about squaring things with Alex to leave the way clear for him to show her how much she wanted him! The ratfink! The evil, callous louse!

'No need to hire a car, Fen. Save your money. I'll drive you down. A couple of days on the coast sounds good to me, too. I'll sort out any business at the studios and then we can both lie low. I'll give you a hand at the cottage, see you're properly provisioned and drive up to Edinburgh until Jean's ready to come back. We'll both come down and pick you up when you're ready to leave.'

So no, she couldn't wait until tomorrow.

She stared broodingly at the mug of coffee on the work surface. She didn't want it, so why had she made it? Then the phone rang and she went through to the sitting-room to answer it, relieved because she had something to do. It was probably Jean and they could have a nice long natter. But dismay sent her stomach plummeting down to her shoes and back up into her throat as Saul Ackerman said, 'I need to see you. I'll pick you up at eight this evening and give you dinner. It's up to you whether you tell Alex where you'll be.'

'No.' She snapped the word out without having to think about it at all. His arrogance took her breath away. She would have slammed the receiver down because just hearing him speak put her in turmoil, but he said quietly, 'I have something to discuss with you, regarding Alex and his future with VisionWest, and I refuse to do it over the phone. Eight o'clock.'

'No.' But this time not quite so decisively. He was threatening Alex's future, through her. She didn't have the right to refuse to listen to him, regardless. Not when it was her uncle who would have to pay the price. But dinner? Probably not here in Tavistock, either, but in the more intimate setting of his lovely home. 'Lunch,' she temporised.

'If you say so.' He sounded faintly amused, as if he had been tuned in to the thoughts that had scurried through her brain, and she pushed in warily.

'And not at your home, either.' She couldn't stand to be alone with him there. He shouldn't be allowed to live in such a breathtakingly lovely place. It was like plucking a perfect blossom and finding a hairy black spider deep in the heart of the scented petals.

'Scared, Fen?' She could hear him smiling, damn him! 'Don't be. I'll pick you up in a couple of hours.'

Which would make it around one o'clock, she thought as the line went dead. She wiped her sweaty palms down the sides of her jeans. There was no need to feel quite so nervous. He couldn't make her do a thing she didn't want to do.

But telling herself that didn't help because he had already forced her to agree to have lunch with him! Groaning, she wondered whether she should use the next couple of hours shopping for something for supper. There was nothing in the fridge. But she felt far too unsettled to concentrate on buying meat and vegetables. Besides, her hair was a mess and needed washing, and she had to ferret out something suitably restrained to wear...

She didn't have a lot of choice but she eventually settled for black leggings topped by a loose-fitting, silky black T-shirt that came down to her thighs. She looked, she congratulated herself, like a beanpole. And the spiky black heels she was wearing merely emphasised the effect. Not even the sex-mad Saul Ackerman could find a black beanpole alluring!

Not bothering with make-up—just a hint of copper-toned lipstick—she flicked a comb through her newly washed hair, the thick golden fringe bouncing against her eyebrows. Then she was as ready as she would ever be for the coming ordeal.

But, as the fingers of the clock in the guest room moved nearer to one, her heart began to hammer against her breastbone, her stomach tying itself in knots. And she knew she wouldn't have been quite this nervous if he hadn't told her not to be! She didn't trust him, with very good reason. And although she had no idea what he wanted to discuss—or only loosely in that it was to do with Alex's professional future—she tried to comfort herself with the thought that there was very little he could do to her over a lunch table, in full view of all the other people around.

But even that small solace was denied her when the imperious ring of the doorbell had her stalking fatalistically down the stairs. He handed her into the sleekly expensive perfection of his car and gestured to a tote bag on the back seat.

'I had Prinny pack us a picnic. I thought we'd go up to the edge of the moors.' And he whisked her away before she could begin to object.

Slumping in her seat, Fen wondered when luck would start running with her, instead of against her. The way he looked didn't help, either. A soft-as-butter fawn leather jacket covered a black T-shirt and snug-fitting black denims. The formal authority of the hard-eyed business giant had been sloughed off along with his impeccable formal suits, making him appear younger, more approachable. Someone she could relate to. Like. Like?

Utter nonsense! How could she ever come near to liking such a man? A man who hadn't turned a hair when his wife died. Even if their marriage had been on the rocks he should have felt some grief and regret.

She slanted him a withering sideways glare and caught her breath. It was still there, all right; all the authority in the world was stamped on that austerely impressive profile. How could she have imagined that the casual clothes could make a scrap of difference?

She looked away quickly, not seeing anything through the window at her side, brooding darkly to herself as he negotiated Tavistock's one-way system. And only when they were heading for the open road did she negotiate a shaky way through the atmosphere of unbelievably forceful awareness that smouldered between them in the intimate confines of the car by muttering at him, 'I'm not dressed for tramping on the moors. And I'm not hungry, either. So why don't you pull into the next lay-by and tell me what this is all in aid of?' She had no intention of spending the long afternoon with him on the empty moors, with only the silent and vaguely sinister standing stones to keep them company, the great purple masses of the high moors crowding against the skyline, shutting her in. With him.

Fen shuddered with chilling remembrance.

She'd been fourteen and too adventurous for her own good. Six years before, when she'd been around eight, her parents had bought the cottage on the Cornish coast, west of Polperro, largely, she believed, because Alex and Jean had hounded them into having somewhere that could loosely be called a home base, for her sake.

Until she'd finally cut loose from her parents, able to fend for herself, she had spent several weeks each summer there. Sometimes her parents had come along, too, and sometimes not. It depended on whether her father could tear himself away from wherever he hap-

pened to be on the planet. But Alex and Jean had
always been there, without fail, and they'd made it a
family holiday, reinforcing the bonds that had been
forged on that beach in Jamaica.

But for a few weeks of the summer when she was
fourteen they'd all been there together. The atmosphere between her and her parents hadn't been good.
In fact it had been rotten, with her father laying the
law down and her mother backing him up and Fen
alternatively raging or sulking.

They had decided she was to spend the next two
years in an English boarding-school, spending her
holidays with Alex and Jean. Fen hadn't objected to
that part. But boarding-school? Staying in one place
for two whole years?

Moving from place to place with her parents, from
country to country as her father researched his travel
books, had become her way of life. Attending local
schools wherever they happened to be, picking up
languages with no trouble at all, she had never known
any thing else and the foundations had been well and
truly laid for a footloose existence. She would never
put down roots, and certainly not in an English
boarding-school!

Out of humour with the whole world—even the
people she loved most in the world, Alex and Jean,
had been on her parents' side—she had taken the bike
she kept in the shed and had set off at dawn for the
moors. Bodmin Moor.

She hadn't bothered to check the weather forecast
or take extra clothing. All she'd been interested in was
a day of freedom, away from the adults who seemed

set on making her do the thing she least wanted to do. But freedom had turned into a prison when the mist had come down, disorientating her, turning Bodmin into a vast tract of isolation and danger.

It had been long, cold, miserable hours later before she had stumbled on to a deserted and definitely minor road, more by luck than by judgement. Too exhausted even to think of tackling the long ride home, she had trudged on until she'd stumbled across a roadside cottage where she'd begged the use of a phone.

It had been Jean who had fetched her in the Land Rover, complete with blankets and forceful remonstrances. Didn't she know how foolhardy it was to go. so far on her own? Bodmin, too! Even if by the time she'd cycled there she hadn't had the energy to penetrate much beyond the edges of all that wildness, it had been a stupid thing to do! Didn't she care that they had all been worried witless because she'd been missing all day, leaving no clue to where she might have gone?

'You're fourteen years old and capable of making your own decisions—or so you keep telling us!' Jean had remarked sternly. 'Yet you behaved with about as much common sense as a four-year-old today. Don't you think the adults who care about you know what's best for your future?'

Fen had known what she was talking about, of course. That wretched boarding-school. And although she had doubts about her parents, she knew Alex and Jean loved her and cared about her future. So, on that day, she had given in, accepted parental dictates. And, amazingly, hadn't regretted it.

But she had been left with a fear of the moors. And
the Devon moors would be much the same as the
Cornish Bodmin. And because Saul had ignored her
request that they stop at the next lay-by to discuss
whatever it was he wanted to say she repeated, 'I don't
fancy a moorland hike and a cheese buttie. Please pull
in to the side of the road.'

'Any time now,' he promised soothingly.

A sneaked sideways glance revealed the amused
quirk of his mouth. She'd been right he was laughing
at her. Finding her strictures funny because he had
every intention of doing exactly as he pleased, and
planned. Regardless. She shuddered, and put the reaction down to memories of another time, another
moor.

But Dartmoor today was smiling, rolling green and
gold beneath the endless soft blue sky and Saul eased
the car off the road and on to a narrower, stony track,
then, where the track dipped, off on to the short,
springy grass, and cut the engine, turning to her.

'The best of both worlds—just for you. The benefits of the view and the air without having to walk
more than a yard on your four-inch heels.'

Twisting her reasons for objecting to the outing.
He had to know she wouldn't willingly share a thing
with him—a view, a picnic, whatever.

He was a manipulator, almost too self-assured to
be believable, and the only way she could hope to
combat him was to stay exactly where she was, glued
to the leather upholstery, until he recognised the fu-
tility of having brought her here and headed back
to Tavistock.

But now that the car was stationary it was impossible to stay cooped up inside with him. Impossible. The smouldering awareness was growing, assuming terrifying proportions. With a soft anguished gasp she reached for the door release and scrambled out, taut as a bowstring as the early summer sun stroked her tense body, pulling in steadying breaths while she waited for him to join her.

'Couldn't be more tranquil, could it?' He came to stand beside her, carrying a soft woollen blanket and the bag. Even wearing her highest heels the top of her head only reached a fraction above the level of his wide, rangy shoulders. She took a teetering step away, her breath coming raggedly despite all her attempts to stay calm and in control. Was he trying to impress their isolation on her? Only a few hundred yards away from the road she knew was back there somewhere, they might as well be alone in the great sprawling loneliness of the moors. He had no need to hammer home the obvious!

'You said you had something to discuss,' she pointed out, turning away as he draped the rug on the ground and shrugged out of his leather jacket. The soft black T-shirt clung altogether too lovingly to his impressive torso. He was in peak condition, superbly fit. She couldn't look!

'So I have. But let's be civilised about it, and eat first.' She felt his eyes on her and shivered.

She wouldn't be able to eat a thing, but the more she tried to push him into telling her what he had wanted to talk to her about, the more he would resist.

Just for the hell of it, just to let her know he was in charge. Now and always.

No, not always, she contradicted herself. Only until Alex's future with VisionWest had been decided. When Laurence Meek had made his decision Saul Ackerman wouldn't see her for dust!

Grudgingly, she sat on the very edge of the rug, staring into the distance, and he said softly, 'I don't bite, Fen. Or only when provoked.'

She shot him an unguarded look from beneath her fringe and met that mocking, slanting smile, felt the power of those silver eyes latch on to her own and couldn't look away, not even when he added warningly, 'So try not to provoke me. At least, not until we've eaten.'

'I . . .' Her voice was too thick, her mouth too dry. She couldn't get a word out, couldn't look away. Did he fascinate every woman he met . . . ? Did he have that much power . . . ?

'Drink this.' He put a can of Coke into her nerveless hands, dealing with the ring-pull for her, his fingers touching hers, scorching them. Fen pulled away, her golden eyes mirroring panic, and his smile was carelessly amused although, she noted shakily, his eyes were speculative.

She moistened her lips with the tip of her tongue, desperate to find the words that would make him understand he didn't impress her, or scare her. But nothing would come and she lifted the can to her mouth, hiding her hopeless inadequacy, unable to murmur even the smallest acknowledgement when he handed her a fat Cornish pastie wrapped in a heavy linen napkin.

She had made a scathing reference to cheese butties but privately had expected his offering to be more of the caviare and champagne variety. But the simple, wholesome food was not going to make her change any of her denigrating opinions of him.

But she did begin to relax, just a little, helped by a cheery greeting from a group of hikers who came down the track, heavy boots clattering on the stones. She watched them tramp away, and even when they had disappeared into the distance she no longer felt quite so isolated, relaxed enough now to draw her knees up to her chin and squint sideways at Saul as he flopped down full-length on his side, propping his dark head up on one curving hand.

'Do you have any deep feelings for Alex at all?' Asked with impeccable politeness, his question took her breath away. Just for a moment she had been beginning to unwind, enjoy the play of the soft warm air on her face, the silence which had, to her retrospective astonishment, turned companionable and easy.

How to answer? Truthfully, or in character? Bearing in mind the scandalous lies she and her uncle had planted inside Saul's head, and the fact that after tomorrow the so-called affair would be over, with Alex going to Edinburgh to be with Jean once he had helped her settle in at the cottage, proving to Joe Public that his heart belonged to his wife, and no one else, Fen opted for answering in character.

'He's quite a guy. Great fun, and sexy with it.' The words tasted foul in her mouth, and she couldn't look at him. If their so-called affair was supposed to be a thing of small substance, as it must be if he were to 'return' to his wife after so short a fling, then she couldn't admit to more.

It was an utterly hateful situation to be in! And made doubly so when Saul said, a tinge of deep disgust in his voice, 'He's much too old for you. But I suppose that doesn't matter to you, so long as he can show you a good time and pay the bills.'

'You're disgusting!' Fen rounded on him furiously, remembering, too late, that she and Alex, aided by the gutter Press, had put that idea in his head. He wasn't to blame, they were!

Her eyes fell, thrown into confusion by the derisory gleam in that clever silver gaze. And she mumbled, dropping her chin to her knees again and sheltering her bright head with her arms, 'It's not like that. You can't begin to understand.' And that was the truth, but feeble. Why wasn't she telling him to mind his own damn business? Why wasn't she stalking back to the car with her head held high, demanding to be taken back to town?

Suddenly, Fen didn't understand herself at all and it made her feel confused and miserable; there was a wretched lump in her throat, forbidding any hope of vocal reaction, when he said softly, 'Then make me understand, Fen. Tell me how it is.'

She simply shook her buried head, her eyes tightly closed against her leggings-clad knees, and when she felt the brush of his fingers against the exposed and vulnerable nape of her neck she went into shock.

It had to be shock; nothing else could explain why she endured his touch. Endured the caress that found the sensitive hollow behind her ear and slid down the fragile curve of her neck to tuck in beneath the neckline of her T-shirt. Shock that set up the quivering chain reaction inside her, holding her weak and immobile, then making her gasp as his arms snaked around her, pulling her down on to the rug beside him, keeping her there by the power of the ruthless need she saw glinting in his eyes.

Fighting back shameful excitement, she said huskily, 'Let me go, damn you!' and saw his mouth curl in a tight feral smile as he answered with dark menace,

'Only when you really want me to.' And he slid his hand beneath the hem of her T-shirt, gliding upwards to close possessively over one firmly peaked naked breast and then its twin, his thumb rolling tellingly over her revealingly taut nipples, his actions making her fully understand where his words had failed.

Fen moaned, her mind in anguish. That decidedly independent mind of hers rebelled at the thought of his effortless sexual domination. But, with his own special brand of dark, masculine magic, he made her female body crave to surrender to his potency.

'Don't fight it, Fen,' he murmured, those silver eyes heavy-lidded now with desire. His hand smoothed a honeyed track down over the soft swell of her stomach, which feathered with a treachery that matched the traitorous need deep inside her beneath the waistband of her leggings. 'You want me; your body gives you away. Tell me you don't and you'll be telling me you're a liar.'

'No!'

Her head thrashed heavily, spilling bright hair against the soft dark wool of the rug, her body alive with shaming pleasure, her breath rushing out of her lungs as he brought his dark head down to hers, his mouth a statement of male sensuality, his kiss a foregone conclusion as he whispered heavily, 'Don't turn a simple physical attraction into a three-act drama, Fen. There's no problem. Leave Alex and come to me.'

CHAPTER SIX

THE kiss seemed to go on forever. It was the only reality. Fen was breathless and giddy and the more thoroughly Saul kissed her, the more her lips clung to his, aching for their repossession when he briefly lifted his head, inviting her, or so it seemed, to drown in the slumbrous depths of his suddenly darkened eyes.

There was, she recognised with a tiny gasp, complete physical rapport between then, a drugging sensation of oneness that made her whole body ache for his possession. Madness, but a magical madness that had nothing to do with logic. Her fingers tightened on his shoulders, digging into hard muscle and bone, and he dipped his head, reading her message, and her eyelids fluttered down on a sigh as his mouth brushed hers, tantalising, teasing, opening her lips and sipping at the inner sweetness.

She had never felt like this before, weak and filled with wickedly desirous sensation, clinging to him as if he were the only reality in her universe. Nothing had prepared her for this. Nothing. Certainly not Ray's clumsy lovemaking. That had left her feeling nothing but embarrassment and distaste, leavened just briefly with regret, a hint of sadness, because all that talk of love, of the physical wonder that could exist ween a man and a woman, was nothing but a fable,

PLAY
HARLEQUIN'S

LUCKY HEARTS

GAME

AND YOU GET

★ **FREE BOOKS**

★ **A FREE GIFT**

★ **AND MUCH MORE**

TURN THE PAGE AND
DEAL YOURSELF IN →

PLAY "LUCKY HEARTS" AND YOU GET ...

★ **Exciting Harlequin Presents® novels—FREE**

★ **PLUS a Lovely Simulated Pearl Drop Necklace—FREE**

THEN CONTINUE YOUR LUCKY STREAK WITH A SWEETHEART OF A DEAL

1. Play Lucky Hearts as instructed on the opposite page.
2. Send back this card and you'll receive brand-new Harlequin Presents® novels. These books have a cover price of $3.50 each, but they are yours to keep absolutely free.
3. There's no catch. You're under no obligation to buy anything. We charge nothing — ZERO — for your first shipment. And you don't have to make any minimum number of purchases — not even one!
4. The fact is thousands of readers enjoy receiving books by mail from the Harlequin Reader Service. They like the convenience of home delivery...they like getting the best new novels months BEFORE they're available in stores...and they love our discount prices!
5. We hope that after receiving your free books you'll want to remain a subscriber. But the choice is yours — to continue or cancel, anytime at all! So why not take us up on our invitation, with no risk of any kind. You'll be glad you did!

©1991 HARLEQUIN ENTERPRISES LIMITED.

NOT ACTUAL SIZE

*This lovely necklace will add glamour to your most elegant outfit! Its cobra-link chain is a generous 18" long, and its lustrous simulated cultured pearl is mounted in an attractive pendant! Best of all, it's **absolutely free**, just for accepting our no-risk offer.*

HARLEQUIN'S

With a coin— scratch off the silver card and check below to see what we have for you.

106 CIH A6PC (U-H-P-01/97)

YES! I have scratched off the silver card. Please send me all the free books and gift for which I qualify. I understand that I am under no obligation to purchase any books, as explained on the back and on the opposite page.

DETACH AND MAIL CARD TODAY

_____

NAME

_____

ADDRESS   APT.

_____

CITY   STATE   ZIP

Twenty-one gets you 4 free books, and a free simulated pearl drop necklace

Twenty gets you 4 free books

Nineteen gets you 3 free books

Eighteen gets you 2 free books

Offer limited to one per household and not valid to current Harlequin Presents® subscribers. All orders subject to approval.

© 1991 HARLEQUIN ENTERPRISES LIMITED.   **PRINTED IN U.S.A.**

THE HARLEQUIN READER SERVICE®: HERE'S HOW IT WORKS

Accepting free books places you under no obligation to buy anything. You may keep the books and gift and return the shipping statement marked "cancel". If you do not cancel, about a month later we'll send you 6 additional novels, and bill you just $2.90 each plus 25¢ delivery per book and applicable sales tax, if any.* That's the complete price—and compared to cover prices of $3.50 each—quite a bargain! You may cancel at any time, but if you choose to continue, every month we'll send you 6 more books, which you may either purchase at the discount price…or return to us and cancel your subscription.

*Terms and prices subject to change without notice. Sales tax applicable in N.Y.

If offer card is missing, write to: Harlequin Reader Service, 3010 Walden Ave, P.O. Box 1867, Buffalo, NY 14240-1867

BUSINESS REPLY MAIL
FIRST-CLASS MAIL   PERMIT NO. 717   BUFFALO, NY

POSTAGE WILL BE PAID BY ADDRESSEE

HARLEQUIN READER SERVICE
3010 WALDEN AVE
PO BOX 1867
BUFFALO NY 14240-9952

NO POSTAGE
NECESSARY
IF MAILED
IN THE
UNITED STATES

ocal people had wrested a living of
a. The tiny village itself was a scant
, up the steep narrow track, taking
shelter of the gentle, wooded hills
view. The only indication that it was
l plume of smoke from some of the
g up through the trees.

uld be a pity to see the cottage sold,
he pushed open the front door and
e great slabs of granite that covered
d floor. She had spent some won-
ummer here as a child with her uncle
holidays had been the one constant
ears, the cottage the only place that
ar to resembling a permanent home.
d come near it during the last couple
ean and Alex, who had driven down
e to check on it. Her mother would
n and she, Fen, had no use for a base.
dn't afford to buy it from her mother.
st couple of days she and Alex had
ouse, flinging the windows wide and
worst of the accumulation of dust.
ocked up with enough provisions to
two weeks. If she ran short of any-
had to clamber up the lane to the
ad nothing to distract her from the

of the twisty, uncarpeted stairs she
room she had chosen to use during
a child she had been consigned to
ttle bigger than a cupboard, while

stood where she was, the shock of the insult making
her feel as if she'd just been flattened by a ten-ton
truck.

Wildly, her eyes searched his features, looking in
vain for some hint of redeeming sanity behind his
motivations. And when he added drily, 'However, I
am sure you will find compensations,' her sense of
outrage was complete and she slid her long legs into
the car and informed him haughtily,

'Don't bank on it. You may be used to buying your
women—it's probably the only way you can get them.
But I can't, and won't, be bought. Or blackmailed.
And if you ever manage to grow a heart, ever begin
to understand that there's more to a relationship than
a quick tumble, give me a call and I'll see if I'm
available.'

And that, she decided with a strange dredging sensation around the region of her heart, was that.
Judging by the thick black silence as he drove back
to town, he would never even contemplate having
anything to do with her ever again.

'Now, you're sure you'll be all right? You've got
everything you need?'

'Of course I'm sure.' She had space and freedom
and solitude, which was all her muddled mind craved
at the moment. Fen leaned forward to kiss her uncle's
cheek, moving back from the open car window as he
started the engine. 'Drive carefully. And be sure to
make an overnight stop—no trying to drive to
Scotland in one go!'

He grinned at her. 'We'll phone you in a couple of weeks, when we're back in Tavi. And we'll come and fetch you just as soon as you've finished here.' And then he was gone, the car bumping up the precipitous, narrow lane which had grass growing all down the middle and big shaggy hedgerows that encroached on either side.

They had been at the cottage for the best part of two days and he couldn't wait to get to Edinburgh to be with Jean. They had missed each other dreadfully. Although childless, theirs was a marriage many would envy. The exception rather than the rule, Fen dismissed too easily as she waved him out of sight.

Frowning, she kicked a pebble along the dusty track and stuffed her hands into the pockets of her jeans. Although her uncle had tried not to let it show, she knew he'd been worried about the renewal of his contract. Saul hadn't attended that board meeting, he'd confided, so he hadn't been able to have a word with him and convey his apologies for the way they'd driven away from his home without so much as a thank-you. But he'd left a note with his secretary, and hoped that would suffice.

And Fen hadn't had the nerve to tell him that she knew Saul had absented himself from that meeting, and why. That he had spent the time with her, trying to persuade her to become his mistress, offering a cast-iron contract for Alex as an extra inducement. And how could she possibly confess that the scathing things she'd said to Saul meant that a renewed contract was about the last thing Alex could look for?

It was all o—— brooded. If Sau—— lusted after her, b—— mistress who cou—— conditions were r—— happened.

If he had simply —— dalous reports in t—— himself and got all —— he would have just s—— not such a dull old —— confirm, watched the —— has-been' with those col—— thing would have gone——

And she wouldn't h—— discovered that she c—— wild, instinctive pas—— have continued to —— pendent life, relyin—— damn thing. But n——

But nothing!

Firming her m—— Ackerman, of w—— he had made h—— pushed open the —— callonia hedge —— breathed in the —— morning air. S—— to get on with ——

The stone c—— green hillside —— slate roof, an——

where once —— sorts from —— half a mile —— advantage —— and hidde—— there was —— chimneys——

In a w—— she thou—— stepped —— the ent—— ana-l—— in her —— had eve——

But n—— of years —— from tin—— never cor—— Besides, s——

During —— aired the l—— sweeping o—— And they h—— last for at l—— thing she o—— village. So s—— task in hand.

At the hea—— walked into th—— her stay here. —— the box room,

Jean and Alex had had what had been grandly termed
the guest room. This room had been used by her
parents whenever they had decided to spend time with
her here during those long-ago summers, and even
now she felt an interloper.

But that was nothing to get maudlin about. It was
nothing new. She had always felt an interloper in her
parents' lives. What she should be getting depressed
about right now was the heap of classy carriers stacked
guiltily at the bottom of the old-fashioned wardrobe!

When Saul had dropped her off in the centre of
Tavistock, at her terse request, she'd had nothing more
in mind than a quick trip to the market to buy fish
for supper. Only somehow she'd got side-tracked and
had ended up in the boutique Jean had told her about,
and, her state of mind being what it was after what
had happened up there on the moors, she had predictably gone on a wild spending spree. Her bank account would be empty and she would have to hunt
around for a private tuition job.

And it was all Saul Ackerman's fault! If he hadn't
got her into such a turmoil she wouldn't have suc-
cumbed to the panacea of impulse shopping. He ought
to be shot!

Muttering to herself, and still too guilty even to
think of unpacking those carriers, she stuck her head
in a dusty cupboard and began to sort through her
father's books and papers.

Unknown hours later, she was still at it, the things
she knew her mother would want kept stacked in a
neat pile on the floor, ready to be taken back to
Tavistock to be carefully packed for the long overseas

journey, the rubbish pushed into a bin bag. And this was only the start of it.

Wearily, Fen pushed her dusty fingers through her fringe and sat back on her heels, frowning just a little as the oncoming sound of a car engine broke the drowsy afternoon silence.

Not a local, for sure. If the villagers came down to the cove they came on foot, although they rarely did, seeming to prefer the busier delights of Polperro or Looe. So it had to be a car full of holiday-makers, though they were rare in this quiet area. Few of them ventured through the winding tangle of narrow lanes to the village above, and the precipitous track leading down to the tiny cove was enough to put anyone off.

Not giving the hapless adventurers another thought, she got stiffly to her feet and tried to ease her aching back. It was time for a break. Her throat was parched. And she was halfway down the stairs when she registered the silence again. The car had stopped. Or backed away up the track. Then she sighed resignedly as someone pounded heavily against the door.

Lost. Looking for directions. Or, as had once happened, asking if they could get a cup of tea. And whoever it was they needn't sound so irate about it. It wasn't her fault they'd landed up at the back of beyond instead of in some bustling holiday centre!

'I'm coming,' she muttered under her breath as the pounding began again, and tried not to scowl as she covered the distance to the door in a few long strides and pulled it open. The Cornish were known for their friendly hospitality and she didn't want to let her adopted county down by appearing to be anything less.

But her hastily assumed friendly smile died the death when she saw who was filling her doorstep, his elegantly cut business suit and gleaming handmade leather shoes looking totally out of place against the backdrop of exuberant escallonia.

'You!' Fen knew she sounded as if she was being strangled, but couldn't help it. After the things she had said to him she had never expected to see him again. But whether she had secretly hoped to see him again was brought into question by the way her heart wrenched painfully inside her, her pulses pounding out a wild drumbeat that made her gasp for breath, made her toes curl in her sensible canvas shoes.

He gave her a cool look, his features frozen. And his voice was pure ice as he drawled, 'So Alex learned some sense and decided to conduct his affair out of the limelight.' His narrowed eyes pierced the interior of the cottage. 'Secluded—even for a love-nest. Where is he?' He clipped the question out, almost rocking her back on her heels, and when she'd recovered she dragged in a very firm breath and set her mouth in a straight, ungiving line.

How could she have wondered if she had secretly been hoping to see him again? He was nothing but a waste of space as far as she was concerned.

Alex had once told her of an ancient Cornish saying, that the devil never ventured to cross the Tamar from England into Cornwall for fear of being caught and put in a Cornish pastie. Well, they'd been wrong. The devil was here, on her doorstep! And if she had her way she would make him into mincemeat!

'Well? he prompted impatiently, his brows thundering together in the face of her obduracy. 'Where is he?'

'Not here.' Her response was as clipped and cool as she could make it but her voice fractured as he brushed past her, striding into the living area and glaring around as if he expected to find Alex cowering behind one of the shabby but comfortable, overstuffed armchairs.

'You can't just barge into my home without so much as a by-your-leave!' Being around him was giving her lots of practice when it came to huffing and puffing she thought, half hysterically, as she noted the way one strongly marked brow drifted elegantly up towards his hairline. She braced herself to receive his scathing comment.

'So he set you up here, did he? Got the deeds safely stashed away, have you?' Cool eyes raked over the homey surroundings, the stack of logs Alex had carried in yesterday and piled up for her beside the open fireplace. 'I'd have thought a penthouse apartment in the glitter of big-city lights would have been more to your taste. But I can see the attraction of complete isolation—from his point of view.'

Fen had had more than enough. True, she had given him every reason to believe she was no better than she should be, but was there any need for him to insult her so often and so heavily? It was, she decided, pulling herself up to her not insignificant height, high time she put him right on one or two things.

'Alex isn't here, so you're wasting your time and mine. And this house belongs to my mother. I am here, at her request, to get it ready to go on the market. And I'm asking you to leave.'

Which earned her a long, level look, an almost imperceptible softening of that slashing mouth as he told her softly, 'And I'm not going.'

Which left her floundering, almost admiring his barefaced arrogance as she sought for a way to make him. She could always phone for the police to come and evict him, and she would have done if it weren't for her uncle and Saul's position of clout at VisionWest! As it was, she was left with nothing to say except a grouchy, 'What is it you want?'

She held her breath, a band tightening around her heart as the very walls seemed to close in on them, enforcing a dreadful intimacy, the air she was trying to breathe becoming a warm, smiling sigh of wicked amusement as, long, unendurable seconds later, he said predictably, 'You know what I want. I've told you often enough.'

WRITING TIME

CHAPTER SEVEN

'How did you find this place?' The question came out on a rush. Well, she had to say something. They couldn't just stand here, staring at each other! The fraught silence, the way Saul was looking at her, as if he had just accepted delivery of a new piece of property, was shredding Fen's nerves into tiny protesting pieces.

'It wasn't difficult. Alex didn't bother to cover his tracks.' Saul patted the breast pocket of his suit jacket, his smile unnerving her all over again. 'He left phone numbers and addresses where he could be contacted during the next fortnight with Meek's secretary. I tried here first. I imagined the Edinburgh address was insurance. He can't have been too sure of you, can he? He couldn't be certain of where he'd be, and he must be fairly desperate to hear that decision.'

He walked further into the room and Fen shuddered then held herself stiffly, refusing to let him see how his presence affected her. But he didn't come too near, seemingly more interested in the few framed watercolours on the walls, bought from a struggling and not very talented artist in St Ives simply because Jean had felt sorry for him.

'I heard Jean went to Edinburgh when your affair with her husband first hit the headlines. One of the tabloids stated she'd gone back to her mother.' He still seemed far more interested in the paintings than in her, or in what he was saying. His wide shoulders looked supremely relaxed, his dark head tilted slightly to one side, as if he was trying to see more in the watercolours than was immediately obvious at a casual glance.

Fen didn't trust this sudden mood of relaxation, the soft reasonableness of his tone. And she knew she was right when he swung round on his heels, his eyes almost crippling her with their searing silver intensity as he shot out the question, 'Did he go to Jean in Edinburgh?'

She nodded, unable to look away from those glittering eyes. Her heart was hammering like a wild thing. It would be a very long time indeed before she allowed herself to get into a situation like this again. An eternity, in fact.

But never mind, she fretfully consoled herself, in a short while it would be common knowledge that the straying Alex Fairbourne was 'reunited' with his wife. So letting Saul know that her uncle was already on his way back to Jean wouldn't hurt, surely?

She wanted the whole misguided deception over and done with so that she could get on with her life without Saul Ackerman verbally branding her as some kind of high-class prostitute. She wanted to be able to tell him the whole truth, but she couldn't. Not yet. Not until that decision had been reached.

Not that the truth could make any real difference, because the wicked, almost overwhelming attraction between them wasn't going anywhere. She just hated the way he viewed her.

And something of her turmoil must have shown on her face because he, the pitiless, found pity from somewhere and he asked, with just a softening trace of compassion, 'Did he go because he wanted to, or did you push him out? It won't be easy for you to admit it if he walked out on you and left you standing. But I'd be grateful for the truth.'

Fen stared at him blankly. What possible difference could it make to him? She pushed her hands into the pockets of her dusty old jeans as the wish that she weren't looking so unkempt and grubby came out of the blue.

'The decision was mutual,' she said, sounding breathless, catching his frown of impatience when he thought she wasn't going to answer. 'We parted on friendly terms.' And that was no lie. A couple of days to help her settle in here and then he'd be off up to Edinburgh. That was what they'd planned. And she couldn't remember a time when she and her uncle hadn't been friends.

And then, catching the gleam of triumph in his eyes, she saw the trap she had lobbed herself into. She should have been quicker on the uptake and burst into tears, and wailed, and said Alex had tossed her out because he had grown tired of her, and that she would never get over it, and her heart was breaking. And would he please go away and leave her alone to grapple with her grief . . .

Instead . . .

'Then it seems you and I have a whole lot of talking to do.'

Which wasn't what she wanted to hear. Because now that he thought her 'affair' with Alex was over he would see no reason why he shouldn't take the older man's place. She should have thought of that.

Suddenly the room seemed airless, despite the breeze moving the curtains at the open windows. Fen set her teeth and walked outside, sinking down on to the wooden bench seat which, together with the picnic table, took up most of the space in the tiny front garden.

She could hear the rush of the stream as it raced its way to the sea, deep in the gorge below the narrow lane, hear the gentle, summer sound of the sea itself as it murmured on the sandy shore and lapped against the rocks. But the hypnotic sounds, the warmth of the sun as it stroked her body through the cotton shirt she wore and shimmered green and gold against the opposite hillside, failed to soothe her.

Nothing could combat the spiralling inner tension, the feeling that she was being stalked by an expert hunter; that the predator had marked out his prey; that it was only a matter of time . . .

So when he followed her, as she had known he would, the urge to scream at him and throw things was almost uncontrollable. But she gritted her teeth and took hold of herself and, carefully not looking at him, suggested, 'I think you should go, don't you? I can think of nothing we need to talk about.' She held herself rigid with frustration because as an exercise in self-assertion it wasn't going to cut any ice with Saul Ackerman and she hated this feeling of shameful impotence.

'Can't you?' His voice was a dark drift of warm amusement, raising the fine hairs all over her body. He arranged himself in front of her, half sitting, half leaning against the table, his long elegantly clad legs stretched out, almost touching hers.

Giving away more than she knew, Fen twisted her legs away, tucking them safely out of his reach beneath the bench, flushing to her hairline as she saw the slow white grin that told her he'd noted her knee-jerk reaction.

'Relax,' he instructed, the silver eyes all smiles now. 'We'll talk when you're ready. There's no rush.'

Her ability to relax went out of sight when he was around. But she couldn't admit to that. It would re-inforce his opinion that he was in total charge; that, with the odd shove and push, he could make her do whatever he wanted her to do.

And they both knew what that was!

Forcing her eyes away from the terrifying appeal of his face, she fixed them on the horizon, the glimpse of bluey green sea that could be seen from here, glittering through the V-shaped opening between the opposing hillsides of the gorge where they ended in high granite cliffs.

'You might have all the time in the world, I haven't,' she told him stiffly. 'I'm not here on holiday, but to work.'

'Doing what? Sweeping chimneys?' The lazy curl of his voice told her he hadn't missed her filthy appearance, and he sounded as if it didn't matter, and suddenly it didn't matter to her, either, so when he tacked on, 'If you're working, maybe I could help,' she shot straight back, her mouth tugging up at the corners,

'What, in that suit?'

'That could be remedied. I could be home and back with a change of clothing in an hour.'

In that car, she didn't doubt it. But why couldn't she get it into his skull that she didn't want him anywhere near her?

'You'd be wasting your time.' She got to her feet, pretending to stifle a yawn, tapping her fingertips delicately against her perfectly even white teeth. Maybe if he thought he bored her senseless he would go away. His over-developed ego wouldn't be able to take that. 'Only I know which of my father's books and papers my mother would like to keep.'

She skirted him, trying not to look wary, more than half expecting him to put out a detaining hand. But his voice alone stopped her progress back inside the house. He didn't need to touch her at all.

'So you were telling the truth. Alex didn't set you up here. The cottage belongs to your parents?'

'My mother. I do have one, believe it or not. I didn't come down in a shower of rain.'

'I didn't imagine you did.' He pushed himself to his feet, his movements, as ever, contained and elegant. 'More like a shower of expensive perfume and starshine—despite the char-lady disguise. I thought you were lying, trying to paint the love-nest with an acceptable and homely coat of respectability.'

'I know you did.' Fen sighed. Would he always think bad things about her? A kept woman, a husband-stealer, a liar. Her soft mouth quivered but she bit down hard on her lower lip to stop it. What did it matter what he thought of her? She headed for the door, but he was there before her, barring the way.

'And she's not here? Your mother, I mean.' Narrowed eyes fastened on her mouth. The quivering started up all over again and Fen quickly dipped her head, staring at her feet because it was easier than watching the way he looked at her mouth—as if he was about to possess it with his own.

The temptation to lie, to say that yes, she was very much here, taking an afternoon nap, and would be waking at any moment, trotting down the stairs to demand an introduction, inviting him to tea and talking his head off, was very strong because it might just get rid of him.

But she knew she wouldn't lie to him, not even by omission as she had done in the past. Why deliberately set out to merit all those truly dreadful things he thought she was?

'She lives in Australia. Why the interest?'

'And your father?' He ignored her taut question, supplying another of his own. Fen gave him a bleak look. Did he never give up?

'He's dead.'

'I'm sorry.' The flare of sympathy in his eyes was the last straw. She didn't want it and wouldn't accept it. In any case, it had to be completely spurious.

'Don't be. We were never close. As far as he was concerned I was nothing more than a nuisance. Save your sympathy for my mother. She's having difficulty coming to terms with life without him!' She snapped her mouth shut, her face flooding with angry colour.

What in the name of sanity had made her sound off like that?

Her sterile relationship with her parents, particularly her father, was nobody's business but her own. She had never discussed it with anyone, not even with her uncle and aunt, because they had been there whenever Alex could spare the time from his busy schedule, watching the uncomfortable relationship at first hand, doing their best to compensate whenever they could. There had been no need actually to sit down and talk about it.

So what had possessed her? Why tell him?

'Excuse me.' Her voice was as tight as she could make it. 'You're in my way. I've got work to do. Close the gate on your way out.'

She had no very clear idea of what his reaction would be. But she certainly hadn't expected him to take her at her word. She had expected... She didn't know what. But not the sound of his car turning in the lane, the engine far too well-bred to sound in the least bit laboured as it soared away up the steep incline towards the village.

She hadn't expected him to go, to give in without a fight—no matter how laid-back and half-hearted that fight might have been. Suddenly aware that she was standing stock-still in the exact centre of the room, listening to the silence, she gave herself a mental shake and headed back upstairs.

So he had lost interest. So what? So deep joy and thank heavens—and all that stuff. She wasn't at all sure she could have trusted herself to keep him at arm's length if he had decided to put on the pressure, to subject her to his own special brand of arrogant, devilishly powerful persuasion.

He had come here, or so he had made it seem, with the express intention of talking to her. About what he hadn't said, but she would have guessed it would be more of the same—precise and, to him at least, logical reasons why she should become his mistress. But he had left without making her listen to a single thing.

Except that he had got a darn sight more out of her than she had ever intended giving.

Fen shivered, suddenly cold. She walked over to the chest of drawers and began to go through them systematically. It wasn't a task she relished, but it was the least she could do.

'We never left anything much in the way of clothes at the cottage,' her mother had said, and had added with a poignancy that had made Fen's throat close up, 'But if you come across a blue and white spotted silk cravat, send it on to me. I gave it to him for good luck. He was recording a series of talks for radio, in London. When they were done we came down to spend a weekend at the cottage with you. It was the last time we were all there together, you remember? I think he must have left it behind; it isn't among the rest of his things.'

She had made it sound as if finding that cravat was one of the most important things in the world, one more piece of memorabilia to add to the collection that kept her in close, almost physical touch with the man she had loved above all else.

Fen knew she would never love anyone with that intensity. She would never leave herself open to that kind of destruction of self.

In any case, she hadn't found it, not so far. Just odds and ends, stuff they hadn't bothered to pack and take away, tatty old gear that might come in useful on their next flying visit.

Only there hadn't been another flying visit, for any of them. Fen had been busy making her own life and her father had been doing a lecture tour in the States, her mother with him, of course.

Sorting through the drawers and dressing-table in the room they had always used when they'd been here only seemed to reinforce her growing sense of isolation, something she'd believed she had come to terms with many years ago, when she'd learned and eventually accepted that neither of her parents had ever wanted her.

So the recognition that she was hungry came as a relief, an excuse to finish up for the day, to carry the bin bag of discards down, ready to be disposed of, to decide what she would have for supper while she was having a shower, and perhaps eat outside and watch the sunset.

Dragging the unwieldy plastic bag out of the room, she started down the stairs and was halfway down, the bag bumping behind her, when he stepped into her line of vision and said, 'Let me help you.'

Fen watched in stunned silence as he took the remaining stairs two at a time, took the bin bag from her suddenly nerveless fingers and carried it down. The formal business suit had been replaced by white

jeans and a black shirt, making him look too mag-
nificently male to be true. She was too shocked by his
unexpected reappearance to make a sound and when
he asked, 'Where do you want me to put it?' she could
only chew on her bottom lip and walk slowly down,
clinging on to the banisters because her legs felt too
weak to support her.

Silently, she opened the cupboard underneath the
stairs and watched, wide-eyed, the play of muscles
across his back as he bent to push the bulky bag into
the confined space and straightened to re-close the
door.

Quickly, Fen stepped back, away from him, her
heart giving an unexpected, treacherous leap as she
recognised the unpalatable fact that she was glad he
was here. Actually glad!

Which made her a fool.

'What are you doing here?' She didn't want to be
pleased to see him, to experience this shuddery
awareness of him, to feel this sweet sensation of relief
because he hadn't, as she had told herself, lost interest
in her.

'You must have known I'd be back.' His eyes slid
over her ashen face, noting the compression of the
soft mouth, as if she was swallowing back the words
she really wanted to say, the tension that held her tall,
slender body very upright, very rigid. And he said
with a softness that surprised him, 'We were going to
talk, remember? But as I said, there's no real hurry.
We've got all the time in the world.'

All the time in the world.

He made it sound so simple, as if they were two people getting to know each other, putting the vital physical attraction they felt for each other on hold because if the relationship were to grow and flourish it would need to put down roots, have something stronger and more meaningful to feed on than the transient desires of the flesh.

She gave him a bleak look. It wasn't like that; of course it wasn't. All he wanted from her was her body in his bed, to be used until he grew bored and moved on to someone else. And, by all accounts, he had a low boredom threshold where his women were concerned. And the talk, when it came, would be nothing more than a hundred and one reasons why he should take Alex's place.

Or what he believed to be Alex's place.

She didn't want it to be like that. She didn't want to have to listen to all those 'reasons'. And she felt nothing but a sagging relief when he said briskly, 'Why don't you go and freshen up while I put supper on the table? I brought the makings with me, courtesy of Prinny.'

Not trusting her voice, Fen shrugged and turned away, the sweet relief that flooded her making her feel giddy as she went back upstairs. She had expected him to resume his attempts to get her to move in with him. And she would never have put him down as a man who would waste time. He would decide what he wanted and go right ahead and take it. He wouldn't be interested in the waiting game.

His unpredictability worried her, but she wasn't going to waste her energies tying her brain in knots as she tried to solve the enigma, she decided as she stood under the shower, sluicing away the grime of the day. She would simply be grateful for the respite, for the relaxation of the pressure he'd exerted on every former occasion and pretend, for as long as the strange truce lasted, that they were two intelligent, mature adults who were capable of enjoying each other's company. Time enough to get back on her high horse if and when he began to try to pressure her into his bed again.

She rough-dried her hair and pulled on a pair of well-worn, clean jeans, topping them with a baggy, fine wool sweater. And didn't bother with make-up. Why go looking for trouble?

And her lack of prinking seemed to have paid off because the smile he gave her when she ventured back downstairs was nice and friendly, nothing sexual about it at all, and nothing to take exception to in the brief appraisal of his eyes as they took in her appearance.

'Better now? Ready to eat? I've put it outside—it's too lovely an evening to waste.'

She followed him, almost as if she had no will left of her own. And why argue? The evening was lovely, gold-shot with clear egg-shell blue and rich amethyst, the chunky picnic table set with four different kinds of cheese, a crusty granary loaf and a bottle of wine. He had cooked a bunch of asparagus spears and they ate it dripping with butter and Fen said, cutting herself yet another slice of the crumbly Cheshire, 'Delicious. I'd have put you down as a smoked salmon and cold pheasant man, with perhaps a few quail eggs on the side.'

She was remembering the simple picnic on the moors, too, and felt herself go warm all over as he refilled her wine glass and remarked softly, 'Perhaps life still holds a few surprises, Fen. I wouldn't have expected to find you in such isolation, cleaning out cupboards and covered in dust.' His eyes gleamed, rivalling the stars that were putting in an appearance overhead. 'Maybe the preconceptions we both started out with need rethinking.'

No 'maybe' about it! He thought she was a high-class tart, and he couldn't be more wrong. But he couldn't be blamed for that, she thought. She was beginning to feel uncomfortable now, which was a pity, because up until this moment she had been enjoying the evening and his company, marvelling in the fact that she had never felt so relaxed around him before.

But could her preconceptions about his character be way off mark, too?

Unconsciously, she shook her head. No, of course not. He was rarely seen with the same woman twice; Alex had been quite definite about that. And, even worse, his affairs had continued right through his marriage. And he hadn't turned a hair when his wife had died, which made him worse than heartless.

So she wasn't going to let herself get all relaxed and receptive. She swallowed the remains of her wine and hardened her heart. The devil was simply trying another tack, trying to get her to lower her guard. She wasn't going to forget what he wanted from her. This new, softly-softly approach wasn't going to get him anywhere. But her heart missed a beat when he told

her, 'When we were on the moors you said something
that made me stop and think—when I'd cooled down,
anyway. You were quite right. I'd been treating you
like a commodity. You deserve better than that. I'd
like to apologise.'

It took her a few muddled moments to recall what
she had said to him. Something about contacting her
if he ever developed a heart! And that in direct response to his cutting comment that he couldn't like
her because he didn't respect her, his insulting offer
to pay her bills and keep her if she agreed to give Alex
the push and move in with him!

So maybe he had had a rethink, decided that the
crudely direct approach wouldn't work. Did he really
think she was incapable of working that much out for
herself? Did he think she had fluff between her ears?

'Apology accepted.' She gave him a meaningless
smile and wondered why she felt betrayed. She got to
her feet. 'An apology plus a delicious supper. Aren't
I the lucky one! Who could possibly ask for more?'
She walked the few paces to the wicket gate and held
it open. 'I think we can call it quits now, don't you?
Goodnight, Mr Ackerman.'

For a long, agonised moment she thought he was
going to stay exactly where he was. But he did move
at last, uncurling himself from the bench seat, coming
towards her, his features unreadable in the growing
darkness.

And when he reached for her she wished he had
stayed where he was because then she could have
slipped inside the house, barred the door and closed

all the windows, and left him there, knowing what it was like to be outmanoeuvred for a change.

But the capacity for coherent thought left her brain as his arms dragged her roughly into the lithe hardness of his body, and the moment his mouth touched hers she was lost in the wild passion they incited in each other.

Lost. And consumed by the fiery invasion of his tongue, drawn deeper and deeper into a dark whirlpool of drugging sensation. This was what she'd once believed a kiss should be. Magic and mayhem all rolled into one, a giving and taking, a blending of two people—heart and soul—into one perfect whole.

And this was what she'd believed could never happen. After her short and monumentally disappointing relationship with Ray she had cynically disbelieved all those stories of a romantic love which somehow rapturously transported the lovers on to a plane where no one else existed, where the need to be together was paramount, as just so much wishful thinking, a lie to ensure the continuation of the species, at best, while, at worst, to subjugate the victims and make them lose their precious independence.

She had believed it to be a lie because she had believed she had loved Ray. And there had been no rapture, merely discomfort and deep embarrassment when she had lain in Ray's arms.

But now, wrapped in Saul's arms, his body pressed against hers, his hot, hungry kisses blocking her mind to everything except this wild need, she was not so

sure about that. Perhaps she hadn't loved Ray at all.
Maybe she simply hadn't wanted to be alone any more.

But she wasn't sure about anything, was she? How
could she be, when she responded, body and soul, so
completely to a man who had as good as said he despised her?

She moaned softly, in distress and confusion, and
Saul's feverish, possessive mouth gentled, drawing
slowly away, just a breath away. And he searched her
wide and frantic eyes in the glimmer of starshine, his
fingers weaving through her hair, his mouth made
tender by passion as he asked her thickly, 'Did I hurt
you? I'm sorry.' He leaned forward, taking her swollen
lower lip between his teeth, nipping gently, his dark
voice wry as he told her, 'I want you so badly. It makes
me behave like an uncontrolled boy. And I can't remember when that last happened, Fen.'

'No!' She could hear the brittle thread of control
in his voice and knew that the check on his desire was
only just manageable. And if that thread broke,
snapped by her own unbridled response to his passion,
then nothing on this earth would prevent him from
becoming her lover.

She wouldn't be able to stop him. She wouldn't want
to stop him!

'Please go!' she pleaded wildly, snapping her head
back on her slender neck, pounding his wide, rangy
shoulders with her fists. 'I don't want you here—I
don't!'

She was sobbing with panic. Dry sobs that tore at
her throat. She couldn't believe she was acting this
way, she who had always been so together, so self-

assured and calm. She was behaving hysterically and couldn't help herself because, at some deep level of consciousness, she knew her whole future was on the line. Allow him to make love to her once and she would be forever changed. Nothing would ever be the same again.

'You don't mean that.' There was a hint of steel in the soft dark voice as he captured her flailing fists and held them tightly against his chest, drawing her closer. 'You know you don't.'

She could feel the heavy beat of his heart through the white knuckles of her clenched hands and the temptation to unfurl her fingers within his iron-hard clasp was enormous. She needed to lay her palms against his chest, touch his heartbeats. But she was fighting for her own survival and she forced out shakily, 'I've never meant anything more. Just get away from me. Stay away from me.'

Saul went very still. Fen raked his face with wide, apprehensive eyes but it was too dark now to see his expression. But she knew he would be furious. And then he released her and her hands fell to her sides, and his voice was perfectly calm, not one trace of anger there at all as he told her, 'Still playing games, I see. Let me warn you, though, such games can be dangerous. A few moments longer and I would have lost control and nothing would have stopped you from becoming mine.'

Idly, he trailed a finger down the side of her face, tracing from the fine flare of her cheekbone down to her jaw, lingering for a tiny moment before dropping away. It was as much as Fen could do to prevent herself from shuddering with delicious reaction to that lingering, seductive touch.

'Maybe you like to play it rough? Is that what it is? Do you goad a man until he is out of his mind and takes you by force? Leaving you free to pretend that none of it was your fault, that you were a victim? Is that the way it was with Alex? Did the act of subduing you make him feel young and virile again? Did it make him feel responsible for you? Is that the way you get your men to pay your bills? Let me warn you again—I don't operate that way. And I don't force my women. You'll come to me because you want to, because nothing can keep you away.'

'I hate you!' She turned away, her eyes brimming with tears, but he walked past her to the gate, his voice very assured as he turned, his hand on the latch.

'No you don't. You just hate the things I make you face. And just remember—I'll be back. And I don't want you seeing Alex again. Ever. And you won't, not unless you want to ruin what's left of his career.'

He'd perched himself on the stool, looking totally
wicked. 'One night. And don't think even *that* won't
seem so short a time that we have to—'

Ripped through! However far you wanted that one to
finish! And this time, when she woke completely,
certain that that kind of sensation—or some such that
she'd...

CHAPTER EIGHT

FEN really didn't know what she was doing sitting
beside him in this car, being whisked away to heaven
knew where. Some place neutral, he'd said, and, like
the idiot she was now convinced she must be, she'd
once again allowed him to dictate terms.

It had been—and still was, of course—a beautiful
morning. But she'd woken feeling as if she was
smothered in dull grey rainclouds and hadn't been able
to get herself into gear and dive into the chores which
were her reason for being here at the cottage, and had
spent a couple of hours aimlessly mooching, miserably wondering what was wrong with her.

She very rarely felt depressed and was almost never
at a loose end. There was always something to do,
even if that something was merely relaxing and re-
charging her batteries. So just why she should be
feeling as if she was a thousand years old she didn't
know.

But when Saul strolled up the garden path, looking
as if he owned the place and everything in it, including her, she suddenly noticed that the sun was
shining, the sky a cloudless blue and the verges of the
narrow lane awash with wild flowers.

'Truce,' he'd said, smiling the smile she was beginning to find irresistible. 'I'm taking you to lunch.
Not my place, or yours. Neutral ground, equal terms.'

He'd parked himself on the bench seat, looking totally relaxed. 'Get ready. And don't take ages; we don't want to waste more time than we have to.'

Equal terms? He was far too confident and sure of himself. And of her. She didn't know where equality came into that kind of equation. But somehow that didn't seem to matter quite so much as it had done.

A fleeting query as to why she was giving in and letting him tell her what to do was all she had allowed herself as she'd trotted up the stairs she had trudged so heavily down a couple of hours earlier. What the heck? She hadn't been achieving anything, had she? Simply dragging herself around the place, not doing anything anyone could call remotely useful, looking and feeling like a very long, very wet weekend.

She was obviously not in the mood for clearing out the cottage. She would work better after a short break.

And she hadn't questioned the way she'd dived for the carriers she'd felt too guilty to unpack until now, tossing the garments on to the bed, her bright, glossy head tilted to one side as she considered her wickedness.

Her mouth curving, she'd selected a one-piece trousers and top in swirling psychedelic patterns in soft amber and cream with highpoints of scarlet and russet. The sleeveless bloused bodice had a cool scoopy neckline and the trouser part was softly pleated around the waist and hipline, narrowing dramatically to tight ankles.

Slipping on the highest heels she owned, she'd twisted this way and that in front of the mirror, pleased with her purchase even though she knew she should have resisted the temptation. The garment wasn't right for a pootle round the countryside but that wasn't at all important because the elegant lines, the softness of the fabric and the styling, disguised the leggy length of her and the boyishness of her figure, and that was what mattered. And wearing it made her heart lift and that was nice because it was such a contrast to the way she'd been feeling up until now.

Up until Saul had arrived, a mocking voice inside her head reminded. But Fen blithely ignored it. She was only too glad she was feeling great again and didn't much care why.

They had left the coast behind and Saul had said little apart from a few easy comments as they'd passed through a series of huddled villages, sleeping in the midday sun. And Fen had been content with that, because when they talked they usually ended up fighting, but as the car swept down into a deep tunnel of green where the hedgerow trees met in an arch overhead curiosity began to wriggle around inside her brain.

She knew, only too shatteringly well, how he could make her feel when he touched her, but that was all. She knew nothing about the man himself except what he had allowed her to see, the little her uncle had told her, and what she had learned from the few rather soulless magazine articles her uncle had kept and which Jean had given her to read when trying to persuade her to take part in the charade that had led her to the mess she was in now.

Was there anything remotely redeeming behind the mask of the ruthless predator, the mask of the man who set out to get what he wanted, who was direct to the point of insulting rudeness when he set out his needs, and his terms?

Was there a warmer, more caring and considerate character somewhere behind that mask? There was only one way to find out, and she asked, 'Did you really mean it when you said you'd see Alex's career ruined if I saw him again?'

Without realising she was doing it, Fen held her breath and silently prayed that she wouldn't be disappointed. She wanted, quite desperately, for him to deny that he could ever really be that coldly ruthless, no matter what the circumstances.

'Can it matter to you? Now?'

He sounded bored and she gave him a frowning sideways glance. So much for not wanting to be disappointed! Now that her short 'affair' with Alex Fairbourne was over she could have no further interest in the man. That was the way his mind would work. Did he lose all interest in and concern for his women as soon as the door had closed behind them after he'd kicked them out?

Of course. What else?

She shot him another dark look. They were deeper into the seemingly endless green tunnel now and the undergrowthy light made him look sinister, poles apart from the charming, charismatic character who had walked up to her this morning and declared a truce.

Heigh-ho, she thought with a deep and dreadful feeling of resignation, yet another bitter fight was obviously in the offing. And she informed him cut-

tingly, 'Of course it matters. Whatever my faults—
and according to you they're legion—I'm a loyal soul.'

She sat squarely in her seat, staring straight ahead,
and allowed him to make what he liked of that. A
ten-round verbal punch-up, she had no doubt. And
so was quite unprepared for the bleakness she heard
in his voice when he remarked, 'If you're worried
about his future, you must care a hell of a lot for
him.'

So why wasn't he plain angry? Or conceitedly
rubbing in the fact that he would make a far more
satisfactory lover than Alex Fairbourne? Much
younger, more virile, far wealthier, and free!

Fen didn't know, and she wasn't going to ask because she didn't really want yet another fight on her
hands. She had come along with him because,
strangely, there had seemed to be no choice and, even
more strangely, she had wanted to be with him. And
then they crested a hill and emerged into sunlight,
above the deep wooded valley, and everything changed
back to the way it had been before she'd asked about
Alex's career. No darkness, no undertones, merely
simple enjoyment as he told her gently, 'Arguing the
toss is pointless. Why spoil a relaxing holiday? Alex's
capabilities alone will determine his future career with
VisionWest. But as far as you're concerned, Fen, he's
ancient history.' He gave her a sideways glance that
was so uncharacteristically gentle and warm that her
toes curled in her shoes and a *frisson* of some sensation that was entirely new to her trickled its way all
down her spine. And then he added levelly, 'Forget
him; he's back with his wife, which is where he should

be. You've got to start getting your own life together, decide what's best for you. I'll gladly help, if I can.'

Help? By installing her as his mistress? A huge help that would be! If she were ever to be so foolish she would never survive the inevitable parting. She hunched her head into her shoulders, loathing the way her thoughts were leading her, telling herself that she would never behave in such a self-destructive fashion. And he couldn't make her do anything against her will. So she would waste no more time brooding about it.

She got her thoughts back in order as they passed over the brow of the hill and swooped down over a hump-backed stone bridge which crossed a shallow stream that chattered in its stony bed, and there, in the green hollow, stood a white-washed stone inn, all alone, not a village, hamlet or church tower in sight.

Fen mentally crossed her fingers. If Saul really meant what he said and her uncle's future rested on his talents, then everything would be fine. He had a lot to offer, and hopefully the big bosses would see that. For all she knew there had been no reason for him to put himself in the public eye quite so drastically.

But desperate problems called for desperate solutions, and poor Alex had been distraught over the prospect of having his programme axed. And to be on the safe side maybe she should phone him and warn him to stay well away from Cornwall—and, by implication, her—until that decision had been reached. Saul hadn't actually said he hadn't meant to carry out that threat . . .

'This is where we eat. I booked a table.' Saul eased the big vehicle into the car park and Fen squashed the thought that he must have been very sure of himself. He always was, and as she couldn't change that state of affairs she wasn't about to grumble about it. It was too nice a day and she was feeling really relaxed, despite her disquieting thoughts about the seriousness of his threat and his ominous offer to 'help' her.

They weren't the only customers, she noted. Plenty of other cars, which was probably why he had thought it necessary to book a table in advance. And although she tried not to she did flinch a little as he took her arm to lead her inside. Really, the touch of his firm, lean fingers on the bare skin of her arm was far too disturbing. It made her think things she didn't want to think. Which was why she didn't make a single protest when he calmly instructed, 'You can tell me all about yourself while we eat. I know next to nothing about you, and I intend to see that remedied.'

'There's not a lot to tell.' She sounded blithe, and she was. If telling him about herself meant she didn't have to listen to all those reasons why she should become his mistress now Alex had returned to his wife—always presuming, of course, that that rather troubled scenario still occupied his mind—then she would talk until her jaw dropped off.

He would probably die of boredom before then, though. Compared to his power, position and wealth her doings would seem totally insignificant.

But there wasn't a hint of boredom in the intelligent silver eyes as they lingered over a lunch that was fabulous enough to explain why the isolated inn was full to capacity.

'So that's why picking up languages came so naturally to you.' He smiled as he poured cream into his coffee and stirred reflectively. 'Did you mind not having settled roots?'

Fen lifted one shoulder in an elegant shrug. She had told him more about her life than she had ever told anyone. It hadn't been difficult, strange to say. Confiding in him seemed to come naturally and it was a relief not to have to watch what she said. She wasn't used to lies and deceit, all the false attitudes that had clouded their relationship—if such it could be called—from the moment their eyes had met over that restaurant table back in London.

'No, not really,' she answered truthfully. 'Maybe a little, sometimes. But travelling round the world became a way of life and I got so that even when we were settled some place—for two or three months, say—I started to get itchy feet, even though I might have made a whole lot of new friends at whatever school I was attending. I was the first to get excited when Dad had to move on. Oddly enough, my mother didn't like travelling. But her life began and ended with Dad, and she went where he went. Once she's able to come to terms with his loss I'm pretty sure she'll be more content with a proper, settled home.'

'She never wanted to make a settled home for you?' Saul put in quietly, and she shook her head, smiling easily because her parents' lack of interest in her had long since ceased to hurt.

'She never wanted me, full stop. Neither of them did. I was an encumbrance. That's not to say they failed in their duty,' she defended. 'I was adequately educated, clothed and fed.'

'But not loved,' Saul said astutely, and Fen bit her tongue because she couldn't explain about the visits from Alex and Jean and, later on, the Cornish cottage where they had spent the long summer holidays with her. Her uncle and aunt had always made time for her, taught her what a loving family life was all about.

But she couldn't tell Saul that. Not yet. But she could tell him, 'Don't feel sorry for me. I was happy. I spent four years at boarding-school here in England and then went on to get the qualifications I needed to set up as a freelance commercial translator. And during that time I only rarely saw my parents—we met up for short holidays at the cottage. So you see,' she informed him with a glint of mischief in her big amber eyes, 'I am capable of being totally independent and earning my own living. I don't need a man to keep me.'

It was as far as she dared go towards putting him right about his wrong and insulting supposition that she made a career out of being a kept woman, but she could have bitten her tongue out when she saw his eyes go bleak, caught the thread of bitterness in his voice as he beckoned the waiter over for the bill, remarking, 'So your affair with Alex was based on something deeper than his ability to pick up the tabs. I wonder if that explains your almost virginal and strenuous efforts to keep me at arm's length?'

Fen could have kicked herself as she watched the brief transaction with the credit card. Why had she reminded him of her supposedly torrid affair with Alex Fairbourne?

During the past couple of hours they had talked as they had never talked before, developing a closeness she would have believed impossible to achieve before today. And she had spoiled it with a few thoughtless words, brought all the bad things crowding in again, and knew she was going to have to suffer the aftermath when they left the inn in deep silence, the happiness suddenly drained right out of the day.

And by the time they were back at the cottage she was ready to burst into tears with tension. And telling herself that this was par for the course, that things couldn't be any different and they would always end up at each other's throats—given the type of man he was and the type of woman he thought she was, but wasn't—didn't help at all.

'I'm sorry. I've been behaving like a spoiled brat. Forgive me.'

He had pulled the car into the narrow parking space at the side of the small house and Fen stared at him, battling with a sensation that was akin to shock. Saul Ackerman actually admitting he was in the wrong? Actually apologising?

Cutting the engine, he twisted round in the driver's seat, his mouth indenting wryly as he confessed, 'I don't want to face the fact that you could have any deep feelings for Fairbourne.' He lifted a hand to touch her cheek. 'Can you understand that? I want to be the man in your life. More each day I want that.'

The touch of his fingers scorched her skin and her eyes brimmed with tears. For one crazy moment she thought she was falling in love with him. She couldn't bear it! And that melting tenderness deep in those silvery eyes was purely imagination. Of course it was. Just the effect of looking at him through a haze of stupid tears.

So she turned her head away abruptly and when he said, 'Look, let's walk ourselves into a happier mood, shall we? Come down to the beach,' she was out of the car like a shot, glad of the distraction, because if he'd said he wanted to be her man, one more time, she could well have ended up saying, Oh, yes please! instead of, Oh, get lost!

The narrow track dipped steeply down towards the shoreline, reaching the level of the rushing stream a hundred yards or so inland, and the going was difficult in the type of heels Fen had chosen to wear, but even so, when Saul scooped her up in his arms, she had to protest, 'Put me down. I don't need carrying.'

'Stop arguing, woman. At least give it a try. You might find you like it.' His arms tightened around her, giving her fair warning that he had no intention of doing as she asked, and, her body pressed so closely to his, Fen wound her arms around his neck—simply to feel more secure, of course—and gave up the fight. And maybe, just maybe, he was right. She could so easily give in entirely and let the dark tide of his passion carry her where it would.

But she wouldn't. She would find herself falling in love with him, needing him to make her complete. And that would be a very silly thing to do. She valued her freedom and independence far too much to risk losing it to any man, especially a man who had no heart.

At last he released her, sitting her down on top of one of the tumbled granite blocks that had once formed a quayside of sorts. Long out of living memory fishing boats had tied up here, trawling in and out of the narrow cove to wrest a living from the sea, their catches hauled up the steep track to the sheltered village in rough carts pulled by wiry ponies. But other cargoes had come this way, silently at night...

'When I was a child, I used to come down here sometimes, when everyone else was asleep, trying to imagine it the way it would have been when smugglers slipped in under cover of darkness,' she confided nostalgically.

Her eyes were smiling as she looked out over the little bay, the sunlight dancing on the azure sea, the golden sand, the bright rays even managing to soften the intimidating aspect of the great granite cliffs. Difficult to imagine muffled hoofs of burdened ponies, the dark shapes of men as they silently unloaded casks of brandy and tobacco, bolts of silk...

'And did you succeed?' There was warmth in his voice as he sat in the sun-warmed sand, his back against the block of granite she was sitting on. He had removed his footwear and his eyes were closed against the glare of the sun as it bounced back off the water and Fen's heart skipped a beat. The light picked out the forceful lines of his spectacular features and showed, far too clearly, the softening of the severely sculpted lines of his mouth. But even so she recognised—felt—the pulsing throb of danger that was such an intrinsic part of him.

Her throat closed up. Every time she saw him the danger escalated and the more approachable and human he seemed, the worse it got. She would do well to remember that.

'All I succeeded in doing was scaring myself half to death,' she confessed and, in spite of her determination to sound amused and at the same time impersonal, she only managed to sound breathless.

'I can imagine.' One of his hands moved lazily to remove one of her impossible shoes and then the other, and his fingers were still idly stroking a delicately arched instep as he added huskily, 'You were a lonely child. I don't like to think of you being lonely. Or afraid.'

Fen closed her eyes on a sudden pang of anguish. Did he really mean that? Did he? Or was he simply shooting a line?

And did it matter?

Frantically, she pulled her foot away from the openly erotic drift of his fingers and dropped it to the hot golden sand.

'I thought we were going to walk?' She pinned a big bright smile to her face and knew how empty it was. She was nearly crying inside.

'There's no mad hurry.' He caught up with her loping, ragged-breathed strides in no time at all. 'We have all day—and all night, too. We could stay down here and watch for your eighteenth-century smugglers. They won't frighten you if I'm holding your hand. So take it easy.' His arm went around her

shoulders, comforting, warm, promising... Fen
thought briefly that no, nothing would frighten her—
not even a ghostly band of smugglers—if he were
holding her hand. But how could she take it easy when
he appeared to be doing just that? She knew him well
enough now to know that when he appeared at his
most relaxed he was at his most dangerous.

She must be mad to be here with him at all. She
knew what he was like, what he wanted from her. So
why was she here? Why wasn't she telling him to take
a jump? After carefully avoiding any hint of the
emotional in her casual and decidedly platonic
friendships with the opposite sex ever since her farcical
affair with Ray, why did every cell in her body leap
with wild response every time Saul came near her?

They had reached the edge of the water, their bare
feet making sharp footprints in the wet sand, and to
escape the unendurable feeling of closeness engen-
dered by the casual weight of his arm around her
shoulders she bent and scooped up a pebble and with
a flick of her wrist sent it skimming over the bright
and glittering sea. She repeated the performance, like
a mindless automaton, until he caught her round the
waist with both hands, swinging her round, drawing
her into his body.

His bare feet were planted wide, and the jut of his
hipbones burned her up, made her heart beat too
madly, her breath leave her lungs in ragged gasps.

'Fen——' His silver eyes were limpid beneath all
those thick black lashes, his body told hers just how
much he wanted her and she felt intolerable excitement build up inside her, feverishly expanding until

it met the fierce need she felt in him, and he smiled at her, slow and sweet, sharing a secret, and his voice was thick as he told her, 'Don't keep running away. I want you in my life; you know that. But perhaps you don't know that I won't rush you, or try to make you do anything you don't want to do. We'll take things at your pace—and if that means nice and slowly, then it's fine by me.'

The hands that had dropped and were now splayed across her buttocks curved gently and pulled her more firmly into his body, his hips moving with a slow suggestiveness that threatened to blow her mind.

And it was that very threat, that very real danger, the knowledge that she was within a hair's breadth of throwing all caution to the four winds and matching his seductive movements with wilder and wantonly willing ones of her own that gave her the strength to tug herself painfully away and grate, 'One day you're going to learn that you can't always have everything you want. You've never known failure in your life, have you?'

A cold little wind whipped up out of nowhere, tossing her hair around her face. Fen brushed her fringe out of her eyes and glared at him. He looked shocked, as if he wasn't used to being told he couldn't have exactly what he wanted. It was high time he learned that lesson and, to punch her message home, she added, 'You were born knowing the world was your oyster—your father founded the hugely successful publishing company you inherited, and the profits from that helped you to buy into a failing airline and make it a legend, and the profits from that helped you grab the majority of shares in a highly competitive communications business and lash out enough cash to secure you the top position in the VisionWest consortium!' Fen shuddered with reaction, folding her arms around her tautly held body. A cloud had covered the sun but she knew that wasn't entirely responsible for the way she suddenly felt so icily cold.

'You have done your homework.' He wasn't smiling.

'It's not classified information,' she shot back. 'There have been enough articles written about you.' Lacy ripples of cold sea water were washing over her feet and she turned to head back across the beach, but his hands came down on her shoulders, swinging her round. And his eyes were bleak as he told her, 'There are other types of failure.' His voice was abrasive. 'Where human relationships are concerned I'm right down at the bottom of the class.'

Fen caught her breath and she went very still, making no attempt now to move away. That he should admit to any kind of failure was utterly new in her experience of him. His hands gripped her shoulders as if she were the rock he was clinging to as he floundered in deep, troubled waters, and she knew, with a clarity that was almost painful, that it would be fatally easy to give in to him, let him take what he wanted from her because she desperately wanted to answer the need she sensed in him, to comfort him and take away the sobering look of bleak pain she saw in his eyes.

'Do you want to talk about it?' she asked gently, moving closer to his body warmth because the wind from the sea was stronger now, colder. But he gave her a puzzled glance from clouded silver eyes before he shook his head roughly, as if to rid his mind of his own particular devils, and then was definitely back in control again as he answered with husky confidence,

'There's only one thing I want to discuss with you, Fen, and that's our future relationship.' He dipped his dark head and lightly brushed her lips with his. 'And there will be one; make no mistake about that.'

He eased her closer to his overwhelming male strength and she went without a murmur and the way her body turned to incandescent flame in his arms was completely inevitable.

She gave a fluttery sigh as their breath mingled and his mouth moved over hers with a slow, drugging sensuality that made her feel as if she was melting, melting into him, becoming one with him.

And nothing else existed. Nothing but the quivering need deep within her as it called out to the primitive arousal of the hard male body pressed so closely to hers. And she was lost, abandoning her will to his, the molten fire in her veins consuming her as she felt the increased rapidity of his heavily beating heart, the gasp of hunger that came from deep down in his throat when she instinctively twined her fingers in the thick black hair at the warm nape of his neck and responded feverishly to his kiss.

A deep shudder rocked through him as his hands moulded her pliant, eager body, his touch a mixture of impatience and heart-breaking tenderness. And as she moaned his name, her body squirming against his in a riot of blind sensation, she admitted all over again that she was lost. Her independence had been surrendered to him, and it wasn't important, not any more.

'God, how I want you, Fen!' His voice sounded ragged, starved of oxygen as he reluctantly broke the drugging kiss, cupping her flushed face with his hands, the flame of desire in his eyes meeting and holding the slumbrous passion in hers. His mouth twisted in a quirky smile, his thumbs moving roughly over her delicate cheekbones, his hard fingers twining in the bright softness of her hair. 'If you don't put an end to this I won't be able to stop myself taking you here and now.'

With the waves already swirling around their calves? A bubble of laughter broke inside her as she slowly, unconsciously, shook her head. She couldn't help him, could she? She was already lost in the type of world-shattering sensations she had never believed existed.

She knew she could break away now, walk back across the beach, and he wouldn't try to prevent her. But how could she? She hadn't the will-power. Or the desire to move out of his arms. Slowly, she ran her hands down his body, from his wide shoulders to his narrow waist, and felt him go quite still, as if he was trying to leash and control all that rampaging need.

Fen knew she was playing with fire, but she'd already been burned out of all recognition by his devastatingly hungry kisses, and, being lost, she had nothing to lose, and he gave an anguished groan and dragged her more closely into his arms, as if he would absorb her body into his if he could, smothering her face with the fierce passion of his mouth.

Slowly, stumblingly, they moved together, clinging blindly to each other, inching through the water towards the sand, beyond the reach of the rapidly incoming tide. Nothing could part them now, Fen knew that and accepted it. She was committed to him. There was no going back. Not now.

Not until an incoming wave, much higher than the rest, swept over them with a deluge of cold water and left them clinging together, gasping with the shock, and when he had his breath back Saul laughed into her big wide eyes and told her wryly, 'You know what they say about a bucket of cold water? Well, it's true. But don't expect the effect to last too long.' He took her hand and tugged her back up the beach. 'Let's go and get dry. I'll share a hot shower and warm towel with you, any time.'

CHAPTER NINE

FEN eyed the colourful, sodden garment on the bathroom floor without a great deal of interest. It had cost far more than she could sensibly afford and the sea water had ruined it. But she couldn't raise even a tiny flicker of annoyance over the extravagant loss.

Still shivering, she stepped under the shower and let the hot water chase the goose-bumps away.

Her body still ached for Saul and no matter how fervently she congratulated herself on her lucky escape the wanting wouldn't go away. So it was just as well he hadn't—as she had feverishly expected—insisted on sharing the shower with her but had simply asked, 'Have you a drier I could put my things in? And a towel? And you'd better get out of your wet clothes.'

An expectant and delicious shudder had snaked through her and she'd almost presented him with her back and the buttons that would need undoing, but he'd misread her reaction because he'd advised blandly, 'A shower should stop you shivering; don't hang around, just show me where to go, first.'

So she'd pointed him at the lean-to utility-room where the washing machine and drier were housed, handed him a towel and gone to take that shower. And all the time wondering if he would try to take up where they'd left off. But even though he'd said he'd share a hot shower and warm towel with her any time—and sounded as if he couldn't wait!—he hadn't made any attempt to join her.

Which meant she should be shouting, Hallelujah! giving thanks for the deluge of sea water that had dampened their ardour and saved her from her hormones.

Only the soaking in cold water hadn't dampened her ardour, she thought crossly as she stepped out at last and smothered herself with a towel. She actually still wanted him; at least, her body did, no matter how strenuously her mind dispatched all those cool and logical warnings about allowing herself to become involved with him.

Saul only wanted one thing: her body in his bed until he tired of her and moved on to the next female to take his fancy. He had been brutally honest when he'd spelled out his needs as far as she was concerned, had said not one word of love or commitment. And that wasn't good enough for her; it never could be.

But it didn't matter, surely it didn't? His lack of any genuine, lasting feeling for her was neither here nor there. She would never make love with a man unless she truly loved him. And she would never let herself fall in love because she valued her freedom and independence far too much to put herself willingly into that kind of trap.

That Saul's touch, his kisses, had demonstrated that the sexual magic she had believed to be a myth was, in truth, very real indeed only served to show her that her experience with Ray Gordon had been an unfortunate mistake. But that didn't mean she had to make another, cheapen herself by allowing all the normal feminine needs and desires she had bottled up since she'd said goodbye to Ray to lead her to indulge in a sordid affair with a man who had openly admitted he couldn't like her because he didn't respect her.

Pulling on an old pair of jeans and a soft wool shirt, she congratulated herself on sorting everything out to her own satisfaction. It wouldn't take long for his clothes to dry and when they had she would send him on his way, with a word or two of polite regret regarding her recent thoroughly wanton behaviour.

She could put all those rapacious responses of hers down to the wine she had drunk with the lunch he had given her. And hope to hell he believed her.

But the sight of the wood fire crackling in the hearth when she opened the door to the sitting-room brought a wreathing smile to her lips and she said an enthusiastic, 'Oh—how nice!' without stopping to think, looking at him without thinking, either, and then wishing she hadn't because wearing just that smallish towel wound around his narrow hips, and not another single thing, was a sexual hammer-blow of the very severest kind.

All the need, the aching, the wanting came flooding back, saturating her with the shattering desire to fly into his arms, smother that superb and almost naked body with hungry kisses and recapture the ecstasy that had recklessly whirled her into the world of the magic they had made together down on the shore.

Fen gulped, her throat feeling tight and painful as she turned away, afraid to let her eyes dwell on all that tempting masculinity for one moment longer. Her body was a traitor, and she didn't know how best to fight it. But she tried, oh, how she tried!

'Your clothes should be ready soon.' She could hear the rumbling grumble of the drier from the other room. 'Would you like a hot drink while you wait?' And now she could hear the violent drumbeat of her heart as his voice drifted over her like a cloud of lazy velvet.

'Not now. But you can feed me later.'

How late was later? Just how long did he intend to stay? Unwanted ripples of agitation skimmed over her skin. How could she tell him to go—without a hint of ferocity? How could she tell him she wasn't interested in his plans for their short-term future without betraying the fact that her wretched body had very definite and insistent ideas of its own?

'It's too comfortable here to think of moving. I'll see if my clothes are ready.'

He passed her on his way out of the room. She didn't look at him; she couldn't. Expelling her pent-up breath, Fen walked to the window and looked out. The English weather was living up to its reputation, blue skies and sunlight obliterated by thick grey cloud, rain coming in from the sea on a scudding wind. Saul was right; the little room, cosy in the light of the fire he had made, made the outdoors easy to avoid.

To insist that he left would perhaps be too extreme, she told herself, watching the rain blow inland in great grey swaths. It would be foolish to place too much vehement importance on his offer to install her as his mistress. Better—if the subject were to be broached again—to state politely but very firmly that she had no intention of becoming his mistress, now or ever. She could even smile while she said it, she told herself, trying to feel like the calm, sophisticated adult she had always believed herself to be.

And she would try to make sure he didn't touch her again. She now knew her own weaknesses where his kisses and caresses were concerned. Mind over matter, she instructed herself staunchly, bracing herself to turn and behave naturally as she heard him walk back into the room.

He was fully dressed now, thank the lord, in dry if crumpled trousers and shirt, and he said, his straight mouth quirking as if he understood her relief, and the reason for it, 'Happier now?' and then at a tangent, sinking down on to one of the comfortable arm-chairs, his endless legs stretched towards the hearth, 'Do you mind having to sell this house? Didn't you tell me it's the only remotely settled home you've ever had? And what's to happen about the furniture—are you going to have to dispose of that, too?'

'No.' Fen didn't know whether to tell him to mind his own business or not. Not, she decided, perching on the edge of a chair that was the identical twin of the one he was sprawled in. Being contentious around him didn't pay off. 'Whoever buys the cottage can have the furnishings thrown in with the purchase price, to use or dispose of as they think fit. Mother's no use for it——'

'I would imagine not—living in Australia. But you?' The softly insistent question hung on the air, demanding an answer. She didn't know why he was subjecting her to the third degree—especially over a topic as unexciting as old and rather battered furniture.

But she would answer because she would do all she could to avoid another fight, because to have that type of tension stinging through the air wouldn't be at all sensible. And against all her wary expectations he wasn't pressuring her now; it was her own treacherous body which was doing that, every centimetre of her flesh burning with the need to be in his arms again.

She was just going to have to hide that sorry state of affairs from him so she answered, hoping she sounded cool but pleasant, 'I've never had much use for material possessions. Enough clothes to fill a couple of suitcases is all I need. Anything else gets in the way and slows you down.'

'And ties you to one spot?' he inserted, watching her from hooded silver eyes, his arms crossed behind his head as he lounged back in his chair.

'Exactly,' she agreed with cool precision, but her precarious composure disintegrated, making her face burn as he enquired astutely,

'The way you were brought up turned you into a wanderer; did the lack of parental love lead to a need for emotional independence, too? Is that why you move from lover to lover—to assuage your obvious physical needs without emotional commitment?'

His question took her breath away. How dared he imply she was a promiscuous trollop? Who the hell did he think he was? All set to launch into a scathing denial, plus a blistering counter-attack because his morals were highly suspect, when all was said and

done, she remembered that he had cause to believe it
and felt a chill slide its way through her skin.

She couldn't tell him the truth, not yet, not until a
decision had been reached about her uncle's future.
And even when she did—if she did—would he believe
her?

She couldn't make an answer and she couldn't
simply sit here, his mesmeric eyes probing right into
her soul. So she said, sounding wooden, 'You wanted
me to feed you. Excuse me...' And she pushed herself
out of the chair and into the kitchen, asking herself
what she thought she was doing, offering to give him
supper when all she'd wanted was for him to go and
leave her in peace, give her the space she needed to
get over this monumental physical attraction.

It had been a knee-jerk reaction, she mourned.
Desperate to get away from him and his probing insulting questions, she had grasped at the excuse of
preparing a meal without thinking it out.

And her tactical retreat hadn't achieved a thing because he was right behind her, big and dark and much
too masculine, his voice dry as he remarked, 'A
subject you don't want to pursue, I take it. Not to
worry; I'll root out your motivations some other time.
What are we eating?'

His words, if she had any say in it! she thought
bitterly. His close proximity in the small kitchen, the
mess she was in—a mess of her own and her uncle's
making—made her want to relieve the stress she was
under by lashing out. At him. But she controlled the
dangerous urge and said ungraciously, 'Omelette. And
only by helping do you get to stay in the kitchen.' She

dived in the fridge and came out with a bag of mush-rooms. 'You can peel and chop these.'

'Whatever you say, little cat. Things might be different later. In fact I can guarantee they will. But for now, at least, you're the boss.'

His eyes were laughing at her and her breath clogged in her throat. She felt punch-drunk whenever he looked at her and she wished she'd been determined enough to give him a glass of wine and send him back to sit by the fire, out of her way. Because the hands that were now busily preparing the mushrooms were beautiful, strong, deft and sensual. And try as she would she couldn't stop thinking of the way they had made her feel as they'd stroked her body into mindless capitulation.

And what had he meant when he'd said things would be different later? She wouldn't give herself three guesses because she already knew the answer, and quite how she was going to be able to fight both him and her own instinctive response to him she didn't know. But she'd come up with something. Somehow.

Edgy, and showing it, she thought self-disgustedly as the plates she was sliding into the warming oven rattled together like castanets. And Saul would know it, too. She sometimes felt he knew exactly what she was thinking, how she was feeling, as if there were a bond between them. Which was nonsense.

Not looking at him because she couldn't bear to see the speculative smile in his eyes, she got on with what she was doing, her growing uneasiness responsible for the song and dance she was making of the simple chores. And it was Saul who actually eased the tension that was gripping her by the throat, eschewing the formality of eating at the table, finding trays, the modest stock of wine Alex had insisted on bringing here for her, selecting a Valdepeñas and ushering her through to the sitting-room where they ate from the trays on their knees in front of the fire.

And it was Saul who removed the plates they had finished with, poured her more wine, revitalised the fire with an armful of dry logs and drew the curtains against the darkness and rain.

Strangely enough, she felt secure with him, like this. Just the two of them and a strand of unforced conversation that ranged over topics that were as diverse as they were interesting. And with his own brand of devilish ease he had seduced her into total relaxation, so that not even one alarm bell sounded when he asked smoothly, 'What will you do and where will you go after you've finished here?'

Fen shrugged dismissively, her tawny eyes like gold jewels in the firelight, lazy and warm. She twisted the stem of her wine glass slowly between her long, slender fingers and told him, 'Look for a way to earn my next crust and, when I've found it, go to wherever it is.'

She was too contented to be bothered to tell him that her next scheduled job didn't start until later in the summer, in Italy, or that, due to her own extravagance, she would probably have to find something to fill the gap. And she was totally unprepared for the harsh rasp of his voice as he admitted, almost reluctantly, as if the words had been torn from him against his will, 'I worry about you. Don't ask me why, Fen, but I do.'

It was then that the treacherous feeling of relaxation he had so cleverly induced flew right out of the window, and her heart was thudding like a steamhammer as he said through his teeth, 'Why run round the world like a gypsy when I can offer you a roof over your head and a bed to sleep in? You know the way we are together—one look, one touch and we both go up in flame.' He went to straddle the hearth, his eyes dark and frowning, his mouth a straight line, and cut off her automatic protest with an impatient slash of his hand. 'Don't even think of trying to deny it. I hate it when women lie. Together, you and I could make magic, Fen. And you know it.' His mouth twisted in a smile that held no warmth, no humour. 'This may not be the most romantic offer you've ever had—I don't believe in dressing basics up with pretty words to make them seem more palatable—but I need someone permanent in my life. Not just anyone with a beautiful face and endless legs. I need you. And I think you need me.'

Could he hear the thunder of her heart in the sudden silence of the room? The things he said made her want to cry. She gripped her wine glass until her knuckles went white and he took it from her, putting it down on the hearth, his movements taut, as if he was under some kind of strain.

Fen closed her eyes as anguish surged through her. Need him? How could she possibly need him?

If she agreed to what he was suggesting she would be pushing the self-destruct button with a vengeance. So now was the time to haul herself together, finally to get things straight, let him know that in no circumstances whatsoever would she agree to become his live-in lady. And she looked at him then, held the intensity of his narrowed eyes and forced a vinegary note into her voice as she derided, 'Why should I need you? What could you possibly offer that I couldn't get from any one of a hundred other men in a hundred other places?' and watched his face go tight with rage.

But he was good at controlling it, she had to give him that, because his tone was perfectly level as he came back, surprising her all over again, 'I said I wanted to help you, and I meant it. You need someone to take you in hand, and I could do it. I understand why you are the way you are. You must have loved your parents when you were a young child, and you would have felt deeply hurt and insecure when you discovered you weren't wanted.'

Even before he moved she knew he was going to touch her and she did nothing to stop him when he took her hands in his and drew her to her feet. How could she stop him when every fluttery beat of her heart was telling her how much she wanted to be near him, to feel his hard body burning against hers, to know again the way his mouth felt against hers?

But the touch of his hands around her small waist was loose, almost careless—as if he knew she had lost all will to fight him, that he held her, now and always, with the simple power of his presence; knew, with that wicked insight of his, that his being near her was enough to subdue the waywardness in her. He was masterful, he was magic, he was spawn of the devil...

He held the dreaming, desire-hazed gold of her gaze with the silver intensity of his eyes and the tone of his voice alone told her of his heightened need as it deepened to a husky caress.

'Without knowing that they did it, your parents taught you to back off from any emotional commitment. I could teach you to give that commitment, help you to learn that giving doesn't mean losing, that giving can only help you to grow as a human being.'

Seductive words to match the light, seductive touch of his beautiful hands. She felt as if she was drowning in warm honey. So sweet, so soft, so tempting . . .

Biting down hard on her lower lip to remind herself that the devil was well-versed in saying the things that poor misguided mortals wanted to hear, Fen queried, just to set the record straight, because he couldn't care for her, not the essential her within what he saw as the nubile outer packaging, 'You said you wanted me in your life. So how permanent is permanent?' And, without knowing she did it, she held her breath. And expelled it on a pang of pain as he told her what she now knew she hadn't wanted to hear.

'Nothing lasts. I've learned that the hard way. I suppose I mean for as long as we both want to stay together. We would be good together, good for each other, and you could learn what it's like to put down a few roots. You've already seen my home. It's a happy house, Fen. You would be content there.'

There. With him. Oh, she could be happy, blissfully so if things were different. If he loved her, if he wanted her for always . . .

As soon as she'd walked into his home she'd had the strangest feeling that the place welcomed her, that there, if anywhere, she could put down roots. But there would be bitterness, too. And fear. Both clouding whatever joy was on offer because sooner or later he would tire of her and ask her to go. She would never put herself through that type of hell.

'You want me to replace all those one-nighters.' Her mouth went hard as she fought the overwhelming need to agree to anything he said, everything he said. 'Feeling your age, Saul? Is the chase getting too much for you and losing its thrill?' She tried to pull away; whatever distance she managed to put between them would be welcome—far more than welcome, it was vitally necessary—but he refused to let her escape, his hands tightening around her body, making her go rigid with distress.

'I don't go in for one-night stands, if that's what you're implying. I never have. Sanchia was the expert in that field.'

The bitterness in his voice caught her unawares, reluctant curiosity easing the rigidity from her body as she asked, 'Who is Sanchia?'

All the tension that had drained from her seemed to have entered into him because the big body so close to hers was taut with it now, his voice hard and clipped as he answered shortly, 'My wife, past tense. She died.'

The wife whose death had, by all accounts, left him totally unaffected. Alex had said something about that short-lived and troubled marriage—that there had always been someone else in it, muddying the waters. She had automatically assumed that Saul and his womanising had been responsible for the breakdown.

Had she been wrong?

This tension, this bitterness, seemed to suggest that she had and she searched his closed features for some further clue but he turned away, his hands releasing her. And, far from feeling grateful for the respite she had so recently craved, she deeply regretted the chilling distance that he had put between them and said quickly, with instinctive sympathy, 'Do you want to tell me about it?'

The ruthlessly handsome face was hard as he faced her again, the black brows frowning. Then he shook his head, as if he had reached a decision, and took the two paces back to her again, his brow clearing as he told her, 'Do you know, Fen, I think I do?' He took her hand, his lean fingers twining with hers. 'My marriage isn't something I discuss. Ever.' His tone was dry. 'But I've got the feeling I can break that rule for you.'

He sank down into the armchair and would have taken her with him but she wasn't stupid enough to let herself get that close and compromised by dropping to the hearthrug by his feet. Her palms were damp with sweat, her pulses racing. Was he breaking his own rules because he thought she was in some way special to him, worthy of his confidences? Or was this to be another of his master-strokes?

One of his hands was resting on her shoulder, the strong fingers burning through the fine wool of her shirt. Fen stared into the fire, at the yellow flames licking around the logs, her mind in turmoil. She ought not to crave his confidences—they would only burden her further with this fateful feeling of closeness, the closeness that seemed to grow with sneaky inevitability each time they encountered one another.

She should never have invited him to talk about his marriage. She should have told him it was getting late and asked him to go. Would she ever learn sense where he was concerned?

No. She answered her own question with a delicate shudder as his hand gently stroked the nape of her neck. No. Never. To her own deep shame she was as weak as water when his terrifying sexual magic came into play. She leaned back against his knees, despising herself yet incapable of acting any other way, and heard the abrasive note in his voice as he told her, 'I'd never considered marriage as a viable option before I met Sanchia. I was an achiever, and proud of it, and I couldn't foresee the day when a woman could take even a small part of my mind away from my business career. Being married, I always knew, would mean that there would inevitably be circumstances when my wife would have to take first place. So I played the field—never anything serious and no hearts broken.'

'But that changed when you met your wife,' Fen put in dully, hating the feeling of being hurt. Why should his admission that he had once loved a woman so deeply that he had willingly relegated his meteoric career to second place cut her like a sharp-pointed blade? All she should sensibly feel was a mild surprise that the hard man was capable of any kind of tender emotion.

'No, not at first. It wasn't a case of love at first sight. Far from it.'

She heard him drag in a sigh. His fingers were playing with the lobe of her ear, but absently, his mind obviously far away. Fen ground her teeth and stared blindly into the fire. His mind might not be on what he was doing, but hers was!

The soft and tormentingly erotic—even if mindless—pressure of those sensual fingers was responsible for the rising tide of fever through her blood. And if there had been any strength left in her limbs at all she would have scrambled to her feet and walked away, away from all that danger, but her rioting feelings went unnoticed by him because his voice was dull, showing no emotion whatsoever as he went on, 'I met her at a party. She was South African, paying a visit to the old country to stay with an aunt and some cousins in London. I barely noticed her. Then we started to run across each other socially quite regularly, and I began to pay more attention. She wasn't beautiful—she was barely even pretty. A little too short, a little too plump, her blonde hair too fluffy. Nothing like the women I'd dated up until then. She would never turn heads but she made me think of home-cooked Sunday lunch, gardens and apple pie and babies in nurseries.' He shifted his knees apart, his hands going to her shoulders to settle her between them, his fingers resting lightly on her collarbone. 'And it suddenly occurred to me that I was missing out. I'd amassed a fortune but wasn't using it. All at once I wanted to hunt for a house I could make into a home, have children to inherit what I had made. Quite suddenly marriage seemed sensible. And when

I made my wedding vows I meant them because, in spite of what you may think, I do have some integrity.'

But he hadn't said he'd loved his wife, Fen thought on a note of ignoble exultation as she trawled backwards and forwards through his words. Then she flattened the feeling because she knew it shouldn't matter. Mustn't matter. And she asked, sympathetically, she hoped, 'So what went wrong?'

'What always goes wrong with dreams? You wake up eventually,' he said, the bitterness back in his voice, self-derision, too, and that showed her how badly he'd been hurt, and she dragged her lower lip between her teeth, thankful he couldn't see her face. 'I married the illusion and had to try to live with the reality. There was nothing sweet and wholesome and domesticated about my wife. She was rotten with disease and the disease was sex. Any man, any time, anywhere. I tried to get her to seek qualified help, tried to make the marriage work and although she was always suitably contrite when her indiscretions were discovered it would never be very long before she got involved with another man. She didn't know the meaning of love, only lust. I was never enough for her and I later discovered, after her death in a road accident, that her parents had shipped her back to England because the scandals she was creating back home were becoming impossible for them to live with.'

'I'm sorry.' Fen couldn't think of anything else to say. And what use was 'sorry'?

'Don't be.' He was leaning forward now, his head dipping so that his dark hair mingled with the gold of hers. 'I lived through it and came to terms with it.

Kept it all private, as far as I could—but I'm glad I told you. I was married, and it was a total failure. I wanted you to know. Now...' He drifted into a silence that was thick with things unspoken and Fen tried to find all the iron resolve that seemed to run away and hide whenever he was close.

But the pads of his fingers were stroking the upper curves of her breasts, branding her through the soft fabric of her shirt, and her pulses raced out of control and a great sob built up in her lungs because she now knew the reason behind his bleak statement touching on his failure in human relationships.

He'd been talking about his marriage, blaming himself for the breakdown when it hadn't been his fault. Just as she had leapt to all the wrong conclusions and heaped all the guilt on to his wide shoulders.

'Shall we just forget about it?' he was saying, the fingers of one hand busy now with her shirt buttons, and she found the strength of will from somewhere to drag herself to her feet and say with breathless haste, the words tripping over each other,

'That's the most sensible idea I've heard in a long time! And the second is a nice hot cup of coffee. Stay right where you are. I'll get it.' And she rushed into the kitchen as if the devil himself were on her heels.

And he was, she thought as she subsided weakly against the work surface. Oh, he was! Insinuating himself right into her heart.

'Oh, knicker elastic!' she growled under her breath as she made a shaky attempt to fill the kettle. How could she have let this happen? In spite of her long-held determination never to fall in love, be cheated of her freedom and independence, he had trapped her. She had fallen in love with Saul Ackerman and she would never be her own woman again. The prospect didn't bear thinking about!

CHAPTER TEN

SHE would get over it, of course she would, Fen assured herself with more fire than conviction as she made the coffee. She would have to, if her chosen way of life were to make any sense, be at all tolerable.

All she had to do was act her heart out, not let him even get a hint of what she really felt. If he even guessed she had fallen in love with him he would move in on her with all the deadly charisma at his command and she knew she would never be strong-minded enough to fight him.

Frowning at her still-shaky hands, she loaded a tray, squared her shoulders and dragged in a very deep breath.

She would be bright and breezy, letting him know she was quite definitely her own woman, and proud of it. But not unsympathetic, of course, because by taking her into his confidence, when he had never mentioned the true misery of his marriage to another living soul, he had bestowed on her a very special kind of honour.

But she would remind him of all his own affairs, following on the death of his wife, and, in doing so, remind herself, ram the facts firmly into a brain that seemed to have gone temporarily on the blink.

And she would definitely keep distance between them, even if it meant drinking her coffee while she walked backwards round the room. It would be fatal if he touched her.

Swallowing the lump of utter desolation brought on by the crippling knowledge that she would never again know the bliss of his kisses and caresses, must send him away and never see him again, she carried the tray through to the sitting-room, gave him a cup and handed him the cream. Then she took her own cup to the far side of the room and sat on one of the straight-backed chairs that stood beside the gate-legged table under the window.

'Don't try to look prim, Fen. It doesn't suit you.'

He was regarding her with something that looked suspiciously like amusement. And tenderness? Whatever—it curled her toes. She looked quickly down at the cup in her hands and the sexy, warm drift of his voice enclosed her, and a sweet stab of desire shafted deep inside her; his voice alone could beguile her, and almost did as he commanded softly. 'Come here. Come to me.'

The temptation to obey was wickedly strong, and had to be resisted. She knew only too well what would happen if she went anywhere near him. He wanted her and she loved him and the equation was danger-ously explosive.

Putting her cup down on the table at her side be-cause the trembling of her hands was a certain give-away, she gazed at a point beyond his head and told him with a lack of heat that did her credit, 'I won't be your mistress. So do us both a favour and don't mention it again.'

'No?'

He didn't sound disturbed by her statement and her eyes were clouded with suspicion as she flicked a look at him through her lashes. A hint of a smile played round his slashing mouth and she could have drowned in the look in his eyes.

'No!' She shook her head then dragged herself together. She was beginning to get too vehement and that wasn't the way she had planned to play this scene. She had to stay cool and in command of the situation. If she lost her temper then things could get out of hand. 'I know what you think of my morals, but I don't hop in and out of men's beds as if I've got springs under my feet, believe me. And by all accounts the women in your life don't hold your interest for longer than yesterday's newspapers. I mean,' she tacked on hastily in case he thought she hadn't believed a word he'd said about the reason for the breakdown of his marriage, 'the women you've had since your wife died.'

'Ah.' He shook his head slowly, his eyes glinting. 'All three hundred and sixty-five of them—one for each day of the year.'

Fen swallowed painfully. She wasn't getting the message through. He wasn't taking her seriously. He had talked glibly about her being a permanent part of his life and had gone on to admit that meant only for as long as they wanted to stay together. Which, in turn, meant until he grew tired of her. He wouldn't put up with a mistress who was beginning to bore him.

And she didn't want to be his mistress, always wondering if today was the day he would tell her the time had come to split. She wanted . . . she wanted . . . what

she could never have, and she would do well to remember that and act accordingly, she growled at
herself. And told him more tartly than she had ever
intended, 'I won't be one of a long, long line. I'm
sure you meant your offer to flatter, but I'm going
to have to decline.' Even though being with him, close
to him in every possible way, was the one thing her
poor silly heart craved above all else.

His face was tense as he got to his feet and walked
towards her with slow deliberation. And his voice was
biting as he threw out, 'Sanchia died four years ago.
And the last woman I took to my bed left it after an
affair that lasted for a little under a week. That was
more than two years ago. I have a normal man's needs
but I found that I took little joy in such cold coup-
lings. You won't be one of a line—long or short. You
are, and will be, unique. Satisfied?'

He was standing right over her, naked anger in his
face. She had obviously touched him on a very raw
spot indeed, but she shook her head speechlessly yet
very emphatically, the wetness of tears on her lashes.
Only his love, a lifetime's commitment, could satisfy
her. And that she was not about to get.

And then the anger sluiced from his face, leaving
it grey and drawn. And he said in a voice she scarcely
recognised, 'Am I really so unlovable, Fen?'

And during the fraction of time it took her to rake
his anguished features with the pained compassion of
her eyes she knew what he meant.

He had not meant love in the literal sense. Rather,
she knew, he was referring to the failure of his marriage, the failure of the relationship he'd entered into

with the woman he'd spoken of, over two years ago
now, the way he'd corrected her when she'd said he'd
never known failure in his life.

And right now he believed that he had failed again,
with her, that he could never sustain a close human
relationship. And, loving him, she couldn't bear it.
And she was on her feet and in his arms before she
had time to think, his totally unexpected display of
vulnerability making her ache to comfort him.

'You mustn't think that. Not ever!' Her hands
looping behind his head, she covered the side of his
face with tiny, feather-light kisses, not a single thought
of self-preservation in her mind, only thoughts of him,
of what he was feeling. His skin felt grainy beneath
her lips, and it tasted slightly of salt, and of something that was indefinably masculine.

Fen heard the rough sound as his breath caught in
his throat, and then his arms pulled her close and his
mouth covered hers in feverish possession. She whim-
pered, not from panic but from sheer blinding
pleasure, and he knew that, because his mouth
gentled, the pressure lighter but even more erotic as
his tongue parted her lips, making her drown in a
whirlpool of dark delight as she clung with wild
abandon to the strong, predatory passion of his hard
male body, exulting in the thrusting evidence of his
arousal, the crazed tumult that sang through her blood
as he crooned hoarsely against her lips, 'Oh, yes, oh
yes, Fen!' then slipped his hands beneath the hem of
her shirt, finding her small yet pertly firm breasts and
holding them in the palms of his hands, caressing the
silky soft flesh until she arched her spine, mewing

softly in her throat until he disposed of her shirt with lean, impatient fingers and gave her the wild pleasure she had unconsciously been begging for, suckling each taut nipple in turn, guiding the erect, rosy buds to the moist wickedness of his mouth with gentle, insistent, stroking fingers.

Her own eager fingers threaded in the soft springy darkness of his hair, Fen moaned with the pleasure that was almost a pain and knew there would be no going back. Not for her. Not ever. Her principles, the self-preserving need to protect herself from emotional damage, slipped out of sight. Because she loved him as she had never believed it would be possible to love any man, and this was right. It was good. So good...

And while his mouth paid homage to her breasts the fingers of one hand dealt with the button at the waistband of her jeans, easing them down over her hips, his hands following, stroking the satin flare of her hips, the slender lines of her thighs until she thought her heart would burst with wanting him, needing him, loving him.

'You are so beautiful, Fen,' he said softly. 'You are perfection, a hymn of delight. Every inch a poem.' His eyes devoured her unashamed nakedness, as if storing away the image for all time. And he was all possessive, demanding male as he growled throatily, 'And you're mine. All mine.'

He swept her into his arms, and she went willingly, with tumultuous exultation in her heart, her blood singing as he carried her upstairs and placed her with almost reverent care on the bed, looking down at her, his eyes black with passion as he removed his own clothing and joined her, gathering her to the aroused and savage masculinity of his body, covering her face with kisses, his voice low but triumphant as he whispered, 'From the moment I first saw you I knew we were meant for each other. And I knew you'd be mine—willingly, wantonly, wickedly...'

And then there were no more words, no need for them when hands and lips said all there was to say, when body worshipped body and flesh adored flesh, when he showed her the meaning of ecstasy beyond description and her fevered, loving body answered his with glorious, unstinting generosity.

Fen woke as the sunlight shafted in through the uncurtained window and touched her face, her lids lifting dreamily. She felt radiant with love and had lost count of the number of times they had made love to each other during the long, glorious night.

What price her freedom and independence now? she thought dazedly as she gently extricated herself from a possessively outflung arm. She belonged to him, now and for all time, enslaved by a depth of passion and love that was impossible to deny.

He was sprawled out on the bed, the deep, slow rhythm of his breathing barely disturbing the olive-toned magnificence of his broad chest. Unable to resist, she traced the outline of flat male nipples with the tip of her finger, felt him stir and made herself stop what she was doing. If he woke now they would make love again, and there was a lot she had to say to him before that happened. So much to clear up, so much to straighten out before they could move forward into their future.

Momentarily, her golden eyes clouded. How much future would he allow them to share together? Until they no longer wanted to stay together. The answer was cold, solid fact, but facts could be altered, given a different perspective, couldn't they?

It would be up to her to make damn sure that he wanted to stay with her always, she vowed with soaring optimism.

Gingerly, she wriggled off the bed and crept out of the room, gathering fresh clothes as she went. She would love him always, stay with him always, go where he went. The only freedom she needed now was the freedom to express her love. And if she were ever to bear his children she would never allow her love for him to freeze them out. Between them, she and Saul would give them the security of knowing they were loved and wanted, that having them cemented and strengthened their own love, making it grow, ensuring that there was enough to spill over and encompass them, too.

Fen pulled her dreaming thoughts up short. There would be no children without marriage and she was definitely leaping too far ahead, allowing the blissful aftermath of a night of passionate, glorious love to blind her to reality.

He had never mentioned the word marriage in connection with her. And why should he? He believed she changed lovers as regularly as other women changed library books. But he might change his mind, the treacherous voice of optimism put in, when he learned the truth about her relationship with Alex.

Hugging the hope to her, she hustled under the shower, not taking time to dry herself properly, so that the light T-shirt and skimpy shorts she dragged on clung revealingly to her woman's body.

She felt more alive, more feminine, more meltingly soft than she had ever felt before. Ecstatically happy, too, the only slight niggle in her mind the question of whether he would want to commit himself permanently to her when he learned that, apart from Ray—who had come nowhere near awaking her true potential as a woman—she had had no other lover.

But even that question mark couldn't quell the bubble of sheer joy that ran through her veins like champagne. And the sky was a brilliant blue again, the early morning sun already warm, and through the door she had flung open she could hear the surf pounding against the shore as last night's storm still swelled the ocean.

Utter perfection! And she was humming under her breath as she took breakfast things out to the picnic table and when Saul padded up behind her and wrapped his arms around her waist, pulling her back into his body and nuzzling his lips to the side of her neck, her heart trembled with excitement.

'I'd intended to bring you breakfast in bed. And lunch. And supper.'

She felt the warmth of his breath, the warmth of his smile against her exultantly sensitised skin and when she twisted round in his arms she felt the potency of his arousal and almost lost her resolve.

But she clung to it, even when the slow, suggestive movements of his hips threatened to drag it from her and fling it to the four winds.

'I've got something I want to talk to you about.' If she sounded breathless she had the perfect excuse. The sweetly tender sensation in her loins was sent soaring to full, demanding life by the things he was doing to her, making her feel.

He smiled, his sinful silver eyes gleaming as he put a slowly lingering kiss on her swollen mouth. 'You certainly do have something, but I can think of better things to do with it than talk about it.'

'No—be serious!' She was flushed, her mouth trembling on the brink of laughter, her body trembling on the brink of something else entirely, and he silenced her protest with a series of tiny linked kisses, assuring her huskily.

'Oh, I am, I am. I've never been more serious. Come back to bed. Let's celebrate the start of a relationship that's going to be fantastic for both of us.'

'I mean it.' Her voice was hoarse as she twisted out of his arms, her loins throbbing in time with the hectic beat of her blood. 'There's something I need to say to you first.'

'I take heart from that "first"!' He grinned at her, his hands on his hips. He looked totally magnificent despite the rumpled clothes, his tousled black hair and shadowed growth of beard making him look dangerously piratical. 'Go right ahead.'

'Over breakfast.' She could be firm when she had to be, she congratulated herself giddily, hurrying back into the kitchen, her heart nearly tripping over itself.

And back with the steaming filter jug, a rack of fresh toast, she edged round the table, choosing to sit opposite him, her eyes checking that everything was present.

Orange juice, butter in a brown earthenware pot, honey. Did he like honey? There were so many things she didn't know about him, and each new discovery would be a joy. As her eyes met his across the table she was swamped with her love for him, too swamped to get a word out as she shakily poured coffee and chilled juice for them both and watched him spread butter on hot toast, the devilishly clever, lean fingers moving with uncalculated precision.

Cutting his toast into four equal quarters, one dark brow drifted upwards. 'Well? What's so important, sweetheart?'

The easy endearment took her breath away, implied something far gentler, more loving than lust. Fen grappled for words and told him, her love for him making her voice ragged, 'Alex Fairbourne is my uncle, my mother's brother. Our "affair" simply didn't exist, needless to say. The only substance it had was in the minds of those people who chose to believe the salacious innuendos coming from the Press.'

Up until this morning she had been determined to keep the truth from him until her uncle's future with VisionWest had been decided. But falling in love with Saul, giving herself to him, accepting him as her lover, had changed all that. The most important thing now was for him to know the truth about her. He wouldn't punish Alex for the deception; he was too strong a character to indulge in that kind of spite. And, even if he didn't love her, he wanted her desperately, felt some tenderness for her, and she was sure he would do nothing to hurt her uncle and, through him, her.

She was watching him closely and he had gone very still. His unforgettable features were quite without expression. His breakfast abandoned, he regarded her from dark, sombre eyes.

'And? There has to be more than that.'

There was, and she told him, her voice going thinner as she realised that something was going drastically wrong. Told him that, far from being a career-mistress, she had only had one lover before him, and that fiasco had happened a long time ago. Told him of her uncle's very real fears that falling viewing figures meant the inevitable axing of his show; of Jean's hare-brained idea to get him back in the public eye, present him as the sexy heart-throb who had once had women swooning in the aisles—and could do again if the female viewers could somehow be persuaded to see him as a mature and macho male who could still attract a much younger woman.

'It was a silly idea,' Fen conceded weakly, wishing he would say something, inject some comment of his own instead of looking at her with those cold, dark eyes. Even the warm sunlight failed to soften the harsh austerity of his hard, slashing features. 'And once the story got out we simply went along with it——'

'Laughing behind your slender white hand.' He left the table, his movements perfectly controlled. His eyes met hers with the impact of an electric shock. 'No one makes a fool of me, not even a woman. Especially not a woman. Never again.'

He was talking about Sanchia, the way she'd acted during their marriage. Fen could excuse his bitterness. But she, Fen, had never set out to make a fool of him. Circumstances had overtaken them and had made a confession, until now, out of the question. She had to try to make him understand that. If it was the last thing she did, she had to do that.

But he was leaving, striding down the path as if he couldn't get away from her quickly enough, and she followed just as soon as her stunned and bewildered brain allowed her to jump to her feet.

'Saul!' He was already unlocking the door of his car and her mouth went dry with fear. This couldn't be happening, it couldn't. How could he walk away from her, after last night? How could he do this to her?

Her huge eyes pleading, she wrestled with the wicket gate, her movements clumsy and uncoordinated in her panic. He didn't even look at her, and her anguished, 'I love you, Saul——' was drowned in the hungry growl of the engine as he backed the car up the steep incline of the track, sending pebbles flying, scattering stones beneath the wheels.

In the grey-green shadow of the rock Fen dabbled her toes in the soft salt water of the pool, watching the glimmer and glitter, the refractions of gold and silver light on the broken surface. She dragged in a long breath of sparkling air and tried to relax.

Tomorrow she would be leaving this lovely and secluded place forever and she would never come back. Jean and Alex had arranged to collect her and the things her mother would want sent on to Australia, and that would be that. She would be saying goodbye to a chunk of her past. And finally, irrevocably, to Saul.

It had been a week, almost to the hour, since he had walked out on her, too bitterly angry to listen to another word from her. And he'd left her dying inside, rigid with shock. It had been quite some time before she'd felt able to pull herself together and then, by some miracle, she had found the energy of twenty, tackling the remainder of the chores like a tornado, rarely stopping to eat and only falling into bed when exhaustion forced her to.

She hadn't cried, and that hadn't surprised her. She was too empty and drained to find tears. All the emotions he had forced into wildly erupting life seemed to have atrophied.

But who needed emotions, anyway? They only made people make a mess of their lives. She could live without them. She would darn well make sure she lived without them!

Wading through the rock-pool, her bare feet found firm, warm sand and she headed for the line of breaking surf, sunlight falling on her bright hair, caressing the bare skin of her long, long legs beneath the tiny cotton shorts, burning through the shabby, oversize T-shirt that came down to her thighs.

The only crumb of comfort she could pick out of the sorry tangle of her situation was the fact that, contrary to the dreadful fears she'd had when she'd emerged from the shock of Saul's reaction to her confession, Alex hadn't been booted out of VisionWest.

Twenty-four hours after Saul had stormed out Jean had phoned from Edinburgh, barely sounding sane.

'Alex can't talk to you—to anyone! He's too hyped up, bless him! Just think—a weekly chat show—not a series—weekly! They're offering him a long contract. Laurence Meek phoned half an hour ago. They've been viewing tapes of his shows, apparently. Laurence said he was a natural interviewer—remember he always did a short celebrity interview slot on *Evening With Alex*? They've decided he's to host his own chat show; we're beside ourselves with excitement...'

At least she could be thankful that Saul hadn't taken his bitter anger out on Alex; she would never have forgiven herself if he had. So there were no loose ends to tie up now, and there would be few regrets. Saul had worked his wizardry and compelled her to fall in love with him. And, in doing so, had underlined her former and definitely saner opinion that it was safer and less complicated to travel through life alone. Footloose and heart-whole.

And she would be that again, she assured herself tightly as she flung a pebble far out into the surging waves. She would put Saul Ackerman out of her mind just as soon as she started out on the rest of her life.

And the rest of her life began tomorrow.

And as for today, she would simply relax and soak up the sun, try to unwind and decide what to do with the next few weeks. She could always stay on at the cottage—being on hand, she could show any prospective buyers around—but she couldn't afford the luxury of such idleness and she couldn't afford the pain. Everything reminded her of Saul, of the way he had touched her, made love to her, the things he had said, the silver gleam of his eyes, the eloquent beauty of his strong, lean hands... And the pain was fierce. So staying on here was not the way to cut him out of her mind.

Jean and Alex had said she could stay with them until it was time to take up her next scheduled job in Italy. But she was too independent to accept charity, even from people she loved, and their other, almost grudgingly offered suggestion seemed the best she could hope for at the moment. Two of their friends owned a small hotel near Truro and were desperately short-staffed; they needed someone who was willing to turn a hand to anything in return for bed and board and a small pay packet.

They had made it sound like hard work but hard physical work was what her restless body craved right now; she needed to fall into bed each night too tired to think. Too tired to dream. Besides, looking for something in her own line of work would take too much time. She needed to launch straight into a job, no matter if she was over-qualified.

So tomorrow, back in Tavistock, she would get the Truro phone number from Jean, check that work was still available, contact a house agent in Plymouth and put the cottage on their books, and sling her hook. And never, ever look back.

The next few weeks decided, Fen put them out of her mind and tested the temperature of the water with her toes. Chilly enough to take her breath away. No one but the most stout-hearted would take to the Atlantic breakers until midsummer.

But Fen wasn't faint-hearted and she stripped down to her bra and pants and waded in, letting the rollers and breakers buffet her, alternatively fighting them and going with them, glorying in the way her tussle with the elemental force of the ocean drained her tired mind of everything else. And at last, wading back to the shore, her hair slicked to her skull and a million droplets of sea water glittering on her skin, she felt free again. Her own woman again.

And then everything changed and the illusion of freedom blew out of existence because Saul was there, watching her, waiting for her where the waves creamed against the shore. And it all came back again, the wanting, the loving, the desperate need.

And the fear. The fear of the emotional pain he could inflict, the joy he could give and thoughtlessly, carelessly take from her again.

A few scraps of wet silk offered no barriers to hide behind and Fen instinctively crossed her arms over her breasts, wishing the small, virtually inaccessible cove weren't quite so secluded. If people had been in the habit of coming here she wouldn't have gone into the water so scantily clad. If there were other people around she wouldn't have had to face him alone, wouldn't have felt so vulnerable, so much at the mercy of what his eyes alone could do to her...

But she couldn't stand here all day, cold sea water surging around her knees, her arms crossed over her heaving bosom as if she were some improbably Victorian virgin. She walked on, tearing her eyes away from his bleak and unreadable features. But his image was printed on her retina, his tall, strong frame shatteringly sexy in body-hugging white denims and a loose-fitting sleeveless black shirt, standing as solid as one of the granite rocks, his feet slightly apart, thrust into the pockets of his denims, just watching her. Watching her...

Her heart was an excruciatingly insistent hammer, battering her ribcage, and her legs felt as if they were made of cotton wool, but she forced herself onwards, trying to look as if his presence was neither here nor there as far as she was concerned.

He had walked out on her a week ago, trailing bitterness like a black cloud, refusing even to talk to her despite the wild and loving intimacies of the night before. And she wasn't going to forgive him for that, forgive him for treating her like a tramp without a feeling to her name.

Always presuming he wanted to be forgiven, of course. He had probably come back to give her another taste of his bitter contempt. No doubt he would tell her, in his own good time.

Her eyes sliding sideways, she located the discarded clothing she'd left above the high-water mark and wondered if she could reach it, pull the baggy T-shirt over her head before she had to confront him head-on. But no, wouldn't you know it, he had moved since the last time she had looked at him, intercepting her line of retreat, his powerfully intimidating body directly in front of her as she walked on to firm sand.

Slowly, her eyes swept up to meet his. She had never wanted to have to see him again, to increase the anguish, and she didn't want to look into his eyes now, but she couldn't help herself.

His face was as still as if it had been carved from rock; only his eyes gave an indication of his feelings. Just a dark flash of something that might have been pain. Or anger. Whatever, it was gone before she could pin it down and make the right interpretation.

He stared into her eyes for a long, silent moment and her breath sobbed in her lungs. It was, she thought with wild incoherence, as if he were drawing her soul right out of her body and into his own. As if she belonged to him, now and always, and he had come to claim his possession.

Fen shuddered in aching reaction and the tiny, revealing movement brought him to life because he touched her then, taking her hands in his and drawing them down, away from her body, the silver gleam of his eyes only just visible beneath the hooded lids as they claimed unspoken yet undeniable ownership of her virtually naked body.

There was no resistance, none whatsoever. As ever, his presence sapped her will, left her a victim of his power. She closed her eyes, trying not to hear the frantic beat of her heart, concentrating instead on the sound of the sea as it surged against the shore and boomed among the outflung rocks that sheltered the cove, on the closer babble and gurgle of the stream as it sped headlong over its bed of stone and sand to merge with the ocean.

She was like that stream, she thought jaggedly as she felt her body's betrayal, the peaking of her aching breasts as they pushed against the inadequate wet silk covering, the hot, hurting magic of the ache in her womb... Yes, just like that happily gurgling stream she felt herself rushing heedlessly towards an almighty, untamable force, flinging herself into wild and elemental danger, never stopping to consider the aftermath.

But it needn't be like that. She could stop it happening. And she would. She opened her eyes on a snap, meeting the steady, mesmeric regard of his, and said thickly, trying to tug her hands out of his grasp, 'Let me go. I don't know why you came here, and I don't want to know. Please leave.'

But he didn't release her, simply took her hands and wrapped them around his waist, his own arms cradling her close, holding her head gently against his chest.

'Don't fight me, Fen. I made a bad mistake. I hurt you, and I'm sorry.' He felt her shudder of emotion and rained kisses on her face, her neck, and her heart gave an anguished leap.

She couldn't let him hurt her again. He had walked away from her, not giving a damn for her feelings, treating her as if she didn't have any. And maybe he had thought things over, calmed down, and decided to come back for more of what she had so willingly given.

Well, it just wasn't on!

She brought her arms round and pushed at his chest, lashing out verbally, 'Come back for another romp between the sheets, have you? Nothing better to do? Well, I'm sorry, I have!' Far better things to do with her life than endure the kind of pain he could dole

out. Maybe his need for her was greater than his reluctance to bed a woman who didn't regard sleeping
around as a way of life, a woman who might ask for
something more permanent than he was able to give,
but, just the same, the time would come when he
would again walk away. And the second time, the final
time, would be far worse than the first. She would
never survive it.

She renewed her ineffectual battering of his chest
and he caught her hands between his own, his eyes
caressing her flushed and angry face, one brow slowly
drifting upwards as she scorned, 'You couldn't move
fast enough when you discovered I don't make a career
out of being a mistress. Can you only function with
a woman you know you can pay off and no hard
feelings? Are you frightened of the other type—a
woman who would make love with her emotions and
not a pocket calculator? She'd be a liability, wouldn't
she? She might start asking for things you couldn't
give, like love and respect and a normal family
life——'

'Don't.' Amazingly, he was smiling. She saw the
curve of his mouth just before he cut off her tirade
with his kiss. A swift, possessive branding that sent
the fight draining straight out of her body, leaving
behind a mish-mash of hopes and yearnings, needs
and confusions. 'Don't say another word. And put
this on.'

Two long strides took him to the little heap of her
clothing and in one second more he was tugging the
concealing T-shirt over her head.

'That's better.' He brushed her fringe out of her eyes. 'We need to talk and I can't even think straight with all that tempting flesh of yours in front of my eyes. Back to the house, I think.'

Sliding an arm around her waist, he pulled her close and set off slowly towards the head of the cove, and she wondered why she was letting this happen, why her will-power disappeared when he was around, why her need for emotional survival, at all costs, became extinct.

The brush of his thighs against her own as they walked was torture and heaven all rolled into one and when his feet dragged to a halt she was glad to stop, too, and lean against him, her legs too weak to hold her upright.

'I walked away because my pride was shattered,' he said, his voice thick. 'I wasn't thinking straight. Can you forgive me?' He eased her round, pulling her into the heat of his body, his hands looped behind her waist. 'Making love to you had been the most beautiful experience of my life, and all I could think was that you had been laughing at me—letting me believe a lie and thinking what a fool I was. That you must have thought me ridiculous when I started to behave like an amateur psychologist.' He shifted his feet in the sand making her very aware of his physical arousal as his body moved against hers. 'You see, Fen, I thought I understood you, that I knew you—really knew why you were incapable of committing yourself to one man, preferred to play the field, never staying anywhere, or with anyone, for long enough for any real feelings to develop. You must have thought me

a pompous fool. And so I walked out. I didn't want
to hear you laughing at me.'

Fen couldn't bear to see the bleak residue of pain
in his eyes. She traced the severity of his mouth with
the tip of one finger, shaking her head.

'I'll laugh with you, never at you. And you weren't
wrong. As a psychologist you were doing fine. I didn't
sleep around to stop myself becoming emotionally
dependent on one man, I never let a man get near
me. Or only once, and that was a disaster that simply
reinforced my opinion that I was far better off alone.
I never wanted to get like my mother. She was so dependent on Dad, so much his creature, that there was
nothing of herself left, not even a tiny corner she could
give to her child.'

'Yet you made love with me.' He cupped the delicate
oval of her face with his hands, his eyes watchful.
'Does that tell me anything?'

Fen shivered. She was treading dangerous ground.
Oh, he had told her that the night they had spent
together had been the most beautiful experience of
his life, that hurt pride had made him walk away from
her in bitterness and anger. But that didn't necessarily
mean he wanted her in his life for a moment longer
than it took for him to tire of her.

'What do you want it to mean?' she prevaricated,
gasping as the ball of his thumb slowly rubbed the
soft pout of her lips.

'That you've found a man you could live with, that
you're not necessarily better off on your own, that
giving yourself doesn't mean losing yourself. That
you'll marry me.' His eyes searched hers with burning

intensity and his voice was rough as he added, 'I'll give you two minutes to think about it. I want you here, and I want you now. But something that beautiful demands a commitment. You've got two minutes. I can't hold out longer than that.'

Two seconds would be more than enough. Tears shimmered in her golden eyes. 'Do you love me?' she asked, unconscious of the wistful plea in her voice.

'Always.' His mouth sealed the statement and Fen responded dizzily, everything inside her going out of control with sheer joy, exploding, and when he demanded, 'And you? Tell me you love me. Tell me you'll marry me,' she could only cling to him, lost in the closeness of him, her voice a tiny patter of sound as she murmured his name, her affirmatives over and over again.

And somehow, without her being truly aware of how they had got there, they were back at the house, the utter silence of drowsy midday surrounding them, and he said as he carried her up the narrow staircase, 'Tomorrow I'll take you home and install you there. We shall be married from there, despite the conventions. We'll leave a note for Alex, pinned on the door, and he can finish up here, do whatever's necessary. But the rest of today, and tonight, my darling, is ours, and ours alone.'

It was almost dark when they emerged at last from the isolated little house, wandering down to the cove, hand in hand, haunted by love, bemused and bewitched by it. Fen felt as if she was walking in a dream, or in paradise, on a journey that would go on until the end of her life, and Saul would walk with her, sharing everything, every splendour and joy.

'You know,' she said lightly as she dropped to the soft sand, gazing out to where the sea should be to view a blanket of black silk, spangled with starshine, a blanket that whispered softly to itself in its sleep, 'I still don't really know how this all happened. Loving each other, I mean.'

'Fate, my darling.' He dropped to his haunches in front of her and she could hear the smile in his voice. 'You must have heard of it. And you can't fight it. When I first saw you I frankly lusted after you and vowed I'd take you from Alex. I wanted you in my life, not his—or any other man's. Then things shifted gear and I started to worry about you, what would happen to you and the rest of your life. I found myself wanting to take care of you, teach you not to be afraid of emotion. Oh, I still wasn't thinking in terms of a lifetime together—I'd been bamboozled by one woman and didn't intend making that mistake again. What I didn't realise was that I was already in love with you, in so deep I couldn't get out, that I would have devoted the rest of my life to you, despite what I believed to be your dubious past.'

He reached out to touch her face, the touch of his hands so tender, she wanted to cry. 'My heart had already accepted that you were an indivisible part of me. And then when you told me you weren't what you seemed I felt—unfairly—that I had been made a fool of yet again. It took a while to get that pride under control and admit that you were the only woman for me, that being made a fool of, as I saw it, didn't matter a tinker's cuss. That, my darling, is what fate is. So let's drink to it.'

He had collected a cool-box from the boot of his car and now he extracted champagne and two tall crystal glasses. And the liquid exploded in a fountain of bubbles, just as Fen's love for him exploded within her heart. He touched his glass to hers and settled beside her, his mouth a whisper away from hers as he murmured, 'To fate. And our life together. Our love.'

'Our love,' she echoed, her glass slipping from her hand, watering the sand with vintage champagne.

Fen didn't notice the loss as she reached up to pull his dark head down to hers. She didn't need intoxicants, all she needed was Saul, and he left her in no doubt at all that he was hers for a lifetime as his lips answered hers with tender promise.

HARLEQUIN PRESENTS®

A new story from one of Harlequin Presents' most
popular authors

#1863 ONE-MAN WOMAN
by
Carole Mortimer

Ellie was only interested in one-to-one relationships,
so Daniel Thackery wasn't for her. But she had
to keep him talking: he seemed to be up to no
good and—even more important—he knew the
whereabouts of her sister's estranged husband.
Only Ellie's persistence seemed to encourage
Daniel to think that she could yet
become his woman!

Available in February wherever
Harlequin books are sold.

Look us up on-line at: http://www.romance.net   TAUTH17

Take 4 bestselling love stories FREE

Plus get a FREE surprise gift!

Special Limited-time Offer

Mail to Harlequin Reader Service®

3010 Walden Avenue
P.O. Box 1867
Buffalo, N.Y. 14240-1867

YES! Please send me 4 free Harlequin Presents® novels and my free surprise gift. Then send me 6 brand-new novels every month, which I will receive months before they appear in bookstores. Bill me at the low price of $2.90 each plus 25¢ delivery and applicable sales tax, if any*. That's the complete price and a savings of over 10% off the cover prices—quite a bargain! I understand that accepting the books and gift places me under no obligation ever to buy any books. I can always return a shipment and cancel at any time. Even if I never buy another book from Harlequin, the 4 free books and the surprise gift are mine to keep forever.

106 BPA A3UL

Name	(PLEASE PRINT)

Address	Apt. No.

City	State	Zip

This offer is limited to one order per household and not valid to present Harlequin Presents® subscribers. *Terms and prices are subject to change without notice. Sales tax applicable in N.Y.

UPRES-696   ©1990 Harlequin Enterprises Limited

HARLEQUIN PRESENTS®

Read the first story in Robyn Donald's intriguing new trilogy:

Olivia Nicholls and half sisters Anet and Jan Currethers
are all linked by a mysterious portrait that is meant to
bring love to the lives of those who possess it—but
there is one condition....

This is Olivia's story:

#1865 THE MIRROR BRIDE

Available in February wherever
Harlequin books are sold.

Look us up on-line at: http://www.romance.net

MM1

You're About to Become a **Privileged** *Woman*

Reap the rewards of fabulous free gifts and
benefits with proofs-of-purchase from
Harlequin and Silhouette books

Pages & Privileges™

It's our way of thanking you for
buying our books at your
favorite retail stores.

✂

| 📖 PROOF OF PURCHASE | HP-PP21 |

Offer expires March 31, 1997

Harlequin and Silhouette— the most privileged readers in the world!

For more information about Harlequin and
Silhouette's PAGES & PRIVILEGES program call the
Pages & Privileges Benefits Desk: 1-503-794-2499

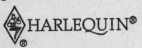

◈ HARLEQUIN®